SALFORD MURDERS

The Private Investigator Gus Keane Trilogy

BUD CRAIG

Paperback published by

The Book Folks

London, 2017

© Bud Craig

This book is a work of fiction. Names, characters, businesses, organizations, places and events are either the product of the author's imagination or are used fictitiously. Any resemblance to actual persons, living or dead, events or locales is entirely coincidental. The spelling is British English.

All rights reserved. No part of this publication may be reproduced, stored in retrieval system, copied in any form or by any means, electronic, mechanical, photocopying, recording or otherwise transmitted without written permission from the publisher.

ISBN 978-1-5207-9128-9

www.thebookfolks.com

Book I
TACKLING DEATH
Page 1

Book II
DEAD CERTAINTY
Page 213

Book III
FALLING FOUL
Page 459

BOOK I

TACKLING DEATH

CHAPTER ONE

I dashed across the road and began to follow the girl along the street. My long strides kept up with her easily. One of the few advantages of being six foot four, I thought. I peered into the murk through smeary glasses. The sky glowered, the wind blew rain into my face, down my broken nose and, somehow, under the hood of my waterproof jacket. A late March morning in Salford. Pissing down. Who'd have thought it?

I kept her in my eye line as she wheeled a pushchair through the puddles. We splashed past a 1970s one-storey concrete building with 'Ordsall Tanning' written in orange over a glass panel in the front door. The smell of gone off food wafted from fast food wrappers. Empty packets blew along the pavement. The rumble of the morning traffic from the dual carriageway on Regent Road behind me accompanied the slap of my trainers on the pavement. I swerved past a man with a suitcase on wheels coughing his way into McDonalds.

I turned right on the corner, still within sight of the girl. The railings of Ordsall Park on the other side of Ordsall

Lane stood to attention, showing off their fresh coat of green paint. I passed an Edwardian pub with 'Hardy's Crown Ales' chiselled in brown cement two thirds of the way up the wall. 'The Park Hotel' was etched in the frosted glass of the windows. On the corner of West Park Street, a wooden sign advertised town houses for £149,500. Here the girl turned right and then right again, seeming to double back on herself until she arrived at Princess Street. Her bare matchstick legs turned down the garden path of a pale brick council house. I made out a number twenty-seven on the front door. Walking towards her, I stopped and hesitated.

"Er, Tanya, is it?"

I looked at the pushchair where I could just see a sleeping toddler through the plastic cover. Tanya turned to stare at me, her sad face scarred with experience and spots. Her close-cropped hair, dyed jet black, was sculpted to her head by the downpour. She looked nineteen going on forty-five. The skirt and white sleeveless T-shirt covered perhaps fifty per cent of her body. A necklace of assorted love bites adorned her neck.

"Yeah, I'm Tanya," she said in a rasping, 'are you talking to me or chewing a brick' voice. "What do you want?"

"It's, er," I said, lowering my voice and looking from side to side as two bulky men went by, "it's confidential."

"I won't be a minute."

She banged on the open door of the adjoining house and unceremoniously pushed the chair into the hall, unhooking her handbag from the handle.

"Shannon! Can you mind Madison for a bit?"

A girl of about Tanya's age waddled down the hallway to take the child in. Tanya began to open the door of her own house.

"Come in," she said, turning her head towards me.

I followed her in. Pulling back my hood, I ran my fingers through my hair then shook drops of water from my hands.

"You've never gone out with wet hair," I could almost hear my mam say from beyond the grave.

We went into the living room, where I sat down on the shabby sofa. I unzipped my waterproof, sending a sheen of rainwater onto the suede jacket underneath. Tanya kicked off her shoes and put her bag on an armchair. She picked up a child's vest from a chair and dried her hair and face, before standing over me.

"Well love," she said, chucking the vest back on the chair, "we may as well get on with it eh? I haven't got much time. Twenty quid and you have to use a Noddy."

She immediately turned to draw the curtains and, turning back to face me, removed her T-shirt, revealing pointed breasts. She began to unhook her skirt. I put my hand to my chest and felt my heart pumping. Nausea bubbled up from my stomach to my mouth.

"I think..." I stammered, "I think there must have been some mistake."

"You'd better get your kecks off, we've not got all day."

Allowing her skirt to fall to the floor she stepped out of her shoes and walked towards me. By now she was wearing only a pair of tight red knickers. She smiled again and pouted, licking her lips. I froze as she sat on my lap and threw her arms round my neck. I caught a whiff of unwashed flesh.

"Don't be nervous love. It'll be all right, you'll see."

Stop reacting like a shy teenager, Gus, I told myself. You're all grown up now; on the verge of early retirement for God's sake. Yeah, but I've led a sheltered life.

"No, no, this isn't what I've come for at all."

Pulling a face, Tanya got up. My eyes struggled to focus as I took my glasses off and wiped them on my T-shirt. She looked down at me.

"You mean you're not business then?"

I shook my head, putting my glasses back on. Sulking like a schoolgirl, she got dressed again.

"Shit!"

"Sorry," I shrugged.

"Thought you was a bit posh for round here."

"Posh! I've never been accused of that before," I said. "I was born and bred in West Park Street."

"Never."

"It's unrecognisable from when I was a kid," I said.

She put her hands on her hips and rolled her eyes.

"What the fuck do you want?"

"I'm Gus Keane, from Children's Services at Ordsall Tower."

I pulled my wallet from my jeans and showed my ID.

"What?"

"It used to be Social Services' I said, putting my wallet away. "I'm looking for Michael Askey. Mick."

There was no visible response to this.

"Who's he when he's at home?"

"I think you know who he is," I said, resisting the temptation to say 'the same as he is on holiday'. "He lives with you, doesn't he?"

She shrugged and looked down, a little shamefaced.

"Come on, Tanya, there's no point in lying. You're not in any trouble. I just need to get in touch with Mick."

She took a packet of Lambert and Butler and a gas lighter from the bag. I shook my head as she offered the packet to me before taking a cigarette and lighting up. Blowing out smoke she refused to meet my eye.

"It's urgent," I went on. "I've been trying all week to see him. I came yesterday as you were going out. I just missed you."

She shrugged and looked at the ceiling.

"Then this morning I saw you walk past the office and followed you here. Just tell me when and where I can get hold of Mick and I'll be out of your way."

She sighed and blew a smoke ring with remarkable skill.

"Yeah, he moved in about a week ago. I've been trying to get rid of him ever since."

"Is he still living here?"

"Yeah, but he's out at the moment. What do you want him for?"

"It's confidential, I can't tell you."

She tutted at the standard answer.

"Do you know when he'll be back?"

Silence. I glanced at my watch. Tanya looked at me, folding her arms.

"He could be back later on," she said. "Hard to say."

I thought for a moment. I was on office duty that afternoon. I could come back anytime before lunch, leave a note if he wasn't in.

"If he gets back before I call again, can you ring me?"

She shrugged.

"Here's my number," I said, taking a card from my jacket pocket and handing it to her. "Just in case."

"I might do," she said, glancing down at the card.

"Right. I'll be off."

"Don't tell him you've been talking to me," she said, as I got up to go.

I nodded.

"I won't."

"And you want to watch yourself and all. He can't stand fucking social workers."

"I'll be careful," I said.

As I got out of the house, I let out a bellow of laughter. Why do things keep happening to me, I wondered. And tomorrow was April Fools' Day.

CHAPTER TWO

Half an hour later I sat typing at my desk, wanting to make sure I got the letter done before I forgot. The strip lights in the low ceilings cast a gloomy light over the open plan office. Twenty years in this place, I thought, no wonder my eyesight's so bad. I watched the screen as the words appeared:

Dear Mick
I called today to talk to you on behalf of a young woman who thinks she may be your daughter. She would like to get in touch with you. Please ring me at Ordsall Tower (number at the top of the letter) or call in this afternoon. If you can't manage to get in touch today, please contact the duty officer any time during working hours – unfortunately I will not be available from next week.
I look forward to hearing from you.
Yours sincerely
Gus Keane

I'm retiring today and won't have to bother about toe rags like you anymore, I was tempted to add. I printed the letter, signed it and put it in an envelope. I could have left it for someone else to sort out but I had promised Charlotte. Just time for a cup of tea before I go out again, I thought, as I wrote the address on the envelope.

As I got up, I took in the partitions that divided the room into team sections. Most desks were unoccupied. What was it that woman had said to me a few years ago?

"Every time I try to get in touch with you, you're on holiday, in a meeting or on the sick."

She'd omitted to mention 'out on visits' and 'not at his desk' (in the bog). As I went over to the kettle, the usual posters were stuck on the wall seemingly at random: Casual Clothes day for Cancer research – it made no difference to me, I was in my normal gear – a Unison quiz, a meeting about the Department's new structure.

Back at my desk with my mug I picked up the staff magazine, idly flicking through the pages and sipping tea. On page seven I saw a photograph of a man with greying brown hair, blue eyes and glasses grinning stupidly. He held a rugby ball in his hand. It took a few seconds to realise it was me. I read the accompanying article:

"Social worker, Gus Keane is retiring after more than twenty years with the Council. Gus, who played Rugby League for Salford in the glory days of the nineteen seventies, will devote some of his time to TRYS, a rugby charity."

Makes me sound a right do-gooder, I thought.

"He is also looking forward to the birth of his first grandchild in May."

I looked up to see a slightly built, thirty something woman rushing in and cursing the rain as she hung her coat on a hook. The phone on the desk next to mine rang.

"Hiya, Karen," I said, as she dashed over to answer it.

I read on:

"'I've had an eventful few months,' says Gus, 'so it will be nice to have time to relax.'"

'An eventful few months' was a euphemism if ever there was one, but I hadn't particularly wanted to tell all the council's employees my wife had left me in September. Or that I'd had a stroke the following week. I saved all that soul baring for my counsellor. I turned my attention from the magazine to Karen.

"Gary, all I'm asking you to do is pick me up after work," she was saying.

She covered the mouthpiece, turning towards me and shaking her head.

"I've told you, my car won't be ready until Monday."

She fell silent for a minute or so.

"It's not my fault if some silly bugger smashed into me in the car park."

She tapped her fingers on the desk.

"For God's sake, we'll survive a weekend with one car," she said, forcing the words out between gritted teeth.

Another pause followed before she spoke again.

"So we'll say 4.30, shall we? I'll see you then."

She slammed the phone down, sighed and grinned at me. In her white blouse and navy blue skirt she looked like the secretary she used to be. 'I could never bring myself to wear jeans to work,' she had said when she heard about Casual Clothes Day. Her dark hair shone with health in contrast with the harassed look on her face. And to think a few months ago her brown eyes had showed the enthusiasm of a newly qualified social worker. Her frightening efficiency made her a force to be reckoned with though. Give her a few years and she'd be running the bloody place.

"Sorry about that," she said.

I shrugged as she picked up an envelope on her desk and ripped it open. She took out the document inside and began to read.

"A letter from the new director," she said. "She starts on Monday. What a shame. You'll miss her."

"Yeah."

Karen looked over to me.

"Didn't you say you know her?"

"Yeah, we were on the same social work course."

"Don will ask you to put a word in for him."

A man's voice was heard in the office on our left.

"You bastard."

"Talk of the devil," she said.

"That was never Don swearing," I said. "I thought he was very religious."

Karen took a chocolate digestive from the packet on her desk. "In theory," she said.

"How do you mean?"

She sipped more tea and looked at me. "Did I never tell you Don tried to get off with me?"

I nearly choked on my cuppa.

"What?"

"Oh, yes. I think it was when you were off after your stroke."

"The bloody hypocrite. What did you say?"

She looked askance at me.

"Gus! Do you even have to ask? I mean, who'd fancy Don?"

We turned towards the room where the voice had come from to see a door open. A man of about Karen's age, taller than me, emerged. Looking towards us briefly, he attempted a smile of greeting, which was more of a grimace. His flushed cheeks contrasted with his unruffled exterior. The striped, open neck shirt and neatly cut fair hair gave him the appearance of a City whiz kid. What had been going on in there? Best not to ask, I decided.

"Boss and deputy fall out," said Karen with satisfaction, jerking her head towards Don as he moved rapidly away.

"Not for the first time," I said.

"You're well out of it," said Karen.

"Yeah."

"We'll all miss you when you go," she smiled, as her phone rang again. "We'll have nobody to confide in."

I wouldn't really miss hearing about Karen's difficulty conceiving, I thought guiltily, her husband's low sperm count and the way it had virtually destroyed their marriage. All my life people had told me their troubles. Maybe that's why I had gone into social work, I thought. May as well get paid for it. I said the words 'early retirement' to myself and looked at my watch. Not long to go.

CHAPTER THREE

Ten minutes later I put my anorak on, putting the envelope in one of the pockets. Going out of Children's Services towards the exit I passed Reliable.com on the right as a man in his forties came out of the door.

"All right, Rob," I said.

"Gus, hi," he said in a public school drawl, looking up at me and fiddling with the collar of a green polo shirt. "So, your last day today."

I nodded and smiled.

"All right for some."

He flicked his fingers through his flop of blonde hair. He looked like a California surfer who had joined the business world.

"Sorry about missing your leaving do," he said.

"That's OK."

"Should be a good night."

I thought about sidling away.

"You know I'd be there only Emma's away."

He proceeded to tell me for the third time – or was it the fourth? – that his wife was flying to Dublin today for someone's hen night. Though I had never met her I knew his wife was Australian and worked in marketing.

"Hen weekend more like," he said.

Again.

He was taking the afternoon off to drive her to the airport. Yes, I know, Rob. His weekend would be dedicated to 'a bit of quality time with the kids.' I began to move past him before he got into doting father mode. I love my kids but Rob always makes me feel neglectful and inadequate. It struck me for the umpteenth time that even with OK people there are things that irritate you. It was impossible to dislike Rob though. There were worse thing than loving your kids.

He was a bit of a wheeler-dealer of course, always popping into Children's Services touting for business. The funny thing was nobody minded: he must have made a fortune out of us. Think of all those social workers needing car insurance. The women certainly liked him: he had a subtly flirtatious way with him that even the die-hard feminists lapped up. It was the old story: either you've got it or you haven't. The effortless confidence and the Home Counties charm helped of course. In Salford it tended to stand out more. I couldn't help wondering how someone from Guildford – or was it Godalming? – felt working on the edge of a council estate.

"Great stuff," I said. "Better be off. Things to finish off."

"Yeah. Have a good one anyway."

By the time I returned to Princess Street, the rain had stopped, but I kept looking suspiciously at the sky. Approaching number 27 I saw a black cab outside the house with its engine running. On the pavement Tanya struggled towards the taxi, carrying her little girl, a folded pushchair and a battered holdall. I quickened my pace when I saw a bloke with long, blonde hair staggering down the path pointing toward Tanya.

"You're going fucking nowhere," he shouted, showing bad teeth, "get back here."

I rushed past Tanya down the path towards the man.

"It's OK, Mick," I said, stopping a couple of feet in front of him.

He stopped and looked at me, breathing hard. Behind me I heard a taxi door open and slam shut.

"Who the fuck are you?" he slurred.

I heard the taxi pulling away.

"Gus Keane," I said. "Social Worker."

"I might have fucking known," he said, lunging at me, breathing out stale beer and tobacco fumes.

My stomach turned over. I gulped anxiously, trying to get some moisture into my mouth. This is all I bloody need, I said to myself, wondering what the hell to do. I was buggered if I was gonna let him thump me but landing a left hook on his jaw wouldn't go down well in the inevitable investigation that would follow. Anyway, I hate violence.

With a sudden inspiration I thought of an old rugby trick. Standing sideways on from Askey, I stuck out my right foot just as he reached me. He sprawled headlong on the path. He clutched his head like a footballer feigning injury and closed his eyes as if in sleep. The last time I'd tried that, my nose had collided with a Featherstone Rovers fist ten seconds later.

His mobile phone clattered to the ground. He swivelled his head round, his eyes spinning. For a few seconds I stood still. That was a close one. I looked down at Askey, whose white t-shirt squeezed his paunch. A serpent tattoo snaked under the sleeves of his donkey jacket.

"I just want to talk to you," I said, "but I get the idea this isn't a good time."

"What?"

I stepped over him, taking an envelope from my jacket pocket. I walked up to the front door and put it through the letterbox.

"It's all in the letter," I explained on my way back. "Give me a ring."

He craned his neck to look at me.

"Fuck you on about?'

Things are still happening, I thought.

"See you, Mick," I said as I left.

On the way back to the office, I got my phone out of my jeans and dialled. I let the number ring until it went into voice mail.

"Charlotte, it's Gus. I managed to contact Mick Askey. I wasn't able to talk to him – he wasn't in the mood. I'll ring again over the weekend and explain. Cheers."

I snatched up my diary, a referral form and notebook from my desk and got up. I ran my hand through my hair. Don walked past on his way out. Karen looked up from her computer screen as I muttered 'bugger' under my breath. I walked over to Bill's office, the legs of my jeans rubbing together, my feet scuffing the lino. I looked at my watch. 4.30. Shit. Giving a peremptory knock, I went in.

"Bill, I…" I said as I heard a female voice shout:

"And you can leave her out of this for a start."

I saw a short, stocky woman with grey hair standing in the middle of Bill's office, smoothing down her pleated skirt, tension on her face. Under her raincoat she wore a string of pearls over a beige jumper.

"Oh, sorry."

"It's OK, Gus," said Bill from behind his desk. He scratched his chest through his Elvis T-shirt. "Have you met my wife?"

"Yes, hi, Jean."

"Hello, Gus," said Jean, looking me up and down. "You've lost a bit of weight, haven't you?"

"Your husband's such a slave driver," I said, "I never have any bloody time to eat."

Jean almost laughed.

"I can see you're busy," she said, "I'll get out of your way."

Sitting down, I picked up a statuette of a footballer from Bill's desk. I felt the weight of its base as I read the inscription: Salford City Council Fantasy Football League: Winner Bill Copelaw.

"I'm looking forward to your leaving do," said Jean.

"Yeah, should be a good night," I said.

"That reminds me," Bill chipped in, turning to Jean. "You'd better get some cash out. I have none."

"That's right, leave everything to me. What would you do with him, Gus?"

I smiled, glancing towards the Jailhouse Rock poster on the wall.

"I'll see you later."

With a nod and half smile to me she left.

Bill took a deep breath and slumped back in his seat.

"That's what I like about married life," he said, "nowt."

We exchanged awkward smiles. If he were looking for marital counselling I was no expert, I thought, as I pictured Louise on her round-the-world trip. When last heard from she'd been staying with my sister in Sydney. I put the statuette back on the desk next to this month's Professional Social Work magazine. I glanced down at the front cover. A coffee stain in the shape of a map of Ireland decorated the words Social Workers Killed at Work: a PSW Investigation.

I held up the referral form.

"Right," he said, sitting up straight like a schoolboy, "that looks like trouble."

I shrugged.

"It's Friday afternoon. What else can you expect?"

His foot tapped out a rapid rhythm on the threadbare carpet.

"Everything's fucking trouble this week," he said.

"What's up with you lately?"

"Take your pick. Four solid days of pissing rain," he suggested. "Or thirty years of sodding social work."

He held his face in his hands.

"What have you got for me?"

I passed him the referral form. He put on his reading glasses. He shook his head as his brown eyes quickly scanned the information.

"Young baby, unexplained injury," said Bill. "Poor little bugger won't have done it playing football, will she? Who's referred this?"

Bill looked over his reading glasses at me.

"It's one of the lads from TRYS," I explained, "Paul Winston."

"I can't picture him," he said.

"I don't know if you've met him. Tall, black…"

"Not the lad who knows Viv Richards?"

"His granddad reckons he does. He's from Antigua."

"Anyway, go on."

"Paul wants to do a bit of coaching for us, so he came on that child protection workshop I ran last week."

Bill nodded.

"I stressed the importance of reporting any concerns you have, you know."

"And he sees this little girl with a dodgy looking leg," said Bill, "and rings you."

"Yeah."

"And on the day you retire," he sighed. "It could be 'I've been on a course syndrome', but you're gonna have to go and have a look at it, mate."

"I know. Nothing like going out with a bang."

"It's not far, that's one good thing."

I nodded.

"Will you be around later," I asked.

"Should think so," said Bill. "I've got someone coming to see me at half five. And I need to make some inroads into that lot."

He gestured towards the wobbly pile in his in-tray.

"Not good for your health."

"It's only angina."

"'Only angina,' he says. I'm surprised you didn't go for early retirement when they announced this restructuring."

"Can't afford it," he sighed, scratching his head. "A few unexpected expenses."

"Bugger."

"I can't work out how you can afford it," he added.

"Health wise, I can't afford not to," I said.

"But financially? If you don't mind me asking."

"No, that's OK," I said.

I paused for thought.

"I suppose what swung it was when I inherited some money from my cousin, Vince."

"He left you money in his will? Nice cousin."

I shrugged.

"No, it's just that me and my sister were his closest living relatives. He died intestate."

"Yeah?"

"Still," I said, "once they've chopped your balls off life's not worth living anyway."

He laughed with gusto.

"Who's gonna cheer me up when you've gone?"

"Not my problem, Bill. Still, if you are staying on, it's good news for everybody."

"Flatterer."

"No, I'm serious. Apart from anything else, if you go young Don might take over."

He looked at me and raised his eyebrows.

"Young Don. That makes him sound like the heir to a Mafia dynasty."

"The Mafia'd kick him out for being too ambitious."

"I thought you liked him."

I pursed my lips.

"Oh, he's not too bad, a bit humourless, I suppose. And too much of a go-getter. I can imagine him as one of those bankers who ruined the economy."

"I know what you mean. Tell you what, Gus," he said, "Don won't be taking over if I have anything to do with it."

My eyes opened wide. I let a smile slip out as Bill went on.

"And he knows it."

"Oh? Was that what he was so upset about this morning?"

"How did you know about that?"

"I heard him."

"Yeah, he did get quite cross."

"Anyway," I said. "I'd better get a move on. I still need to contact the police."

"I'll ring them for you; get someone to meet you there. And any problems, ring me."

"Thanks, Bill."

"Just think, in a few hours we'll be at the Park Hotel, having a pint at your party. I hope you've got some decent music lined up."

"Fifties band, A Lop Bam Boom. My daughter's in it."

"Oh, aye? You must have brought her up right."

"Marti Pym's the lead singer.'

"Marti? The solicitor?"

I nodded.

"She kept that quiet."

"The band put an advert in the paper for a vocalist and got Marti. Brilliant voice. Looks good on stage."

We looked at one another, each knowing what the other was thinking.

"Looks good anywhere," he grinned.

Ten minutes later I dashed outside into the rain, struggling with my briefcase and a baby-seat. Automatically pulling my hood over my head I scurried across the road to the car park. Opening the boot of my red Peugeot I flung the baby-seat in and slammed it shut. I got in the car and chucked the briefcase onto the passenger seat. I turned the engine on and eased the car through the potholes. Out of the corner of my eye I thought I saw Jean Copelaw in a posh car with a much younger woman.

That made me think of what Bill had said about his financial troubles. How could he be short of money? He and Jean had well-paid jobs; their daughter was independent. Not that it was any of my business, I acknowledged, as I thought of my own financial situation. Louise and I had made a big profit on the house in Worsley we'd lived in for 30 years. With my share I had bought the flat in Salford Quays, with enough left over to pay for the improvements. My pension wouldn't be great but with the lump sum and Vince's money I'd be OK for a while. I'd need some part time work eventually but I'd worry about that some other time.

I switched off from monetary matters to more immediate concerns as I reached the address I was looking for. I'd had to pass Tanya's place, where there was no sign of life. I could have walked but I had a feeling I'd need the car. I pulled up outside the house and got out clutching my briefcase. The rain pelted down as I walked past a flash motorbike parked outside. I approached the front door and knocked hard, taking my wallet out in readiness.

"Come on, you bugger," I muttered, "I'm drowning out here."

After what seemed like a long time a girl with a fading black eye opened the door.

"Sharon Winters?"

"Yeah."

"Gus Keane. Social worker from Children's Services at Ordsall Tower," I said, showing my ID.

Sharon stood staring at me.

"I wonder if I could come in and have a word about Rebecca."

Sharon gawped a few moments longer then stood aside to let me in. I put my wallet back in my jeans and pulled my hood down. As we walked along the hallway, I took my notebook from the briefcase. In the sitting room a fair-haired young man sat on the sofa watching The Weakest Link and swigging from a can of Special Brew. Without waiting to be asked I sat on a wooden chair with a biker's jacket thrown over the back. Sharon balanced on the edge of an armchair.

"You must be Liam...Bentley," I said, looking down at my notebook.

"Social Services," said Sharon.

"What do you want?" he asked without taking his eyes off the screen.

He spilled lager on his grubby white T-shirt. He took a long drag on his cigarette, squinting his brown eyes against the smoke. I told them why I was there: report expressing concern about a swelling on Rebecca's knee. Sharon stood impassive with a dead look on her face, her faded jeans and pink top hanging off her bones. Smells of dried sweat and fried food fought for supremacy.

"We haven't done anything to her if that's what you're saying," she said.

I went through my well-rehearsed explanation: I wasn't accusing them of anything; I would need to have a look at Rebecca and if I were concerned about her we would have to take her to hospital to be examined. Liam got up and began to pace the room. He looked at me, moving closer, invading my personal space, before turning to his girlfriend.

"You know what he's trying to do, don't you Sharon," he said, blowing out smoke. "He wants to fit us up for hurting the baby."

"Liam, please," said Sharon, crossing her legs as if bursting for a slash.

"Why not sit down again? Let's talk this through properly," I said.

"He wants our kid in care, you know, Sharon," Liam said, waving the beer can in the air. "They have monthly targets."

He sat back down on the settee.

"It really would be best if you both co-operate," I said, trying to take control. "If you could just let me have a look at her before we go any further. Where is she?"

"She's upstairs asleep," said Sharon. "I've only just got her off."

"I'm sorry. It's got to be done."

"It's the only way to get rid of you, I suppose,' said Liam, scowling.

Muttering from Liam accompanied us as they took me upstairs to Rebecca's bedroom. I took in the bare walls and lack of toys or any other evidence of whose room it was. Going over to the cot, I pulled back the cover and looked at a baby with hardly any hair in a pink sleeping suit. I smiled at her. Rebecca opened her blue eyes.

"Hello, Rebecca," I said, "aren't you lovely? Sorry to disturb you."

"She can't understand you," said Liam, "stupid twat."

"Could one of you get her out of the cot, please," I asked.

Sharon picked her up.

"Could you undress her, please?"

Sighing, she lay her daughter on a changing mat on the floor and did as I'd asked. I knelt down and continued talking gently to the baby.

"There's quite a swelling round the right knee," I said. "Any idea what might have caused it?"

Sharon shook her head, her mouth open wide.

"Wasn't me," said Liam.

"Could you turn Rebecca on her tummy?"

Again Sharon obeyed.

"There's quite a few bruises on her back as well," I said, "how did they get there?"

They shrugged in unison. Fingertip bruising, I thought, that familiar sick, helpless panic attacking my stomach. I'd rather be anywhere but here right now, I admitted to myself. Thank fuck for procedures. At least I knew what I had to do without agonising about it.

"If you could get her dressed," I said, "We'll talk about it downstairs."

"We need to get Rebecca checked out at hospital," I said a few minutes later in the living room.

Liam stabbed his finger at me.

"You're not taking my fucking baby away," he shouted, dropping the can and cigarette. He reached across and snatched Rebecca from Sharon's arms. He held her against his chest. As lager spilled out on the carpet, Rebecca let out a howl, her screams increasing in volume the longer her father had hold of her. Where were the police when you needed them, I thought. They should have been here by now.

"Liam, you're not helping. Whatever you think of me, Rebecca needs proper treatment. And we need time to find out what happened to her."

Liam squared up to me before, with a petulant pout, he shoved the baby roughly into Sharon's arms.

"You won't get away with this," he said.

"Liam" I said, "right now we need to concentrate on your little girl. I'll take you all to hospital in my car."

"Fuck that. Tell him, Sharon. Tell him you're not going to no hospital."

She looked from me to him and back again while trying to comfort Rebecca, whose sobs were slowly dying down.

"It can't do any harm to get her checked out, Liam."

"Right! You're on your own then."

He grabbed the leather jacket and ran out of the room. Rebecca flinched in her mother's arms as the front door slammed.

Things are still happening, I thought, as I heard a motor bike start up outside.

***

At the front steps of Ordsall Tower I stepped back to let two teenage girls pass. Smoke from their fags made me want to sneeze. I approached the main door and punched in the security number. I entered the building. I breathed in the salt and vinegar tang of somebody's fish and chips. My stomach rumbled, reminding me how long it had been since I had eaten. Going into the office, I removed my waterproof, watching it drip water past my jeans onto the floor. I looked at my watch. Six thirty. Stifling a yawn I stretched my arms over my head. One good thing, Rebecca was safe for now. Sharon was staying with her in hospital. Someone else could pick up the pieces on Monday morning.

The deserted office smelt of damp and stale air. It had an air of abandonment, matching the way I felt. The only sounds were a background hum of traffic and my footsteps pattering along. I gave a start as a vacuum cleaner burst into life on the first floor. I noticed a light under the door of Bill's room. As I approached my desk my mobile beeped and I pulled it from my jeans pocket. I opened the text:

> Hi, Dad, train has still not left London. Nobody seems to know why. Will let you know when I'm on my way. See you soon. Danny.

Shit! The party would be over by the time he got here at this rate. Hanging my waterproof on the back of my chair I flopped down and dumped my briefcase on the desk. Logging on to the computer I began to update my case notes. No good leaving it until Monday. Ten minutes later I sat back in my chair and looked out of the window. Rain clouds accentuated the darkness of the sky and the gloom that surrounded me.

My usual logic was no comfort. You've got early retirement, I kept telling myself. An ambition fulfilled. By eight o'clock tonight you'll be in the Park Hotel sinking your first pint. It didn't work. Thinking I ought to make sure there was nothing in my desk when I left tonight, I opened one of the drawers. I pulled out a packet of fig rolls with two biscuits left in; a brand new notebook never used and a PG Wodehouse paperback: Very Good, Jeeves!, this week's lunchtime reading. I opened the flyleaf, reading Gus Keane 167 West Park Street Salford 5. How long must I have had it for God's sake and how many times had I read it? Looking through the yellowing pages I read the title of the first short story: Jeeves and the Impending Doom. A suitable title, I couldn't help thinking. What was the matter with me? In the interval between the vacuum cleaner being switched on and off there was an unnatural quiet. Goose bumps ran up and down my spine. No sound at all seemed to come from Bill's office. Whatever he was doing, he wasn't making much noise.

Getting up, I strolled to the other end of the office again, accompanied by the sound of the Hoover above me. Arriving at the door of Bill's office I noticed it was slightly ajar. Pushing it open I saw a small packet on the floor, and picked it up. Durex Fetherlite, I read. For customers of Maxwell's Hotel, York. So that's what he got up to on that course last week. Wasn't our new director a keynote speaker? Smiling, I pushed the door wider and went into the room.

"You must have dropped these…" I began, holding out the packet with a grin.

An abrupt silence hit me as the vacuum was switched off. On the floor I saw an overturned chair, a chipped Salford City Reds coffee mug and a sheet of white paper with typing on it. A letter? I stared straight ahead and a shiver trembled through me.

I felt a sudden dizziness, clutching at the wall for support. My eyes flitted at breakneck speed from one spot to the next round the room. I took in the Swiss cheese plant knocked sideways so that it leant gently against the window, like a drunk pausing on his way home. A buff file hung precariously over the edge of the desk, its papers hanging loose. The studio portrait of Bill's wife standing to attention. In all this my eyes avoided him, seeing him but not seeing.

"Bill," I called out, walking over to the desk, "you OK?"

No response. I walked round to the other side of the desk towards the window. Bill lay crazily across his chair, his right hand hanging limply, head down on the carpeted floor, grey hair dishevelled, denim jacket hanging open, T-shirt riding up to reveal his beer belly. On the desk in front of him lay a Manchester Evening News, an open wallet bulging with banknotes and a half-eaten Mars bar.

Averting my eyes for a moment I looked out. Rain whooshed against the window. A clapped out yellow camper van farted blue exhaust fumes past the Park Hotel. Come on, I instructed myself, you've got to look at him. Really focus on his face. Take it in properly. The mouth gaping open as if in amazement, the brown eyes protruding alarmingly. I forced myself to examine the bruise on his forehead, the congealed blood. On the carpet I saw the statuette from Bill's desk, the football trophy, with blood spots on the player's head.

"You were so proud of that thing. Poor Bill."

Catching a hint of aftershave, I walked over to him and shook him by the shoulders. Nothing. I sniffed, feeling tears run down my cheeks. I licked my lips, tasting the salt. I'd been prone to tears these past few months. Vulnerable, that's how my counsellor described it, a mild case of post-traumatic disorder. A bit dramatic, that, I thought. The expression 'blood drained from his face' came to mind as I passed a clammy hand over my forehead. The cold made me long to huddle up to a hot water bottle; at the same time I wanted to wipe the sweat from my brow. Momentarily, I closed my eyes. Quickly I opened them again to drive away an image of my mother's dead body on the kitchen floor all those years ago. About to pick up Bill's phone, I realised I still had the condoms in my hand. Dropping them on the desk, I dialled 999. My bottom lip trembled as I tried to speak. I had the same constriction in the throat I had had the day my mam died. I tried again and succeeded in giving my name and location and telling the operator someone had been attacked. Then, in response to a question, I said:

"His name's Bill Copelaw. I think he might be dead."

CHAPTER FOUR

"Hi, Gus, you still here?"

I looked up from my desk, where I had sat staring into space for maybe three minutes, wondering who the young woman with the foreign accent was. The cleaner, of course. I had forgotten there was anyone else in the building.

"I did your apartment," she said, "it's as good as new."

"Ania," I said, "sit down, I've got something to tell you."

She bent down to plug in the vacuum cleaner.

"I need to get on."

"No, this is important."

She walked towards me, stuffing a yellow duster into the pocket of her navy blue overall.

"What is it, Gus, you don't look too good."

She tucked her brown hair behind her ears as if to tidy herself up in readiness for something. She sat down.

"Listen, Ania," I said, struggling to find the right words. "Something terrible has happened."

"What do…"

"I went into Bill's office a few minutes ago and…"

After a pause for breath, I told her Bill was dead. I explained the circumstances. She sat with her hand over her mouth, trying to stifle the tears welling up in her brown eyes.

"I'm just waiting for the police," I said. "They'll want to talk to you. And the other cleaners."

"It was that guy, I know it was."

"What guy's this?"

She took a deep breath.

"About an hour ago it was. He barged in just as I opened the front door. I never had a chance to stop him. I am sorry."

"There's nothing to be sorry about."

She fished a tissue from her pocket and wiped her eyes. She probably wishes she were back in Warsaw, I thought. I knew she had come over last year to do an English degree at Manchester University. The cleaning helped pay for her studies.

"He was waving a piece of paper in his hand. He was looking for you, Gus."

"Me?"

"'Where's Keane', he said. 'I'm gonna kill him.' He used the F word."

I sat up and watched as she took a deep breath.

"I told him the office was closed," she went on. "'He sent me a letter,' he said, 'something about my daughter. Well, I haven't got an effing daughter.'"

"I think I know who it is," I said.

"I said he'd have to come back on Monday."

"What happened next?"

She gripped the arms of the chair.

"Bill came out and said he'd deal with it. He said to the man, 'Calm down, Mick, come into my office and we'll talk about it.'"

Mick Askey. I knew it.

"And that was the last I saw of either of them."

We spent the next couple of minutes getting the other two cleaners together then sat down again near my desk to wait. I took my mobile out of my pocket and dialled.

"Hiya, Rachel," I said when she answered, "there's a bit of a problem."

"What's that?"

"We're gonna have to cancel the leaving do."

"What? You can't do that. We've only just arrived…"

"No, listen, Rachel. It's just that…"

How to put this?

"Well, Bill Copelaw, the boss, you know, has been found dead at his desk."

"Oh, my God."

"Yes, I got back from a late visit and…"

I struggled to find the right words.

"It looks like someone assaulted him."

"Bloody hell."

"I'm with the cleaners now. We have to wait for the police and everything."

"Are you OK?"

"Yeah, fine. It just wouldn't be…appropriate to go ahead with the party now."

"Of course. I'll tell the rest of the band. And the landlord."

I wouldn't be popular with Arthur.

"Thanks. You can go home and have an early night."

"No way. I'm coming to see you," she insisted.

"Let me finish off here, love. Why not come round to the flat in an hour or so? Say eight o'clock."

Ten minutes later a uniformed constable arrived. He said he'd been in the area when he got the call. After having a look in Bill's office he asked a few questions and got our names and addresses. He parked himself outside Bill's office and asked us to wait for CID to arrive.

Ten minutes after that, I had just made a pot of tea in the kitchen. I took mugs out of the cupboard and put them on the table. The sound of someone sniffing made me look towards the open door. A woman of Asian background with a leather handbag slung over her shoulder was just coming in.

"Mr. Keane?" she asked.

I nodded. She sniffed again, holding up an ID badge.

"Detective Inspector Ellerton."

I noticed she had a Scottish accent and a husky voice. We shook hands and she sat on a hardback chair opposite me. She plucked a tissue from a box on the table and wiped her nose. She used this movement to stifle a yawn. Her business suit had a few more creases than it had started out with that morning, I guessed. She had her dark hair up but stray wisps had escaped. She'd had a long, hard day, I surmised, as she coughed and cleared her throat, and it wasn't over yet.

"You OK to answer a few questions," she said.

"Sure. I've just made tea," I said, "you sound as if you need one."

"Please," she said.

We sat at the table with our tea. She took out a pen and notebook from her handbag. She was probably thirty-five or less but right now she looked older. Poor sod, I thought, feeling quite fatherly. She gave what I took to be an oft-repeated spiel: the death of a colleague in such circumstances must have been a shock but it was important to gather whatever information I could provide as soon as possible. Like a keen pupil she opened her book at a clean page and straightened her shoulders. She asked me if I'd seen anyone or anything suspicious in the vicinity of Ordsall Tower.

"No," I replied, "but do you know about Mick Askey?"

"Mick Askey?"

She wrote the name down. I explained my connection with Askey and what Ania had said.

"One of my colleagues is talking to the cleaners at the moment, but thanks for mentioning it. Now perhaps you could tell me how you came to find Mr. Copelaw."

I told her about coming back after a late visit and finding the body. She was careful to check the times.

"I see. When and where did you last see Mr. Copelaw alive?"

That last word reinforced the finality of Bill's death.

"About half four or so in his office. I had to see him about an urgent case."

"Was anybody else around at the time? Colleagues perhaps?"

"Well, he was talking to his wife, Jean, when I went into his office."

"His wife? A bit unusual surely?"

She wrote more notes and looked expectantly at me. It was probably my imagination but I sensed a heightened interest.

"Not that unusual," I said. "She occasionally pops in to see him."

"Really? Doesn't she work?"

"She's the manager of Marks and Spencer somewhere, Wigan, I think. I presume today was her day off."

Was anxiety making me say too much? What was she getting at? Whatever it was I couldn't think of anything more to say about Jean's visit to the office. The Inspector looked at me with intense concentration. A sudden sneeze and a grab for another tissue rather spoiled the effect. She apologised.

"What other family did he have?"

I thought for a second, sipping tea.

"There's a daughter. I can't think of her name, sorry. I think she lives down south somewhere."

Inspector Ellerton scribbled away in her book. I wondered why Bill hardly ever talked about his daughter. On reflection it seemed strange. Rob, the insurance bloke, talked of little else and I often referred to Danny and Rachel in everyday conversation. Most parents did. But not Bill.

"Who else was in the office this afternoon," she asked.

I shrugged.

"We were pretty thin on the ground," I said. "There's quite a few taking their last few days of annual leave. And people tend to come and go in any case. What time are you talking about?"

"Say from lunchtime onwards."

I tried to list the people I had seen that afternoon: Don and Karen, a couple of typists, a bloke from IT who was doing an inventory of computers. 'Infantry', he'd said in his e-mail. What was the point of all this, I asked myself.

"What about when you last saw Mr. Copelaw? Who was around then?"

"Well, it was past home time. Nearly everybody had gone home."

"I have to ask you, can you think of anyone who would want to kill Mr. Copelaw or attack him?"

"Nobody," I said, "though I can imagine Mick Askey lashing out in anger at anyone who happened to be around."

"How did you get on with Mr. Copelaw?"

"OK."

"Just OK?"

"Yeah, we weren't close friends but we got on fine."

"I see. Did everybody else get on with him?"

"Yeah," I said, thinking momentarily of Don. "As far as I know. Bill has ...had only been here about nine months and for a large part of that I was on the sick."

"What was the problem?"

"I had a stroke last year. I only got back to work in January," I added. Is this relevant, I said to myself. I wasn't going to argue. The whole thing was a bloody nightmare – for once not a misuse of that word – and I wanted to get it over with and go home.

"This won't help," she said.

I nodded, wanting to say 'I am aware of that' through clenched teeth.

"It's OK," I said, "I'm retiring today."

"You don't look old enough."

"I feel it."

"I bet you don't feel much like celebrating though."

"Not exactly."

"I'll let you go then," she said, trying to smile. "If I could have your full name, address and phone number."

I recited the details to her, feeling like a lost child, then remembered I'd already told the constable where I lived. She handed me a card from her bag.

"If anything does occur to you perhaps you could give me a call."

"Of course."

As she got up to go, I remembered something else.

"Oh, the condoms."

"What?"

I explained about finding the noddies.

"It was funny at the time," I said.

I picture myself walking into that room, about to take the piss out of Bill.

"Not funny now," I added.

She shook her head.

"Life's a bitch."

I nodded in agreement. She smiled half-heartedly.

"Well, that's it. You can get yourself home."

That's where you should be, I almost said.

I left the building accompanied by the uncomfortable thought that the Inspector must be viewing anyone who knew Bill with suspicion.

CHAPTER FIVE

An hour later I was home in my third floor apartment, feeling more human after a quick shower and shave. I looked out of the window of my new, state of the art kitchen at the science fiction world of Salford Quays. Like stage lights, balloon bulbs on black lampposts lit up a couple walking hand in hand into the Holiday Inn. Swans glided on a section of the old Ship Canal, cordoned off with blue and white locks and bridges. Benches with wooden slats in black metal frames sat by the water. Beside them rubbish bins with 'Salford' written in gold on their sides stood ready to receive the city's litter. In the distance Old Trafford with 'Manchester United' lit up in red dominated the skyline.

"Past, present and future in one package, Gus," I said to myself.

I remembered when Salford Quays was Manchester Docks and got that ache of longing in the guts for things I would never get back. I closed the blinds and took my mug of tea to the kitchen table. I put it down by a three quarters full bottle of Chilean Merlot.

Looking round the room I noticed for the first time how tidy it was. Just as Ania had promised. There was still a smell of paint – her boyfriend had done a good job too. May as well read the paper while waiting for Rachel, I thought. Maybe I'd have time to read the bloody thing properly from next week. After a bit of a search, I located the Guardian on the bookshelf where the PG Wodehouse autograph edition and the complete works of Delia Smith took pride of place. My eyes focused on the headline at the bottom of the front page:

Kylie's Mother: 'I have not given up hope'.
Elaine Anderson believes she will one day be re-united with her daughter, Kylie. The forty-one-year-old was speaking last night at a press conference to mark Kylie's 18th birthday. Kylie was abducted at the age of 4 months, and has not been seen since.

I looked at a blurred photograph of a blue-eyed baby girl next to one of what she would look like now. Allegedly. Beneath it were 'Then and Now' pictures of her glamorous mother. With a sad shake of the head, I read on:

The distraught mother recalled the rainy day eighteen years ago when she was looking forward to a night out with friends in Chorley, her home town. Planning to leave Kylie with her mother, she set off with her in her pushchair. She stopped at First News, just a matter of yards from her mother's place. In the shop she bought Woman's Weekly and a packet of cigarettes. People were calling into the shop on their way home from work. Elaine left the pushchair outside because the inside of the shop was so crowded. When she came out the pushchair and Kylie had gone. There were conflicting reports at the time of either an overweight woman or a middle-aged couple pushing a pushchair away from the shop. Several vehicles were sighted and a camper van was seen moving away at speed a couple of streets away.

Today there would probably be CCTV footage, I thought. Before I could read any more my mobile rang and I took it out of my jeans pocket.

"Hiya, is that Gus," said a woman's voice struggling to be heard over what sounded like pub noises.

"Yes."

It wasn't one of those cold callers who wanted to lend me money, was it? They didn't usually sound pissed.

"It's me, Tanya."

"Tanya?"

I didn't know any Tanya.

"You know, from Princess Street."

Bloody hell, that Tanya. So much had happened since then.

"You all right," I asked half-heartedly.

"Hey, it was dead funny, what happened this morning, wasn't it?"

"Yeah."

"I can laugh about it now," she went on. "Any road, I just wanted to thank you for helping me, you know what I mean?"

"That's OK, Tanya."

"I've finally got away from that bastard."

"Good, I'm glad," I said, wondering whether to tell her he had killed my boss.

"If I can ever do owt for you, just call me, know what I mean?"

"Yeah, I'll do that."

"Gotta go, see you."

As the call ended, I wondered what circumstances could possibly lead me to ring her. I saved her number anyway, just in case. I was a 'just in case kind of guy' according to my counsellor. She was right, of course. It was truer than ever now: recent events proved you never knew what was round the corner. And child protection social work had strengthened my natural caution. As I went back to the Guardian I heard the sound of someone calling:

"You there, Dad?"

Rachel walked into the flat, her flat, black shoes squeaking on the laminate flooring, her hands protectively on her bump. She took off her anorak, revealing cotton trousers and a Beatles hoodie. Putting the coat and her handbag on a chair, she joined me at the table. She put her arm round me and kissed me on the cheek. Pregnancy had darkened her long, brown hair so that it was now almost black. Faint lines around her blue eyes showed the end of week strain of teaching special needs kids. Guilt about worrying my pregnant daughter added to my anxiety. A few seconds later a black woman, even taller than Rachel, strolled in after her on trendy walking shoes.

"Hello, Marti," I said.

Marti smiled and said 'Hi'.

"Marti offered to come with me," explained Rachel.

"I hope that's OK," Marti added in a scouse accent.

"Course it is. Nice to see you. Sit down."

Dumping a canvas shoulder bag on the table, she took her leather jacket off and put it on the back of her chair. I glanced at Marti craftily as she sat down. Rachel had told me Marti was nearly fifty though I would have put her at late thirties, forty at the most. Whatever her age she looked well on it in her tight jeans and white T-shirt. Slim but not too slim, I thought to myself. Understated make-up except for perfectly applied red lipstick that made her mouth even sexier. Intricate dreadlocks – at least I thought they were dreadlocks – framed a face with too much character to be called pretty. You'd look twice though. A smile that would light up the world. Skin as smooth as deep brown velvet. Fantastic bum. Not that I was really looking. Or was I? Was this my long-lost libido making a comeback? Another box ticked in the recovery checklist?

"Tea," she said, pulling up a chair, "I thought you'd have been on the Scotch by now."

"I can't stand whisky," I explained.

Before I could offer drinks, Rachel demanded information. I explained in a bit more detail about finding Bill. As I gave my account, images of Bill lying dead invaded my mind. These were followed, for some reason, by pictures of me running out of the office in a confused state the day I'd had a stroke. What would my counsellor make of that?

"Oh, my God," said Marti, while Rachel sat in horrified silence. "Poor guy. And poor you, Gus."

I'd like to have bottled the loving sympathy in her voice. Pity she's out of my league, I thought.

"So what happened after you found him," asked Rachel.

"Just what you'd expect," I said. "I rang the police and had to wait for them, not touch anything and all that."

"Do they know who did it?"

"They're looking for a suspect, an angry client."

"Well, that's something," said Marti.

"I can't believe this. You actually found..." said Rachel.

"Yeah, but it's over now. Let's talk about something else."

I really didn't want Rachel thinking about any of this. She had enough on her plate. I decided to try and lighten the mood.

"I reckon Bill would have wanted me to celebrate my retirement somehow. We can start by finishing that."

I pointed at the bottle on the table. I went over to the dishwasher and got out three clean glasses.

"Just a small one for me," said Rachel.

"Large one for me, Gus," said Marti, "I'm not pregnant and I'm not driving."

When the glasses were filled and we'd clinked glasses, I noticed Rachel yawn.

"You look tired, love."

"I am a bit," she said.

I took another mouthful of wine in the pause that followed.

"You should get yourself home early."

"I don't like to leave you."

"Rachel, I'm OK, just had a bit of a shock. You should go home and rest. Kev will be waiting to look after you."

I thought of the handsome Frenchman my daughter had married last year. Knowing Kevin – pronounced in the French way though his dad was Irish – was a Rugby League fan was a source of great comfort to me. More importantly, he was a good bloke – bon type in French, he assured me. Pity he was always so bloody cheerful.

"You sure you'll be OK?"

"Rachel, worry about yourself. And about George or Georgia."

"Who," asked Marti.

"If it's a girl it'll be Georgia. George if it's a boy," I explained. "Whatever it's called, you need to go home and rest. Marti, tell her."

"Listen to your father, Rachel," said Marti, wagging her finger.

Rachel smiled.

"Now you're ganging up on me."

"Because we care about you. And you know we're right."

"I can't win," said Rachel but I could see she was weakening.

"I'll keep an eye on your dad for a while," Marti said.

Rachel and her friend looked at one another for a few seconds.

"Oh, I see," said Rachel eventually. "Right. OK."

Marti swallowed another gulp of wine and exchanged another smile with Rachel before looking away.

"You'd better keep an eye on her as well, Dad."

"It'll be my pleasure," I said.

I was vaguely aware of being in the middle of a private joke I didn't fully understand.

"Don't worry, Gus, I won't stay too long," said Marti.

"Stay as long as you like," I said, hoping she would realise I wasn't just being polite.

"I'm due in Liverpool at ten tomorrow morning. I'm taking Mum to Chester for her birthday."

After more conversation about nothing in particular – I hate long good-byes – Rachel finished her wine and got up.

"Oh, by the way, Dad, Danny's train has only just left Euston," she added as a parting shot. "I told him to come straight to my place. I'll ring tomorrow about meeting up."

She left and I was alone in my flat with Marti. After dark.

CHAPTER SIX

I thought of what I knew about Marti Pym. After 25 years as a solicitor in London she'd moved to Manchester a few months back to be nearer her mother. She and a friend from University days had opened their own business on Salford Quays. She'd popped round for coffee a few times when I was on the sick – at Rachel's instigation, I couldn't help but think. Sometimes she'd suggest going to Tony and Dino's for a change. Rachel again, I reckoned – 'don't let him stay indoors all the time, he'll get depressed'.

I felt my stomach rumble.

"I've just realised I'm bloody Hank Marvin," I said, after a bit of chat about Rachel, the new baby and my excitement and anxiety about becoming a grandfather. "Do you fancy something to eat?"

"I thought you'd never ask."

Fifteen minutes later we sat down to Venison steak with red wine and dark chocolate sauce with stir-fried veg. During the cooking, we'd talked about music, the evils of the Tory government and her visit to Bruges at Christmas.

She took her first mouthful, swallowed and murmured with pleasure.

"My God, this is gorgeous," she said.

"Glad you like it," I replied with suitable modesty.

"Rachel told me you were a good cook but she didn't tell me you were this good."

I recalled someone telling me years ago that being able to cook added to your pulling power.

"So," she said, cutting up another bit of meat, "tell me about this murder."

I wondered whether I could handle this. Maybe if I steered clear of dead bodies and just told her the rest of what happened it would be OK. Anyway, people were going to be interested. I had to admit I would be if someone else had found the body. Most importantly I wanted to keep Marti here as long as possible.

"After I'd phoned the police I spoke to one of the cleaners."

"Right."

"She told me a bloke called Mick Askey had been in the office about an hour before I found the body."

"Who is he, this…"

"Askey. He's the angry client I told you about. Effing and blinding, he was apparently, threatening all sorts."

"And?"

"Bill took Askey into his office to try and calm him down."

"Shit! What was his problem, do you know?"

"Don't tell Rachel but he was after me."

"God. What did he have against you?"

"Well, I am – was – the social worker for a girl who's been in foster care most of her life. She's 18 now."

"And?"

"She thinks Askey's probably her father. I went to his house to tell him she wanted to see him."

I explained about Tanya's escape in the taxi and my tripping Askey on the front path.

"I ended up sticking a note through his door. He had it with him when he came to the office."

"And?"

We exchanged glances.

"He was saying he didn't have an expletive deleted daughter. Seemed pissed off I had even suggested such a thing."

"I presume you told the police this?"

"When I could get a word in edgeways," I said. "Before I had a chance to mention Askey, I was given a grilling by a Detective Inspector. Not much older than Rachel, she was."

"Who was it?"

"Oh, what's her name? Elliott, I think it was. No, Ellerton. Asian, Scottish accent."

"That'll be Sarita. Married to Jake Ellerton, he's a copper too. Yorkshireman. They're trying for a baby."

I laughed.

"How do you know that?" I asked.

"All part of the job. I have to deal with the police so it's a good idea to befriend them."

For a moment I wondered what Marti had found out about me without my realising. She went on with her questioning.

"What did Sarita have to say for herself?"

She picked up the wine glass in her right hand, twirling the stem with her left. Telling myself not to stare, I watched her long fingers, the plain gold ring on her right hand. As she sipped her wine, I noticed a cluster of freckles above her top lip.

"First I had to account for my movements. Next it was, 'And how did you get on with Mr Copelaw?' She asked that one with just a slight inflection in her voice. You know, as if that would induce a confession."

"Nightmare."

She looked in my direction, intense concentration on her face. I thought back to the office and the young policewoman sitting across the desk from me.

"'Who was in the office when I last saw Bill - I couldn't remember all that well."

I leant forward, putting my elbows on the table.

"She got interested when I told her Bill's wife had popped in to see him."

She looked at me with raised eyebrows. I went on with my story.

"I didn't tell the Inspector but they were in the middle of a row."

"Who, Bill and his wife?"

"Yeah. She said, 'leave her out of it' or words to that effect. I've no idea who she was talking about."

"Oh, it'll be one of Bill's women," said Marti. "He liked them young apparently."

"What?"

Marti sipped her wine before going on.

"That's what people say."

"People?"

"Social workers," she said, "you can't beat them for a good gossip. It helps to pass the time while we're hanging around the family courts."

I thought about this while we drank our wine, wondering, not for the first time, why I was always the last person to hear any gossip.

"I suppose the spouse is always the main suspect," I said, "but that doesn't seem relevant in this case."

"No, although…"

"What?"

"Well, if it was you he was angry with," she said, "why attack someone else?"

"Well," I shrugged, "To Askey me and Bill both represent the same thing. Officialdom, authority, whatever. I've had people threaten me for something somebody else has done plenty of times."

"Yeah?"

"I remember one bloke who took a swing at me because his benefits hadn't been paid. And I was trying to help him."

"It's a dangerous job, yours."

"Yeah," I said, "more social workers than police are killed at work."

"God."

There was a thoughtful silence.

"You know, Marti," I said, "when I found Bill..."

"Yeah?"

"There was...well, it was like those things you see in the paper: what are the differences between these two pictures?"

"I'm not with you."

"Well, I had been in Bill's office earlier and when I went back – the time I found his body…"

"Yes?"

"Well, this is going to sound stupid, but it's as if something was there that shouldn't have been or something wasn't there that should have been."

"Right," she said uncertainly.

I finished my wine, beginning to doubt myself. It wasn't as though any of this was relevant.

"Probably imagining things."

"So, retired, eh," said Marti later that evening.

I nodded. We had finished our meal and retired to the living room. From the iPod speakers in the corner came Billie Holiday's huskily caressing voice.

"You don't look old enough."

"You know I've always liked you, Marti," I grinned.

"Good," she said, looking at me, then looking away again.

She sipped her brandy, resting her glass on the arm of a leather armchair. Drinking spirits is one of the many things I don't see the point of. I'd only had the brandy in for a recipe. I sat in a matching armchair, close to hers. I had stuck to red wine, the only thing I drink unless I'm in a pub with really good beer. She stretched her legs in front of her and lay back with a smile of satisfaction on her face. Quietly she joined in the song for a few seconds.

"Fine and mellow," she sang. "That's just how I feel. Good food and drink and good company."

Was she talking about me, I wondered, tempted to look round to see if there was anybody else in the room. She turned towards me and smiled.

"You know, this is the longest time we've spent in one another's company," she said.

"Yeah, it's nice."

I smiled and sat back. She lifted her glass to her lips and drank.

"When I've popped in to see you these past few weeks," she said, "I was afraid I might have been making a nuisance of myself."

"Anything but."

"It's just that sometimes you seemed so guarded."

She was right, I realised, though I hadn't thought of it like that before.

"I have been guarded, I suppose," I went on. "My counsellor thinks I need to get back into mainstream life, you know."

I thought of those sessions when I'd talked about my loss of self-confidence. When she had made me list the things I was most proud of.

"You're still having the counselling then? How's it going?"

I nodded, drinking more wine and noting the look of interest on her face.

"It's brilliant," I said, "It's helped me a lot."

"Great."

She drank her brandy and looked at me, as if weighing me up.

"Are you ready for mainstream life?"

I nodded and smiled.

"You need to let go,' she said, reaching out and laying a sensuously comforting hand on my arm.

"Good idea."

I watched, fascinated, as she ran her elegant fingers along my arm. I looked her in the eyes. Awkwardly, we moved our heads closer together across the arms of the chair. We kissed.

"At last," she said, leaning forward to entwine her arms round my neck. "At bloody last."

* * *

"A lot's happened today," I said at around midnight in my double bed, "but this is definitely the best bit."

"I should think so," she said, cuddling up closer and stroking my stomach.

We kissed.

"Who'd have thought I'd end the day in bed with a gorgeous woman."

We kissed again and lay back in silence for a while. Then, I'm not sure how, we got talking about Marti's musical career.

"I was in the charts once, you know," she said.

"Really?"

"Number seven back in the eighties. An Original Way, composed by yours truly."

"I remember it," I said. "The band was…Side Parting. So that was you?"

"Yeah."

"Hey, I was lusting after you even then. I bet I wasn't the only one."

"Flatterer," she grinned.

"I didn't know you were famous," I said.

"Famous for fifteen minutes," she said disparagingly. "The follow up was a flop."

"What was it?"

"As I never managed to write another hit, we released a cover of Just A Little Loving, you know, the old Dusty Springfield number."

"A sexy song," I said, as the lyrics ran through my mind. "In fact nearly as sexy as you."

"You're a bit of a smooth talker beneath that rugged exterior," she said.

"One does one's best."

Just A Little Loving, I thought, a good song for right now. I found myself wondering what other songs would be suitable. What about the archetypal sixties song: I'm into Something Good? Was I into something good? I took a deep breath and savoured the moment. It certainly felt like it.

Afterwards we must have dozed for a bit, but suddenly we were wide awake again. I made tea and toast and brought it back to bed.

"What are you gonna do with your time," she asked, crunching toast, "now you're retired?"

"Well, I'd like to spend quite a bit of it with you," I said.

"Good idea."

She gave me a buttery kiss on the cheek.

"From now on I'm thinking of devoting my life to selfish pleasure."

"You've made a good start," she giggled.

"At one time I just wanted a better world."

"Don't we all?"

I sipped more tea and put the mug on the bedside table.

"I've been a Trade Union activist in my time," I said, "got involved in Amnesty International, Anti-Apartheid, the Peace Movement. You name it."

"I've done some of that," she said.

"I went on so many demos, I had to pay the cobbler by direct debit."

"Selfish pleasure sounds better."

"Yeah, but I'm gonna have to do a bit of part-time work now and again to maintain my lavish lifestyle," I said. "I could do part-time social work but…"

"You don't fancy it?"

I sighed.

"You know what I really want to do?"

"What?" she asked.

"Don't laugh but I've always wanted to be a Private Eye."

"Really?"

I thought of the Humphrey Bogart character in The Maltese Falcon. What was he called? Sam Spade, that was it.

"Yeah, you know, like in the old black and white films. I'd get myself a Fedora and a trench coat."

"I can just see it. You could do it, you know."

"What?"

"Set yourself up as a Private Investigator."

"I'm too old to retrain."

"No, it's completely unregulated. Anybody can do it."

"Can they?"

"Social workers certainly could. You must have done plenty of investigations in your time."

"True."

"I could get you work easily enough."

"Yeah, I suppose you could."

She lay back as a grin crept over her face. She took my hand.

"We'd have to see more of one another, of course," she said, "but we've worked well together so far."

"We certainly have."

I squeezed her hand.

"Have you got any contacts in the police?" she asked.

"Not really, though my mate Steve is a retired Superintendent."

"That'll have to do then. Now, we need to decide what you're gonna call yourself. Initials are good. GK Investigations, how about that?"

"GRK Investigations," I said.

"Even better. What's the R for?"

"Risman."

"Risman? I like it. Is that a family name or what?"

"My Dad named me after Gus Risman. He was a Salford Rugby League legend."

"Right. So, GRK Investigations. It's got that JFK ring, you know, President Kennedy."

"As long as nobody tries to assassinate me."

* * *

Coming into consciousness the next morning I looked at the alarm clock and did a double take. Half ten, the latest I'd slept for years. I didn't remember going to sleep – I'd wanted to stay awake forever – but I must have done.

I got up and sang in the shower. The bathroom showed signs of being used already this morning. Ten minutes later I put on jeans and a shirt and, fancying some music, ambled into the living room and took the iPod and speakers into the kitchen. I opened the blinds and, disbelieving, looked out on the sun shining in a clear, blue sky. Things were looking up. Turning round, I saw on the table a hand-written message on a page torn from a notebook:

Gus,
I had to leave at eight. I didn't like to wake you – you were sleeping like a baby. Something must have tired you! I'm back Monday. Call me on the mobile number on the card and maybe we can meet up when I get back. Hope to see you soon.
Love
Marti xxx
PS Don't forget GRK Investigations

Looking down at the table, I noticed a business card near where the note had been. I picked it up and read the name at the top: Pym and Sigson, Solicitors. Another thing had happened to me. I thought about Marti's PS and pictured myself as a private investigator. I could do it – never mind 'could', I would do. I'd do it today. My ambitions were interrupted by my mobile.

"Hi, Dad."
"Oh, hello, Rachel. All right?"
"Fine. How did last night go?"
"Last night?"
"You know, you and Marti?"
Surely she didn't want a blow by blow account.
"Well..."

"Did she stay long after I'd gone?"

"Er, she left quite late actually," I said, hoping my embarrassment wouldn't show over the phone.

"She's nice, isn't she?"

"Lovely."

"She likes you, you know."

"How do you know?"

"Oh, just things she's said."

An inkling of what might have been going on without my knowledge filtered through my brain.

"I see."

Rachel carried on with her cross-examination.

"Did you go out at all or…"

"No, we stayed in. I cooked a meal."

"Does that mean…"

"Yes, it means we were hungry."

"Dad, don't be obtuse," she demanded. "You know what I mean."

"What do you mean?"

"I mean, are you gonna see Marti again. See as in 'seeing someone', going out with them."

"Yes," I said, deciding to put her out of her misery.

"Result!" she yelled. "About bloody time."

I shook my head. If I'd asked Rachel about her love life she'd have gone mad.

"It was obvious you two liked one another," she said. "Why do you think Marti has been coming to see you so often these last few weeks?"

She told me in a variety of ways what a dickhead I had been. That, in a strange sort of way, put me in an even better mood. Going over to the iPod I tried to think of a suitable song. Of course, I said to myself, the Happy Play List. First track: Good Day Sunshine.

CHAPTER SEVEN

Coming out of my apartment building six days later, I turned left, looking at my watch. The warm weather had continued into the second week of my retirement. It was the morning of Bill Copelaw's funeral, eleven days after his death. I needed to catch the next tram if I were to have time to call on my dad beforehand. Hurrying past the old Docks Office, sweating in my suit, I got to the tramlines just in time to hail the tram to Weaste. I could visit my mam's grave while I was at the cemetery. There was no point in asking my dad to join me.

The sleek, turquoise doors slid smoothly open as the tram pulled in. It brought to mind images of the trolley buses that had trundled along years ago, metal poles sparking against the overhead wires. They were already being phased out when I was a kid sitting upstairs on the front seat and pretending to drive the bus. These modern trams, though, were cool and continental, a symbol of a 21st century city on the move, I'd heard someone say. I climbed on board. Using the orange handrails to help me along, I found a seat at the back.

As the tram moved away, I thought about Marti. I thought of her a lot. It took my mind off Bill's death, which still haunted me from time to time. My brain kept telling me there was an inconsistency at the murder scene. I would mull it over now and again without working out what it was.

Once in the cemetery I walked along a straight path, flanked by trees on either side, fields of gravestones spread out ahead. A whole history, I thought, was etched on those stones. I adjusted my tie and looked straight ahead. My shoes crunched on the gravel path. I was dimly aware of bird song somewhere in the background. When I got to my mam's grave, I stood up straight and prepared myself as if for an ordeal.

"I suppose you know I found a dead body," I said, looking at my mother's headstone as though expecting it to speak. "That brought back a few unhappy memories, as you can imagine."

I closed my eyes and in an instant I was travelling back in time, to a Mid-summer Friday. Coming home from my last 'A' level paper – English Literature: Shakespeare. Looking forward to a drunken celebration. Making my way into the kitchen. Calling her name. Thinking of the plan for the evening: I would go out for fish and chips as soon as my dad got home. Then a bath, get ready and out to meet Steve in the Park Hotel at seven. I remembered saying something like 'thank God that's over' before I saw the figure slumped against the gas cooker.

For maybe ten seconds I had observed myself watching the scene. In that time I registered the twisted expression on her face, the grease on her pinny from the floor, her grey hair in disarray. I felt for a pulse on my wrist so I would find the correct spot on hers. I must have thought she was dead even then. Then the panic overtook me and the numbing realization that, yes, she was dead.

"This time it was different though," I said. "Well, you were my mother, weren't you? A bit more important than your boss."

I waited a few seconds before continuing.

"There was something strange about it. Something different about what I saw compared with the time I'd seen Bill earlier. What do you reckon it was?"

If she knew the answer she kept quiet about it.

"You never answer at all, do you, Mam. Ever. I didn't believe in ghosts and all that malarkey. Nor in life after death. You won't approve."

Pausing for thought, I read the inscriptions on the stone:

PAULINE KEANE AGED 22 MONTHS

HER MOTHER MAUREEN KEANE AGED 53 YEARS

Pauline, the sister I never knew. I thought of my dad's response to the Kylie Anderson disappearance. He knew what it was like to lose a daughter, to know he would never see her again. Parallels to my own family's experience were all around me.

"Life's a bugger, Mam. Still, you don't need to worry about any of this, do you?"

Looking at my watch, I realised I'd better be going.

* * *

Later as I watched Bill's coffin being lowered into the grave, I looked at the mourners gathered around. I recognized Jean and a few people from work.

The burial over, I walked over to the car park to see if I could cadge a lift to Bill's house from somebody. I saw Don Bird standing by his car, talking to a woman, who had her back to me. He glanced towards me as I approached.

"Hi, Gus," he said in a good impression of a man with social skills. "Have you met the new director?"

The woman by his side turned towards me.

"Gus," she cried, throwing her arms around me.

"Pam," I said, returning the hug.

Don stepped back a pace. He looked as though he didn't know whether to shit or be sick as my dad would say.

"Sorry, Don," she said as she unravelled herself. "Gus and I go back a long way."

Don nodded and smiled weakly. If I were any judge, there was one question he was asking himself. Why couldn't I be old friends with the Director of Children's Services?

"We were students together," said Pam.

She still spoke with a slight West Country accent.

"A long time ago," I added.

Now Don would be telling himself that such a relationship would be wasted on me; whereas he would know how to make good use of it.

"I didn't recognize you for a minute," I said to Pam a little later as she drove me to Bill's house.

I looked at her hair, which was now shoulder length and blonde. She had also been on one of her crash diets since I'd last seen her a year ago.

"Oh, God, I haven't aged that much, have I?"

"No, but you change your appearance with such bewildering frequency I'm surprised you recognize yourself at times."

She grinned at me and stuck her tongue out. Suddenly she was the young woman I had met a couple of decades ago.

"Left here," I said, as we passed the house I had lived in until a few months ago.

She parked her Audi outside Bill's house. When we got out a man who must have been Bill's brother greeted us. He seemed to have taken on the role of host and ushered us into the garden. He pointed to a long table draped with a white cloth at the far end. We were to help ourselves to drinks. Food wouldn't be long. Having poured myself a glass of red I dropped a tenner in the collecting box on the table. I didn't look too closely at the cause I was supporting but it was a local children's charity.

Joining Pam in a shady corner, I took in my surroundings. I was struck by the incongruity of the scene. The dark, sombre clothes and the solemnity of the occasion clashed with the bright sunlight, the blue sky and the spring flowers. The tables and chairs were laid out as though for a party. Yet somebody had died.

"I asked Don to take over Bill's job temporarily, you know," said Pam.

Did I really want an update on developments at Ordsall Tower, I wondered as Pam began to give me just that.

"He's complaining about staff shortages and increased work load," she said. "As if I could do anything about it."

We were interrupted by the arrival of a woman with dark, curly hair, tending to plumpness. She introduced herself as Cal, Bill's daughter.

"Dad would have loved being here today," she said in a decidedly un-Mancunian accent after handshakes and expressions of condolence, "showing off his garden."

"It's certainly looking lovely," said Pam.

"Gardening was the great love of his life – after Elvis of course."

Pam and I smiled. I thought of what Marti had said about Bill's women and wondered where they would come in the pecking order.

"How's your mam," I asked.

Cal puffed out her cheeks.

"OK, I suppose," she said. "A bit flaky, you know. She might be better if things weren't still a bit up in the air."

I drank more wine and wondered what she meant.

"I suppose you know that Askey character is still on the run," said Cal.

Pam nodded though this was news to me.

"All this uncertainty doesn't exactly help," added Cal.

"They'll get him, don't worry," I said, knowing how stupid the average criminal was.

"I do hope so," Cal said, "at least the police are confident he did it so once they find him…"

We stood in silence for a while.

"Anyway," said Cal. "We should be celebrating Dad's life. I hope you're hungry. Mum's prepared mountains of food. Part of keeping busy therapy – a bit obsessive actually."

We stood in awkward silence for a moment.

"I'd better go and help her," said Cal as she left us to it.

A few minutes later I was walking towards the house in search of the toilet. I was thinking of how my life had changed since I had first met Pam Agnew. Your life's changed in the past week and a half, I reminded myself. Marti and I were now an item. GRK Investigations was set up but there hadn't been time for Marti to give me any work. I was in no hurry. I was too busy enjoying myself. I'd even fitted in a day's walking with Danny before he had to go back to Brighton. My son being so far away was the only downside I could think of.

I got to the back door of the house that led into the kitchen. I was just about to turn the handle when I made out Jean Copelaw's voice. I thought back to the scene at the graveside earlier. It had been hard to decide whether the lines etched on her face were a sign of grief or just the everyday misery that always seemed to accompany her.

"At least that bitch has had the decency to stay away," she said.

"What did you expect?"

It took a few seconds to realise the second voice was Cal's.

"I wouldn't have put it past her to turn up all sweetness and light, saying how sorry she was."

I stood still, my hand on the door handle. Going inside was out of the question but what else could I do?

"I'm sure you'd have coped," said Cal.

"I don't suppose you'd have been much help."

The sigh that followed spoke volumes.

"How many more times? I don't want to get involved in this shit. I don't even want to be here."

"Charming."

"I've turned up, haven't I," hissed Cal, "done my duty."

"For a change."

"Listen Mummy, I'll play the part of the grieving daughter for today. Tomorrow I'm going home to get on with my life."

Deciding I had heard more than enough, I turned away, and walked about twenty yards away from the house and went back. Rattling the handle as hard as I could, I opened the door quickly and went in. The two women were taking cling film off plates of sandwiches. They turned to look at me as I smiled and said hello. I had expressed condolences earlier so couldn't think what to say to Jean. Cal came to the rescue and told me the way to the toilet.

Arriving back where I'd come from, I saw Pam closeted with a smiling Rob from Reliable.com. He was probably trying to sell her insurance or singing the praises of his children. I may as well circulate. I spent half an hour saying hello to a couple of people from work before I noticed Don sitting alone with a glass of water. I sat in the chair next to him and asked him how things were going.

"OK," he shrugged. "You know I've been given Bill's job."

I nodded.

"I'm beginning to wish I'd said no," he sighed. "Short staffed; an increase in referrals; everything needing to be done yesterday. And that's before the cuts begin to bite."

It wouldn't help to tell him it had always been like this or that it didn't affect me any more. I said nothing.

"Now Helen wants us to start saving to put the kids through private school."

Like I wanted to know. He went on with his tale of woe.

"Save, I said. What with?"

I knew his children were pre-school, but that was about it. He only referred to them as a chore. Enjoying life wasn't a priority for Don.

"And there's all the fall out from Bill's death. Everybody's been affected."

"I can imagine."

He looked into the distance for a second and sipped from his glass.

"I feel bad because the last time I saw him wasn't exactly pleasant."

"How come?"

I recalled the scene on the morning of Bill's death when Karen and I watched Don come out of Bill's office.

"Well," he said, looking round furtively, "I was thinking of applying for a job in Bolton."

"And?"

"He said he couldn't give me a good reference."

"Oh."

"I'm afraid I blew my top."

He averted his eyes for a second.

"I promised myself I'd apologize on Monday morning."

He shook his head.

"You know, try and talk it through reasonably and see if he'd change his mind."

We were interrupted by the voice of Cal from the other end of the garden. She had a guitar round her neck.

"If I could just have your attention for a moment," she began, "I'm sure you realise that Mum and I came a poor second to the King of Rock'n'roll in Dad's affection."

Polite laughter greeted this. I thought of the expression about many a true word being spoken in jest.

"I thought I'd sing an Elvis song as my personal farewell to Dad."

We sat through Cal's rendition of Loving You. Was I embarrassed by the obvious hypocrisy or was I just embarrassed? When the applause died down, Don looked at his watch.

"I need to get back soon," he said. "Time and tide and social work wait for no man. If you're ready to go, I can give you a lift."

For the first few minutes of the journey back to Ordsall, conversation didn't exactly flow. Silence built up as Don looked around at the traffic as though surprised that there were other cars on the road. He finally spoke as we approached the slip road to the M602.

"Gus," he said, "I'm in a position to offer you some work if you're interested."

In a position to? Pompous pillock.

"Depends what it is."

"Remember the family you visited on the day Bill died," he said, "the little baby."

"Rebecca," I said, "I remember her well. Poor little mite. What's happening with her?"

"The injuries were definitely physical abuse. She's in foster care and we're going for care proceedings."

"Where do I come in?"

He passed a lorry before continuing.

"Well, Karen was supposed to take it over. I don't know if you know but she's on long term sick."

"Oh? What's the problem?"

Don shrugged.

"Stress, depression or something."

I detected a distinct lack of sympathy. I couldn't help thinking about him trying to chat up Karen. It wasn't until I started in social work that I realised how many affairs start at work. I wondered if Don had tried it on with anybody else. Or if he had been any more successful.

"And you want me to take it on?"

He nodded. We travelled on in silence for a few seconds. Was this too soon to be going back to work? It would at least save me the bother of looking for it. If I said no, when would I get the chance to earn a bit of extra money? Don wouldn't ask if he weren't keen so I sensed my bargaining position was strong. I said I'd consider it on a self-employed basis.

"Well, we've got a private solicitor in – two of ours are on maternity leave at the same time – so why not a private social worker?"

"And as long as it's only a couple of days a week maximum," I added.

"We can't afford to pay you for any more than that."

He sounded defeated and downtrodden. How long before he succumbed to the effects of the thankless task he was lumbered with? Stress had definitely been one of the factors in my stroke.

"And just for this one case," I insisted.

"Fine. I could only pay you twenty-five pounds an hour," he said with an air of regret.

Or more than I've ever earned before.

"OK," I said, trying to sound reluctant.

"The court will be impressed with an experienced practitioner like you. You don't need me to tell you it's a high risk case."

"Certainly is."

"And it means the solicitor stops giving me grief."

"Who is it?"

"Marti Pym. She says she knows you. She's heard you're a good worker. Which you are of course."

Compliments from Don Bird and the chance to work with Marti. I struggled to keep a grin from my face.

CHAPTER EIGHT

Two days later I got off the tram at Timperley at quarter to seven. I was about to text Marti to say I was nearly there when my phone rang.

"Hiya, Gus, it's Tanya."

Now what did she want?

"I wanted to ask you something, right?"

I walked along the pavement a little way before stopping. It still felt weird talking on the phone while walking. Perhaps I was just an old git at heart.

"Go ahead."

"It's about Mick Askey…"

Great. Just what I needed.

"Is it right he's in clink?"

"Yeah."

I had no need to plead confidentiality this time. It had been reported in the paper in an article about the size of a postage stamp. Still, it was only a social worker he'd killed.

"Any chance of him getting out?"

I thought for a few seconds, scratching my forearm.

"Well, the case won't come to trial for months so he'll be in till then if not longer."

"Great."

"And if he's found guilty he'll be away a long time."

"I could move back into my house, couldn't I, know what I mean? I never did get round to giving the keys in."

"I suppose you could," I said. "Anyway, Tanya, I've got to be off."

"Ok. See you then. Ta ra."

With that I ended the call, texted Marti and went on my way. Timperley was just a few stops from Salford Quays but until Marti and I had got together I couldn't remember having been there before. I thought of it as being in Cheshire – and therefore a bit posh – and knew from Rachel that the Stone Roses started there. On my first visit I'd been disappointed not to see Ian Brown swaggering down the street.

I got to the cul-de-sac where Marti lived, admiring the terrace of Georgian town houses in the evening sunlight. Marti stood at her door in blue jeans with turn-ups and a pink top, smiling and waving. She really did look good in that outfit, I thought, but she could wear anything. Her Mercedes was parked outside as usual. A posh car and a house worth about half a million, I'd been in the wrong job all these years. She gave me a smile, a hug and a kiss when I got to the doorway, followed by a 'good to see you'. I could get used to this, no bother. Taking out my phone, I got her to pose seductively on the doorstep and took a couple of photos. There were worse ways to spend a Thursday evening, I thought. Our plan was to go for a curry at a restaurant a ten-minute walk away. We were both hungry so we left straightaway.

"I hear we'll be working together," I said.

I looked down at her red-painted toenails peeping out of her sandals, as we strolled along.

"Yeah, brilliant isn't it," she smiled. "I didn't think Don would get round to doing anything about it. The poor guy doesn't know whether he's coming or going."

A group of teenagers rushed past outside Currys, laughing at nothing. I thought of the joys of youth. Then I looked at Marti and told myself you don't have to be young to enjoy life.

"I'm not surprised."

"So, when do you start?"

She had to shout as a bus went by.

"The sooner the better as far as I'm concerned."

"I'm going into the office on Monday morning," I explained. "Just to read the file, talk to a few people, arrange home visits."

"Right. And we'll have to have several long planning meetings to prepare for court. In a relaxed environment."

"Relaxed yet completely professional, I'm sure," I said.

"Oh, completely. Of course it might be better to work from home sometimes."

We grinned at one another and she squeezed my hand.

"Anyway, I've got something else to tell you."

She looked at me, taking a deep breath and swallowing hard.

"It's about Mick Askey."

I looked expectantly at her.

"What about him?"

She walked on half a dozen paces before explaining.

"The police finally caught up with him this morning."

"Good."

"He was arrested and charged with Bill Copelaw's murder."

"Predictable."

She looked away for a few seconds.

"I'm gonna be representing him."

"How come?"

"Well, I was contacted at half nine to attend a PACE interview. I was on call, you know, duty solicitor."

"Right."

"When it was over Askey decided he wanted me to be his solicitor."

I didn't know what I was supposed to say. Marti went on.

"You don't mind, do you?"

I shrugged. "Why should I mind?"

She let out a sigh.

"I thought you'd be, you know, annoyed. In the circumstances."

"Not really."

"People always ask me how I can defend these monsters."

"You seem to forget I'm a fully paid up wishy-washy liberal."

"True, but…"

"Anyway, I know how these things work," I said, "you have to take him on regardless of how you feel."

She nodded as I thought for a moment.

"Even toe rags like Askey deserve a fair trial," I went on. "I'm sure you'll do a good job for him. It sounds a bit of a lost cause though."

"Probably. His best hope is to plead guilty to manslaughter."

"Yeah?"

"Bill suffered from angina: we could argue the blow on the head brought on a heart attack."

"I suppose so," I said, "but he's still dead."

We turned left by the Co-operative funeral parlour.

"Askey denies point blank he was responsible for Bill's death. He admits he was in Bill's office – he could hardly deny it – and had a bit of a row with him."

"And?"

"Well, he says Bill was alive when he left."

"Then who killed him?"

"Askey claims he passed a man going into the building as he was on his way out of Ordsall Tower."

"Yeah, right."

"Don't be cynical."

"Well, it's a bit convenient."

She shrugged.

"The guy Askey saw was wearing a leather jacket."

"Oh, well, that clinches it."

She looked at me and smiled.

"I know it sounds unlikely but I do have a slight doubt he actually did it."

"You must be joking."

"Well, there were no fingerprints on the murder weapon – the football trophy."

"He wiped them off."

"That's a logical deduction," she said, "but think about it. This is Askey we're talking about. His brain is addled by years of alcoholic excess. Is he going to think clearly enough to worry about forensic evidence?"

"I don't really know. I'm just glad it's not my problem."

We walked on for a while enjoying the sunshine before Marti spoke again.

"Gus, I've been thinking…"

"Oh, no," I put in, "My dad has always warned me about women who say, 'I've been thinking…'"

"No, listen. When I realised you would be going back to Social Services and I was representing Mick Askey, I had a brilliant idea."

That didn't sound too good.

"I don't like the sound of that," I smiled. "I swore I'd never again get involved with a woman who has ideas…"

She chuckled.

"I can see you're interested so I'll tell you all about it."

I tried to pay attention.

"When you go back into the office, you'll be talking to your colleagues, won't you?"

"Yeah," I said, sounding puzzled because I was.

"You know, chatting of this and that."

"A certain amount of social intercourse is expected," I said.

She grinned, leaning towards me and kissing me on the cheek.

"As long as it's only social," she whispered in my ear.

I could definitely get used to this. Or was I too old for this sort of thing? And in the street as well. I didn't feel too old.

"The murder will still be on their minds so it will seem quite normal for you to discuss it with them."

"I suppose so," I said hesitantly. "What exactly are you getting at?"

"It's a golden opportunity for you, with your Private Investigator hat on, to look into the murder."

"I won't have time."

"Course you will. You can do it while you're at work."

"I don't fancy cross-examining the people at work."

"It's not cross-examining. They don't need to know what you're doing."

"So, I'm working undercover?"

I couldn't keep the scepticism out of my voice.

"Nothing as dramatic as that. You just find out subtly if they saw anything or anyone suspicious at the relevant time."

"But..."

"Especially if anybody saw this man Askey claims to have passed on his way out."

I sighed.

"Leather jacket man?"

"That's as good a name as any."

"It's a pointless exercise. There is no leather jacket man."

"Maybe there isn't but you said yourself Askey is entitled to a fair trial. And to someone defending him who does more than go through the motions."

"Mmm," I said, "I'm not sure."

"Fine. If you don't want to get paid twice for the same work…"

She left her words hanging. Getting paid twice did sound good. And I could do it, no bother. I knew how to make my questioning sound natural. And I had to admit, at least to myself, I fancied the idea of working undercover. No matter what Marti said that's what I'd be doing.

"It's a legal aid job, so I could only pay you thirty quid an hour," she said.

Making £55 an hour in all for some of the time, I thought, as we approached the Taj Mahal.

"Oh, all right," I said with faked reluctance, "I'll do it. Now let's go and get something to eat. I'm bloody starving."

The next day, in my TRYS tracksuit, I ran in the sunshine, trying to keep up with twenty-six young men. A light breeze blew over Lancaster Road playing fields, where I had played rugby and cricket at school. A promising move was in progress on the right wing. A beefy youngster trudged over the ground, looking round for someone to pass to.

"Come on, Ryan," I shouted.

A tall West Indian lad, all elegance and power, ran into open space. He was good, that Paul. Spotting him, Ryan slung the ball his way. Without breaking stride, Paul took the ball with one hand, making it look easy. He wrong-footed two defenders and sped through to touch down under the posts.

"Good support play, Paul," I shouted after blowing the whistle and signalling a try. "Great awareness, Ryan."

I watched the two teams struggle on in the heat. It was now easier to fit in these Friday afternoon training sessions with TRYS. I unzipped my tracksuit top, wondering if this summery weather would last. When I had played for Salford I'd preferred mud and rain. It gave an advantage to anyone born within ten miles of Manchester. There were worse things than being paid for something that brought me such joy, I thought, as I looked back on my career. I did OK at school but Rugby League had been the one thing at which I'd excelled. Physical and intellectual satisfaction of the highest order, each move the solving of an intricate puzzle. Seeing patterns of movement in my head, influencing them through my skill. It was beautiful. I would never forget the day dodgy knees had forced me to give up. Never.

As the play started again I thought about the assignment Marti had given me. What did I need to do to find leather jacket man? Who apart from people who worked there might have seen something around Ordsall Tower the night Copelaw was killed. How could I reach the locals who lived around there?

Looking at my watch I blew my whistle. I thought about Paul Winston, the try scorer. The lad was impressive, there was no doubt about that. Natural talent, an eye for an opening. And boy, was he quick. Speed of thought, speed of reaction and speed of movement. He had them all. The three things you needed to make it in any sport. Most of all though Paul was bright. If anything pissed me off it was the common misconception that sportsmen were thick. Especially those who had the temerity to come from working class backgrounds and speak with regional accents.

I reran the sight of Paul running through the defence like it wasn't there and making a beeline for the spot between the posts. Great stuff. A bedraggled band trooped off. Paul walked over to me.

"Hey, Gus," he said. "What happened to that little kid I called you about?"

"Rebecca? She's safe, that's the main thing. And you did the right thing."

"I've noticed she's not at home anymore," he said.

"I can't say too much about that but you can draw your own conclusions."

He nodded.

"Yeah. That Liam's not been seen for a while. He should stay away if he knows what's good for him, know what I mean?"

We walked on.

"So, what you doing, Gus?"

"Well, I'm back at Ordsall Tower part time…"

"Back there? I thought you fancied something different."

"Well," I said, "I've set myself up as a Private Investigator as well."

The chance of impressing Paul was too tempting to resist. Gus Keane, I said to myself, you're pathetic, what are you?

"Private Eye," he enthused. "I've always wanted to do that."

We walked on towards the changing room.

"You don't want an assistant, do you?"

"Well," I shrugged.

"I'm serious," he insisted.

"What about your new job?"

"I don't start until next month."

Why not, I thought. I could trust Paul and it would be nice for him to earn a bit of extra money. I could claim what I paid him back on expenses. What could I get him to do though?

"It's a thought," I said.

Then I remembered he lived in the area where the murder took place.

"OK," I said. "You probably heard a feller called Bill Copelaw got killed in the Social Services building on Friday."

"That welfare bloke? I heard Askey did that."

"I've been asked to do some investigation. Do you fancy helping me out? I'll pay you of course."

Paul shrugged, as though he'd realised his original enthusiasm wasn't cool.

"Why not?"

I explained about leather jacket man.

"So ask around," I said as we went inside the changing room. "Someone might have seen this bloke."

"All right."

"Don't make it obvious, you know. I'll give you a ring in a day or two."

As I left the changing room later, I saw Marti waving at me at the entrance to the playing fields. I watched her walking towards me. God she was sexy. She came over to me and kissed me. Paul walked past and said, "see you, Gus."

"Who was that," asked Marti.

"Paul," I said. "A success story for TRYS. He was heading for a life of crime until we got hold of him."

"Sounds impressive."

"We got him back in education. He moved in with his granddad. He's done 'A' levels."

We got into the car.

"The expense put him off university so he's got himself an apprenticeship."

"Good stuff."

"Now he's a role model for the other TRYS lads."

"Pity I missed the game," she said as we went over to her car.

"I thought you didn't see the point of sport."

"But I do see the point of watching hunky men run around."

We stopped while she got her car keys out.

"You're a very naughty girl."

"And aren't you glad?"

CHAPTER NINE

The following Monday morning at 8.30 I arrived at Ordsall Tower in a light drizzle. Only two and a bit weeks since I had last been there. As I went in I was wondering if it was a good idea. The bad weather had returned to mark my first day back at work. Within a few days of my last day at Ordsall Tower, I had decided work had no part to play in my life. Furthermore, that work was unnatural and not what we were put on this earth for. This particularly applied to sensitive souls like myself.

Since retiring I'd settled into a routine. Except when I was seeing Marti, I was in bed by ten o'clock, awake about six, up by six thirty. Then I would throw on some clothes and go for a brisk walk round Salford Quays for half an hour or so. Then back for a shower and a leisurely breakfast before taking my medication. Two or three evenings a week I'd go for a swim. This rigid timetable was the only way I could maintain my healthy lifestyle. The night before my return to work I hadn't got to sleep until one a.m. Woken by the alarm clock only to doze off again, I'd had to drag myself into the bathroom for a quick shower. I barely had time to get dressed before dashing out breakfastless, grumbling about the weather and anything else I could think of. Now, as I got into the office kitchen and put the kettle on, I wondered where all my energy had gone. My phone beeped. Opening the text, I read the name: Steve Yarnitzky.

Any chance of putting me up on Tuesday night? I'm en route to Glasgow. I'll get you a pint in the Park Hotel. Cheers. Steve.

It would be good to see my old friend, I thought, as I texted back, as long as he didn't want to tell me about his new Jag.

I was halfway through my second cup of tea and third slice of toast when Wendy on reception rang through to tell me Charlotte Stephens was here to see me. I only hoped I could stay awake while I talked to her. Even the caffeine had failed to liven me up. At least seeing Charlotte would postpone my reading of Rebecca Winter's case file. The only thing more boring than social work records, I decided a long time ago, is Steve going on about cars.

Two minutes later I was sitting in an interview room opposite a young woman with purple hair. She had dumped a leather rucksack on the table. Skinny jeans on skinny legs concertinaed onto blue baseball boots. She fidgeted with her fringe for a few seconds.

"I heard you were back," she said, twirling one of her long plaits in her right hand.

"Yeah, just part time…"

"So you can…

"Just to deal with a particularly complex case."

"So you're not gonna be my social worker again?"

"No," I said.

I could have told Charlotte that, as she was 18 now, someone in the care-leavers' team would be responsible for her; that she'd be offered advice about employment and education. Not that she needed it. What she needed, she would say, was somebody she knew and trusted. Anyway, she knew the system better than I did. We chatted about her new boyfriend, her foster carers, her 'A' level revision and her plans for next year. I waited for her to get to the real point of her visit. She looked down for a few seconds before speaking again.

"I heard about, you know, my 'father'," she said. "Going to prison and stuff."

"Yeah," I said

It already seemed a long time ago.

"I had an idea what he was like," she said, "but I never expected anything like this."

Charlotte looked down at her bag on the table. "I'm really sorry about the man who was killed."

"Bill Copelaw? He was my boss."

I decided not to tell her I found the body.

"It's terrible," she said.

She went quiet for a while.

"Listen Gus, I wanted to talk to you about something."

"Go on," I said.

"Well, I'd like to go and see Mick Askey in prison. What do you think?"

"Well, if it's what you want and he agrees."

She tugged at her other plait.

"I've got to know if he's my father. I've got to."

"He denies even having a daughter, you know."

She nodded.

"It might be different if he actually sees me. I want to ask him if he'll do a DNA test."

"It's worth a try," I said though I couldn't see Askey co-operating with anything. "You might want to take someone with you."

"Suppose so," Charlotte shrugged. "Actually Gus, I was wondering…"

I knew what was coming and what I was going to say.

"…if you would come with me."

"OK," I said.

* * *

"I can't believe you've got yourself mixed up in a murder, Gus," said Steve as we left my flat to go to the Park Hotel the following night.

On his arrival he had told me about his new Jaguar until my eyes started to glaze over. He had followed this up with a match by match analysis of United's chances for the rest of the season. I like football and of course I support United. I'm from Salford, aren't I? But to me football is a poor third behind Rugby League and cricket. And the bad sportsmanship, inflated wages and the way it dominates everything did my head in at times.

Then we'd got onto the far more fascinating question of how many pints we had supped in the Park Hotel since we'd first set foot in the place. We'd both been 18 at the time so a fair few, I thought. I didn't tell him about Marti – it was early days yet. I also kept quiet about GRK Investigations: it only existed on paper at this stage. Anyway, he would only laugh. Bill Copelaw's death was, ironically, a much safer topic.

"Neither can I," I replied.

We crossed Trafford Road at the pelican crossing. Steve's movements were as neat as his Manchester United polo shirt and Chinos. He was a few inches shorter than me, his wiry frame the product of cycling, climbing and golf. He'd lost a bit more hair since I'd last seen him, I thought smugly. The cropped style he'd adopted about ten years ago was a big improvement on the various versions of the comb-over he'd tried.

"I can believe Mick Askey did it, though," he went on. "I know him of old. Nearly every copper in Greater Manchester must have come across him at some point.

"And social worker."

Steve turned to me.

"He was always a vicious little bastard."

I nodded.

"Put a squaddy in hospital a few years back. Only got five years. Then some silly sod let him out after three."

I braced myself for a blast of Daily Mail reasoning that never came. Maybe he had mellowed.

"He was in care as a kid if I remember rightly," he went on, "for all the good that did him."

"I don't know much about his background."

"You went to see him about this daughter then," he asked.

"Yeah, well, according to the file he's her father and his name's on the birth certificate."

"Where is she now, this lass?"

"She's been with the same foster carers since she was a toddler. She was born in Salford, but the carers live in Altrincham now."

"Yeah?"

"I was her social worker for years until a few months ago."

We walked on.

"Why was she in care?"

"Neglect," I said.

"Poor little bugger."

"Things have worked out for her," I said. "She's doing 'A' levels this year, got a place at university."

"Nice to hear a bit of good news."

"She still sees her birth mother from time to time. I think she feels sorry for her."

"Is she worth feeling sorry for, this so-called mother?"

"It's a matter of opinion," I said. "At first we worked hard trying to get Charlotte back with her but to be brutally frank Tracy turned out to be a total waste of space."

I wanted to say something else but my mind suddenly emptied as though someone had scooped out its contents. Just when I thought I was over the stroke one or more of the effects would return. Difficulty with words; unaccountable lapses in memory. I was already resigned to the residual weakness in my right arm.

"With a useless mother and Askey as a father," said Steve, "she's done well."

I instructed my brain to get its arse into gear. I tried to concentrate on what Steve was saying and gradually it got better.

"Askey's probably her dad," I said, "but Tracy put it about a bit. A DNA test is the only sure way of knowing."

I told Steve about the prison visit I'd arranged for next week and my doubts about Askey's willingness to undergo a DNA test.

"If he says no, there's nothing we can do about it, I suppose."

"Depends," said Steve. "With his record he's bound to be on the database but that can only be used if we're investigating a crime."

"I thought as much."

"She's not making any allegations against him, this girl, is she?"

"No."

"So, he didn't abuse her as far as we know?"

"Well, he could have neglected her."

"That's a crime," said Steve.

"True," I said. "Come to think of it, Tracy was convicted of child neglect."

"Well, he must have played a part in that, mustn't he?"

"He'd left Tracy before we got involved but I suppose he might have been."

"Well, if we proved he was her father that would be evidence if we wanted to charge him with neglect."

I smiled.

"That connection's a bit tenuous."

"Rules are meant to be bent," he smiled back, as we got within a few yards of the pub. "If he won't play ball when you go and see him, let me know."

"That's never Steve Yarnitzky, is it, Gus," asked the landlord when we entered the Park Hotel. "We are honoured."

Taking in the CAMRA PUB OF THE YEAR pennant over the bar, I felt that buzz you get from being somewhere familiar and welcoming. Customers sat around the room eating and drinking, putting the world to rights. Photographs of old Salford on the walls were interspersed with horse brasses, toby jugs and a warming pan.

"Give us two pints of Red Devil, Arthur, and less of it," said Steve. "And a couple of menus. My belly thinks my throat's been cut."

Arthur handed over the menus and manoeuvred his bulk along the bar to the beer pumps to pull our pints. His long, grey hair flopped over his shoulders. I wondered how he carried all that weight around every day. Arthur's baggy shirt, worn over his trousers, made him look like two darts players who had collided at high speed and somehow merged permanently.

"Your wish is my command, Chief Superintendent."

"Not Chief Super any more, remember," said Steve.

"Oh, yeah. How's retirement in Dog Leg or whatever it's called?"

"Dolgellau," Steve corrected him.

"Oh, speaking the lingo now, are we?"

"Have done for years, Arthur."

I often wondered if Arthur had made a conscious decision to put on weight when he took over from his dad twenty-five years ago. He looked the archetypal pub landlord in the archetypal pub. He had managed to preserve the traditional features while keeping up with the times. There were the nooks and crannies with the nostalgia evoking names – snug, public bar – with the main bar doubling as a restaurant. Upstairs were a music room, snooker room and a sports room with the biggest telly in the world. Heaven.

"To what do we owe the pleasure of this visit then?"

"Just stopping off for a night with Gus," said Steve. "I'm on my way to a golfing break in Glasgow."

"And here's me thinking only posh people play golf," Arthur replied.

"I'll ignore that."

"You're not here to solve this murder in Social Services then?"

Steve shook his head.

"No way. I'm well out of it. Did you know Gus found the body?"

Don't remind me, I said to myself. I didn't really want to talk about it. But then I had to accept people have always been fascinated by crime.

"Never," said Arthur. "You'll need this pint then. It was supposed to be your leaving do that night and all."

"Yeah, sorry about that, Arthur."

Arthur shrugged.

"That's all right. A fair few stayed on as it happened. Drank themselves stupid, ate all the pies and danced to the jukebox."

"In the midst of death there is life," said Steve.

"Shouldn't wonder," said Arthur. "Then in the middle of it all, I had the police round."

"What did they say?"

"Not a lot. Asked me if I'd seen anything suspicious whatever that's supposed to mean."

"So you couldn't tell them anything?"

"No, I was busy in here, wasn't I?"

He looked pensive for a moment.

"I thought to myself, you know, just an ordinary evening in here and while we was having a drink and a natter and that, just a few yards away some poor bugger's been done to death."

He breathed deeply.

"Makes you wonder, doesn't it?"

He shook his head sadly.

"Hey, I've just thought. One of your lads was in that night, Gus. Early doors."

"Who was it?"

"One of the social services lot. What's his name now?"

Was I meant to guess?

"Well, it can't have been Copelaw."

Arthur dismissed the idea with a flick of his hand.

"He took his birds to all the posh places. No, it was that other one. Copelaw's assistant, so he reckoned anyway."

He straightened a towel on the bar while waiting for the beer to settle.

"To hear him talk he ran the place single handed while Copelaw took a back seat. Wanker."

That sounded like Don.

"Long stringy fucker. Right gormless looking get and all. Buggered if I can remember his name."

"Don Bird?"

"Aye, desperate Don, that's it."

"What on earth was he doing in a place like this? A nice boy like him."

Arthur let out a sigh, puffing out his cheeks.

"Started coming in a few months back. Boring bastard. Tries to be one of the lads and fails miserably. Thinks we all love him and can't wait until the next time he graces us with his presence. Stupid sod."

Arthur held the floor. Having gone through wanker, fucker, get, bastard and sod what expletive, I wondered, would Arthur now use against Don? I was almost beginning to feel sorry for him.

"I wouldn't mind but he sups sod all. Normally makes half a pint last about an hour then skedaddles home to the wife."

He topped up our glasses, watching the froth bubble over the top.

"Come to think of it," he went on thoughtfully, "on the night of the murder he was different."

I went into Private Eye mode. This is what they did, wasn't it? Befriended people in the local, lulled them into a false sense of security and pumped them for information. This could count as part of my investigations. I should charge for my time. Were the beer and food legitimate expenses?

"In what way," I asked.

Arthur tilted his head to one side as if contemplating infinity. Perhaps he was getting to the point at last.

"That night he did put a few away. Comes in all of a work, in a right state with himself."

"Oh, yeah?"

"Nervous like, you know. As if he needed a drink. He must have had, oooh, three pints."

Arthur handed us our pints.

"There we are, gents," he said, "named after Salford Rugby League team, the original Red Devils."

Arthur winked at me. I responded to his cue.

"Some people think the Red Devils are a collection of overpaid prima donnas who kick a ball about at Old Trafford," I said, looking at Steve.

"Salford were given the name on a 1930s tour of France," added Arthur.

By then Steve was studying the menu with renewed concentration, pausing only to say between yawns:

"Yeah, yeah, Les Diables Rouges, Gus may have told me that two or three thousand times."

* * *

"Did you see that stuff in the papers about Kylie Anderson?" Steve asked later as we got stuck into home made steak pie and chips.

"I had a quick look at it," I said, "amazing how it's stayed in the news all this time."

"Yeah. That's down to Elaine, of course."

"Her mother?"

"Yeah. I was involved in the original investigation, you know."

"Yeah, I remember you telling me. It happened in Chorley, didn't it?"

"Yeah, I was a DS with Lancashire Constabulary then."

Steve drank more beer and swallowed a chunk of pastry.

"Her mother left her in her pushchair outside a newsagents while she went to get some fags. When she came out Kylie was gone. Never been heard of since."

"Eighteen years ago," I said, thinking of what Elaine had missed in that time.

"Yeah."

"Different world," I said, "Was Thatcher still in power? Either her or Major."

"I'm not sure. One thing I do know, we were a hell of a lot younger."

"You even had hair, didn't you?"

"You know how to hurt a man," he said in a camp voice.

I drank some more beer.

"I read about her mother thinking Kylie's still alive. Not very realistic."

"No." Steve shook his head sadly. "But you've got to remember Elaine has to believe that to keep going. I reckon if she gave up hope she'd top herself."

I shook my head sadly as Steve went on.

"They're doing a Crimewatch special soon."

"I might watch it," I said, finishing my beer. "I'd better get us another pint."

On my way to the bar I thought of Kylie, wondering sadly what happened to her. When I ordered the drinks from Arthur my mind turned again to what he had said about Don. But Don couldn't have killed Bill Copelaw. Could he?

CHAPTER TEN

On the Wednesday of the same week after a day off, I knocked on Sharon Winter's front door and waited. And waited. At least the sun was shining this time, I thought, unlike the first time I had come to the house. Looking at my watch I wondered if I could afford to waste any more time out here. She knew I was coming. I'd told her twice and written it down for her. Still, playing silly buggers was Sharon's main talent.

"All right, Gus," said a female voice from behind me.

I turned round to see a teenage girl with a bag slung over one shoulder.

"Oh, hello, Tanya," I said, taking a few seconds to recognize her.

We exchanged a bit of small talk, as I tried not to picture her in her knickers on the day Bill died. She wore jeans and a long sleeved sweat shirt. It was a relief to see her covered up. She even smelt better.

"Where you off," I asked for something to say.

She leant slightly to the right, putting her weight on one leg.

"Just on my way to work. Just a couple of hours in the paper shop, all cash in hand."

"Every little helps."

She suddenly looked worried.

"Oh, shit, me and my bigmouth," she said. "Hey, you won't grass me up to the social, will you?"

I shook my head.

"I haven't got time, Tanya. Think of all the paperwork."

She laughed, shifting her weight to the left.

"How's Madison?" I asked.

"A lot better now Mick's gone. I had to keep her out of his way, know what I mean?"

I nodded, having a good idea exactly what she meant.

"She's at the Sure Start centre while I'm at work. She loves it there."

"Great."

"If you're looking for Sharon," she said, "I saw her go out about half an hour ago."

I sighed, preparing to say my goodbyes to Tanya. Then I had a thought.

"You don't know where Liam is, do you?"

She shrugged.

"No, not seen him for ages. Have you tried his mam and dad?"

"I've no idea where they live."

And Sharon denied all knowledge of them. Or was she just being awkward?

"Didsbury somewhere," she said.

I raised my eyebrows.

"Didsbury?"

She grinned.

"Oh, aye. Dead posh, his family. He thinks he's a cut above. Wanker."

Ten minutes later in the office, I took out the phone directory and opened it out on the desk. Sipping tea as I scanned the long list of Bentleys, I picked out three that looked promising. The first turned out to be a woman who wanted me to allow Jesus into my life. Wondering if she said the same to every random caller, I tried the second.

"Derek Bentley," said a well-spoken voice.

"Is Liam there, please?"

"I'm afraid he's out at the moment. Can I take a message?"

"Can you tell him Rick called. I'll try again later."

I put the phone down, not wanting to tell Liam's dad who I was. I couldn't see him being impressed by a social worker phoning him at home.

The next morning nine o'clock found me ringing a doorbell in Didsbury, miles from my normal stomping ground in more ways than one. When Steve moved into a house in Didsbury thirty years ago, it was a sign he'd made it. Now, in yet more April sunshine, here I was calling on a man whose child was in foster care.

Putting my briefcase on the front path, I pressed the bell for a third time. I held my left hand on it, while banging on the door hard with the right. The motor bike parked outside suggested there was somebody in there. If that were the case they'd have to answer. I didn't have time to come back and try again. I heard movement inside the house and the clinking of the chain on the PVC door. A key turned and a handle cranked before the door was flung open. Liam Bentley, in white T-shirt and Simpsons boxer shorts stood there in all his bloodshot glory.

"Who the fuck…"

"Morning, Liam," I said with a grin, picking up my briefcase.

He blinked his eyes as if focusing on an optician's chart. It had taken us three weeks to locate him. I was convinced Sharon could have told us where he was if she'd wanted us to find him.

"Oh, it's you," he said. "What do you want?"

"I want to come in and talk to you."

"What about?"

I sighed and tapped my foot on the ground.

"It's confidential, Liam," I said with exaggerated patience. "As you well know. Not for doorstep conversation."

"I'm not really sure…"

"The neighbours will be wondering what's going on. I can't see your mam and dad being too chuffed about that."

"Oh, come in then."

I followed him into the lounge, where he sat me down on a pink leather sofa. The stainless steel legs of a glass-topped table in front of me sparkled.

"Do you want a cuppa, mate? I know I do."

"Tea, please."

He went off to put the kettle on. I got up and wandered round the room. On a sideboard was a picture of a fifty something couple, Mr and Mrs Bentley, I presumed. In his check slacks and short-sleeved shirt Liam's dad looked like a model for a smart/casual catalogue. His wife was dressed in similar trousers to her husband and a maroon sweatshirt with a Didsbury golf club logo. Wondering, not for the first time, what the point of golf was, I sat down again. I looked at a flat-screened television hanging on the wall like a mirror. Liam came back in.

"Kettle's on," he said. "I'll take a shower, yeah? Back in a minute."

Ten minutes elapsed before Liam emerged, dressed in jeans and a striped jumper. He carried two mugs of tea and a plate of toast and plonked the lot on the table, spilling tea in the process. He sat down opposite me and drank a mouthful of tea.

"I need this. Heavy night last night."

I took a notebook and pen out of my briefcase.

"So, what's it all about, then?" he asked through a mouthful of toast crumbs. "I suppose you want to talk about the kid and everything."

"I'll bring you up to date with what's happening," I said, putting the cup down. "The medical opinion is that the injuries to Rebecca were the result of physical abuse."

"Don't look at me, mate," he said, "I'd never hurt a kid. The police haven't charged anyone."

I knew that only too well. There wasn't enough evidence to pin it on any one individual and a variety of people had cared for Rebecca during the period when the injury could have happened. I explained that the local authority was taking care proceedings and the court had made an interim care order. This would be reviewed in four weeks.

"The care order means we can decide where Rebecca lives."

"So she stays with foster parents?"

"At least for now."

I explained I had to do an assessment for court and I wanted to include him in it.

"Not sure I want to get involved in anything like that, know what I mean?"

"No?"

"Not really. I may want to move on, you know, not really sure where."

"Can I just clarify a few points while I'm here?"

"Why not?"

We went back over what had happened since the night I took Rebecca and Sharon to hospital.

"What did you do after you ran off?"

"Sorry about that, mate," he said. "Not very bright, was it?"

He looked down at his hands.

"I just, like, got on the bike and drove around for a bit. After a while I calmed down and started to think straight."

"And?"

"I thought I might as well go back home. I thought maybe Sharon would, you know…"

He shrugged as though completing a sentence was too much trouble.

"What time did you get back to Ordsall?"

"Dunno, after five, maybe half past."

The time of Bill Copelaw's murder, I thought.

"Did you go to the office?"

"Office?"

"Ordsall Tower."

"What for?"

"To try and find out what happened to Rebecca."

Another shrug.

"I knew I'd find out soon enough."

He drank more tea, while I seethed. No wonder some kids went wrong.

"It wouldn't have been too much trouble," I said, annoyed at his casual attitude. "You would have gone past Ordsall Tower on the way."

"I did, aye. I parked near there. Thought I might as well get some chips while I was there."

He grinned and picked up his tea cup.

"There was summat weird going on at your place, you know."

"Something weird?"

"Yeah, some head banger was running up the steps towards the front door."

"Head banger?"

Moving into private eye mode again, I tried not to sound too interested.

"Yeah, looked as if he'd just got out of bed. Mad, staring eyes. Feller with long blonde hair. Banged on the door just as it was closing."

It sounded like Askey.

"You know, as if he was after someone. Looked dead funny. Then he went inside."

"Did he? I wonder what he wanted."

"Search me, mate. I stood and watched him for a bit, know what I mean? There was a feller at the cashpoint on the corner just as interested as me in what was going on."

"Was he?"

"Yeah, he kept looking towards this lunatic."

It could have been Don, I thought.

"What did he look like?"

"What does anybody look like? Pretty average, I'd say."

"Old, young? Colour hair, clothes?"

He screwed up his eyes in concentration.

"Older than me. Fair hair, wearing a leather jacket."

"Did he go into the office?"

He shrugged.

"No idea. I went off to the chippy."

"Right."

Where did that get me? I already knew Askey had barged into the office. A man in a leather jacket was near the scene of the crime at the time Bill was killed. I didn't recognize the description. It could have been almost anybody so I wasn't a lot further forward.

"Do you know that Mr. Copelaw, my boss, was killed that night?"

"No."

His voice throbbed with indifference.

Over the next ten minutes my powers of persuasion got Liam to answer some questions about his own background. He had dismissed his daughter and her future by simply saying he wasn't going to take any part in her upbringing from now on. Not the way one would like a father to talk about his only child but I was used to it. Nearly.

He told me his parents considered he had let them down. They would let him stay with them for the time being but would not offer anything more than food and shelter. He got up and started walking backwards and forwards around the living room, his feet sinking into the cream shag pile carpet.

"I've always been a bit of a disaster to my mum and dad, to be honest," he went on.

He went through a catalogue of difficulties. Problems at a snobby, private school. A waste of money, according to his dad. He scraped through one GCSE pass in English Literature. Packed in Sixth Form half way through the first term. Went 'down South somewhere'. On his return he joined the Army.

"Well, no-one was more pleased than my dad," he said. "He reckoned it would give me a bit of discipline, thought I'd carve out a career for myself."

Predictably Liam's army career self-destructed.

"What about your relationship with Sharon?"

"Relationship? Is that what you call it?"

He took a couple of paces and stopped by the fireplace, as if posing for a photograph to show off this feature.

"It wasn't meant to be this way. It was just a bit of…well, you know, when it's laid on a plate."

I waited while he stood deep in thought and sat down again.

"Don't get me wrong, I'm not trying to run the girl down. She comes from a rough family and all that."

What's your excuse, I thought. He passed his hand over his chin.

"I'll be honest with you, she's not the sort of girl I thought I'd, you know, settle down with."

"What are you intending to do now?" I asked.

"Hard to say, know what I mean? A mate of my dad's might have a job for me."

He went on to tell me Sharon would have a better chance of getting Rebecca back without him. In one way he was absolving himself of his responsibilities; in another he was right.

"So, that's about it, Don," I said later that day, looking up from the case file on my lap.

I sat in Don's office, having just updated him on Rebecca's situation: she was thriving with foster carers. Liam was out of the picture it seemed. It was hard to say what Sharon could offer her daughter. Some days she made an effort; some days she didn't.

"How's your health, Gus," he asked.

I looked round the room, thinking back to when it had been Bill's. At some point the Elvis posters had been taken down. Don hadn't thought to do anything to personalize the office. Typical, I thought.

"Fine," I said. "I've just had my latest check-up. Everything OK. I feel better for working part-time."

"What about finding Bill? Has that affected you at all?"

He looked at me trying to look caring. All I got was an impression of indifference.

"Yes," I said, "up to a point. It seems terrible to say it but the rest of my life is pretty good. That goes a long way towards countering any fall-out from that night."

"You could have counselling, you know. It's been offered to everyone else."

I had never told Don I was having counselling, though I'd been happy to confide in Bill. I knew Don was just doing his duty, going through the checklist in his head.

"I'll think about it," I said, knowing I was still entitled to two more sessions in any case.

I closed the case file and put it down on Don's Desk.

"The police questioning is what keeps coming back to me," I said.

This was becoming a habit, finding a way to investigate the murder without it being obvious.

"If it's any consolation," he said, "they spoke to everyone."

"Including you?"

"Oh, yes," he said.

"Weird experience, isn't it?"

He smiled.

"Yeah, a bit like something on television. Especially when they asked me where I was around the time Bill was killed."

"And where were you?"

"At home as far as I could recall. I left on time for once. Traffic wasn't too bad."

"You didn't nip in for a quick drink?"

"No," he said.

"Don't you sometimes call in the Park Hotel."

I was sure that was the beginning of a blush creeping down his face.

"Now and again, but not that night."

I shook my head, trying my best to look puzzled.

"It's just that I thought Arthur, you know, the landlord, said you were in the Park Hotel that night."

I waited for a response, hoping I had just stopped short of confronting Don. He shrugged.

"Don't think so. I mean I suppose I could have been and forgot about it."

I left a few minutes later to go back to my desk. Thinking about Don as a suspect still seemed bizarre. I had met a lot of ambitious people in my time but didn't know any who'd killed to help their career. But why did he lie about going to the pub that night? It had been the day of his row with Bill. He would have been upset about that and worrying about his career. Maybe he was ashamed of drinking to excess because of his Christianity. One of the many things I couldn't understand about some Christians was their opposition to alcohol. Wasn't Jesus supposed to have turned water into wine? Before my mind could take me on an anti-religious rant I thought again about what made Don tick. The truth was I hadn't a clue. Why should someone choose to do a job like social work when their main motivation was climbing the organisational ladder?

I was still hard at it that evening long after official knocking off time. I was thinking about Rebecca and the responsibility of making decisions about her future. This led me to think about Liam. Was he a suspect for Bill's murder? He would have a motive for having a go at somebody from Social Services. Despite his indifference to Rebecca's welfare he was angry about what he saw as this unwarranted interference. Liam thought somebody else was to blame for whatever went wrong in his life. He already had a long history of failure and disappointment. Had that left a legacy of frustration? Did that explain the barely concealed anger that could kick in any time?

Did he come out of the chip shop as Askey was leaving Ordsall Tower and sneak in while the door was open? Then I remembered the salt and vinegar smell as I went in the office. Yet Liam was only too willing to admit he had bought chips that night. And there was no smell in Bill's office. This needed thinking about.

A few minutes later Ania walked in with her cleaning stuff. Plugging in her vacuum cleaner, she yawned and put her hand over her mouth. Smiling, she came over and sat next to me.

"Don't work too hard, will you," she said with a smile, indicating the notes littering my desk.

"No, once I've finished this, I'm off until next week."

I sat back on my chair and stretched my hand above my head.

"That's good," she said. "You know, this is the first time we've met since, you know, Bill dying and everything."

"Yeah," I said.

"Coming here just brings it all back. It's hard to stop thinking about it."

I nodded. Impossible, I would have said, rather than hard.

"People are still asking me about it," she went on, seeming eager to talk.

She pulled up the sleeves of the grey, woollen top she wore underneath her overall. I noticed a chipped nail on her right index finger.

"Yeah, me too."

"They think it's exciting being interviewed by the police."

I shook my head.

"It made me feel guilty," I said.

"Yes. You wonder what's behind their questions."

"What did they ask you?"

"Oh, mostly about Askey. And had I seen anybody else?"

"Had you?"

"I told them I saw a couple of men outside the building when Askey forced his way in."

She got up and, taking a duster from her overall pocket, she polished Karen's desk.

"Anyone you knew?"

I was getting used to changing my role whenever an opportunity to investigate Bill's murder presented itself.

"I don't think so," she said. "One was dressed in leathers, you know, motorbike clothes. I didn't know him."

"The other one?"

"Well, I only saw his back. I know it sounds stupid," she said, "but he looked familiar."

CHAPTER ELEVEN

"Now then, Gus," said Pete Jenkinson two days later, as I entered Worsley Premium Butchers.

Pete was a walking advert for his produce, looking plump and self-satisfied. He wore a collar and tie as usual, a white hat covering his thinning hair. The doorbell clanged behind me, evoking memories of going on errands for my mam. Cheese and bacon aromas mingled with a background smell of cleanliness and disinfectant. We exchanged greetings and small talk as I gave him my long list. Glancing down he pulled the cord tighter round his striped apron.

"Bit of a shipping order, this."

"Well, I can't get over that often these days," I said.

"Glad of your custom, Gus. Not a lot of loyalty around these days."

"You're hard to beat on quality, Pete. Do you think you could have it ready for me if I call back in half an hour or so?"

"No probs. Getting stocked up for the weekend?"

"Yeah. I'll leave you to it. I just need to call on someone," I explained.

"Not Mrs Copelaw by any chance, is it?"

If there was once thing Pete liked as much as a well-hung sirloin, it was a good gossip.

"Yeah. I thought I'd see how she was while I was here."

I had already decided to use my meat buying trip as an opportunity to call on Jean Copelaw. I told myself I would have gone to see her anyway but deep down I knew it was part of my investigation. She was around on the day of Bill's death. I'd talked to her about an hour before he was killed. Maybe she'd seen something. I was only hoping she was in. I hadn't been able to phone her as I didn't have her home number.

"A sad business," said Pete. "She was telling me her daughter has gone back home."

"Yeah?"

"Good riddance to bad rubbish," he went on.

He folded his arms and made an almost imperceptible movement of his head from side to side.

"What a little madam she was as a kid. I don't suppose age has improved her."

"I only met her at the funeral."

"On her best behaviour no doubt. Butter wouldn't melt."

"Hard to say."

"Still, not the happiest of homes, I wouldn't have thought," he went on. "They tried to buy her affection, you know. Not good news."

Five minutes later I made my escape. The morning sun glinted through the trees as I walked through Worsley. The warm weather had returned after overnight rain but the breeze was cool enough for me to put on a V-necked jumper over my t-shirt. I recalled my boyhood, when Worsley had always seemed miles away and a trip to Worsley Woods was like an expedition. The village, with its expensive black and white half-timber houses had once seemed out of my league. Now it was a place where I used to live. I'd grown to like it over the years. Quiet and secluded, with a village green, it was still not far from the city. Two minutes later I was approaching the large 1930s semi I had last visited on the day of Bill's funeral. I saw a woman coming out of the front door. She zipped up her jacket and walked towards me with the aid of a stick.

Jean gave me her nearest equivalent to a smile. Even so, her stick and the pinched expression on her face gave her the appearance of a bad-tempered granny.

"Hello, Gus," she said, "what are you doing here?"

I explained about being in the area shopping and deciding to call round.

"I'm just having my morning walk," she said, "why not join me?"

We walked briskly as though it were part of an exercise routine. I took deep breaths, enjoying the smell of trees and grass after the rain. At Worsley Court House we turned left. Traffic noise and the footsteps of the few dog walkers accompanied us as we strolled along Barton Road.

"How have you been?" I asked to break the silence.

She shrugged, avoiding a puddle as she marched on.

"As well as can be expected as they say," she said. "It's been one shock after another."

We walked on to the Packet House and Boat Steps. The latter spot was where passengers boarded the packet boats. I thought of the boats carrying the Royal Mail down the Bridgewater Canal. I enjoyed memories of walking here when Rachel and Danny were school age. I had learned local history for their benefit. At this time of day only elderly couples and mothers with toddlers and pushchairs passed us.

"Yeah?"

"That business with Karen knocked me for six."

"Karen?"

"That young lass you work with."

"What about her?"

"My loving husband had been having an affair with her."

"Never."

"Why else would he leave her a load of money in his will."

"What?"

A load of money, eh? Where had Bill got hold of that? And what exactly constituted 'a load of money'?

"From some insurance policy apparently."

"Oh."

I was tempted to ask for more information, but Jean would probably have said the details weren't relevant. And, having started talking, she showed no sign of stopping. A question and answer session would only put her under pressure. We passed a white house that I thought might be the old nailmaker's shop. More irrelevance, I thought.

"You mean she hasn't told you? I thought she'd have been gloating all over the office."

I told her I hadn't seen Karen since Bill died.

"She's been on the sick for a while," I explained.

She turned her head slightly towards me.

"On the sick? Probably exhausted from counting her money."

Turning left on Worsley Road we went back towards the Court House, passing the library and a roundabout.

"I tried to find out if the will was kosher, you know. He changed it quite recently."

"Right."

"There's nothing I can do about it," she shrugged, trying without success to sound philosophical.

I pondered this as we crossed the road, again going uphill under the motorway bridge. The traffic on the M62 whizzed along while we enjoyed our relative tranquillity.

"I'll be OK. I've got some savings and I can sell the house, get a smaller place. Bill was always against moving."

Jean took a deep breath as though getting a second wind.

"You know about all his other women I suppose."

"No," I replied, being economical with the truth, remembering Marti saying something similar about Bill.

"You're the only one then."

Life has always seemed more or less straightforward to me. Everyone else had a complicated love life. Did 'everyone' include Louise, I wondered. If she had had somebody else I wouldn't necessarily have known. I hadn't thought of her for a while. Could be Marti's influence.

"Quite a few times he'd been going to leave me," she said, sounding almost pleased as she led the way towards St Mark's church. "Always for someone younger."

I didn't bother to answer. Jean was on a roll.

"Some of them had kids," she said, "We only had the one."

"I met Cal at the funeral."

"Cal," she said scornfully. "Trendy nonsense. Carol's her name, always was, always will be."

"Sorry."

"Not your fault, Gus," she said. "She became 'Cal' when she went to university down South."

We walked on with no let up in the pace.

"Typical of her self-indulgence. Of course, we spoilt her rotten, I can see that now. Private school, the lot. For all the thanks we got."

She put on a spurt at this point as though she were in a race.

"Me and Bill were brought up in Little Hulton and we wanted something better for our daughter."

"I can relate to that," I said.

"She started to look down on us."

That I couldn't relate to, so said nothing.

"We hardly see her these days. When she did deign to come and see us, she and Bill hardly exchanged a word."

How did people get into that situation? The idea of hardly seeing my kids, not speaking to them, made me come out in a cold sweat. I remembered Cal's hypocrisy on the day of the funeral.

"It's just a pity they can't pin Bill's murder on Karen," she said out of the blue.

She stabbed her stick into the ground.

"She had a bloody good motive after all."

So did you, I thought.

"On the whole," I said, "I think it's a good thing we know who killed Bill."

She nodded. Already I was finding out things about Bill and his life that could have got him killed. Instead the events that had led to his death had been purely random. If I hadn't sought out Askey on that day; if Askey had been in a fit state to talk to me; if Bill had gone home early.

"Did the police speak to you at all?"

"Yeah. They wanted to know if I'd seen anyone around the office. Particularly that Askey feller."

We went over a road bridge and I looked over to the Delph. Its name was derived from 'the delved place'. Stone had been quarried from this place to construct the canal. How had that managed to stick in my mind?

"I couldn't help them. I left soon after I'd seen you, Gus."

Maybe she wouldn't be much help, I thought.

"Carol was paying us one of her duty visits. She was waiting in the car outside."

It must have been her I'd seen in the car park when I came out of the office that night.

"I'd just picked her up at Piccadilly station. She was staying at the Marriott Hotel of course. Her own home isn't good enough for her."

Jean breathed in as if taking in more air for a final onslaught.

"I'm a fighter, always have been, I've had to be all my life. I've seen off all the others. I would have done the same with Karen."

* * *

Three days later, I met Charlotte outside Haddon House Remand Centre in Sale where she was waiting for me in a steady morning rain. I had vowed never to work on Mondays when I retired but it hadn't worked out like that. After muted greetings, we approached the entrance of the grey, concrete building. I could have thought of more pleasant places to be, but the job had to be done. After giving our names at reception, we had to deposit keys, cash, mobiles and bags in a locker. Even my pen and the paperback I had read on the tram journey had to go. We then trailed along endless corridors, claustrophobia and a feeling of not being welcome accompanying us.

Eventually we faced Mick Askey across a table in a poky, whitewashed interview room. His face was less flushed since I had last seen him and, in the kind of striped shirt that would go with a suit, he looked almost smart. "Now then, Mick," I said.

He nodded.

"All right."

"This is Charlotte."

Again a nod.

"Now then love."

"Hi," she said, nibbling her bottom lip.

This place raised my liberal hackles. Why are people dumped in these warehouses that smelled of wee and school dinners? Some of them shouldn't even be here. Though Mick should, I reminded myself.

"I just wanna say from the start," said Mick. "I'm innocent. I want you to tell everybody that, you know what I mean?"

"That's not what we're here for, Mick."

He lowered his voice.

"I don't give a fuck what you're here for. I'm only here for two reasons: to get out of my cell for a bit and to tell you I never touched that Copling feller."

"Copelaw."

"Whatever his name is I never laid a finger on him."

"Somebody did," I said, "he didn't bop himself on the head."

"Listen, Mick," Charlotte said.

"No, you listen. You've got to help me, mate. It's doing my head in, this place."

I looked at Charlotte, who shrugged.

"You're talking to the wrong person," I told him. "I can't interfere in a case like this."

"Just listen to me," he said, "that's all I ask. I've got to talk to someone. It's going round and round in my head. I'm cracking up."

"Mick, please…"

"I've been forced to stay in places I don't want to be all my life. I got took into care when I was four."

Oh, no, here comes the hard luck story. We didn't have time for this.

"Foster parents, care homes, secure units, I did the lot. Now this. And for something I didn't even do. Just listen to me, will you?"

I took a deep breath.

"OK, say what you've got to say, but when you've finished me and Charlotte have some questions for you."

"Thanks, mate."

"And remember we haven't got much time."

"Well, that night I was coming to see you, mate. I got into social services just as some bird was going in…"

"The cleaner?"

"Yeah, I nipped past her through the front door."

I knew all this.

"And?"

"Well, she started having a go but Copelaw came along and took me into his office."

"What happened between you and Mr Copelaw?"

That was what I really wanted to know. I hadn't thought Mick would give me the chance to question him about the murder. I'd better take advantage while I could.

"It's hard to remember. He said summat like, 'Sit down and calm down, we won't get anywhere shouting and bawling'."

I could imagine Bill saying that. Mick flexed his fingers.

"So I sat down," he said. "I told him I'd calm down when he stopped people like you hassling me."

"What did he say to that?"

Mick leant back and folded his arms across his chest.

"He must have asked me what it was all about cos I definitely gave him that letter you sent me."

He closed his eyes as if trying to bring it all back to his mind.

"He read it and handed it back to me."

"Anything else happen?"

"I lost my rag again at one point," he said.

Surprise, surprise.

"Why?"

"Well he was trying to fob me off, know what I mean? You know, 'I won't be able to talk to Gus until Monday. I can't do anything till then'. Load of bollocks."

He scratched his head before going on.

"I said, 'he's got a fucking mobile, hasn't he?' Phone him."

A look of scorn spread across his face.

"He said you were tied up with an urgent case. Tied up with a pint more like."

"What happened next?" I sighed, thinking better of telling him I really was on an urgent case.

"I got fed up and got out of my chair. I lost it a bit, got a statue off his desk and threw it at him."

He's admitted handling the murder weapon, I thought. He shook his head in dismay.

"It missed. He just picked it up off the floor as calm as anything and put it back on the desk."

"Then what?"

"He said, 'fuck off out of it, Mick, I can't be bothered with you.' Well, a feller in his position shouldn't be talking like that."

I struggled to hold back a smile. At least Bill went out with a bang.

"What did you do?"

He shrugged.

"I fucked off."

"So he was alive when you left?"

And the trophy was still on the desk. Unless he were lying. Would an upstanding citizen like Mick Askey tell me fibs? Surely not.

"Yeah and as I was running out the front door, this bloke brushed past me."

"Which direction was he heading?"

"Towards Social Services," he said. "He was about my age, I reckon. Average height. Fair hair. Had a leather jacket on."

"Any idea who it was?"

"No, but my brief's looking into it."

"Who's your brief," I asked as if I didn't know.

"Coloured lass, good though, seems to know what she's about, know what I mean? Pym, she's called, Martina Pym."

Using your Sunday name, are you, Marti, I said to myself.

"If you've got a good solicitor that's half the battle," I said. "She'll sort it out for you, but you'll have to be patient."

He nodded.

"Now, Mick," I went on, "while there's still time let me explain why we're really here."

"Fair enough."

"According to our records," I said, "and her birth certificate, you're Charlotte's father."

Mick unfolded his arms and leant on the table. Behind him on the wall I noticed an AIDS poster that looked as if it had been there since the disease was first discovered. He said nothing.

"Are you gonna talk to me?"

He looked up at the ceiling. I waited.

"I can't help you, mate."

"You could start by telling me whether you are Charlotte's father."

He breathed hard through his nose and drummed his fingers on the table.

"No, I'm not," he said, "I haven't got a daughter. I've got a lad. He was in Birmingham last I heard."

"Do you want to say anything, Charlotte," I said, looking towards her.

She shook her head.

"Let me go through the facts," I said, "Charlotte's mother is Tracy Stephens. She lives in Little Hulton. You lived with her for about a year."

"I might have done," he shrugged. "Hard to remember. I've had a few birds, know what I mean?"

What Mick was saying was probably true. I was willing to bet he had had 'a few birds'. Sometimes I thought a handful of men like him had fathered most of the problem kids in Salford. Not for the first time I wondered what the attraction was with these blokes. Was the secret of success not to wash from one week's end to the next; to cultivate broken and discoloured teeth; to behave as if you'd never heard of safe sex? Deciding not to pursue these thoughts any further, I got back to the point.

"Now, during that year, Charlotte was born. Tracy put you down as the father on the birth certificate. Why would she do that?"

He sat still for a moment, as if deep in thought.

"Tracy, I remember her now. Lying cow. And I know for a fact she's had more cock than I've had hot dinners."

"If you're not my father, who is?"

We both looked at Charlotte, taken aback by her intervention.

"Take your pick," he said.

A silence descended. Mick rested his chin on his hands and sighed.

"There's things you don't know, things you don't want to know. It's just…it's not as simple as you're making out."

"So explain," Charlotte demanded.

He pursed his lips and shook his head.

"I'd like to help you love," Mick went on, "I would honest, but take it from me, I'm not your dad."

"Listen, Mick," said Charlotte, sounding more confident now. "There's only one way to find out for sure. Would you take a DNA test?'

He puffed out his cheeks, letting air out slowly. He shook his head again.

"No way."

"Please," said Charlotte, "I'm begging you. I don't know who my real father is. Imagine how that feels."

I wondered if Mick knew who his father was, as Charlotte appealed to him.

"Take the test and we'll know one way or another."

"No. No. I'm telling you love, you are not my daughter. Leave it, it's for the best, I promise you."

CHAPTER TWELVE

I sat back in my seat on the half empty train. It was still t-shirt weather and I'd even risked wearing shorts for the first time since last August. I checked that I had everything I needed. I'd put my iPod in its case on the table in front of me. Next to them there was a set of headphones. I took the book I'd brought – Fly in the Ointment by Anne Fines – out of my rucksack. It joined the other stuff. I'd nearly finished it so had brought Rugby Renegade by Gus Risman as well. I took my ticket out of my shorts pocket and looked at the date. Thursday 28th April. Bloody hell, April was nearly over. Where had the previous twenty-seven days gone? I thought of the weather forecasters saying it was the driest April since the year dot. And my dad worrying about the lack of rain on his allotment. Thinking of the irony of a Salfordian complaining when it didn't rain, I took out my mobile and texted Steve:

> 20 minutes late out of Piccadilly. Should still make the connection at Shrewsbury. Due in Barmouth 15.52

A couple of days in Wales would go down well, I thought. Steve and I would go walking, get drunk, argue politics and listen to Creedence Clearwater Revival. Not necessarily in that order, I said to myself as I thought about last night's Crimewatch programme. It had gone over the Kylie Anderson case again. Elaine Anderson had appeared to talk about her daughter's abduction. She had made an emotional but controlled appeal. She had worked tirelessly for 18 years to keep the story alive. In the process she had become a media star herself, travelling the world and developing a slight Californian accent in the process. She had written books, hosted a TV series, Keeping Hope Alive, about missing children and set up a trust fund for Kylie from her earnings.

Her looks, charisma and sincerity had in general won over the sceptics. There were those who thought it unnatural that a grieving mother should be able to play the role of TV personality. Others blamed her for exploiting the tragedy to become famous. There had been intermittent speculation that she had had something to do with Kylie's disappearance, even killed her. Me, I just felt sorry for her. It didn't take much imagination to know how I'd feel if that had happened to Rachel or Danny.

At Barmouth station four hours later I got out of the train and slung the rucksack over my shoulders. The good weather had continued with no sign of let up. I looked ahead to the end of the platform. I had to shield my eyes with my hand although my glasses had lenses that go dark in sunlight. I saw Steve waiting by the exit. A couple of minutes later we were driving in his Jaguar through the town with its slate roofs and onto the road to Dolgellau. Within half an hour I was sitting in Steve's back garden, a book of walks on the picnic table in front of me. Steve had instructed me to choose a walk for tomorrow.

"You could never get tired of that view," I said as he brought out two mugs of tea.

In one direction Cader Idris towered over the hillside; in the other you could see down the valley of the river Wnion to the coast. I thought of boyhood holidays around this part of Wales. For two weeks every summer I'd go with Steve's family to stay with his maternal grandparents. In return, he'd come with us to my dad's folks in County Kerry. Happy days.

"I take it for granted sometimes," he said.

He sat down opposite me and put the mugs on the table.

"Jackie said she'd try and finish work early."

"How is she?"

"Fine, you know, same as ever."

I pictured Steve's second wife and thought once more what an improvement she was on the first.

"So you're back at work," he said.

I explained about the case I was dealing with.

"It's just part time, as and when, you know."

"Yeah, you don't want to be doing too much."

"I've got another job as well," I said after another mouthful of tea.

"What's that?"

I took out my wallet and handed him a business card.

"GRK Investigations? What the bloody hell's that?"

I told him I'd set myself up as a private investigator. As expected, he laughed out loud.

"Private investigator, you? How do you intend to get any clients?"

"Marti will get me work."

He looked puzzled and seemed to think for a while.

"Marti? Who's he?"

"She is a solicitor I know. And she's…"

I hesitated, drinking more tea.

"Well, we're, you know…"

His eyes opened wide, his grin threatened to split his face in two.

"You've got a bird."

100

I nodded, trying to keep the smirk from my face.

"When did this happen?"

I shrugged.

"Well, it had just started around the time I last saw you but I didn't want to say anything. You never know, it might have just fizzled out."

"But it didn't?"

"Not so far."

"You little bugger," he said. "You always were a bit of a bird magnet, though, before you met Louise."

He grinned.

"So, what's she like, a right cracker, I'll bet."

"Yeah, gorgeous."

Just then I heard footsteps and turned to see a woman with long, red hair, dressed for work, approaching.

"Gus," she cried in a Welsh lilt. "Come here."

She folded me in an embrace, planting a smacker full on my lips.

"I could leave home for you, you know," she said, smoothing down her Wales Tourist Board jacket.

She had said that before.

"Well, don't let me stop you," said Steve.

"I'll just get changed," said Jackie.

"Anyway, you're too late," Steve went on, "he's spoken for."

That stopped Jackie in her tracks.

"Is he now? You mean…"

Steve nodded.

"Got himself a girlfriend."

She sat next to me on the garden bench.

"Maybe I'll get changed later," she said. "Tell me all."

"Well…"

"She's a solicitor," Steve put in. "Gus reckons she's gorgeous."

"Really? Have you got any photos?"

I shook my head then thought of the day I'd photographed Marti on her doorstep.

"Although," I corrected myself, "there's a couple on my phone."

Getting the phone from my pocket I managed to find the pictures. Twisting the phone around until the screen was out of the sun, I held them up for inspection.

"Hey, not bad, Gus," said Steve.

"She's black," announced Jackie.

I hadn't known whether to tell Steve and his wife, that Marti was black. If she hadn't been too busy to come to Wales with me, they would have known. The dilemma of the white liberal was deciding between two opposing positions that were held simultaneously. Of course the colour of someone's skin didn't matter; of course it mattered. Well, I thought, better men than me have tried and failed to resolve it.

"And she's from Liverpool," I added.

Steve was about to drink more tea but he took the mug away from his mouth and put it down on the table.

"A black Scouser, eh? You like 'em exotic, Gus. First a blonde from Darlington, now this."

"Yeah, well…"

After a few more questions about how long I'd known her, how we'd met and what Rachel and Danny thought, Jackie finally started to move off.

"I'm trying a James Martin recipe tonight, Gus," she said. "I'll be interested to see what you think."

"I'll look forward to it."

"And remember, Steve, certain topics of conversation have to wait until I'm in bed."

"Such as," I asked.

"Politics," she replied. "I know what you two are like when you get together."

"Well, he's such a right wing toss pot, Jackie, somebody has to put him right."

"There speaks a typical loony lefty," put in Steve

"That just proves my point."

She turned again to Steve.

"And the only time you listen to Creedence Clearwater is tomorrow morning when I've left for work."

I looked at her in amazement.

"You don't like Creedence?"

"I used to until I started living with this bloke called Steve Yarnitzky. The man's obsessed. If I never hear Proud Mary again, it'll be too soon."

With that she smiled and left us.

"So this new girlfriend, has she given you any jobs yet," asked Steve later.

"She's got me investigating Copelaw's murder," I replied.

"What? How does that work?"

I told him what Marti had said about 'leather jacket man' and how she had persuaded me to look into it while I was working at Ordsall Tower.

"Sounds like the old pals' act," said Steve with a world-weary cynicism.

"Suppose so."

"Have you got anywhere yet?"

I shook my head. Of course I wasn't getting anywhere with the Copelaw case. Admit it, Gus, I said to myself, you never will. Still the thought that there was more to it, that I was missing something, nagged away at me like a strict teacher. Something that would seem obvious when I realised what it was. An image of Bill's room when I found his body kept coming back to me. There was definitely something wrong about it. But what? Just lately I'd also been trying to identify a word I'd heard somewhere. A word that might be significant. Something like 'certainty', it was. Or a word that sounded like it or had a similar meaning.

"To be honest," I said. "I don't really expect to."

"Still, it's a living, I suppose. You think Askey did it then?"

"Almost certainly," I said.

He pursed his lips and clicked his fingers.

"That reminds me, how did you get on when you saw him in prison?"

"Oh, yeah, I meant to mention that. He refused to take the DNA test."

"Bugger. Let's see if I can help you. I could give Sarita a ring."

"Not Inspector Ellerton?"

"Do you know her?"

"She interviewed me when I found Bill's body."

"I suppose she would," he said. "She's one of my protégées."

"Oh, yeah?"

"Do anything for me, she would. Well, nearly anything."

He went into the house and came back with a mobile phone. Sitting down, he admired the view as he dialled. I could finally concentrate on the Snowdonia Walks book while he waited for an answer. I studied the Precipice Walk, thinking it would be a good one to do tomorrow. Despite its name, it was rated as easy.

"Sarita? Steve Yarnitzky here, how are you doing?"

The obligatory chit-chat went on as I read through the points of interest on the walk. Eventually Steve got to the point of his call. It was obvious even to a casual listener that there was some hesitation at the other end of the line as Steve explained what he wanted.

"But this lass suffered neglect bad enough to be taken into care. Askey must have been a part of that. This evidence could help nail him. A bit of justice for Charlotte."

There was a pause. I gave up on the walk to listen to the outcome of Steve's entreaty.

"I know that's not why she wants the test but what's wrong with killing two birds with one stone?"

Obviously impatient, Steve got up and began walking up and down.

"Come on, Sarita, have I ever steered you wrong?"

Another pause, followed by a 'Yes!' from Steve.

"Lovely jubbly," he said in a terrible impression of Del Boy. "You know it makes sense."

Getting his own way was Steve's speciality.

"On a more important point, are you pregnant yet?" he asked.

"Keep at it. That dopy husband of yours does realise that having sex is an essential part of the process?"

He chuckled as he listened to the response.

"There's no need for that sort of language."

A few seconds later he ended the call and came back to the table, putting the phone in his trouser pocket.

"Sorted. Get Charlotte to go down to the station for a swab. Ask for Inspector Ellerton."

"Thanks, Steve."

"Now, have you sorted out a walk?"

* * *

The next day we set off just after ten. We drove a couple of miles north from Dolgellau, heading for a car park on a minor road. Once out of the car, we spent a few minutes on the usual walkers' rigmarole. Boots on, rucksacks packed with essentials, suncream applied, we set off. As we were getting underway, Steve asked after Louise.

"She's due back tomorrow," I said, "she'll be staying with Danny for a few days then coming up to Salford."

"Are you gonna see her?"

I shrugged as we walked on.

"Suppose so. We'll have to meet sometime, not sure when."

"Listen, give her my love when you see her."

"Course."

We walked along the road for a while before taking a footpath into the woods.

"And tell her she's always welcome to come and see me and Jackie."

I nodded. After a pause he went on.

"Is she, you know, involved with anybody else?"

"Not that I know of," I replied. "She said married life didn't suit her any more. She needed her own space apparently."

Whatever that means, I said to myself.

Having said what he wanted to say about Louise, Steve began to wax lyrical about the joys of country living. He even urged me to join him in Wales. I'd never had any intention of moving from Salford. It was home, simple as that. For years, Steve had nurtured a dream of doing what he was doing now. Living here would, I couldn't help thinking, mean the experience would no longer be special for me. And where would I go for a break?

We then talked about Rachel and Danny and the progress - or lack of it - of Salford City Reds. That didn't take long: the less said about my Rugby League team the better. We walked on for a while in silence through the trees.

"So, this murder," said Steve as we climbed a stile at the end of the wood, "how do you intend going about it?"

I shrugged as I swung my leg over the stile.

"Have you got any ideas? You're a real detective."

"Go through what happened with you and Askey that day."

I told him about my second visit to the house in Princess Street, Tanya's escape in the taxi and Askey tripping over my foot.

"Then I put the letter through the letterbox."

"So, he was upset about his girlfriend leaving. He'd partly blame you for that."

"Well, I wasn't gonna let him attack her."

"Fair point but he wouldn't see it the same way. The other significant thing is he was pissed when you saw him. When he got up after you'd tripped him up, he probably went for a kip."

I nodded as we followed the path to the right. I looked down the valley at Llyn Cynwch and the sun glistening on the lake. I breathed in and wondered at the beauty of it all. Could anywhere in the world match this, I asked myself, or equal the feeling of tranquillity it brought me. Mick Askey should have gone on more country walks, I thought.

"He would have woken up feeling like shit when he found the letter," said Steve, breaking abruptly into my meditation.

"I suppose he would."

"So by the time he got to Social Services," Steve continued, "he would have felt like murdering someone."

"Yeah."

"He goes into Bill Copelaw's office still spitting feathers."

"And kills him?"

"Precisely."

"That doesn't get me anywhere," I said. "Let's think about the alternatives."

"It'll pass the time."

I told him I'd been to see Liam Bentley.

"He said something relevant to the murder inquiry," I said, after explaining who Liam was.

"Oh, yeah," said Steve.

"He parked his bike near Ordsall Tower about the time we think Bill was killed."

"Did he see anything of interest?"

"Said he saw a bloke going up the steps towards Ordsall Tower. I'm pretty sure that was Askey."

"Right."

"There was another man nearby. Pretty average, Liam reckoned. Older than him. Fair hair, wearing a leather jacket."

"Leather jacket man. Maybe he does exist after all."

"Yeah, but the description's so vague it could apply to almost anyone. And he was outside. There's nothing to say he went into the office."

"Nothing to say he didn't."

"We have to remember Liam was wearing a leather jacket himself."

"Being a biker."

"Right. He admits being in the vicinity at the relevant time. He had a motive. He was as pissed off with me as Mick Askey."

We walked on.

"So what's he like this Liam?"

"He's what we social workers call a little twat," I said.

"Who else have you spoken to?"

"I went to see Bill's wife, Jean. She didn't see anything but she told me Bill was having an affair with Karen Davidson."

"Karen who?"

"A youngish social worker. She's been in the office a few months."

"And your gaffer was giving her one?" asked Steve. "The plot thickens."

"There's more."

"Very interesting," said Steve when I explained about Karen's legacy from Bill. "What does Karen say about it?"

"I haven't seen her. She's on the sick."

We crossed another stile.

"Money is always a good motive for murder," I suggested.

"Don't start fantasizing," he grinned.

"That's precisely what I need to do. I have to assume somebody else did it or what's the point?"

Steve smiled.

"I know what this is about. What's that film you like? Maltese Falcon, isn't it? You fancy yourself as Humphrey Bogart, cracking the case in the last reel."

"What if I do? They can't touch you for it."

We laughed as we strode on, getting up a nice rhythm now.

"Maybe not," said Steve, "but if Karen is suddenly a suspect that rules out leather jacket man."

"But once you go into it there are lots of people who had reason to kill Bill. That's what I'm beginning to think anyway."

"Who are all these people with a motive?"

We climbed another stile while I thought about Steve's question.

"Liam and Karen I've already mentioned. There's Jean of course."

"The wife's usually at the top of the list."

"Doesn't say much for married life. And there's Karen's husband."

"A fair sized list, I grant you but have you got any actual facts?"

"Well, Ania, the cleaner saw a man in a leather jacket outside Ordsall Tower as Askey was forcing his way in."

"That's two people who have seen him. You could argue that makes it more likely Askey is telling the truth. A bit shaky though."

I nodded.

"Yeah. Askey could have seen someone outside in a leather jacket. He had plenty of time to think up a story, using leather jacket man."

* * *

I left my apartment block five days later. The working week was starting on a Tuesday because of the May Day Bank Holiday. I didn't mind going to work today because of who I was working with. I walked in the sunshine towards the Holiday Inn, its beige brick frontage looming above me. Skirting round the side of the hotel, I passed the ubiquitous swans. I walked on towards Old Trafford for a couple of hundred yards before arriving at a steel and glass tower block. I glanced at 'Dacre House' written over the doorway as I went inside and waited for the lift with two businessmen complaining about air travel. Pity you've nothing better to worry about, I said to myself. As I entered the lift I checked the metal plaque listing all ten floors. Selecting the fourth, I was soon opening the door of Pym and Sigson.

I was at Marti's black ash desk a few minutes later. Filing cabinets of the same wood lined the walls. I pulled out a file, a biro and a notebook from my briefcase and put them down in front of me. Marti and I had arranged to spend some time working on the Rebecca Winters case. The sun shone through the window on my left as I began to read the medical report on Rebecca's injuries. As I worked my way through the medical jargon, jotting down notes as I read, I tried to block out the thought of a baby being assaulted.

Just as I was finishing the last paragraph, Marti came in with two mugs of tea. Looking fantastic of course, even in a formal, navy blue suit. I let my mind dwell for a few seconds on the way she had welcomed me home when I got back from Dolgellau. Having put the tea on the table and given my hand a quick squeeze, she sat opposite me. We agreed the paediatrician's report told us nothing we didn't know.

"It was physical abuse and we still don't know who did it."

She nodded.

"Sharon could have lashed out, I suppose. She didn't have much of a life."

"Yeah," I agreed, "but "Liam's a good bet too."

"Typical Mr Angry. Did you manage to see him?"

"Yeah."

"And?"

I shrugged.

"Basically he doesn't want to know."

I explained what Liam had said about opting out of Rebecca's life.

Later we talked about Bill's murder. She asked if I was making progress with my investigations. I told her what I had discussed with Steve. She didn't seem to think it would get us anywhere.

"There's still nothing to say leather jacket man actually entered Ordsall Tower."

"Except for what Askey said."

"And that's hardly independent and objective."

I sighed.

"It's hard to know what to make of it all. Sometimes in moments of desperation, I wonder if the packet of condoms I found was relevant in some way."

"What?"

I explained about the condoms from Maxwell's Hotel in York I found by Bill's office door just before finding his body.

"And I keep thinking about a yellow camper van that drove past," I added. "Around the time I found the body."

"How could that be relevant?" she asked.

"Dunno. I've come across something else about a camper van since then. I can't remember where."

"Camper van and condoms. What do they tell you?"

"Well," I said, "a hippy driving by stopped his camper van. He went in to Social Services and set about the first establishment figure he could find."

"Bill Copelaw, the big, bad boss."

"He used a fantasy football trophy as a protest against competitive sports and dropped a packet of contraceptives to tell the ruling class to stop breeding."

We grinned at each other.

"Cracked it," said Marti.

CHAPTER THIRTEEN

"Gus, Hi," said a female voice later that morning.

I looked up from my desk and smiled.

"Hello, Pam," I said.

"Hard at it, I see."

She rested her briefcase on the desktop.

"Just finishing off a report. We're due back in court next week."

"Got time for lunch?"

I had suggested lunch to Marti but she was in court.

"Lunch with the director, I am honoured," I said, giving her a wink.

"Well, if you're just going to take the piss," she said.

I put the papers in the desk drawer and got up.

"As if I'd do a thing like that."

We walked towards the front of the office together.

"You did say you were paying," I said as we went out into the sunshine.

"Has anyone ever told you you're a cheeky sod," she said.

"Yeah, you, just now."

"Have you got yourself a girlfriend yet?" Pam asked later over the prix fixe lunch in the Salford Quays branch of Café Rouge.

We'd spent the intervening time talking shop and reminiscing about our days on the social work course. A Facebook addict and avid tweeter, unlike me, Pam was able to update me on the progress or otherwise of our fellow students.

"Yes."

She let her fork drop into her tuna salad.

"Tell me more."

I shrugged, wondering why we hadn't got round to discussing Marti when we met at Bill's funeral. Maybe I'd cleverly avoided it as the relationship had only just started.

"Not much to tell," I said as I ate cheese omelette.

"A likely story," she said. "She'd have to be something special to snare you, Gus."

I wondered how she made that out.

"I don't think you were avidly looking for someone, were you?"

"Not really."

"Anyway, tell me how you met, what she does, favourite sexual positions etc. etc?"

"I met her through Rachel…" I said.

"You're going out with one of your daughter's friends?"

She couldn't have been more shocked if I'd confessed to Bill Copelaw's murder. I would have spoken but was chewing omelette du fromage at that precise moment.

"Cradle snatching, oh, my, god," she went on.

"No, no," I said, after I'd swallowed my food. Maybe the French name made it harder to digest.

I explained about the band.

"Marti's fifty this year – looks younger of course."

"Of course. Does she have a day job?"

"She's a solicitor," I said.

"A solicitor? That's handy. She can handle your divorce."

I smiled at her.

"Hardly."

"Well, you old devil."

I shrugged modestly.

"You haven't told me what she looks like."

"Black and beautiful."

"Really? Even more interesting."

She drank more mineral water.

"You'll have to bring her to my barbecue. I'll text you the date."

"I'll mention it to her."

She looked suspiciously at me for a moment before speaking again.

"Gus, she's not married, is she?"

"Is she heck," I said, "she's been married – twice."

"God. Still that's better than the situation I've got myself in."

"In what way?"

"The guy I'm seeing is very much married."

"Pam," I said, shaking my head at yet another example of her chaotic love life.

She sipped mineral water.

"Don't you look at me like that, Gus Keane, you old puritan. Everyone plays away from time to time. Well, nearly everyone."

I could have told her I wasn't a puritan but we'd had this argument before.

"It's just that..." she said. "Oh, he's just so gorgeous. The funny thing is we met on the day I had my interview for the Salford job."

"Yeah?"

"I can't say too much," she said, tapping the side of her nose.

I couldn't help asking myself if this air of intrigue was a large part of the attraction.

"Everything's so perfect when we're together," she went on.

"But?"

"Yes, there's always a but, isn't there? He's planning to leave his wife but it's difficult..."

"Difficult," I said, wondering if I had kept the cynicism out of my voice.

"Yes. You see the thing is he's too caring for his own good."

I asked myself if this bloke would ever leave his wife.

"He doesn't want to hurt her."

Was this the old, old story of the man who was always about to leave his wife? If he were so caring would he be shagging another woman?

"And when he does finally tell her, he wants to do it at the right time and in the right way."

That translated in my mind as 'never'.

"So it all has to be timed very carefully if it's going to work out."

"I see."

"He wouldn't want her to find out just by chance."

I bet he wouldn't. I wondered once again about Pam. It was obvious from the first day I met her she was going to be a high flyer. Despite being the youngest member of the course she was destined to leave the rest of us far behind. She had always talked a good game and had an uncanny knack of impressing the right people. Most of all she wanted success and thought she had a right to it. Now she was behaving like a love-struck teenager. What a contrast with her professional image. I thought of the disastrous men she'd attached herself to over the years.

"One day…one day we'll be together, I know it."

I watched her pick at her food. The obsession with her weight was partly about attracting a bloke, whatever she said to the contrary. It spoke of an uncertainty that wasn't allowed to show itself in her working life. Pam had summed up one reason I would never have had an affair even if I'd wanted to. I just couldn't be arsed.

Later, with a kind of reluctant inevitability, we talked about Bill's death. It was Pam who raised the subject.

"I'm only just beginning to realise how much it's affected people."

I nodded. She drank more water before she spoke again.

"There's going to be an investigation into how it happened, you know."

"In what way?"

"Well, with all the safety measures we have in place, you know, doors you can only open if you know the security number, a service user shouldn't be able to get in like Askey did."

"I don't see what good an investigation would do. I can tell you how it happened."

"I know," she said, "but…"

She shrugged.

"And asking Ania about it would only make her feel even more guilty. The poor lass feels bad enough as it is."

She nodded.

"I know how she feels, Gus. You know what a load of crap we have to put up with in this job."

"Only too well."

Ten minutes later we settled the bill and left.

"We'll have to do it again soon," I said, as we went outside.

"Yeah, you can update me on your love life."

I grinned, knowing full well Pam would need no excuse to update me on hers. She'd've probably moved onto someone else by then.

* * *

"What's up with you?" I said as I stepped into Bill's old office the next day, looking for Don.

I closed the door gently behind me and went over to Karen, who looked up reluctantly from her seat behind the desk. Tears streamed down her cheeks, onto her chin. She looked up briefly but carried on crying. I went over to the desk and sat opposite her.

"Tell me," I said.

"Oh, you know…Bill and…every bloody thing."

She wrapped her arms around her chest. She had aged since I'd last seen her. Even her hair looked duller. Most surprising of all, though, she looked as if she had put on weight. Comfort eating perhaps, I thought. At the same time she had a neglected look, as though she had given up looking after herself.

"I came here to get out of the way," she said after wiping tears away from her chin. "I knew Don was out."

"Right. Maybe you shouldn't have come back to work."

"There's no maybe about it. Not even back half a day and I'm in bits."

"Right. Lunch." I announced authoritively.

"It's only 11.30," she said, looking at the clock on the wall.

"Irrelevant," I said. "I've pretty well finished for the day. I don't suppose you'll achieve anything useful."

I took a pen off Don's desk and tore a sheet of paper from a notebook. As I wrote Don a note, Karen shook her head, sniffing and wiping her face with the back of her left hand. She got up and picked up her handbag from the top of a filing cabinet and followed me out into the team room. I grabbed my briefcase from my desk and went over to the white board on the far wall. I wrote 'not back' next to my name in red felt tip; 'lunch back 1.30' against Karen's.

"Just give me a couple of minutes to wash my face," Karen asked.

She met me in reception ten minutes later, freshly made-up, obviously having added a splash of perfume.

"Let's go to my place," she said, "give the neighbours something to talk about."

As we drove down Trafford Road in Karen's car, she seemed to snap out of her mood to some extent.

"I'm only working out my notice, you know," she said.

"You're leaving?"

"Yeah. I'll explain when we get home."

We covered the few miles to Prestwich saying very little.

"It's nice of you to come to my rescue, Gus," said Karen later, filling two cups with tea from an old-fashioned brown pot.

"Knight in shining armour, me," I said from the dining room of her posh semi. I looked round the room, almost a parody of good taste, having the antiseptic air of an operating theatre. She put the pot down on the table between us.

"I've got to talk to someone or I'll go mad."

I could see a small back garden through the window. The shaven lawn and carefully tended flowerbeds matched the neatness of the house. On the table she had laid out hummus, cheese, salad, ham and slices of French bread.

I lifted the mug to my lips and drank. She handed me a plate.

"Right. What's bothering you?"

She sipped her tea.

"Help yourself," she said, waving towards the food.

I spread hummus on a piece of bread and began to eat.

"It's about Bill," Karen said after another drink. "I just can't go on as if nothing has happened."

"It's affected all of us," I said.

I had decided to plead ignorance about the money Bill had left and her affair. I couldn't see her being too happy to know I'd been talking to Jean about her. She drank quickly, topping up her mug again.

"No, no, you don't understand," said Karen, shaking her head emphatically. "I loved him."

I glanced at the wedding photos on a Welsh dresser and wondered if Gary knew the truth about Copelaw. If not, how would Karen explain the money?

"Oh," I said.

Karen looked down as if examining the contents of her mug.

"We'd been...lovers for some time."

"You had an affair?"

"It wasn't an affair," said Karen insistently. "We were planning to set up home together."

"So it was serious," I asked, trying to keep the disbelief out of my voice. "Bill was going to leave Jean?"

She looked up and nodded her head.

"He didn't want to hurt her, but..."

Where had I heard that before? She stifled a sob.

"We were starting to look at all the practical stuff: finding a house, getting a mortgage."

I sipped more tea. Karen picked up a piece of cheese and made a half-hearted attempt to eat it. She let out a sigh, attempted a smile, tried to speak then hesitated.

"I'm pregnant," she said finally.

"I thought Gary was..." I began.

Shut up, you silly sod, I told myself, it can't be Gary's. Bill should have used those condoms I found on the office floor.

"Bill and I had talked about having children together and we weren't always too careful."

Obviously, I almost said.

"I wasn't on the pill and you can't always be bothered with condoms, can you?"

She looked down at her hands.

"It would have been brilliant, Gus," she went on, looking across the table at me. "Living with Bill and expecting his baby."

She looked down and laid her hands over her stomach.

"It doesn't show yet but it soon will."

"Do you want the baby?"

"Of course I want the baby!"

Anger flared up then subsided.

"You know how much I longed to be a mother. And it's all I have left of Bill."

I thought of the messes people got into. I still couldn't quite believe that I had joined the club whose members had a broken marriage on their CV. Not me, not solid, reliable Gus Keane. The one everybody brought their troubles to.

"It's just as well I am pregnant," she said, sipping more tea. "Otherwise I'd be hitting the booze."

She stared into space for a while.

"Oh, it's doing my head in, Gus."

"Must be."

"Sometimes I think I just can't handle it."

"Does Gary know?"

"No. I'm going to have to tell him soon. Poor Gary, it's not really his fault."

She drank more tea and sat back.

"I'm thinking of going to stay with a friend until I can get myself sorted out."

She sighed and pushed her hair away from her face.

"The money will help of course."

"Money?"

I tried to sound as if I knew nothing about it.

"Bill left me £50,000 in his will."

"What?"

My surprise was genuine. Fifty thousand! 'A lot of money' Jean had said. How right she was.

"Yes, life insurance."

"Quite a surprise."

"A sign of how much he loved me."

"Did Bill know you were pregnant?"

She nodded.

"It had just been confirmed. I think the insurance policy was for the baby too."

Karen picked up another piece of cheese and toyed with it before putting it down on her plate.

"He always wanted more kids, you know. He was so excited."

I tried to imagine Bill as a proud father and failed.

"He was worried about how we'd manage if anything happened to him. You know, with that heart scare he had."

Karen pulled herself together almost literally by shaking her body as she sat up and straightened her shoulders. She apologised for getting upset. It seemed confession time was over.

"Here I am going on about myself when you've had problems of your own."

"It's OK."

"And then finding Bill like that. It must have been awful."

"Yeah. The weirdest part was talking to the police. It didn't seem real."

Once again I was trying to steer the conversation round to the investigation of the murder. I felt sorry for Karen but not all that sorry. She must have known having unprotected sex could lead to pregnancy. It wasn't her fault Bill had been killed, of course. Unless she killed him.

"Oh, they talked to me as well."

"They probably ask everyone the same thing," I said. "Did you see anything unusual or suspicious around the time of Bill's death?"

"Or anybody hanging about outside," she added, "or someone in the building who shouldn't have been there."

"Had you seen anything?" I asked.

She shook her head.

"You know as well as I do that at that time on a Friday, there's virtually nobody around. You were getting ready to go out on a late visit, I remember."

She looked into space as if trying to remember something.

"Don was around somewhere, but that was about it. Gary got to the office by about twenty to five or so. We were in the car on the way home by quarter to."

"That's the funny thing, Karen," I said. "It was just an ordinary day."

She looked me in the eye.

"Except it wasn't."

* * *

Later, as I walked home after Karen had dropped me off, I mulled over what she had said. As far as Bill's murder was concerned, I was no further forward. The amount of money he had left her was more than I had thought. And she had stressed the seriousness of their relationship. But there was more. I had a feeling she had said something new and significant. At some point during our conversation a word had come into my mind briefly. Then just as suddenly it was gone. It was the nearest I had come to recalling that word that was like 'certainty'.

CHAPTER FOURTEEN

"Hello," I said into the office phone, as I sat at my desk the next morning.

"Is that Gus Keane?" said a hesitant voice.

"Yes."

"It's Gary here."

Gary, Gary, who the hell was Gary? I pondered the name as I made my way to my desk. I scratched my head. It was a common enough name but I was buggered if I knew anyone called Gary. So why was he ringing me?

"Gary Davidson."

Oh, that Gary. Still none the wiser, I sat down and switched on my computer. With my memory the way it had been lately I didn't want to embarrass myself by asking who he was. It could be somebody I'd known for years. I sat down.

"What can I do for you Gary?" I asked.

Suitably neutral, I thought.

"Will you be in the office for the next half hour?"

I looked at the computer screen and clicked open an e-mail.

"Yes, but…"

"Right," he said. "I'll be there in two minutes."

"What's it about?"

Silence greeted this perfectly reasonable question. Presumably he was on his way. Where was this leading to, I thought as I checked my messages. Two minutes later reception rang through to say Mr Davidson was here to see me as promised.

As a tall, skinny man was shown into the interview room, a vague recollection of having met him before filtered into my mind. I didn't think I knew him well though. His jacket looked too big for him. He was like a fifteen-year-old in his first suit at a family wedding. Something told me he wouldn't look right no matter what he wore. After a murmured greeting, Gary hovered as if asking for permission to sit down. I gestured towards the chair opposite me. He looked at it as if wondering what it was.

"A bit of a rough area, this," he said as his bum finally made contact with the chair.

"My dad always says there's no rough areas, only rough people," I replied. If there's one thing that gets my goat it's people slagging off the place of my birth.

"Yes, but…"

"You might come across one or two working class types though," I added.

"It's not that I'm a snob, you understand."

"Heaven forbid, Gary," I said.

"It's just that I've never really been happy about Karen working here."

Karen? Davidson, of course. Gary was Karen's husband. That still didn't explain why he was going out of his way to talk to me. I waited a while but he didn't say any more. There was a diffidence about him, an air of apologising for his own existence that was paradoxically quite powerful. Gary looked around warily as if afraid of being interrupted in some shameful activity. His manner was already beginning to irritate me. He took a deep breath and I noticed a slight tremor in his right hand.

"I understand you were at my house yesterday," he said.

"Yes."

"No doubt you're wondering how I knew?"

"Not really, Gary, no."

There was no reason why Karen shouldn't have told him.

"My next door neighbour mentioned it," he went on. "A nice old dear is Betty."

"Everybody needs good neighbours," I said.

"It's nice to know somebody has my best interests at heart," he said, missing the irony by a mile.

I rested my chin on my left hand while he went on with his tale.

"Once she described you it was obvious who she was talking about. The broken nose is a bit of a give-away."

I looked ostentatiously at my watch and scratched my eyebrow.

"Listen, Gary," I said, "you look as if you're on your way to work and I'm pretty busy. So if you could just say what you want to say, please."

"Right. OK."

He folded his arms like a schoolboy.

"Karen told me last night she was leaving me."

"I'm sorry to hear that but don't see…"

"Sorry!"

The flash of anger stopped me in my tracks.

"Like you care," he sneered. "You've had your fun. As soon as she tells you she's pregnant you don't want to know."

"What?"

He clenched his teeth.

"I'd been pretty certain for a while she was having an affair. Even now she hasn't told me the man's name."

I shook my head.

"Gary, you're barking up the wrong tree. I went home with Karen because she needed someone to talk to. I haven't had an affair with Karen. I don't knock around with married women."

He banged the desk with his fist. Even that gesture of aggression failed to impress.

"You might at least have the decency to admit it now you've been found out."

Why should I have to put up with this first thing in the morning? Or at any time, come to that? I sighed and met Gary's eye.

"I couldn't have got Karen pregnant. I can't get anyone pregnant."

"What?"

Oh, God, I said to myself, now he'll think I've got the same problem as him. I'd better make it a bit clearer.

"I had a vasectomy about twenty-five years ago."

"Oh, my God," he groaned. "If not you then who?"

He ran both hands through his hair, bunching it and pulling hard.

"I don't know," I lied. "She did tell me she was pregnant and the relationship with the father is over. It has no future."

He began to get up from his chair and turned towards the door.

"I'm sorry about this."

I got up too.

"Does Karen know you're here Gary?"

He turned back.

"No, she doesn't actually."

"I won't tell her if you don't," I said, as we left the room together.

"I'm bloody sick of this," I muttered to myself on the way back to my desk. "Why do I get involved with other people's affairs? Why can't they leave me alone?"

Sitting down, I paused for thought. I let out a guffaw. I shouldn't laugh really but it was hard not to.

* * *

Walking through the car park on my way to Ordsall Tower the following Tuesday I recognized Pam Agnew's car. The sun glinted off the windscreen so it was difficult to see the people inside. The woman in the driving seat was presumably Pam but I had no idea who the man in the passenger seat was. This was partly because of the sunlight, partly because Pam was snogging him with all the enthusiasm of a teenager. The 'very much married' man no doubt. Bloody hell. Not the best way to keep a secret.

* * *

Half an hour later, Children's Services staff were squashed in the team room.

"I'd like to welcome Cal McIntyre, Bill Copelaw's daughter," said Pam Agnew.

All eyes were on the curly-haired woman on Pam's left. She was casually dressed in jeans and a dark blue T-shirt, holding a piece of paper in her hand. I looked over at Pam as she went on.

"This has been an extraordinarily difficult period for the family and for all of us who knew Bill as a friend and colleague. We will always remember him."

A mumbled 'hear, hear' from a handful of people could be heard. Pam's good at this, I said to myself. To the manner born, one might almost say. The half-smile said, 'this is a sad occasion but let's remember the good things about Bill'.

"And today's modest little ceremony is another small sign that he is still in our minds and hearts. Mourners at

Bill's funeral were asked to make a donation towards buying play equipment for children in the Women's Aid Refuge."

I looked round the room, picking out Don Bird, looking stern, and Karen at the back of a group near the partition. I wondered how she felt, as Pam went on with her speech. When it was over, Cal, after explaining how her mother had found it 'too difficult' to attend today, thanked everyone for their support and handed over a cheque to the manager of the refuge.

Over tea and biscuits later, I got talking to Cal.

"It's Gus, isn't it?"

"Yeah, well done for remembering."

"Dad mentioned you. You played Rugby League, didn't you?"

"Yes. I played for Salford. A long time ago now."

"Well, it meant you could do no wrong in Dad's eyes. Men and their sport, eh?"

She looked me up and down as if wondering how tall I was.

"Do you always wear a suit?" she asked.

"Hardly ever," I smiled. "I was in court this morning for a case I'm dealing with. And I'll be going to visit my mother's grave in a couple of minutes."

"Oh?"

"I only work part time. I have this idea my mam would like me to wear a suit when I go and see her."

"You're probably right. Which cemetery is it?"

"Weaste."

She looked me up and down again in a way that was becoming disconcerting.

"I hope you don't mind me asking," she said, "but would it be OK if I came with you?"

"Yeah, fine."

She looked me in the eye, her expression giving nothing away.

"My dad's buried there. I'd like to visit him and, well, I'd be glad of some company."

"Fine."

"And mummy's still very fragile."

"Were you close to your mother?" she asked as we got into my car a few minutes later.

There was to be no small talk then, I thought, as I considered my reply.

"Not in the way I think you mean," I said. "I was only 18 when she died."

"How sad."

"Yeah. I suppose I never got to know her. I mean my relationship with my dad has changed out of all recognition since then."

We went on down the dual carriageway along Regent Road, overtaking two over-laden lorries.

"Do you talk to her?" asked Cal.

I nodded.

"It's a mixture of...making up for lost time and trying to have a sort of fantasy relationship with her."

I realised I had never told anyone about this before. Losing a parent, no matter what the circumstances, was a powerful thing to have in common.

"You mean a better relationship than you could have had in real life."

Again I nodded as I bore left into Eccles Old Road.

"Spot on," I said, remembering what my mam was really like and how hard it would have been to confide in someone so judgemental.

"You know Dad and I didn't get on, I suppose," she said.

She glanced out of the corner of her eye, her hands in her lap. She twiddled her thumbs as she waited for my response. I couldn't see the point of lying.

"Your mother said something about it, yeah."

"We weren't exactly at daggers drawn but not the best of pals either. There was a kind of truce."

"I see."

Weird that a social worker should have the same problems as clients, I thought. Not really, I told myself, after quickly re-considering, not weird at all.

"My ex-husband always said I was a control freak. I'm beginning to think the bastard was right."

"I'm saying nowt."

Someone else wanting to open her heart to me, I thought. They seemed to be queuing up to do it.

"A wise man," she smiled. "Dad was the same, always wanting to be in control. That's why we clashed."

I continued to say nowt.

"Of course when daughters and fathers fall out…well, I can imagine what a social worker might think."

Oh, no, I said to myself, what's she gonna say next? Is this why she wanted to come with me today?

"Of course they'd be wrong," she said, putting me out of my misery.

"Nearly there," I said as we turned down Cemetery Road.

In the cemetery, we turned from the main path and approached Bill's grave. Cal smoothed her hands down her jeans as if to prepare herself. For what, I wondered. She lowered her head.

"Listen, I'll leave you to it for a while," I said, "I need to go and see my mam. I'll be back shortly."

Again I approached the grave with the familiar headstone and stood up like a soldier on parade. As I told Cal, I was trying to make up for lost time, to re-create the relationship I had in fact never had with my mother.

"That's Cal over there, mam," I said. "She never got on with Bill, her dad. I don't know why she's here, whether she feels guilty or what."

I listened to the wind through the trees, the birdsong.

"It makes you wonder what goes on beneath the surface of people's lives though."

I smiled at the gravestone as events from my life passed through my mind as though I were dying too.

"Keep everything covered up, that was always your way. All top show. And you know what? Everyone's like that. That could be what's at the heart of Bill's murder, I'll bet."

I shook my head, wondering what she would have thought of me now.

"What would you have thought about Louise walking out? Did you ever feel like walking out, mam? We all do."

"You know I've got a girlfriend now. I know what you'd say: what do you want a girlfriend for at your age, our Gus? And: I've nothing against coloured people but."

I looked over to where Cal stood by her father's grave. "Better go."

"You OK, Cal?" I said, as I arrived back at Copelaw's grave.

She nodded, wiping tears from her face with a tissue.

"It's just...oh, I dunno," she said. "The fact he's gone forever, well, I don't know what to say."

My eyes held her gaze for a moment longer as she tried to smile.

"Not like me to be stuck for words."

I glanced down at the gravestone.

WILLIAM COPELAW
DEVOTED HUSBAND OF JEAN
LOVING FATHER OF CAROL

"Carol," she said. 'How I hate that name."

Funny things, names, I said to myself, thinking of my son. He'd go mad at being addressed as Daniel. It always had to be Danny.

"What am I doing here?" Cal asked.

We stood still as if waiting for an answer to that question. Cal sniffed and wiped away more tears.

"Let's go."

We walked along the path. For a time we said nothing, thinking our own thoughts.

"It's hard to walk and talk at the same time," she said, stopping at a bench and sitting down.

I sat down next to her. She paused as if not knowing what else to say.

"Mum and Dad wanted the best for me. They'd neither of them had much education. Dad did a social work course after being made redundant from Carborundum in the eighties. Mum was shop girl in M&S and worked her way up the ladder."

"Working class heroes," I said.

"Precisely. Not me, though. I won a scholarship to St Edmunds Academy in Cheshire. Suddenly I was flung into a crowd of posh girls who went skiing in St. Moritz every Christmas."

"And you had to adjust?"

"And how. That's how I got this accent."

I had been wondering.

"The trouble was they wanted me to be different and somehow stay the same."

"A tough one."

"Plus I was the most appalling little snob in my teenage years. Mum just took the line of least resistance but Dad and I constantly clashed."

She brushed away some soil that had somehow got onto her jeans.

"I went to uni in Canterbury when I was 18," she said, "I knew I would never come back home."

She drew patterns on the gravel with her boot.

"It's the sort of thing people do."

I tried to remember what was happening to me at that time. Kids growing up, me working in Social Services, Louise climbing the career ladder in Human Resources. Rachel went off to University but only as far as Sheffield. Now she was back in Salford. Back home.

"I wish I could have made it up with him before he died. I never thought I'd say this but I feel guilty."

She got up and we walked away together. On the way towards the exit. I occasionally glanced at the other graves, wondering what kind of lives the people buried there had. Had they left behind people with guilt and regrets?

"I was helping Mum sort through the house the other day. Do you know what I found?"

I shook my head.

"A Manchester Building Society book. I'd had it as a kid. The last time I saw it there was about 10p in it."

I nodded. What was this about?

"It turns out Dad has been feeding money into it bit by bit over the years. With what he's put in plus all the interest that has accrued there's, well, a tidy sum."

She wiped away a tear and looked at me.

"On the day he died Mum picked me up at the station. She drove to Dad's office to see him about something."

"Yeah?"

"I waited in the car so I never saw him again. What kind of behaviour is that from a grown woman? It's the way a teenager treats her boyfriend for not sending her a Valentine card."

"You weren't to know."

"Suppose not, but it wouldn't have taken much to go in and see him. I could have tried to be nice."

CHAPTER FIFTEEN

"Well, Gus," said the woman in the comfortable chair opposite me the next day. "At the last session you said you were kind of moving on."

Not my exact words, Fiona, I almost said but I decided not to quibble.

"Getting there, yeah," I said.

I glanced at the wall clock behind Fiona Pemberton-Wisely. Just after three thirty. We had started dead on time as usual. That had reassured me from the start, seeming to show she could be relied upon. My initial apprehension had increased when I heard her accent – so posh as to be almost incomprehensible – and her double barrelled name. Looking round the room, I saw the table in the corner with leaflets for FPW Counselling Services.

"I feel like I'm getting on with things more," I added.

She pulled a baggy jumper over her voluminous skirt, her chubby hands reminding me of a baby. She fiddled with her grey hair, which was twisted into a sort of bun. Then from a still, upright position she looked up at me over half-moon glasses.

"You're looking well," she said, before looking at me as though about to give a medical diagnosis. "Physically, I mean. You look more, I don't know, purposeful."

I nodded. We had once spent about ten minutes discussing the psychological benefits of regular exercise and a healthy diet. Looking at her now, I couldn't help thinking she should take a leaf out of my book.

"Right," she said, looking down at the notes in her lap. "Last time we agreed we'd have two more sessions, making the one after this the last."

At this, I wondered how I felt about finishing off the counselling. Ambivalent, that's what a social worker would say. For three months now, once a fortnight. I had been getting off the tram at Heaton Park and following a now familiar route east through the park. Memories of the rare treat of childhood visits to what was then a wondrous place would fill my mind. The gentle half-mile stroll between the boating lake and the Parkside Centre onto Sheepfoot Lane brought me here. I would always arrive relaxed yet psyched up.

"Yeah," I said.

I'd be relieved at the thought I would not need it any more. At the same time I would miss it, despite an occasional reluctance to talk about the painful stuff that had brought me here. Where else, after all, can you talk about yourself or whatever you fancied for an hour?

"Now, what's been happening since last we met?"

"Quite a lot," I said with my impeccable grasp of the art of understatement.

A list appeared in my mind. The events ran forward like scenes from a silent film: the misunderstanding with Tanya and my altercation with Askey; finding Bill's body; getting together with Marti; Bill's funeral and Cal's hypocrisy; my return to work and starting the investigation into Bill's murder; taking on Paul as assistant; the DNA test. Charlotte, Liam, Jean, Karen and Gary flitted through the pictures at random.

"Such as?" she asked.

Where to start? Making a snap decision, I began to go through it all in chronological order. I could change the names to protect the innocent. Fiona responded with her usual nods, taking the odd note here and there. When there was a natural pause she would seek clarification.

"Well, now," she said when I showed signs of running out of steam, "that's life in the fast lane all right. Do you feel you're taking on too much?"

Was I? It would be bound to give that impression, I thought. My account had made it sound as though it had all happened at once. In fact, most of the time I was getting on with the ordinary things of life. If anyone had asked me I would have said I was enjoying life more than I had for years. I tried to explain that to Fiona.

"Are you sleeping OK?" she asked.

Sleep or the lack of it, coupled with my reluctance to go to sleep in case I didn't wake up, had formed a large part of our discussions.

"Fine," I said, "though I have been having a recurring dream."

"A recurring dream? How often?"

"A couple of times a week, I suppose."

"I see. What's it about?"

I closed my eyes momentarily and saw the dream again in my mind's eye.

"I'm back playing rugby for Salford again, trying to tackle Gus Risman…"

"Sorry?"

I explained who Gus Risman was and told her about being named after him. For what felt like the millionth time, I wondered about my dad's motivation. He had never given a satisfactory explanation as to why he had called me after his sporting hero. At least it had meant I wouldn't do the same to my kids.

"Anyway, I'm making a right hash of this tackle. To add to the surreal atmosphere Eddie Waring is commentating.

"I remember him. Didn't he used to commentate on Rugby League for the BBC?"

"Yeah."

"The up and under chap," she said, quoting one of Eddie's catchphrases.

"That's right. In the dream he says, 'Gus, lad, you might just as well try and tackle death.'"

"I'm no expert on dreams, but that sounds like it's connected with the murder."

Yes, and with my own mortality, I said to myself. Fiona looked pensive for a moment.

"How fascinating. It does sound as if you're struggling to come to terms with everything. At the same time, you're more capable of doing so now."

After a moment's thought I had to agree. I thought back to the frequent flashbacks that had plagued me in the weeks following the stroke. The way I would relive the events of that day. All that had happened recently would, I couldn't help thinking, test me as severely. The session ran on as I talked about all I had to think about in the coming weeks and months. Before long I would be a grandfather.

"Thanks a lot, Fiona," I said as I got up to leave. "You've really sorted things out for me."

"That's not quite true," she insisted. "I've just listened to you and helped you draw conclusions," she said.

I nodded.

"However it's happened," I said, "I feel a lot more positive about things."

"That's good. Just remember there's no certainty."

"Certainty, that's the word that's been plaguing me," I said, "or something like it."

Her brow creased in concentration.

"Pardon."

"Sorry, it's just this murder."

"Murder?"

"Yeah, the one I'm investigating. I keep thinking something was wrong when I found the body. And the word 'certainty' keeps coming into my mind."

"How intriguing."

"The funny thing is, I know it's not the right word. Something with a similar meaning or that sounds the same. That's what I'm trying to remember. I feel sure it will give me an insight into the death."

I looked around the room again while I thought how to explain. It was built for practicality rather than aesthetic appeal. A flip chart stand leant against the wall. The pale green curtains were too close in colour to the paint on the walls, reminding me of those shirt and tie sets that were fashionable in the seventies.

"This word you're searching for," said Fiona, "will probably only come when you least expect it."

"Right," I said. "I'll see you next time."

* * *

Later at Ordsall Tower I put a mug of tea on my desk and sat down. Don was walking past just as I unlocked the top right hand drawer.

"Working late again, Gus," he said.

"It's a case of having to," I said. "Anyway, it's nice and quiet at this time of day. I can concentrate."

"Too true. I'd better get back to it myself."

After he left I pulled out a buff file from the drawer. I opened it up and began to read. I was due in court for another interim hearing about Rebecca tomorrow afternoon. I spent half an hour refreshing my memory about the salient points in case I was asked any questions. I put bookmarks in the pages I might want to refer to and made sure my latest report was easily available. With everything else that was happening it would have been all too easy to forget about little Rebecca.

As I read and rehearsed what I was going to say, I thought back to my penultimate counselling session. Talking through everything that had happened had crystallized something in my mind. The murder investigation had got me hooked. Whether this was simply a morbid fascination or a desire to do the right thing I preferred not to think about too deeply. Maybe I just wanted to do a good job. Why change the habit of a lifetime? Or did I actually believe there was something significant waiting to be found out? Did I think it would be me who would find it? I looked at my watch.

"Shit," I said out loud.

Marti would be arriving for a meal in half an hour. I got up to go with my mind full of conflicting demands but now the main one was to get home and start cooking for Marti, who was arriving at the flat at seven. As I reached the door I nearly bumped into Ania about to drag her vacuum cleaner into the room. After saying hello, I held the door open while she manoeuvred the machine through the narrow space. As she came into the office, I nipped past her into the corridor.

"You in a hurry, Gus?" she asked.

"Yeah, a friend's coming round for a meal."

"A friend, eh? A lady, perhaps?"

"Yes," I smiled.

"Better not keep her waiting," she smiled.

"No. I'll see you."

I turned to go, seeing Don ahead of me.

"Yeah, oh, Gus, I nearly forgot," said Ania, "you know the guy I saw on the night Bill died?"

"Er, not sure," I said.

Truth be told, I just wanted to get away. I could hear Don talking to someone at the end of the corridor.

"You know, the man in the leather jacket…"

"What man?"

"At the office. On the day Bill died."

"Oh, yeah. What about him?"

I looked in Don's direction as someone raised his voice. There were three other blokes making their way out at the same time.

"I've remembered who it was."

Now this could be interesting, I thought. I turned to look at her as her phone went off. I waited as she spoke to whoever was on the other end. It soon became clear it was going to be a long conversation. I looked at my watch. I couldn't wait.

CHAPTER SIXTEEN

In the early morning sunshine the following day I was on my usual walk through Salford Quays. I crossed the road in front of the Holiday Inn, following the signs to the Lowry. By then I'd built up a good rhythm and was nicely out of breath and sweaty. Must have done four miles this morning, I thought, as I crossed over the bridge towards the Watersports Centre. Better get home soon. My mobile interrupted my thoughts. I pulled it out of the pocket of my shorts and answered it.

A female voice came down the line.

"Gus Keane?"

"Yes," I said.

"DI Ellerton. I need to see you right away."

"At this hour?"

I walked on, keeping up a nice rhythm. I was buggered if I was going let a panicky phone call upset my exercise regime.

"Right away," she repeated.

"What's it about?"

"Never mind. Just get over here."

"Over where?"

"The police station."

"But...what's the hurry?"

"I'll tell you when you get here. I can't explain over the phone."

"Can't it wait?"

"Just get your arse over here now!"

The call came to an abrupt end. DI Ellerton swearing, it must be important. Well, she was gonna have to wait. I would have to have a shower first. I put my phone away and walked quickly back to Palace Apartments. I wondered what the Inspector wanted in such a hurry. She'd sounded pretty pissed off, angry even. As I had only met the woman once I couldn't for the life of me see why she was summoning me so urgently. There was only one way to find out, I thought, as I let myself into the flat.

Twenty minutes later, showered and changed in record time, I was shown into Sarita Ellerton's office. Today she was wearing rectangular glasses. She seemed to have got over her cold and her hair was under control. Her suit looked as if it had just been dry-cleaned. Not that she looked happy about any of those things. She gestured to a seat on the other side of the desk from where she was sitting. I sat down. Her jaw was clamped tight shut like she was angry with me and giving me the silent treatment. We looked at one another. She twisted her fingers together and swallowed like someone at a job interview. Finally, with a visible effort, she spoke.

"Well, er," she said, her Scottish accent stronger than usual, "we've done the DNA test on Charlotte Stephens."

There was an atmosphere in the room but I could not have said what it was. Sarita looked at the notes on the desk before continuing.

"And we've found a match."

"Is Askey Charlotte's father?"

Sarita looked down at the papers on her desk again though she must have known the answer to the question.

"No," she said, untangling her fingers, "Charlotte Stephens is Kylie Anderson."

A silence descended from the ceiling, filling every corner, seeming to suffocate the two people in the room.

"What?"

My cry broke through the tension. Sarita took up the narrative again. "Charlotte Stephens' DNA matches exactly the DNA of Kylie Anderson."

I opened my mouth to speak.

"Before you ask," Sarita said quickly, "we are sure. It's been double checked and triple checked."

"Right."

"Octuple fucking checked," she added.

"Bloody hell. It can't be true can it? I mean, Kylie's been missing for…how long?"

"Nearly eighteen years."

I breathed out and shook my head.

"How the bloody hell did it happen?"

"We don't know," said Sarita, "we've checked Charlotte's records. She was born in Salford Royal Hospital. Her birth was registered. The hospital records confirm it. Her date of birth is two weeks before Kylie's."

"But she is Kylie," I said, completing the crazy story. "Well, this leaves a few unanswered questions."

Well spotted, Gus, I said to myself. Sarita pointed at me as though pronouncing me guilty of some heinous crime.

"That's the last time I do any favours for Steve Yarnitzky, and you can tell him that when you see him."

"What's the problem?"

"Where can I start? The main thing is how the fuck we're going to explain this. Any thoughts, Gus?"

"What do we have to explain?"

Sarita gave an exasperated sigh. Before she could speak I put in another point.

"Won't everyone be so pleased to have found Kylie that they won't care how it was done?"

"Not unless we can answer a few questions. Like how we came to be testing this girl's DNA for no apparent reason? And how come she turned out to be Kylie bloody Anderson?"

"Oh, is that all," I said, "write this down."

Sarita picked up a pen and prepared to write.

"I had a hunch she might be Kylie," I said, thinking on my feet. "She looked a bit like the picture in the paper, you know, the one of what she would look like now."

Sarita scribbled notes and looked up at me.

"With you so far."

"I spoke to Steve and he came to you and you agreed to help. You thought I was probably wrong but didn't want to take the chance."

"OK."

"You didn't want to say anything beforehand, it would only start rumours."

She nodded, writing furiously.

"And build up hopes," I added.

"Gus, you're a genius."

"I know. So when it hits the press you and Steve get the credit."

She smiled.

"Now all we have to do is tell Charlotte," I said.

"And Elaine Anderson," said Sarita, burying her head in her hands, "and the fucking media."

Without warning she got up clutching her stomach with one hand while the other covered her mouth. Her 'excuse me' was barely audible as she rushed out of the room. I sat for a couple of minutes. I was wondering whether I too should just leave when a deathly pale Inspector returned, murmuring apologies. I looked at her with some concern. Was all this getting to her?

"Are you OK?" I asked.

"Fine," she smiled. "I've never been so happy in my life."

After lunch I got back to the office just in time to accompany Marti to court for an interim hearing in the Rebecca Winters case. I only hoped I wouldn't be too distracted by the news about the DNA test.

"It shouldn't take long," she explained as we made our way to the car park, "but it's a good idea for you to show your face."

"Right."

"At least the court will know we've appointed an experienced social worker."

As we got to Marti's car, I saw Rob coming towards us and said hello to him.

"Have you met Marti," I said.

He shook his head.

"Sadly, no," he purred.

"This is Rob," I said.

He held his hand out and shook Marti's. He held onto it longer than was strictly necessary, making sure he made eye contact.

"What are you doing with this reprobate, Marti?"

"I'm the solicitor on one of Gus' cases," she replied, letting go of his hand.

"I couldn't do your job," he said, "not in a million years. I'd get too emotional, I know I would."

Marti nodded.

"That's why I sell insurance," he went on. "It's more predictable. But I mustn't keep you."

"So that was the famous Rob," she said as we got into the Mercedes.

I would have been quite happy to walk but Marti had insisted on driving. She claimed it made a better impression. And, I couldn't help thinking, she could show off her flash motor. Still, nobody was perfect.

"Famous?"

"Yeah," she said, switching on the engine, "the have a go hero."

I looked towards her as the car went out of the car park.

"What are you on about?"

"You can't have forgotten the time he fought off a burglar in his office."

"First I've heard of it. When was this?"

"Ooh, a few months ago. October, I think. Around then."

"I was still off work then," I explained, "in recovery mode and not taking a great deal of interest in things."

I preferred not to think about that time in my life.

"He was quite the local hero for a while. On the telly and everything."

"Rob on the telly?"

"Yeah, local news. I've got to say he was a natural."

She changed down as we turned left onto the A57.

"A natural?"

"Oh, yeah. I thought he would have been offered a contract to present a documentary on urban crime."

I could see him doing it.

"What did you think of him," I couldn't resist asking.

"Well, good-looking obviously," she said. "Though he knows it."

"Does he?"

She put the car into gear.

"Oh yes."

We turned right into Oldfield Road. I thought momentarily of what this and many other streets had looked like when I was a kid. Anyone who left Salford at that time and came back today would be hopelessly lost.

"I can't help wondering why he's selling insurance in Salford."

"Nothing wrong with Salford," I said.

"I'm not saying there is," she replied, patting my knee. "But you'd hardly say he fits in, would you?"

"No, suppose not."

"He's obviously from a fairly privileged background. You'd expect him to be a Chief Executive somewhere."

"Yeah, he certainly seems like one of the poshocracy who think they have the right to rule us."

"Oh, God, if I'd known this was going to lead to a left wing rant I'd have kept my mouth shut."

* * *

"Can we get you anything, Charlotte?' asked Sarita later that afternoon. She had rung me after speaking to her superiors. They had insisted we get Charlotte over to the station as soon as I had finished in court and tell her the news. I had to be there because I was a social worker and knew Charlotte. Sarita was there because her bosses thought a woman would be suitable. Or to put it another way they were offloading their responsibility onto somebody else.

The inspector was the image of polite efficiency and looked a lot healthier than the last time we had met. There was even a hint of a smile though what she had to smile about was a mystery to me. Not that it mattered.

"A cup of coffee perhaps."

Sarita sipped from a bottle of water. She looked pleased with herself, which was hard to fathom given the task we had to perform.

"No," said Charlotte, nibbling her bottom lip, "let's get on with it."

She sat facing Sarita Ellerton and me in her office. Three comfy chairs were in a casual circle. Charlotte brushed her fingers through her purple fringe, then put her hands on her lap. Then she was back on the fringe again. Her feet shuffled around with a will of their own. In the silence of the room I could hear someone down the corridor giving an off-key but word-perfect rendition of REM's Losing My Religion.

"Sarita and I decided to see you together," I said, tugging at the neck of my t-shirt, "because the result of the DNA test is…complicated."

Charlotte gripped her thighs through her black jeans and swallowed nervously.

"Mick Askey, right," she said, as though staying quiet any longer would cause spontaneous combustion, "is he my dad or not?"

"No, he's not."

A modicum of relief ran through me at being able to answer a straightforward question. How the bloody hell were we going to get through this? Nobody spoke for a little while as the singing continued.

"Shit. So you didn't find a match for my DNA."

"We did find a match, Charlotte." Sarita said, before hesitating and touching her chin with her right hand. "The DNA proves conclusively that you are Kylie Anderson."

For a few seconds Charlotte sat motionless, her eyes blinking rapidly.

"You must be, like, taking the piss," she finally said, gulping hard. "If this is a fucking wind-up it's not funny."

"It's true, Charlotte."

"How can it be true? This is so fucking…oh, my God!"

Abject horror covered Charlotte's face.

"That means Elaine Anderson is my mum. No way, no fucking way."

Charlotte's firmly in the anti-Elaine camp, I thought. Wouldn't you know it?

"She is so not a nice person. God I hate her. She's exploited her own kid disappearing to make herself, like, rich and famous. She went on that Crimewatch when it first happened and thought, 'Oh, I like this'."

I looked at Sarita as Charlotte breathed in deeply then blew air back out.

"Well, if this is true, I'm glad I got snatched. Saved me from being called fucking Kylie. What sort of low life calls their kid Kylie for fuck's sake?"

Sarita and I looked helplessly on. We had, it seemed, come to an unspoken agreement to let Charlotte rip.

"And another thing, what did she think she was playing at leaving me outside a fucking shop. Going for fags, wasn't she? Couldn't wait for a smoke until she got me to her mum's house."

What could I say? Nothing, that's what, Gus, I told myself, just leave her to it.

"Where I would have been fucking safe."

Charlotte, wiping the tears from her cheeks with the back of her hands, paused for breath.

"Sorry about that. I never fucking swear normally."

She tried to smile.

"It's OK, Charlotte," Sarita reassured her.

"So, did... was it..." Charlotte stammered, "what the hell happened?"

"We don't really know."

"But I've got a birth certificate for Charlotte Stephens. Properly registered and everything. I mean, what the hell..."

Sarita leant forward.

"We checked on that," said Sarita. "Charlotte was registered just a week after her birth at a time when Kylie Anderson was definitely in the care of her mother."

There was a desperate need to know what happened to the real Charlotte Stephens. Where is she? That was the question, I thought with more than a trace of sadness. Best not to ask it yet.

"What happens now?" asked Charlotte.

"We need to..." Sarita began, "we need to make some more inquiries. In the meantime, what do you want to do?"

She leant her head back and took a deep breath.

"I need to have a private word with Gus," she said.

"Fine, I'll wait outside, shall I?"

"If you don't mind," said Charlotte, rediscovering her manners.

Sarita got up.

"If you could just put everything on hold until I speak to Gus," said Charlotte.

"Sure."

We watched while Sarita went out of the office. As I turned back towards Charlotte, the penny dropped. Being sick in the morning, saying how happy she was, smiling her way through the tricky interview with Charlotte. Sarita was pregnant.

"Gus, quick, come with me," hissed Charlotte as soon as Sarita had gone.

She got up and took me by the hand.

"Where are we going?" I asked as she pulled me out of the office towards the exit.

"To Little Hulton. I'll drive, I've borrowed mum's car."

"Why Little Hulton?"

"It's where Tracy Stephens lives. My so-called mother," said Charlotte, taking me outside into the rain.

"Bloody hell."

Charlotte let go of my hand and ran towards the car park.

"She spends most of the time getting pissed at home," she said, turning back to me while on the move. "With luck she'll be there now."

"Charlotte, stop," I gasped, struggling to keep up.

"We need to pick up some booze on the way. Boddington's. She'll tell us to get stuffed if we arrive empty handed."

"Charlotte, we maybe need to think about this," I said as I followed her, desperately trying to keep up. "I'm not sure this is a good idea."

"I'll go on my own then," she snapped back.

"An offer I can't refuse," I said, recognising emotional blackmail when I heard it.

"We must speak to her before the police pick her up. I need to know what happened."

CHAPTER SEVENTEEN

"I just can't get my head round this," said Charlotte, hurling the car towards the M602 and screeching down the slip road.

The sky had clouded over and a steady drizzle was falling. The wipers squeaked across the windscreen. My suede jacket wouldn't offer much protection, I thought, as I looked out. Worrying about the weather, though, was just a distraction from more serious concerns.

"You and me both," I said, pinning myself back in the passenger seat.

"I mean, what the hell happened?" she went on.

"I don't know, but when we get there. If we get there," I corrected myself as she overtook a Land Rover on the inside, "let me do the talking."

I watched the motorway signs whiz by, gritted my teeth and decided to close my eyes. When I opened them again, I was surprised to see we were passing through the terraced houses on Manchester Road in Walkden. Nearly there. Charlotte stopped outside an off licence where we stocked up for Tracy's benefit.

A few minutes later we reached Little Hulton and turned left down Kenyon Way. I noticed a one storey building called the Top Club where the Labour Club used to be in my teenage years. I dreaded to think how many traffic offences Charlotte had committed to get us this far so quickly.

"Hello, Tracy, it's only me," said Charlotte as we crept down the hall of the council flat minutes later.

Carrying a 24 pack of Boddingtons, I followed Charlotte to the living room through a door on the right. We saw a rotund woman with straggly grey hair on a sagging sofa. On the television a game show I'd never seen before failed to hold Tracy's attention.

"So you could be arsed to come and see your mother for once," slurred Tracy, swigging from a can. "Who's this twat?"

She nodded towards me before taking another drink. She shook the can and, discovering it was empty, chucked it on a table in the corner.

"This is Gus," said Charlotte.

"Bit old for you, isn't he?"

"Nothing like that. Gus is…"

"Hiya, Tracy," I put in, "I've brought you a drink."

I put the beer on the table next to a whiffy carton of milk and took two cans out. I sat down on an armchair facing Tracy.

"Ta," she said as she took the can I offered.

The cans hissed open. We drank.

"I used to do my first underage drinking round here."

"Did you," she asked.

"Yeah, my mate used to live in Carrfield Avenue."

"Carrfield, eh? Just round the corner."

"We used to get in the Kenyon Arms."

"Old people's home now," said Tracy, taking another long drink.

"Never."

"Aye, Poor Dick's is an Indian Restaurant."

"Bloody hell," said Gus, "the Antelope a curry house. What about the Lancastrian?"

"Pulled down. Just a hole in the ground now."

"No wonder you have to drink at home."

"He's all right, your boyfriend," she said, turning to Charlotte, who had sat down on a rickety hardback chair.

"I'm not her boyfriend, Tracy," I explained. "I'm Gus Keane a social worker. We have met. Charlotte's asked me to come with her today."

"What's she done that for, the little bitch? Bringing a social worker to see me. Nothing but trouble, they are."

"To start with she wanted to trace her father. Now she wants to know what happened to the real Charlotte."

"The real Charlotte, what you on about?"

She spoke in a bored Bolton accent through the gaps between her blackened teeth. A room-filling body odour came off her in waves as she spread herself over the settee.

"Because this 'Charlotte' here, the Charlotte I know, isn't the child you gave birth to."

She wriggled around and scraped her feet along the floor.

"She's not your child – we've had a DNA test done."

"Who is she then, the cat's mother?"

"She's Kylie Anderson as you well know. It was her who was removed from your care by Social Services."

I stared into Tracy's eyes. We were coming to the crunch. I wouldn't like what I was about to hear. That's what Mick Askey had said but I had no idea at the time what he meant.

"The question is, Tracy, what happened to the real Charlotte?"

"I have a right to know," said Charlotte.

"I'm saying nowt," she said, looking to her left.

"In that case, we'll be off," I said, getting up and picking up the case of beer. "We'll take these back with us."

"You can't do that," she whined, "I've run out and I don't get paid while tomorrow."

"Well, talk then," I said, putting the beer back on the table and sitting down again.

Tracy paused to wipe saliva from her chin with the back of her hand.

"It were Mick."

"Who's Mick," I asked.

"He were my bloke, weren't he? You know, living with me. At time, like."

"What's his second name?"

"Askey. Mick Askey."

Now the two of us looked one another full in the face. My stomach tightened and I held my breath.

"Tell me about Mick."

Tracy leant forward and placed her elbows on the table. She rested her chin on her hands like a bored teenager.

"I'm not kidding you. He were gorgeous in them days," she said.

I nodded as she began to cry.

"Oh, God."

She wiped tears from her cheeks with the back of her hand.

"I were gorgeous too. You should have seen me. You would have fancied me, I can guarantee."

She sniffed and wiped her cheeks again.

"I could have had any lad I wanted and I had to pick Mick Askey."

"What was he like?"

"Could be nice except when he were drunk. Or if you crossed him."

"I can imagine."

She sat back again.

"When I first met him I thought he were great. Real tough guy, dead muscly, you know what I mean? He picked me up in the White Lion. I were pissed out of my head."

I tapped my foot on the carpet.

"What was he like with Charlotte?"

Tears fell down her face again and for a few seconds she couldn't speak.

"Listen, right," she said. "It weren't my fault, I couldn't help it. You can't know what it's like unless you've been there."

"What was he like with Charlotte," I repeated.

"Most of the time he just ignored her. Said that were my job, always on at me to keep her quiet. He were worse when he'd been on the piss."

"What was he like then?"

"He said she did his head in. He couldn't stand her crying."

"That's what babies do," I said.

Tracy stopped talking to slurp more beer before resuming.

"I know. I looked after Charlotte all right, health visitor and everyone said she were doing fine."

I nodded.

"I used to try and keep him out of her way," she went on. "I did, honest. Best thing with his temper and that."

Charlotte got up, scraping her chair across the floor.

"I can't handle this, Gus," she said, "I'll wait in the car."

She hurried out, wiping tears from her face with her arms. I looked anxiously after her but knew she would want me to finish this.

"Let me know what she says."

"Go on, Tracy," he said. "You tried to keep him away from Charlotte."

"But I couldn't keep him away all the time."

Again the tears came. This time I thought the sobbing would go on forever.

"What happened?"

"I don't rightly know," she said, calmer now.

I knew this could not be true.

"What happened? I'm not leaving here until you tell me."

"One night she woke us up. He'd had a few so he had a right mood on him."

She drained her can and let it fall on the settee. I opened another one and gave it to her.

"He jumped out of bed and went to her room. Shouting his head off, you know, 'Shut up, you fucking little bastard.'"

A tension shot through the room. She looked round as if searching for an escape.

"Couple of minutes later he came back. Said there'd been a bit of an accident."

"What did you do?"

She rearranged her hair without making any appreciable difference.

"I got up and went and had a look at her. She were lying in her cot all quiet. He said he thought she were dead."

I nodded.

"I goes, 'don't be daft, she can't be dead'…"

She looked pleadingly at me.

"But she was," I said.

She averted her eyes.

"God help me, she were fucking dead. I just picked her up and held her. It just …fucking destroyed me."

She sobbed quietly to herself as though she had no energy to do anything else. The mystery's only half-solved, I said to myself.

"I said get her to hospital but he wouldn't have it."

"Why not?"

"He said they'd fit him up for killing her," she said. "He'd go down for life. He said to bury her in the back garden."

"And you went along with him?"

"God forgive me, I did."

She sat still, breathing shallowly. She buried her head in her hands before looking at me.

"Don't look at me like that," she begged, folding her arms across her chest, "you don't know what he's like, he would have fucking killed me."

I pursed my lips.

"Go on, Tracy," I said with a sigh.

"Mick had one of them vans you can sleep in."

"A camper van?"

"Yeah, that's the one, yellow it were. You can make a cup of tea and everything."

"And?"

"Day after we'd buried her he said, 'let's go to Blackpool. For the illuminations. Take our minds off things'."

"Take your minds off…"

With an effort I choked back my anger as Tracy went on.

"On the way I kept saying 'what if they catch up with us and we haven't got a kid with us? They'll start asking questions.'"

I'm ahead of you, I said to myself.

"He got fed up of me nagging and said 'just grab another kid' then'. Anyway, we came off motorway at Chorley. We went in this pub. He wanted a couple of pints."

He would, I said to myself.

"Anyway we stopped outside a shop on the way back. I nipped in and got some cheap fags and a couple of pasties."

I wanted to tell her to get on with it, get it over with but knew she had to tell it in her own way.

"On my way out I saw a pushchair outside the shop with a kid in it. I didn't think about it, just grabbed it and walked away."

I held my breath again. How a moment can change lives forever.

"When I got to the van he were ready and waiting, revving the engine up. He slid the door open and I got in. Shoved push chair onto the seat next to me."

She took a deep breath and another drink. She shook her head as though trying to wish away the past.

"She looked a bit like Charlotte, same colour hair and that. Good as gold she were, never woke up all night. We drove straight back home, never bothered going to Blackpool."

With some relief I realised it was nearly over.

"Mick buggered off the next day. Told me to say nowt."

"Didn't anybody recognize Kylie? Her picture had been all over the papers and television for twenty-four hours."

Tracy shrugged.

"We never bothered much with neighbours. Our Health Visitor had left and we didn't see the new one for a few weeks."

"I see."

"Any road, as far as anybody else were concerned, I already had a kid. Why should I snatch someone else's?"

We looked at one another while she tried to stop her tears.

"I couldn't cope with a kid after that. I had nightmares and that. Started drinking to forget about it. You never forget though. I were glad when they took her away. I knew she'd be better off."

She wiped her eyes with the sleeve of her jumper. I told her I'd have to report what she'd told me. She barely reacted. On my way out I phoned Sarita Ellerton and told her what Tracy had said. Now I just had to tell Charlotte.

* * *

Charlotte sat hunched up on the passenger seat, twisting her hands together and biting her bottom lip, as I went through what had happened to the real Charlotte Stephens. Tears streaked her face. For ten minutes we sat in silence.

"You know, all my life people have been offering me therapy," she said, finally breaking the silence, "but I've always resisted. Now I'm not so sure."

"I've had counselling, you know."

"You?"

"Yeah. It was brilliant, helped me a lot."

"Do you think I could see the person you did?"

"I'll have a word with her," I said.

"Thanks."

* * *

"The headlines tonight," intoned George Alagiah the next evening.

Drinking red wine, I sat in my living room, watching the BBC news with more interest than usual.

"Sensational developments in the search for Kylie Anderson," the newsreader went on over a shot of a press conference, "as her mother speaks to the world."

After more headlines and a warning about flash photography, the programme moved back to the press conference where Elaine Anderson, formally dressed in the style of an upmarket PA, sat with the Chief Constable on her left.

"I have wonderful news," said Elaine, the controlled emotion in her voice judged to a nicety. "More than I could ever hope for."

The flash bulbs went off as promised and there was a murmur of expectancy.

"Kylie is alive and well."

The murmur took on the character of unruly group of third formers left in the hands of an inexperienced supply teacher. Elaine continued as the hubbub died down.

"For legal reasons, I am unable to explain in detail how Kylie was found or where she is now. This has been a shock for both of us – a nice shock but nonetheless a shock. Kylie does not feel able to go public at this time."

That's one way of putting it, I thought, as Elaine drank from a glass of water and composed herself.

"While I am obviously delighted that my beloved little girl is alive, there are certain aspects of... what has happened that cause me great sadness. The reason for this will be made clear once further investigations are completed."

The conference moved to its end with no clear conclusion. I was about to switch off when the next item came on the screen. A council house in Little Hulton, taped off like a crime scene, appeared on the screen. It was, I reckoned, a few streets down from where Tracy now lived. A reporter stood near Our Lady and the Lancashire Martyrs church. He spoke of police digging in the garden:

"It is believed the current residents have no connection with this investigation. Our understanding is that the purpose of the digging dates back to the nineteen nineties."

There followed several minutes of pointless speculation and obvious remarks about the shock in the close knit community. This was padded out with interviews with neighbours keen to get on telly. I reached for the remote control and switched off, wondering what the police had found.

"Hiya, Charlotte," I said the next morning.

Trying to smile, she came into the interview room at Ordsall Tower and sat down opposite me. She put a plastic water bottle on the table between us.

"You are still Charlotte, aren't you?"

"Oh, definitely."

I nodded.

"I need to up-date you on some things, Gus," she said.

"Right, what's been happening?"

She picked up the bottle and twisted it round in her hands.

"The police have told the press and Elaine Anderson I'm not to be disturbed as I'm revising for my 'A' levels."

She wrung her hands.

"What a time for this to happen," she added.

We sat in silence for a while.

"Have you got anything else to tell me," I asked.

"I take it you saw the press conference?"

"Yeah."

"Brilliant performance, wasn't it," she said with a sneer of disgust.

"Suppose so."

"I'm amazed she didn't plug her new book."

"What book?"

She looked at me with disbelief.

"Oh, there'll be one, don't you worry."

She sipped water and did yoga deep breathing before continuing.

"You saw the coverage of the police digging in that garden?"

I nodded.

"That was where Mick Askey and Tracy lived at the time when, you know…"

"I guessed as much."

"They found a baby's body…"

She wrapped her arms around her chest.

"What about Tracy and Askey," I said. "Have you heard anything?"

"They've arrested Tracy. They've charged Askey with the murder of Charlotte Stephens."

"I see."

She sighed and looked down at her feet.

"Sounds weird put like that."

She shrugged, stifling a tear.

"Bastards," she said, pulling at one of her plaits with her right hand. "Doing that to a little kid."

She sipped more water.

"And what does Elaine Anderson do? Holds a press conference, that's what."

I wanted to speak but Charlotte went on.

"She didn't waste any time," she said, "anything to get her face on the telly."

"I'm sure she's glad you're OK."

"What, so we can write a book, go on a promotional tour? I bet she's got a contract drawn up already."

She sighed, her foot beating out a staccato rhythm on the floor.

"I'm not gonna meet her and that's that."

"It's your choice," I said.

"No way am I going to get caught up in that media frenzy. There's no need for it."

She shook her head.

"I'm going off to France in a few weeks. I'm gonna work over there for a year before Uni."

"Great, but you still haven't found your father," I said.

Charlotte shrugged.

"To be honest I'm not that bothered about going on with it."

She paused, flicking her fringe with her right hand.

"I think I'll just get on with my life," she said, chewing her bottom lip, "which is what I should have done in the first place."

We exchanged glances.

"I've had three mothers. Only one's been a real mother. One out of three ain't bad."

I smiled. "Suppose not."

"Elaine left me outside a shop to be abducted; Tracy neglected me so badly I had to be taken away."

She shook her head.

"Not to mention covering up the murder of another child."

I could only admire Charlotte's realistic assessment of her own life.

"Kate's my real mum. She's the one who's been there through thick and thin. Even when I've been a right prat."

"Some good has come of this," I said. "By the way, I've had a word with my counsellor. She's happy to see you. Here's her card."

"Great," said Charlotte as I handed her the card.

"You need to see your GP and get her to refer you."

A few minutes later I saw her out, still wondering how she would cope with all this.

I worked away at my desk, more to take my mind off things than to achieve anything constructive. It didn't work: thoughts of both Charlottes wouldn't go away. I was even less inclined to delve into Bill Copelaw's death as that would mean I was trying to help Askey. That was the one thing I didn't want to do. And yet, and yet. There was still something bugging me about it. I knew I wouldn't rest until I had got to the bottom of it.

Marti being unavailable didn't help. She'd been busy with urgent stuff at work and had gone to see her mam. I could have done with talking it over with someone sympathetic. She would have helped me see things more clearly with her lawyer's way of looking at things. There was more to it than that. Course there was. Sex of course, but I wanted physical affection as well, some comfort. I'd got used to it in the short time we'd been together. It was a novelty to be missing someone. Well, she'd be back tomorrow.

CHAPTER EIGHTEEN

Marti breezed into my flat the next morning, gave me a bear hug and kissed me.

"It's good to see you," I said.

We kissed again, for longer this time, before she could return the compliment. What a way to start a Saturday, I thought as I admired her white cotton trousers and stripy red top. She kicked off her open toed sandals, looking at me as she ran her fingers through my hair.

"You look tired," she said, kissing my forehead.

I put my arms around her waist, slipping a hand under her t-shirt and stroking her back.

"I am a bit. I have a feeling that spending a bit of time in bed would do me the world of good."

"You know," she grinned, "I have the same feeling myself."

Some time later I lay back on the bed with a silly grin on my face.

"What are you looking so pleased about?" Marti asked, leaning towards me and planting a kiss on the side of my neck.

"You, I suppose," I replied. "I like you being here and...everything."

"That's nice. I like being here too."

I let the words wash over me and stretched out, luxuriating in the sheer hedonism of it all.

"You know," she said, leaning over to kiss me, "after Rachel has had the baby, we should go away together. Somewhere nice."

"Sounds good."

It did too. It meant my life was moving on, a sign that there was more to it than all the shitty things that had been happening lately. And with luck the baby wouldn't be too long in arriving.

"So, it was you who found Kylie then," asked Marti later.

We had dragged ourselves out of bed. Marti had put her clothes back on and I was pulling on a pair of shorts.

"Yeah, I suppose it was."

Marti peered into the wardrobe mirror as she touched up her make-up. We had reluctantly decided we'd better get out of bed and prepare ourselves for going out.

"And it was you who found out what happened to the real Charlotte."

"How did you know about that?" I asked as I put my wallet, keys and phone in the pockets of my shorts.

She shrugged and applied her lipstick.

"I'm Askey's solicitor, remember. I sat in while the police questioned him."

Had I been thinking straight I would have realised that.

"I spent a fair bit of yesterday on that," she continued. "Then I had to dash to Liverpool to see my mother – I'd been promising to take her out somewhere for ages."

"What happened with Askey?" I asked as I put on a green t-shirt. Marti had told me I suit green and who am I to argue?

"He's been charged with killing Charlotte Stephens. The good news is he's pleading guilty to manslaughter."

I breathed a sigh of relief.

"Tracy has admitted her part in it. I suspect it was a relief."

I nodded.

"Charlotte – the girl I know as Charlotte, I mean – has taken it pretty badly. I'm worried about her."

She walked over to me and took my hand.

"You worry about yourself," she ordered. "How are you coping with it all?"

"A lot better now you're here."

She smiled at me.

"This investigation you're doing, you know, into Bill's death. You can call it a day if you like."

As we went from the bedroom to the living room, I thought about what she had said. We sat down on the settee.

"I think I'd like to go on with it," I said. "I'm not getting anywhere but, oh, I don't know, I still feel I'm missing something."

She looked at me, a puzzled expression on her face.

"Like what?"

Good question, I thought. After a pause I went on.

"I've got the stupid idea that if I keep digging, I'll find it."

"Fine," she said.

"And, well," I added, "if someone else did do it they should be caught."

"True. Now let's talk about something more cheerful. Like this barbecue this afternoon."

"That reminds me," I said. "I'd better phone for a taxi."

I took out my mobile.

We got in the taxi at one pm. I gave the address in Woodford to the driver and looked at Marti. In her hand she carried a tiny handbag and a white cardigan. Judging by the sun belting down from a clear blue sky, the cardy might be redundant. My t-shirt, shorts and flip flops were suitable for the weather though lacking something in glamour in comparison with my companion.

The taxi pulled away and we fell silent for a couple of minutes. The sun glinted through the window. Not a bad old life, I said to myself, in spite of all the nastiness. I'd retired, was earning money for work that wasn't too taxing. A grandchild on the way. Even the weather was on my side it seemed. And going out with Marti made me feel young again. Now a day of fun in the sunshine.

"It's usually a good do," I said. "Looks like Pam's gonna be lucky with the weather again."

"So this Pam is, what, the Director of Children's Services?"

"Yeah."

"So what's she doing inviting a humble social worker to her garden party?"

"I told you, she's a friend from way back," I explained. "We were social work students together."

"And you've kept in touch all this time?"

"On and off," I said. "Every now and again a few people from the course get together."

"And she makes a point of inviting you to her annual barbecue."

"She invites me, yes."

She grinned at me.

"She's just a 'friend'," she said.

I could almost hear the inverted commas round the last word as she went on.

"Not one of your exes?"

I wondered what she had been getting at.

"One of my exes? How many do you think I've had?"

She shrugged.

"To answer your question, no, she is not one of my exes."

"So, you didn't have a little dalliance with her?"

"For most of the time I've known Pam, I was married."

Still am legally, I thought, but maybe it was best not to mention that.

"And that makes a difference?"

"Yes, it bloody does."

"Your wife was lucky then. I could go through the deficiencies of my husbands in that regard, but life's too short as they say."

Not for the first time, I had to take account of how influential the sex drive was. I had never thought of myself as a naïve innocent but I was beginning to feel like one. At the back of my mind was the thought that that's what Bill Copelaw's murder was all about. Had I detected a hint of jealousy in Marti's questions about Pam? Could jealousy be connected to Bill's death as well?

Fifteen minutes later we were approaching the street where Pam lived. We passed a house with a monkey puzzle tree in the front garden that was a sort of marker which told me we were nearly there.

"Next left and it's about the sixth house along on the right," I said to the driver.

As the car took the turning I looked over to the right.

"What's going on over there," I said to Marti, pointing in the direction of Pam's place.

We both craned our necks forward as the driver pulled up by the side of the road. Blue and white tape blocked off the entrance to the house and a uniformed policeman stood guard by the garden gate.

"It looks like a crime scene," said Marti as we got out of the taxi.

While Marti paid the driver – my turn on the way back – I looked more closely at the scene in front of me. The white detached house with the red pan-tiled roof looked the same as ever. Only the surroundings jarred. It certainly did resemble a crime scene, I thought. There were even people walking about in those white suits I had only ever seen on telly before Bill's murder. At that thought my stomach tensed. After paying off the driver, we approached the garden gate.

"I'm afraid you can't go in there," said the policeman.

"We're friends of Pam Agnew," I said. "She's expecting us."

Just then a woman parked her car on the other side of the street. She got out and locked it. Seeing us she crossed the road, a frown on her face.

"Mr Keane," she said. "We meet again."

"Inspector Ellerton."

"And Marti. What are you doing here?"

"I'm with him," she explained.

"Oh, you two are…"

She looked from one to the other of us, a smile sneaking onto her face. I decided I'd better say something.

"What's going on?"

She bit her lip and looked around.

"I'm afraid I need to know why you're here before I tell you anything."

"We're here for a party. Pam was having a barbecue."

She tapped her foot a few times, disturbing the dust on the pavement.

"I see. We were hoping it was just neighbours. We've managed to contact most of them."

She gritted her teeth and seemed to be deep in thought for perhaps half a minute. She breathed out through her mouth.

"It would be better to find somewhere private but you can't come in the house. It's a crime scene."

Her foot tapped the ground again.

"If you could just wait by my car," she said as though she were thinking out loud.

We waited, unsure what to do.

"It's just across the road," she said pointing as though we would have trouble finding the way. "I need to have a word with the constable."

Obediently we went to the car and stood by it, watching the inspector speak to the young man. Then she took out her mobile and made a call. She walked briskly across the road, looking both ways, reminding me of those Green Cross Code TV ads they had years ago.

"I'm afraid it's bad news," she said. "Ms Agnew is dead."

I gripped Marti's hand and felt tears prick my eyes.

"Bloody hell, that's terrible."

The inspector nodded. I already had an inkling what all this must mean but decided to ask anyway.

"If you're here does that mean…"

"We are treating her death as suspicious."

"How did she die?"

"I'm not at liberty to say."

Marti and I shuffled from foot to foot and looked at one another. The inspector went relentlessly on.

"Look, I need to ask a few quick questions, if that's OK."

Marti and I looked at one another.

"Sure," I said.

She asked us how long we'd known Pam. Marti had never met her so got off lightly.

"Were either of you around this area between seven and ten this morning?"

"We've only just got here," said Marti.

I wondered if Inspector Ellerton were checking our alibis in a roundabout way. I thought of the questioning I'd endured after Bill's death. All those years since my mam had died I'd had no experience of death. Now two deaths in a short space of time.

"We don't know much about Pam," Sarita said. "We've managed to contact her parents in Somerset. Someone has broken the bad news to them and her sister in Shropshire."

She shook her head sadly.

"I wonder if you know much about Pam."

"I can't tell you too much," I said. "I only saw her once or twice a year if that.

"What about Pam's private life? We know she wasn't married…"

"She was divorced years ago," I said.

"Was she seeing anybody, do you know?"

I took a deep breath.

"She'd said something about a married man."

"I see," said the inspector, though what it was she could see she didn't let on. "Do you know his name?"

"No, she didn't tell me."

"Would you like to hazard a guess?"

"I haven't a clue."

"How old was Pam?" asked Marti a quarter of an hour later.

We had left the crime scene once DI Ellerton had finished with us. Neither of us had wanted to hang around. We walked along a tree lined street. We were heading to the Grey Horse, the pub DI Ellerton had recommended for lunch.

"Forty odd, I suppose."

"No age," she said.

"Yeah, depressing, isn't it?"

I really didn't want to think about it, but what else was there to think about? I could see we were going to have to talk about it too. I knew from Bill's death that the police would delve into Pam's life, talk to her family. Someone had been to see her parents to tell them their daughter was dead. Sarita would be thinking about the married man. They would go to great lengths to trace him so his privacy would be invaded. And what about his wife? Would she find out? And I'd have another funeral to go to.

"You've had a few shocks lately," she said.

I nodded.

"It must be hard to take."

We walked on for a while in silence.

"It is, but I'm trying to hang on to the positives. There are one or two of them."

I squeezed her hand. She turned to me.

"Good."

That holiday Marti had suggested was beginning to sound better and better.

"What do you think happened to Pam?" asked Marti as we tucked into fish and chips half an hour later. In spite of everything we were hungry.

The tables in the pub garden were packed with drinkers enjoying a day off. One family group covered three generations from six months to sixty odd and I tried to picture myself with Rachel and Danny with their kids in a few years' time. Not that Danny showed much sign of becoming a father just yet.

"Hard to say."

"It could have been a burglar," Marti went on.

"At seven in the morning? That would be strange."

"It would at that. Maybe it was someone she knew."

I drank my pint and pondered this.

"You know," Marti continued. "A conspiracy theorist would think it strange that two managers from the same department have been killed within a few weeks of each other."

"There surely can't be any other connection between the two deaths," I said.

"Strange coincidence though."

I drank some beer and thought about this.

"When you think about it, life's full of coincidences, isn't it."

"Yeah."

"Like when you meet someone from your home town on holiday abroad."

She nodded, picking up her glass of wine.

"Even so they were killed several miles apart," I continued. "One at work, the other at home."

"Fair enough," agreed Marti, sprinkling more vinegar on her chips. "Somebody killed poor Pam. The question is who?"

"If it was someone she knows," I said, "he or she must have either been staying at her place overnight..."

Family, friend, boyfriend? I asked myself.

"Or someone who knew she'd be at home at that hour. On a bank holiday Monday"

"They'd also need to be sure they could get in the house without being seen," said Marti. "Or if they were seen, without being recognized."

How the hell would they do that?

"That rules out anyone staying the night," I said. "One of the neighbours would be bound to see him or her."

Marti nodded. I carried on with my meal. The police would no doubt sort it out. At the same time, I couldn't help wondering what would happen next.

* * *

The next morning as I was in the middle of my second cup of tea, a loud rap at the door frightened the life out of me. I wished, not for the first time, that the postman wouldn't bang so hard. My nerves were quite fragile enough as it was.

I opened the door with more force than was strictly necessary.

"Hello, Gus," said DI Ellerton.

'Gus' is it now, I asked myself, as I took in her denim jacket and blue jeans.

"Oh," I said, taken aback not just by seeing her instead of the postman, but by the clothes, the hair hanging loose and the smile.

"Any chance of a word?"

"Yeah," I said, composing myself and ushering her in.

I waved her to a seat at the kitchen table and sat down. I picked up my mug, while I waited for her.

"Fancy a cup," I asked, gesturing towards the pot.

"That would be nice," she said, smiling again.

As I got a mug, filled it and offered milk and sugar, she looked around the room with apparent interest, saying how nice it was.

"It's about Pam Agnew," she said, after taking her first sip of tea.

I nodded. In spite of her casual attire and attempts at friendliness, I didn't think it would be a social visit.

"I can now tell you she was shot."

"What!"

She nodded, while I wondered how the head of Children's Services, how someone I knew, had managed to get herself shot.

"That's a bolt from the blue," I said. "Anyway how can I help you?"

"We're talking to everyone in her contacts list."

"Contacts list?"

"You know, mobile phone. Perhaps you could explain how you came to be in hers."

I drank more tea and put the mug down. It seemed a silly question but I supposed I'd better answer it. I dismissed the idea of saying, 'so she could ring me' as too flippant.

"She would occasionally ring me or text, you know."

"Occasionally? What does that mean exactly?"

"Well," I began, "not that often, I suppose. Sometimes it would be months between contacts."

She had taken a notebook out of her bag by this time, signalling, I thought, the passage from informal to formal.

"Just recently, though, there have been quite a few texts and calls."

What was all this about?

"Yes, about the barbecue. You know, confirming arrangements."

"You told me she was involved with a married man?"

"Yes," I replied, wondering why she was changing the subject.

She looked at me over the rim of her mug.

"You're married."

So that was it. I had always thought social work warped the mind, but the same must apply to the police.

"True, though separated."

"I think you know what I'm getting at, Gus."

I was still 'Gus' then, rather than Mr Keane.

"Of course, Sarita. Though it seems a bit of a roundabout way to tell you I was having an affair with her."

She drained her mug before speaking again.

"You couldn't very well come right out with it while Marti was there."

I shook my head in disbelief. I was supposed to be some sort of Lothario. I had many faults but thinking I was God's gift to women wasn't one of them. I could never quite imagine a long line of them wanting to drag me into bed. Although, come to think of it, it was a nice fantasy.

"I thought you seemed, well, unduly upset about Pam's death," the inspector went on.

"I don't know what 'unduly' means in this context. Of course I was upset. Pam was a good friend for over twenty years."

"Just good friends then?"

I sighed. I'd been through this with Marti.

"Yes. Nothing sexual, romantic, whatever you want to call it."

To my simple mind that was that. I just wanted her to go and leave me alone. No such luck.

"It seems strange you should keep in touch with a woman for so long," she went on, "if she was just a friend."

Another sigh. I was beginning to think I had better things to do: sitting in a bowl of sick, counting the leeks on my dad's allotment, something like that. "You seem to find a lot of things strange, Sarita," I answered.

Well, we were on first name terms, it seemed.

"Do you do much exercise, Gus," she asked.

Was she changing the subject again? She had donned casual gear, adopted a friendly demeanour and tried to lull me into a false sense of security. Clutching at straws sprang to mind. The trouble was I recognised what she was doing all too easily. I'd tried those tricks in my social work career. And I could see something similar on telly any night of the week.

"A fair bit."

"Jogging?"

"No, walking and swimming. Why do you ask?"

"A jogger was seen near Pam's house early in the morning of her death."

Was he now? I was tempted to ask. I decided against it.

"And did he look like me?"

"The description was a bit vague."

"And I never run because of dodgy knees. Plus, I find it boring."

"Just wondered," she said.

And that seemed to be that.

CHAPTER NINETEEN

I looked at my watch, thinking it must be well past time to go home. Ten past six, I was right. I needed to have my report for court done though. I'd have to take it by hand tomorrow to get it in on time. Paperwork was a necessary evil as far as I was concerned. I didn't find it difficult, just didn't like doing it. That was why I left things until the last minute. However, ten minutes later I had finished the report and was waiting for it to print out. I picked up the copy of the Manchester Evening News Don had dropped on my desk as he was leaving. Pam's death had a reasonable amount of coverage on an inside page. Even in a limited amount of space, there was plenty of speculation. The 'mysterious deaths of two social services bosses' led to unanswerable questions: were the killings linked; was a group of disgruntled clients at work; was Salford council somehow cursed? The usual bollocks, in other words.

Putting the pages of my report into a neat pile I slid it into an envelope, wondering what had happened to Ania. She would usually have been in and out by now. As if she had read my thoughts, Polly came in, dragging her Hoover behind her and grinning at me. The grin was more or less permanent. At sixty odd, she had an appetite for life suitable for someone half her age. I knew if I didn't get away soon, she'd tell me about her internet dating adventures. I bet she'd described herself as cuddly and bubbly.

"Hiya, Gus," she said. "You wanna get yourself home."
"Just leaving, Polly. Where's Ania tonight?"
She screwed her eyes up.
"That's the funny thing. I don't know where she is. I thought I'd better do this floor anyway."
"Has she not phoned?"
"No. It's not like her."

Polly was about to plug the vacuum in when her mobile phone went. She took it out of her overall pocket and answered it. She listened intently to the person at the other end. A look of anxiety gradually replaced her chirpiness.

"Never," she said.

Her face went white.

"That's terrible…you're not safe on the streets these days…I wondered why she hadn't been in…such a nice girl too…yeah, I know…I hope she'll be all right…right, I'll just write that down…"

She made a writing motion and I passed her a pen and tore a sheet of paper form my notebook. Leaning on the desk, she wrote as she continued her conversation.

"Right, got that…OK…tara."

She put the phone back in her pocket and turned to me.

"That was my manager. She's had the police round at her house."

Sitting down with a bump, she cleared her throat.

"I can't believe it. Ania's been shot."

"What?"

Polly took half a dozen breaths, shaking her head from side to side.

"She was on the way here about an hour ago," she said. "Someone took a shot at her as she came out of her house."

"Is she going to be all right?"

"Too early to say. She's alive, that's the main thing. In Hope Hospital. I've wrote down the ward she's on and the phone number."

She picked up the bit of paper and handed it to me.

"She's not allowed visitors. We can phone tomorrow."

I nodded, thinking of Ania's family in Poland. They'd have a police officer at their door. I could picture the panic-stricken attempt to get on a flight to Manchester. Another shooting, I thought.

Two days later I walked down a seemingly endless corridor, clutching a bunch of spring flowers. I looked up at a confusion of signs I hoped would lead me in the fullness of time to the right ward. A motley collection of people – the expression 'all colours and creeds' sprang to mind – hurried in every direction as though they, unlike me, knew where they were going. Finding the lifts after only two wrong turns I went up to the fifth floor, wondering how Ania was and what had happened to her. She was allowed to see visitors; that must be a good thing, mustn't it? There'd been a piece in the Salford Advertiser, hinting that she had got caught up in gang warfare. Anyone less likely to be in a gang was hard to imagine.

I walked into the ward and scanned the beds lined along either wall. The patients practically glowed with well-being; their visitors perched uncomfortably on bedside chairs showed more signs of ill-health. I walked to the far end, where Ania sat up in a baggy Winnie the Pooh t-shirt, her left arm in a sling. She was reading a Kindle. Not for the first time I pondered the wisdom of getting one. It would be handy on journeys and holidays, I supposed. And if I ever happened to have my arm in a sling. I stood at the end of the bed for a few seconds before Ania noticed I was there.

"Gus!"

She grinned with delight. Her hair was tied back in a blue ribbon, her face scrubbed clean. She looked younger without make-up but there were lines of pain round her eyes.

"Nice to see you in one piece," I said, leaning over to give her a kiss on the cheek and hand over the flowers.

"Thank you, they're lovely."

She gave me the flowers back and I put them on the bedside table. There were already two vases full and six or eight get well cards. When I asked how she was she insisted she was fine.

"I can go home tomorrow," she said. "The bullet went through my shoulder and managed to miss anything important."

"That's a relief," I said. "We've all been worried about you. Who's going to look after you when you get home?"

"My mum of course. She and Dad got the first flight out when she heard. He's hoping to get tickets for Man U. They are in element. Is that right?"

"In their element," I said, as her unofficial English teacher.

"I will remember that."

"Have the police found out who did it yet?"

"No. It was weird. I came out of my house to get the bus to work"

"Yeah?"

"I live in Walkden," she added, pronouncing the 'l'. "I must have passed out. My neighbour phoned the ambulance."

"Did you see anything? Or anyone?"

She shrugged then winced in pain.

"I was looking in my handbag to make sure I had everything. Then I took my keys out to lock the door."

"Yeah."

"I dropped them on the pavement. I bent down to pick them up."

She swallowed.

"All of a sudden I heard a noise, like a bang. I felt a pain just here."

She pointed to her shoulder where the sling was tied.

"Bloody hell."

Dropping her keys must have saved her life. But who would want to shoot someone as unassuming and, well, nice as Ania?

"Then I had to be questioned by the police again, just like with poor Bill. They asked me if I was on drugs."

I shook my head in disbelief.

"Then they said I must be a prostitute. I nearly told them to eff off."

I smiled at the thought.

"They thought I'd been, you know, what's the word?"

She screwed her face up in concentration.

"I forget the word. It means forced to become a prostitute."

"Trafficked?"

"That's it. They said maybe I had upset my pimp."

I supposed the police had to ask these questions. Gun crime was usually associated with organised crime. They had no idea what Ania was like.

"One thing they asked me was very strange," Ania went on.

"What was that?"

"They wanted to know if I knew Pam Agnew."

"Pam?"

"Yes, I didn't know who they meant at first. They told me she was the Director who got killed."

What possible connection could there be between Pam and Ania? They worked for the same department but the Director would hardly socialise with the cleaner. I doubt if she had known Ania's name. They'd both been shot. That was a pretty strong connection. If you wanted to stretch things even further there was a link between the two women victims of gun crime and Bill Copelaw. I was buggered if I knew what it was. Anyway, the police had charged someone for Bill's murder. Askey could hardly have shot Ania and Pam from his prison cell.

* * *

The next day, just as I was immersed in Simon Brett's latest, I had another visit from Sarita Ellerton. I had been half expecting it. At least this time I had finished breakfast so the teapot was empty. Her dress – business suit and polished black ankle boots – and manner were more business-like. To add to the effect her hair was tied up.

"I wanted to ask you about Ania Bolek."

I realised I had never known her surname.

"Yes."

"As with Pam Agnew, your name was in her contact list."

What now? I asked myself.

"In fact you're the only person who is on the list of both women."

I put a tram ticket on page 93 to act as a bookmark. I closed the book. Sarita ploughed on.

"In fact I could almost say you were the only link between the two women."

Apart from them working for the same organisation, I thought. They must know some of the same people from Children's Services apart from me. They were both women, that was a link. Lived in the same city. Neither was married. I should offer to take over the investigation. Then I picked up on a word she had used.

"Almost?"

"There is another link but I'm not at liberty to reveal it."

I shrugged as she went on.

"Why would a cleaner have your number, Gus?"

"She and her boyfriend did some work for me."

"Work?"

"Yes. I'd had a lot of work done on the flat – new kitchen and things – and I must have mentioned I needed someone to decorate."

"You don't do your own decorating?"

"Not if I can help it," I said, wondering what it had to do with her. "But as I was saying…"

"Sorry."

"She said she and Darren would do it cheap. And she would clean the place afterwards."

"So it was a business relationship? You weren't friends or anything?"

There was no need to ask what 'or anything' meant.

"We're friendly enough when we meet," I said. "She's a nice girl. But we didn't socialise. I'm old enough to be her dad - granddad even."

"Do you own a gun," she said, seemingly ignoring my words.

"No," I replied with a certain emphasis. "Why?"

"Just routine, you know, background."

Just routine, I said to myself. A likely story.

"I don't own a gun," I said. May as well emphasise the point.

"And you had no reason to kill Pam or Ania?"

I decided to get the explanation over with in one go.

"Listen, Sarita," I said. "I need to explain a few things and I'd like you to listen while I do so."

"There's no need to…"

"Six months or so ago, my wife left me. Then I had a stroke."

"Yes, but…"

"Just listen. For several months I wasn't in a fit state to cope with anything but the everyday basics of life. Clear so far?"

She nodded.

"I gradually pulled myself round. In recent weeks I have discovered the dead body of my boss. My friend has been killed. A young girl I worked with has been shot at."

"Quite…"

"In the midst of all this I have become…involved with Marti. That's as much as I can handle. Please rid yourself of the idea that I am some demon lover who shoots any of my mistresses who displeases me."

* * *

Marti came round later on a flying visit before she had to go to court. I told her about Sarita's visits.

"She's only doing her job," she said, as we drank tea at the kitchen table.

"I know, but asking me if I had a gun. What would I have a gun for?"

She shrugged.

"Hang on a minute," she said after a moment's thought. "She's saying you're the link between Pam and Ania?"

"Yeah, but…"

"She says there is another link?"

"Right."

I picked up my mug and looked at her as she continued.

"Now if she wants to know if you've got a gun, that must be the other link?"

"What must?"

My brain was beginning to hurt.

"The gun of course. She wouldn't just be idly speculating about links between the two killings without some forensics to back it up."

"You'd better spell it out."

"They were killed by the same gun."

CHAPTER TWENTY

"Hey, Gus," I heard someone call the next morning.

I turned from the tram stop in the direction the shout had come from. I saw a young, black man come towards me along Salford Quays. A baggy American football shirt engulfed his body. It took a few seconds to recognize him.

"Hiya, Paul," I said.

"Gus, how're you doing?"

"Fine, how are you?"

"I'm good, mate, know what I mean? Where you off to?"

"Off to see my dad. He lives in Weaste."

"Cool."

Was it cool, I wondered, for me to go and see my father or for him to live in Weaste? I came to the conclusion 'cool' had simply become a modern equivalent to the meaningless phrases that people use to fill gaps in conversation.

"I'm glad I caught you," said Paul. "Got some news for you."

Paul stood at the stop with me, surveying passing cars. He tried to make himself heard against the traffic roaring along Trafford Road.

"News?"

"Yeah."

He dug his hands deeper into the pockets of his jeans.

"Remember after rugby practice the other day?"

"Yes," I said, though unsure what I was meant to remember.

"When you asked me to find out if anybody saw anything that day."

"What day?"

"You know," he said, "when that guy got killed."

"Oh, you mean Bill Copelaw?"

"That's the one."

I hadn't expected Paul to do anything about it. Oh, ye of little faith, I told myself. I listened more carefully.

"Well, I might have found someone. With information, you know."

"Who is it?"

"Mate of mine. Stringer. We can go and see him today if you like."

"This afternoon should be OK. Where?"

"He's doing community service in Little Hulton."

My heart sank.

"Community Service? Is he reliable, this mate of yours?"

"Yeah," said Paul, affronted, "sound as a pound."

I asked myself how sound a pound was these days. 'Not very' was the answer I came up with.

"He's not been in any trouble for ages. Well, three or four months anyway."

My heart sank even further.

"Why are you getting mixed up with toe rags like him?"

"I'm not…"

"You've got your future to think about."

"I'm not mixed up with him. I have my own mates. I'm bound to come across wasters like Stringer from time to time."

I nodded. I'd been too hasty. It was just that for him to slide back into his old ways would be little short of tragic. Paul went on with his explanation.

"I just heard, like, on the grapevine that he'd seen something."

* * *

Just after three o'clock that afternoon, I parked near a wooden hut on a patch of grass in Carrfield Avenue, Little Hulton. Paul and I got out of my car. As I looked at the row of council houses opposite, a vivid memory of visiting Tony Murphy here in my teenage years came into my mind. Wondering what the hell became of Tony, I examined the houses more closely. The first two were boarded up; the next two, including Tony's old home, had white front porches and PVC doors. Someone had obviously bought them. In the old days neither boarded up houses nor private homes existed round here, I thought.

As we entered the hut, I looked round at a group of young workers sitting in a cacophony of coughing and a blue haze of cigarette smoke.

"Fuck me, every fucker's got fucking pneufuckingmonia," said a spotty youth.

"Now, Stringer," said Paul to the foul-mouthed one.

The lad sat there looking lost in an ill-fitting t-shirt and jeans that had seen better days. He looked at Paul.

"All right, mate."

"Brought someone to meet you. This is Gus Keane."

Stringer thought for a moment.

"Not the one who played for Salford?"

"Yeah," said Paul.

Stringer's eyes lit up.

"Fuck me. Never."

He stood up, raising his right hand like a witness taking the oath. He high-fived me.

"Respect, Gus," he said. "My granddad used to tell me about you."

"Granddad!"

"Making you feel old, am I? Sorry, mate."

"Nice to be remembered."

"You'll never be forgotten, you, Gus."

"How's the community service going?"

"Not bad," said Stringer, "if you like weeding pavements."

He shrugged and scratched his hair.

"What?"

"Yeah, barmy, isn't it? Clearing all the weeds, you know, bits of grass and that."

"Who thinks of these jobs?" I asked.

"Fuck knows," said Stringer.

"There's probably a pointless task co-ordinator in an attic somewhere," I said.

"I was telling Gus you're quite a tasty inside centre," said Paul.

He'd need feeding up if he were to be any use, I surmised. 'Needs a good tater pie down him,' as my mam would have said.

"Not bad, I suppose," Stringer shrugged modestly. "Nowhere near as good as you, Gus. Fucking legend, you, mate."

I shrugged.

"Best team Salford ever had when you played for 'em."

"You still playing?" I asked.

"No, not played for a while."

"Well it's time you started again," I said. "Here, have a look at this."

He accepted the leaflet I'd offered him as if it were a summons to appear in court. He read the caption, mouthing the letters one by one.

"TRYS. What the fuck's that?"

"Taking Rugby to the Youth of Salford," I said squirming with embarrassment as I did every time I spoke those words.

"What?"

"It's something to keep you out of trouble but we'll talk about that later," I said. "I've got some other stuff to ask you about. Perhaps the other lads could get back to work while we talk."

I sat down on the bench cut into the walls of the hut.

"You heard him, lads," said Stringer. "Need a bit of privacy, you know what I mean?"

The other five in the group got up and went outside into the rain. It was as if Stringer had the voice of authority.

"I understand you saw someone on the night Mr Copelaw was killed at Social Services," I said.

"Yeah," said Stringer, "He was, like, coming out of the building, you know, about the time you said. On the night in question."

Like a ham actor he injected added significance into the last five words. A look of pure smugness crept over his face, as if he were imagining himself on telly. He leaned against the wooden wall behind him, his arms hanging loosely by his side. He shuffled around, sliding backwards and forwards on his seat. This movement seemed to dissipate all his energy.

"I'll need to ask you some questions. You know what this is all about?"

"Yeah."

"Well, Stringer," I said only slightly self-consciously, "can you tell me where you saw him, what he looked like, what he was wearing and what he did?"

Stringer was such an apt name that I couldn't help but smile. He drank from a plastic water bottle. Thinking he may need lubrication before he could speak coherently, I waited. There was a silence and I wondered how much time would elapse before I got any useful information. There was no great urgency but I wanted all this to be over. I felt a strong need to go away with solid information that was actually of some use. Casting aside this thought I got to the point.

"Right. Remember, what he looked like, what he was wearing, where you saw him and what he did. OK fire away."

Stringer took another long drink from his bottle. The water seemed to set his teeth on edge.

"Well not very tall. About average."

That sounded about right.

"He was wearing a leather jacket, I do know that. Pricy, I'd say, know what I mean? He came out of the door and stood at the top of the steps, not for long though. Outside the Welfare like."

"Right, anything else."

"A dark jacket, I'd say, could have been black and he didn't have a hat on."

"No hat. I see. Go on."

"Seemed in a bit of a hurry, know what I mean? Just looked round, dead quick, and then rushed down the steps."

"Rushed down the steps, right. What did he do then?"

"Just walked away fast as he could. Didn't run though."

"What made you notice him?"

"Dunno really. There was no one else around, it was dead quiet. It'd be, what, half five, quarter to six."

This was important. It meant leather jacket man did exist. He must have been in the building at the time Bill had died. The only trouble was would Stringer's evidence hold up in court, always assuming he could be persuaded to go to court in the first place. Finding leather jacket man would be a better idea. Who the hell was he though?

"How old was he," I asked, remembering another vital question.

Stringer took another drink. By now his bottle was nearly empty.

"Ooh, old."

Old? I somehow hadn't pictured an old man.

"How old?"

I would pin him down yet.

"Well, pretty old like," said Stringer, thinking hard, "Oo, at least thirty-five if not more."

* * *

The large sheet of paper, pure white like my t-shirt, lay before me on the kitchen table. It was time to take stock of Copelaw's murder. I'd finally decided to try and pull all the strands of it together. Exactly seven weeks since he was killed, Gus, about bloody time. It would also take my mind off Rachel's baby, who was due any day now.

Even if he hadn't killed Bill, Askey was still a murderer. So he'd still be in prison no matter what. If I turned up information that pinned Bill's death on someone else, I wouldn't feel bad about Askey being at large.

Now, concentrating like a schoolboy, even sticking my tongue out, I wrote quickly and methodically with a felt-tip pen. The red letters stood out as clear and sharp as my mind tried unsuccessfully to be. Come on, Gus, have one last go to see if you can crack the case, I told myself. I could be missing something, you never knew. Would it be worth it? I asked myself. Sod that, Gus; remember you're being paid by the hour.

I wrote the words WHO WHAT WHEN WHERE HOW WHY one beneath the other down the left hand side. Drinking tea and biting a chunk out of a chocolate digestive, I looked through my notes again. Some things were not in dispute. I wrote against four of the headings:

WHAT - Copelaw killed;
WHEN - Friday 31st March between 5.30 and 6.30 in the evening;
WHERE - Children's Services Office, Ordsall Tower;
HOW - Bopped on the head with a statue/football trophy.

So far so good. Just who and why remained unanswered. Oh, was that all? How could I ever have thought it was difficult? Wanting something different from my previous work, I was now doing exactly what I had done before. Using the same skills. Keeping a diary, writing reports, making lists, thinking methodically and logically. It was just like a proper job. But then, why shouldn't it be? Another why question, there had been a lot of those lately. Before I could wonder why I was sitting here with a red felt-tip like a child at play I asked myself why I didn't get on with the task I had set myself. I began to write again, this time in blue.

WHO: Karen, Don, Cal, Jean, Gary, Liam

I stopped and looked at the list of names. WHO and WHY went together, didn't they? I picked up a green pen.

WHY:

MONEY: Karen, maybe Jean
JEALOUSY: Karen, Jean, Gary
AMBITION: Don
REVENGE/ANGER: Cal, Jean, Liam

It was getting a bit Shakespearean. Macbeth was ambitious – I remembered that from 'A' level. Othello was jealous. Who was greedy or revengeful? No, pass. My knowledge of Shakespeare was not exactly encyclopaedic. If I were a proper private eye, I'd find the answer in the works of the bard, a quotation from the metaphysical poets or something equally erudite.

What did I know about? What would be my chosen specialist subject on Mastermind? I'd read the Jeeves and Wooster stories of PG Wodehouse over and over again for more than forty years. And I ought to be an expert on Rugby League. Maybe Gus Risman's autobiography, started on the train to Barmouth and finished on the way back, would offer enlightenment. There was a lot to choose from. If Steve were here he would use his extensive knowledge of the works of Creedence Clearwater Revival. Come to think of it wasn't there a Creedence song called Sinister Purpose? Steve would be able to tell me which album it was from. Would any of this rubbish be of any use to you, Gus? Question expecting the answer no, as we used to say in Latin lessons.

Impatiently I looked again at the names. My eyes lighted on the middle one. Gary, had he had a sinister purpose? If he had known about his wife's affair at the time – a possibility at least – he would have had a motive for killing Bill. He had said he didn't know who Karen had had the affair with but he could have been lying. He may have suspected Karen was pregnant even if he didn't know for sure. Karen getting pregnant to another man when he was not capable of fathering a child would have been twisting the knife.

Did Gary have an alibi for the time of the murder? It would be interesting to know. He had picked Karen up after work. Gary, though, had approached me after Karen had told him about the affair. If he had known the affair was with Copelaw would he have come to me? Or had that been a double bluff? Come on, Gus, you're straying into the realms of fantasy now. How was I going to prove any of this even if it were true? I wasn't.

Copelaw had humiliated his wife, Jean. The spouse was always the prime suspect. What had she told me on that walk in Worsley? That crack about wanting to pin the blame on Karen, was that a way to deflect suspicion from herself? Had she finally got sick of Copelaw's affairs, his incurable womanising?

Even Cal had got some money out of Copelaw's death. She had also left home and never come back. She could hardly have gone further and still stayed in England. She'd hardly spoken to her father for years. Did she have a motive? A lot would say yes. Jean and Bill had been arguing about someone on the afternoon of the murder. 'Keep her out of this,' Jean had said. Had she been referring to their daughter? She'd been waiting outside in the car. Was it an accident that she made one of her rare visits to her mother on the day her father was murdered? Why shouldn't it have been? And in any case, if she were going to snap and lash out at him, why now? Still, murder was often a family affair.

Karen had to be a suspect. Had she told me everything? This was a woman who was determined to get what she wanted. The motive was there. Not just the money; there was no way of knowing whether Bill was really going to move in with her. Suppose he had dumped her when he knew she was pregnant? I wouldn't have put it past him. What time had Karen really left the office on the night of the murder? Had she come back? She had seemed genuinely gutted about Bill's death, but tears could be a sign of guilt. I thought of all the clients, male and female, who could turn on the waterworks without even trying. I reminded myself that this was not a pre-meditated crime. Whoever had done it had reacted on the spur of the moment and wouldn't necessarily have known if Copelaw were dead.

What would Jeeves do? In my favourite story, The Great Sermon Handicap, Bertie Wooster had had a plan to make a small fortune by betting on the vicar who preached the longest sermon. It had been foiled by the favourite falling ill and someone they hadn't even considered won the race. I was back to that feeling I was missing something.

I thought about the way Gus Risman's autobiography dealt with the opposition he had to face when he went from Rugby Union to League. He said 'many people refuse the right of any man to capitalise on his talents'. Was that how Don felt? Putting aside for a moment the fact that he didn't have much talent in the first place, Don thought he'd been treated badly. Copelaw had refused to recommend him for promotion, so Copelaw dying gave him a better chance of achieving his ambition. Had he been so obsessed with his own worth he had lost his temper that night and killed his boss? Was it really a motive? A job in Bolton slightly more senior than the one he already had? People have been killed for 50 pence, but even so. Don would have had to have anger boiling up for ages about more than just his career to have let it affect him like that.

The police would say the murderer was not hard to catch at all. He had already been caught. The sheet of paper, with its handful of words sketched in symbolised starkly and effectively the emptiness of my case. Even the list of names was incomplete. Well, of course it was. Askey's name wasn't on it.

What about Liam? His baby had been taken away; he had been around Ordsall Tower at the time; he could have barged in just like Askey and confronted Bill. It was a spontaneous attack, not a planned assassination. Death was by chance really; Bill could easily have survived.

A lot of people could have killed Copelaw. I was left looking for a lucky break as I so often had been in my sporting career. You make your own luck was a mantra amongst sportsmen. In rugby you had to have a mixture of individual brilliance and good support play. This coupled with a touch of the unexpected would usually win the day. Do something your opponent hadn't thought about. So if someone helped me to see something I had not even considered, would that help me find the killer? I broke off at the sound of my mobile phone.

"Hello," I said.

"Hi, Gus."

"Louise, where are you?"

"I'm staying with Yvonne until I find somewhere more permanent."

"You OK?"

"Fine. I wondered if you fancied meeting up."

"OK."

"We need to catch up properly."

What was she on about? Before I had a chance she asked me out to lunch. I accepted.

Louise sipped her mineral water and smiled at me. In Tony and Dino's in Salford Quays smells of steam, coffee and baking mingled in the air. I looked around. It was as good a place as any to meet my wife, I thought. Quite why we were here, I could only guess. There would be a reason, you could bet on that. Still, we had to meet sometime. We had kids for God's sake; soon we'd have a grandchild. It was difficult to concentrate with the intermittent sound of coffee machines, waiters bustling around and the opening and closing of the door. Or maybe it was just difficult to concentrate.

"Tell me about your trip," I said in a fairly obvious attempt to get some sort of conversation going.

Up to that point we had managed with 'you're looking well' and 'how's the jet lag'. Now she enthused for ten minutes about Thailand, Vietnam and Australia and I made suitable noises of interest.

"I think you would have preferred New Zealand though," she said.

"Yeah?"

She nodded. She was looking fantastic, I thought, remembering why I'd fancied her in the first place. Tanned and blonde (though her hair needed some help these days), she still had a glamour that a lot of women would pay good money for.

"It's not too hot for a start," she explained. "Stunning scenery. It's a very outdoor sort of country."

"Sounds good."

"You should go some time if you can get insurance. It's time you branched out a bit."

Louise had just summed up what I didn't like about her. She'd always tried to bully me into going abroad when there were so many lovely places in this country. Why did I have to branch out? What did it have to do with her? That was the trouble with being married: whatever you did, said and even thought was assumed to have something to do with the other person. But it didn't matter now, I realised with profound relief.

"I'm not sure I fancy a long haul flight," I said.

Not to mention not wanting to be away from home for too long. A short break somewhere not too far away, that would do me. That seemed to bring an end to that part of the conversation. There followed a pause while we ordered from the waitress who approached us at that moment.

"Anyway, I've got something to tell you," said Louise when the waitress had gone.

She smiled like a little girl about to unleash a secret on an unsuspecting world.

"Go on."

"Well," she said, dragging it out so I wanted to tell her to get on with it, "I'm getting married again."

The urge to laugh or say 'you must be bloody mad' was so strong I could feel myself holding my breath.

"We're still married," I said instead, though that wasn't really the point.

Then I wondered who the lucky man was as she struggled on with her news.

"I know, but…well, Brad and I see no reason to wait any longer than absolutely necessary."

"Brad?"

"Yes," she said, "I spent some time with him in New Zealand."

I couldn't help wondering whether that was a good basis for marriage. Apparently it was.

"And?"

"Well, we hit it off, like you do."

Like who does, I was tempted to ask.

"So he's a Kiwi?" I asked.

"Well, no. He's from Knutsford. He's head of HR in Cheshire."

The plot thickens, I said to myself, as she explained the practicalities of ending our marriage. Like she was my lawyer or something. I, however, was thinking about Brad. She knew him before she took her career break and went travelling. I could just picture them meeting at a diversity conference in Warrington or somewhere. She didn't leave me because she needed her own space. She had plenty of space: we led practically separate lives. She was the one with the high powered career. Not that I was bitter. I just didn't fancy the label 'divorced' hanging over me. Add the fact she had been shagging another bloke while I'd been faithful all those years. Another thing I didn't like about her. I tried to examine my feelings about her infidelity. Partly pissed off, partly philosophical, about summed it up. I was surprised I wasn't more angry. I had been making a conscious effort not to get angry. The beta blockers the doctor had given me helped. And I knew getting mad was bad for me.

"So you want to get divorced?"

"Well, I thought it would be best for both of us… I know you have someone so…"

I knew she'd say something about Marti but had no idea how to respond. Saying, 'yes, but I'm not planning to bloody marry her, I've only know her five bloody minutes' would come out wrong. I considered this for a while before realising I didn't want to marry anyone. Nor did I want to move in with anyone, even someone as nice as Marti. Maybe it was a question of 'been there, done that'.

I shook my head. It was more than that. If I said I was happy with just having a girlfriend it would sound immature and shallow to some people. It was to do with living with someone for the rest of your life and being happy with that. Suddenly that was what seemed unrealistic. My thinking was also coloured by Louise's deceit. And what about Marti's two husbands; Karen's affair with Copelaw and his constant womanising? When I thought about all that, marriage didn't sound such a good bet. Why was everything bringing me back to Bill's murder? And why did I think something Louise had said, a passing remark, was significant? Needless to say I had forgotten what it was.

CHAPTER TWENTY-ONE

I wandered round Salford Quays the following Monday after a weekend spent with Marti. She'd gone off to work first thing, leaving me to have a lie-in. The sun was shining and I had finally managed to have a Monday off. The next day I would be back at Ordsall Tower but I wouldn't worry about that for now. Soon I'd be meeting Marti for lunch at Cafe Rouge. I fancied a nice steak, a glass of wine or even two. Why not? As I strolled aimlessly about I thought on and off about my meeting with Louise. Divorce was a big word. The sort of thing that happened to other people. Now, it's happening to you, Gus.

Not just to me. How would Rachel and Danny take to this Brad? They weren't kids any more, but this was bound to affect them. At the back of my mind, the thought that something Louise had said had a different kind of significance just wouldn't go away. What was it? Something she'd said in passing, nothing heavy, but the idea that it might make all the difference wouldn't go away. Nor would it come back to me, no matter how much I tried to remember. Or was I trying to avoid thinking about yet another change in my life? How many more would there be? Plenty, Gus, I said to myself.

I looked at my watch: ten past twelve. As I passed a cash machine I wondered if I had enough money. I took out my wallet and saw just one measly, creased fiver. I went through the usual ritual of putting in my PIN, telling this inanimate object how much money I wanted and waited for something to happen. Money from a machine, when did that start? How easily we had all managed to get used to it. As I took the notes from the slot, and put them into my wallet, something clicked and I stopped musing about the history of banking. It was as if a light went on in my head.

The wallet. That was it. That was the inconsistency I'd been trying to identify. The difference between what I saw when I went into Bill's office the first time and the second visit when I found Bill's body. Why was it different? How had it become different? Where did that get me, I wondered. It showed I had been right about there being an inconsistency. Big deal, I was tempted to say. What was its significance? Was it even relevant? It gave me something else to think about; something that may lead to the answer. And then again...

I walked away, still mulling it over. There was a lot more to do if I was ever going to solve this. I may never solve it. Maybe the bleeding obvious - that Askey had murdered Bill Copelaw - was the answer. I got to Cafe Rouge just as Marti arrived and we managed to find a corner table. I ordered a glass of house red and a mineral water from a passing waiter, noticing Marti's harassed look.

"I can't stay long," she said, taking my hand. "Sorry."

She complained about how much she had to do, there not being enough hours in the day and how stupid her clients were. I nodded sympathetically, resisting the temptation to tell her what time I had finally crawled out of bed.

About half an hour later she dashed off with an apology and a kiss. I hadn't quite finished my steak, but had ordered a second glass of wine. It all felt a bit self-indulgent. I rarely drank at all during the day. I looked round the restaurant. It was less crowded than I'd feared. Monday was probably a quiet day and a lot of people were now short of money. This thought took me back to the money in the wallet and how it got there. How should I know? A waiter brought my wine. I started to think about my lunch with Pam, the last time I had really spoken to her before she died.

I tried to think of something else but the arrival of a young woman with her arm in a sling put paid to that. She scanned the room as if looking for someone. Then, turning in my direction, Ania recognised me and waved with her right hand.

"Ania," I said as she approached my table, "nice to see you."

She was casually dressed in jeans and a long sleeved t-shirt.

"Hi, Gus," she said. "Where's your girlfriend?"

"She had to rush back to work. I've got a day off."

"I'm meeting a friend. She's not here yet."

I asked her to join me and have a drink while she was waiting. I could almost see the cogs turning in her brain. Did she want to be seen sitting with this old guy? Maybe sitting on her own would be worse. And a free drink was not to be sniffed at. She sat opposite me. I ordered her a white wine.

"How's the arm," I asked.

"Improving," she replied. "I can take the sling off now and again."

I drank more wine and thought about the shooting.

"Are the police any nearer finding out who did that to you?"

She shook her head.

"I don't think so. I haven't heard from them for a while."

I wondered again about Pam's death. Would anybody be caught for that? Or would it join the list of unsolved crimes? Ania's wine arrived.

"Cheers," she said, raising her glass.

"Cheers."

We chatted for a while until Ania's friend arrived and she went to join her. It wasn't until I'd paid my bill and gone outside that I remembered I had something to ask Ania.

I left the restaurant feeling mellow. I'd enjoyed my lunch and the two glasses of wine had had the desired effect. I passed a travel agents as I walked home, noticing a poster of New Zealand in the window. I stopped to admire it. Louise was right, it certainly looked beautiful. The bit of conversation I'd had with Louise popped into my head again. She had used a word that reminded me of 'certainty'. What the hell was it? I looked at the other posters in the window as though searching for inspiration. Shrugging my shoulders, I walked away.

My mind went back to the question of the wallet. Bill had no money the first time I had seen him on the day of his death; when I found his body he had a full wallet. He had far more money than he would have got from a cash machine. In any case he hadn't been to the cash machine. So how did the money get there? That needed explaining. It couldn't have been from Jean. Why would she get so much cash for a night out? And why would she come back to the office to give it to Bill? And I still hadn't recalled the significant word, I reminded myself.

At ten past seven that night I was watching Channel 4 News. The first advert break started. As the Go Compare ad came on, I muted the sound. People get paid for dreaming up that rubbish, I thought, and as for that meerkat thing... I stopped and looked at the remote control. "You dozy sod," I said out loud. It had been staring me in the face all this time. I now knew what the word was that had been plaguing me all this time. I hadn't quite worked out its significance but, perhaps wrongly, I felt now as if I were on a roll. The meaning of it all, how everything fitted together, was just out of reach. Would I be able to pull the strands together?

Thinking about Bill's murder brought a picture of my finding his body to mind. Not what I wanted but inevitable. The part that always featured heavily was finding the condoms. From farce to tragedy within a few seconds. Not that a Durex Fetherlite packet would tell me much. Or would it? It came from that hotel in York. Was that relevant? I closed my eyes and events flashed through my mind. It might just make sense. Was I almost there? I realised I still hadn't asked Ania about leather jacket man. Would it be worth ringing her? Before I could think about it too much, I got out my mobile and found Ania's number. Once I had got through to her I came to the point.

"A while ago you were going to tell me about a man you saw near the office on the day Bill Copelaw was killed."

"Was I?"

She sounded puzzled. I wasn't surprised. It must seem a long time ago to her and she would hardly have been thinking about it too much since then. I gave her a bit more information to jog her memory.

"Oh, I remember," she said eventually. "It's funny because I should have recognised him straight away. He's one of the guys who came out to me."

This added a new twist, I thought.

"Came out? You mean he's gay?"

And why should whoever it was tell Ania?

"No, not gay."

She giggled.

"Not 'come out'. He came on to me."

I smiled.

"He tried to...?"

"Chat me up. What is it about married men? Are they trying to prove themselves or..."

"This guy, who..."

"Do they think I'm stupid, that I won't realise they are married?"

"But who..."

"Or do they think I am immoral. I am a good Catholic..."

"Ania if you could just..."

"He begged me not to tell his wife. Pathetic."

I reminded her she had not yet told me who this man was. Then she told me his name.

"Somebody's lying," I said to myself as I ended the call. Surely Ania couldn't be...? Get a grip, Gus, it's really getting to you if you're starting to suspect her.

* * *

The next morning I went to Ordsall Tower at 9.00. By then I thought I had it all worked out. More or less. I had a cup of tea and a chat with Don about Rebecca's progress. Just as it started to rain, I left my desk, telling Karen I was going to sort out my insurance. I went down the corridor to Reliable.com, knocked on the door and went in.

"Gus, hi. What can I do for you?" asked Rob.

He sat back in his chair, adjusting the knot on his red tie. I sat in a chair on the opposite side of his desk, watching the rain fall on the windows.

"I've been thinking about Bill Copelaw's murder," I said.

That was a start at least.

"I think you might be able to help."

"Terrible business, especially for you, Gus. It takes a bit of getting over, but I'm not sure I can..."

I nodded as his words petered out. Rob uncrossed his legs and sat forward. He cocked his head slightly. I too sat forward. I looked round the room. Someone had been putting shelves on the wall to my right and had left the job half-finished. I noticed one of the unused shelves on the desk. Concentrate, I told myself.

"A few things have puzzled me about this whole affair," I said. "There was an inconsistency about what I saw when I found Bill's body."

"You been doing some amateur sleuthing, mate?"

"Not exactly," I said.

I couldn't be bothered to explain about my investigation. It would only get in the way. So I carried on.

"A short time before his death Copelaw had no cash and asked his wife to get some."

"Oh?"

"Yet when his body was found his wallet was bursting with money."

"So?"

"Well, somebody must have given him the money."

He shook his head.

"Sorry, Gus, you're losing me."

"We'll come back to that," I said. "Let's think about Bill's health, shall we?"

"His health? What about it?"

"Copelaw suffered from angina. Had done for years apparently. He made no secret of it. He would often talk about his first attack on holiday in France. Yet just a short time before he died he took out a life insurance policy."

"I really don't see what you're driving at," said Rob.

"It was a conversation with my wife, Louise, that put the idea in my head."

"Your wife, but I thought…"

"We are separated but on good terms."

He nodded.

"She's just got back from New Zealand and suggested I might like to go."

"And?"

"She just mentioned in passing I might struggle to get travel insurance."

"Oh?"

"Presumably because I had a stroke in September."

Rob picked up his coffee cup and drank. He put it down again.

"I remember it. You're looking a lot better."

"It was only later I applied this to Bill Copelaw. Now who would be stupid enough to insure a man in his late fifties with a heart condition?"

Rob squirmed in his seat.

"There's been a word at the back of my mind for weeks," I went on. "Tantalisingly out of reach, you might say."

Rob made as if to get up.

"Stay there, Rob. I haven't finished yet. The word was something like 'certainty'. Something like 'certainty', what could that be?"

"I don't know."

"Certain. Sure. Insure. Insurance."

I almost chanted the words.

"Insurance, that was the word. I'm amazed it took me so long to realise."

I breathed in and made a conscious effort to focus.

"It kept cropping up. Bill took out the second policy not long ago."

Rob shrugged.

"He was getting desperate for money," said Gus. "Wasn't he?"

"How should I know?"

"His lucky day came when he found out about your affair with Pam Agnew."

"How on earth …?"

Rob was genuinely curious now, temporarily forgetting the seriousness of his position.

"You met when she came here for a job interview. A trip to Ordsall Tower to meet the staff was a part of the process."

"He saw you with Pam in Maxwell's Hotel in York. Copelaw had been there at the same time on a course," I said.

There was a look on his face very much like panic.

"He dropped a packet of condoms from the self-same hotel on his office floor the day he died. Or maybe you did."

I was partly guessing now. But I had it all worked out. I must be right.

"You were so terrified your wife would find out you made the mistake of asking him to be discreet."

Rob's head dropped. He looked forlornly at the floor.

"Pam was making a speech, wasn't she," I asked. "Did she suggest you joined her afterwards?"

"I told Pam we shouldn't go there," he said, "but she swore there'd be nobody there who knew me."

Pam was getting tired of all the secrecy by that time, I thought.

"You were amazed when he started to blackmail you. A respectable man like him. Still, you went along with it, had to."

"What do you mean?"

Rob was finding speech difficult. He sounded hoarse.

"I bet he just wanted money at first. Then he thought of getting you to fiddle an insurance policy for him."

"Ridiculous," said Rob, just managing to get the word out.

"You knew about Copelaw's health problem and normally you would have picked up on it."

"Quite."

"But you only had to tick the box or whatever you do to say you didn't need a report from the doctor."

I concentrated hard and tried to control my breathing.

"Not much chance of being caught, was there?"

"This is pure fantasy."

"Is it? There was the money too. Things were desperate."

Throughout this Rob had held onto himself, reminding me of the stiff upper lip hero of a war film. Now his body slumped back in the chair.

"Oh, God," he said.

He looked defeated but I wanted to finish off properly.

"I know you were in the habit of popping in to Children's Services' office, touting for business."

"Yes."

"Bill told me he had an appointment with somebody that evening at 5.30. It was you he was expecting."

All Rob had to do was deny it. There was no real evidence he was there.

"The feller who's accused of the murder saw you. So did somebody else. You were wearing a leather jacket for casual clothes day. That confused me at first."

Rob's eyes gazed emptily. He held his hands up in surrender.

"OK, OK, I was there. Somebody did see me. He rushed past me as I …"

"I thought you were supposed to be at home with the kids."

He shrugged.

"It was easy enough to ask a neighbour to keep an eye on them. I said I'd left something at the office."

I nodded.

"What had you gone to see Bill about?"

"I'd just gone to make another payment. Five hundred pounds."

"Five hundred pounds. Is that all?"

Rob looked indignant.

"Five hundred pounds a fucking week, that's what the slimy bastard wanted. Until I could raise twenty thousand pounds through a low interest loan. I was trying to buy time in the hope that something would turn up."

"I can see it, Rob," I said. "You hand over the five hundred pounds, what was it, twenty-five twenty pound notes?"

Rob averted his eyes and looked at his trembling hands.

"I bet Copelaw stuffed the money into his wallet with a smirk. As I said, it made quite a bulge. Was that when you snapped?"

Rob slumped lower in his chair, then started scrabbling around in his desk drawer. My mobile rang. I took it out of my pocket.

"Don't answer it," barked Rob as I pressed the green button and said hello.

Rob held his right arm out at full length and pointed aggressively at me.

"Kev, hiya…"

"Put the phone down!"

I covered up the mouthpiece with my left hand, still listening to my son in law.

"Bugger off, Rob!"

I took my hand off the phone and continued my conversation, ignoring Rob.

"What was that, Kev? Bugger! The signal's gone."

I ended the call and looked at Rob. I put the phone back in my trouser pocket. I looked more closely at Rob. He had a gun in his hand. What was he playing at?

"What are you doing?"

"Gus," said Rob hesitantly, "I have a gun and I will not hesitate to use it. I'm sorry, mate."

Gradually it sunk into my head that something weird was happening. All would become clear, I told myself. There's time for your clear, analytical mind and irresistible charm to come into play. I looked at Rob's desk, noticing a bunch of car keys next to a notepad, a box of tissues and a wedding photograph.

"Where did you get that thing?"

He looked at the gun as if he had never seen it before.

"From that toe rag of a burglar I disturbed."

"Oh."

As I considered the inadequacy of my response he went on.

"I was in a bad mood to start with that day. I'd had go into the office on a Friday night. When I saw a little scumbag searching the place I just snapped."

So the smooth exterior was only skin deep, I thought. Here was a man on a very short fuse. Bugger.

"As soon as I saw him I kicked him in the balls. Just like that, didn't even think about it."

Thinking doesn't seem to be your strong point, Rob, I wanted to say, despite your expensive education.

"The gun flew out of his hand and landed on the desk. He ran like fuck, I can tell you. He got a boot up the arse to help him on his way."

His eyes looked intensely at me.

"I picked up the gun and just looked at it. I'd never even seen one before except on telly."

That didn't really explain what he was doing with it now.

"I was going to hand it in but then I thought about it. If low life were going to terrorise me in this way, maybe I needed something to defend myself with."

Well that explained that, I thought, for all the good it did me.

"Now I'm going to have to kill you," he said.

I didn't like the sound of that. It wasn't going to happen. No way. I was going to watch my grandchild grow up. George or Georgia was gonna get to know me. We would do things together. Not necessarily sport, Danny had never been sporty.

"So you did kill Copelaw?"

He nodded.

"I didn't mean to. He... Oh, I just lashed out. When I realised he was dead, I was crapping myself, but at the same time I was relieved."

Rob swallowed and his left hand twitched compulsively. Luckily that wasn't the one holding the gun.

"What about the others?"

I watched the rain drip on the windows.

"Pam for a start," I added. "Did she get too clingy?"

He nodded.

"She was too impatient, too demanding. She stopped being discreet. Wanting to hold hands when we were together. She even snogged me a couple of times in public places."

I nodded, picturing the scene in Pam's car the day Bill's daughter came to the office.

"When she threatened to tell my wife, she had to go."

Just like that. Pam would never have gone to Rob's wife. But she had to be killed just in case.

"And Ania?"

"Who the hell's Ania?"

"The cleaner you tried to kill."

"So that's who she was."

"Another woman you tried to get into bed, but that wasn't why you tried to kill her."

He held the gun tighter.

"You heard her about to tell me she recognised you outside the building on the day Bill was killed."

The evening I was rushing off as Ania's phone rang came into my mind. Rob was one of the men leaving the office at the same time as Don. He would have been able to hear Ania through the open office door. Without being asked, Rob now explained how he followed her home one night, then drove out to Walkden the next day and parked half a mile from her home. He jogged over to her house and shot her as she left for work.

"And I'm to be your fourth victim?"

"I can't take the chance of your telling…what you know."

I shook my head, wondering how I had got into this mess. I should have taken my suspicions to Marti or had a word with Steve. Too late now. Rob gripped the gun tighter and stared at me. Where there's life, there's hope, I said to myself.

"Rob, why are you doing this? You cheated on your wife and she might find out, but…"

"I couldn't take the chance of losing the kids. If Emma found out about me and Pam she'd go back to Australia. She told me that after the last time."

How he expected this to stop her I had no idea.

"I'll never see the kids again."

He looked round as if expecting somebody to walk in.

"She left me once before when I…you know…I had a breakdown. I was off work for ages…"

Again he looked down as if exhausted.

"I was at head office in Hampstead in those days…When I recovered they transferred me to this god-forsaken place."

That explained that.

"God knows what they'd do if it happened again."

Time for a reality check, I thought.

"Rob, is pointing that thing at me really gonna help?"

"What do you mean?"

"Bloody Hell, Rob...people know I'm here."

"I'll..."

"You got away with killing Bill, but that was because there was nobody else around. You won't be so lucky this time."

He sat and watched me.

"What are you gonna do with the body – we're in a public building for God's sake. I don't know if you've noticed but I'm a bit heavier than you."

Rob tensed his neck and upper body as if getting ready to take a blow.

"I'll leave you here," said Rob, a look of petulant determination on his face, "say you were a burglar."

"You're not very good at this."

I watched Rob's movements – a twitch of his neck, a tensing of his left leg – while trying to keep perfectly still myself.

"Burglars work nights, not nine to five. And tackling two burglars within a few months of one another. A bit suspicious, isn't it?"

"Let me worry about that."

But I'm the one who's in danger of getting shot, I wanted to say.

"All this seems a bit drastic, Rob," I said.

Master of understatement, that's me.

"You don't understand."

"True," I said.

I began to think about getting out of Rob's office. There wasn't much of a gap between us. I would have to pass him to reach the door. I thought of rushing him but discounted it immediately. The gun might go off. There was no guarantee of where a stray bullet might end up. Keep the bugger talking while I thought a bit more, that was the best plan.

"Tell me about it and I might understand."

"I became a father late in life. Never thought I'd settle down and have kids. But it turned out to be the best thing that ever happened to me."

"Me too."

"So you'll understand. Katie and Will are my whole world."

"I don't get it, Rob," I said. "If your kids mean so much to you why risk losing them?"

"The trouble is, Gus," he said, suddenly confiding, "I...well, I like women and they like me."

I watched the gun in his hand and continued to weigh up my options.

"Not that I'm saying I'm God's gift or anything."

Of course not, Rob. I leant forward imperceptibly and tensed myself. I couldn't wait any longer. I had to do something. I heard a voice outside.

"Are you in there, Gus?"

"Don't come in here, Marti," I shouted.

We both turned towards the doorway. The door sprang open. Marti came in. She looked round the room. Her face showed a modicum of surprise as she picked up the shelf from the desk. She brought it down fiercely on Rob's right wrist. I heard wood on bone and a cry of pain. The sweetest sound I had ever heard. The gun clattered to the floor. I sprang to my feet, then bent down to pick the gun up. Rob brought his foot down on my hand.

"Bastard," I shouted.

I swung my left elbow up and connected with the tip of his nose. Nice one, Gus, I said to myself. Between us Marti and I were doing our best to spoil his looks. I looked at Rob slumped back in his chair. By now, Marti had pulled her phone out of her bag.

"Police...reliable.com, Ordsall Tower, Salford...a man with a gun..."

The words shot out staccato style. Once more I reached for the gun on the floor. Rob got up again. He wasn't giving up without a fight, I'd give him that. He tried to shove me out of the way. I shoved him back. For a few seconds we got involved in an apology for a fight like kids jostling in the school yard. He managed to get his hand on the gun. Before he could pick it up I trod on his hand.

"Tit for tat," I gasped.

Marti stepped forward, wooden shelf in hand, and swung it against Rob's left cheek bone. He dropped like a stone, then tried to get up. Marti smacked the wood across the other side of his face. He slumped down again, two nice bruises forming on his cheeks striated by deep scratches oozing with blood.

"Stay there," she instructed, her scouse accent stronger than ever, "twat."

Still he tried to speak. Marti cut him short.

"Shut it."

He knew when he was beaten. Marti turned to me.

"Police are on their way," she said.

While struggling to get my breath, I flexed the fingers of my right hand. I began to dial Kevin's number.

"If you're calling Kev, there's no need. He called me after you'd been cut off. They should be at the hospital by now."

"You mean..."

"Contractions started about an hour ago. Shouldn't be long now."

"Great."

"Kev didn't know where you were. I knew you were working today so came to Ordsall Tower."

I nodded.

"I looked all over for you. I was getting worried, then Karen told me you might be here."

Marti and I looked over towards Rob, who was trying to speak.

"Gus, I wouldn't have shot you, you know that," he said. "We can talk about it."

"I told you to shut it," said Marti.

She turned back to me.

"Would you care to explain what the hell this is all about?"

So I did.

* * *

I walked down the hospital corridor that evening, following the arrows towards maternity. Silly grin time, I said to myself, just like when Rachel and Danny were born. The events in Rob Dryden's office can't really have happened, can they, I kept asking myself. It took a while to convince Marti. Had she not seen Rob pointing that gun at me, she would have dismissed the idea of him being a killer. Now, even the reality of the police arriving; Marti and I having to make statements; Rob being arrested couldn't change the dream-like – make that nightmare-like – quality of the past few hours.

Going into the ward I took in Rachel lying on a narrow bed, looking knackered with dark circles round her eyes. Kev sat on a chair by her side, holding her hand. He looked as elegant as ever, except for his somewhat tousled, reddish brown hair. He's still smiling, I said to myself.

"Congratulations," I said, going over to Rachel and hugging her. Then Kev got the hugging treatment.

"Let's have a look at her, then," I said, going towards the cot by the side of the bed. "Oh, wow."

"You can have a cuddle if you like," said Rachel.

"I do like," I said, picking up the little bundle and looking down into her face. "Hello, Georgia. Aren't you lovely?"

The door opened. Louise rushed in.

"Here's your grandma," I said to Georgia.

She went over to Rachel.

"Oh, Rachel, I'm so proud of you," she said, kissing her daughter. "Well done. And you, Kev."

She kissed Kev and turned towards me, giving me a hug too.

"Gus, congratulations."

"Congratulations. Come and say hello to Georgia," I said, handing over the baby.

Louise took Georgia from me.

"Oh, aren't you gorgeous?"

"Another beautiful woman in the family, eh, Louise," said Kev in his peculiar hybrid of an accent.

He spoke with a bit of Irish, a touch of received pronunciation, some Salford.

"Just as well," replied Louise, "there's not many of us left."

* * *

Marti took a bottle of champagne out of the fridge to the accompaniment of The Definitive Ray Charles.

"At last we can celebrate," she said.

She took glasses from a cupboard and, removing the silver foil, opened the bottle with a festive pop. It frothed up on the kitchen table as she poured a fair proportion of its contents into the glasses.

"To Georgia," we said, clinking glasses and drinking deep.

I savoured the yeasty flavour and smiled at Marti.

"Congratulations, granddad," she added, giving me a kiss.

"Thanks," I said. "I can't believe how lovely she is."

"She certainly is."

"It's nice to get back to normal," I said, "after all that carry-on with Rob."

"It's hard to believe he killed Bill Copelaw."

"And Pam," I said.

"And he would have killed you," she added.

"Thanks for jumping in when you did, Marti."

I put my arms around her and we kissed.

"Somebody had to do something," she said. "You were just sitting there like a lemon."

"I would have thought of something," I said unconvincingly.

"I didn't know you were going to play Lone Ranger," she went on, rightly ignoring my protestations. "There was no need to do that."

"I know, but I didn't realise he'd have the gun at work." She took my hand.

"You were right, though. You knew there was something wrong somewhere and you worked out what it was."

"Suppose so," I shrugged.

"You know, on the surface he's so stable but…"

"Yeah, I know, but he's anything but. He was a high flyer in the head office in London. He got moved to Salford after a nervous breakdown a year or so ago."

"Really?"

"Yeah, his wife had left him because…"

"He couldn't keep it in his pants."

I nodded and grinned at her.

"You have a way with words."

We fell silent for a while. There was nothing else to say. Or maybe there was too much to say. What would the future hold for Marti and me? And for little Georgia? Would I be around to see her grow up? That meant I would have to stop taking stupid risks as I had with Rob. The rest was down to chance. I poured more champagne. We drank for a while before Marti leaned over and kissed me.

"We haven't finished celebrating yet," she said, kissing me again.

* * *

A very quiet drum roll sounded. The room was in darkness except for a spot on the drummer.

"Attention please, Attention please," he cried.

A buzz gradually died down.

"Here is a very important announcement."

A light flashed on to reveal Marti at the keyboards. Teddy Boy suit bright blue, setting off her black skin, hair gelled into a glorious quiff, stance arrogant.

"A Wop Bop A Loo Bop A Lop Bam Boom," she screamed.

Coloured lights flashed all around her. The band surrounded her with a driving beat, lifting her up like a wave. Dancers flooded the floor.

It was a month later in the upstairs room of the Park Hotel. Starting my second pint of Red Devil, I sighed in contentment at the thought that my leaving do was finally taking place. I was fit and well, had plenty of money to be going on with and the sun was still shining. Not quite perfection but it would do to be going on with.

An hour or so later, the band took a break. Friends, colleagues, former colleagues, family were sitting around chatting. I saw Marti get up on the stage, a guitar slung round her neck. Speaking into a microphone, she called for attention.

"Ladies and gentlemen," she said, as the hubbub died down. "A lot has happened since Gus retired, but I want to tell you about something particularly significant."

I looked round the room, remembering the events of the past couple of months. Since the altercation with Rob Dryden I'd enjoyed a quiet life. Marti and I had been to Brussels via Eurostar; Louise and I had started divorce proceedings; Rachel was harassed and knackered but happy; Danny was thinking of moving back up North.

"I'd like to tell you that Gus has fallen in love."

A loud 'ah' greeted this announcement. What the hell was going on? "He has fallen in love with a beautiful young woman called Georgia."

It was difficult to say whether the audience were relieved or disappointed at this. I was relieved.

"This song is for her."

Marti started to sing *Georgia on My Mind* in the style of Ray Charles. Everyone in the room, especially me, was captivated. Roars of approval broke out when the song was over. Marti came over to me and kissed me on the cheek. I had no clear idea what the future held. That word 'certainty' came back to me. Nothing was certain, I knew that now. I was fairly sure, though, that my career as a private eye was over.

THE END

BOOK II

DEAD CERTAINTY

PART ONE: 2012

CHAPTER ONE

"Is this suitable attire for meeting a paedophile?" I asked my reflection as I looked in the wardrobe mirror.

That was one thing about living on your own, you could talk to yourself without anyone looking askance at you. I straightened the collar of my pale blue open neck shirt. Running my hands through my hair so it looked a bit tidier, I adjusted my glasses. I could just about convince myself I didn't look too bad. I wasn't fat or bald and still had my own teeth. The broken nose added a certain something. Or possibly not. I looked down at the charcoal grey trousers with a crease and black shoes that were almost smart.

I admired Salford Quays out of the bedroom window of my third floor apartment, thinking of the day ahead. The view of remnants of the old ship canal, the swans gliding along, Old Trafford football stadium in the background never failed to give me a nostalgic kick. I put on the jacket of my second best suit and an anorak. Picking up my briefcase, I left the flat.

I walked the familiar route through the Quays past the old docks office to the dual carriageway on Trafford Road. Waiting at the crossing, I watched a lorry rumble by. The traffic lights turned red and a 67 bus, reminding me of schooldays when it was a green double decker, slowed to a stop. A young man came up from behind and ran past me. I crossed the road more slowly and made my way along Ordsall Lane, skirting the council estate. An overcast sky cast a grey pall over everything. A breeze got up occasionally, disturbing the litter in the gutters, blowing cigarette ends and drink cartons around. I carried on past Ordsall park and West Park Street, where I spent my childhood. It looked different then, having since been demolished and rebuilt. I tried to picture my old home and my old street. The cobbled road outside number 167; the back-to-back houses, their dingy bricks spread out into the monotonous distance; a trundling Cheshire Sterilised Milk float the only vehicle in sight.

Then my mobile rang, bringing me back to the 21st century. I pulled the phone out of my trouser pocket. Trying to focus through my varifocals, I noticed the date on the screen. Friday 24th February: 5 days to my birthday. I don't want to be a year older, I thought.

"Is that Gus Keane," said the caller, as I walked on a couple of paces.

A bloke, annoyingly cheerful like all these cold callers. Neutral accent, probably Northern.

"Yeah."

"Tony Murphy here, mate."

Mate? Who the hell was he to call me mate? Some wanker trying to sell me double glazing or car insurance.

"Listen, I don't want to buy..."

"Don't you remember me?" he asked.

Remember him? Why should I re...? Oh, bloody hell, wait a minute. I used to know a Tony Murphy, but this couldn't be him, could it? A vision flashed into my mind: a wide grin, long red hair, a jaunty swagger.

"Not Tony Murphy from...?"

From where exactly? Or should it be from when?

"From way back when? The very same."

"I thought you were dead," I said.

The words were out before I could stop myself.

"Very much alive," he said.

"Obviously."

And now you've come back from another world, from a different life, from the past. I walked on a bit further, then stopped again.

"I'm in Manchester on business for a week or so," Tony went on. "Got here yesterday."

"Yeah? Where do you live?"

"London."

Had he been in London all this time then? It hardly mattered. He may as well have been in Timbuktu for all the difference it made.

"I wondered if you'd like to meet up," he said.

I shook my head as if to clear the fog from my brain and bring reality back. I looked around me, mentally tracing the route to Robert Hall street, where Tony had lived. I am not talking to Tony Murphy, I said to myself, I'm not, it's just too...

"OK," I managed to blurt out, "Where are you staying?"

I believed in getting straight to the point. The telephone wasn't made for chatting, was it? Plus, I didn't know what else to say.

"The Midland."

He must have a few bob, I thought, trying to remember my plans for the next few days.

"Right. I'm busy at the weekend. What about a drink in the Park Hotel Tuesday night?"

I wanted to see Tony, I was sure about that. There were so many questions I needed to ask. At the same time, I was glad of the opportunity to prepare myself. There was a short silence. Maybe my local was too downmarket for him these days.

"Is that place still standing?"

"Yeah, going strong."

I pictured the Edwardian, brick building, unchanged for years, at least on the outside.

"That'll bring back memories," he chuckled. "I used to think Park Hotel was all one word."

"So did I."

For the first few years of my life I had imagined it was called the 'parkatel'. Only when I had read the sign did the truth dawn. Still people referred to it in that way. Nobody ever called it the Park or pronounced the two words separately.

"Anyway, do you fancy it?" I said.

"Yeah. Great idea."

We agreed to meet at 8 o'clock. For a moment it was as though we had only seen one another a few days ago. I stood still, deep in thought, pondering the surrealism of what had just happened. What would Steve think? More to the point, what would Brenda think if she knew? Where was she now? Did Tony know? Was he planning to get in touch with her?

I walked on, wondering how Tony had got my number. Or how he knew I still lived in Salford. I tried to remember the last time I'd seen him. Something told me it had been at a test match at Old Trafford. England v India? Yeah, could have been. Steve was there too; we were having a day off from 'A' level revision. That would have been the 3rd day, the Saturday. A bloody long time ago. Boycott was playing for England, I seemed to remember, Bob Willis too. Both grey-haired pundits now. I thought back to those days when Lancashire were kings of one day cricket; Salford were Rugby League champions; Manchester United were relegated. The world turned on its head.

Where did you spring from, Tony, I asked myself? How did you come to be contacting me after all these years? And where the bloody hell have you been in the meantime? It had been ages since I'd thought about Tony, but there had been a time when I'd thought of little else. Some nights I'd even dreamt about him. Anxiety dreams of course.

I tried to turn my mind to more immediate concerns when my phone beeped. Modern technology was all well and good, I thought, but this constant communication could be a bit wearing. Then I looked at the phone, saw the name Marti above the text and smiled. She'd been in London all week, staying with a friend while dealing with a case in the Crown Court. I could imagine her there now, a rare black face among all the lawyers, looking important and dead sexy. She was always busy, was Marti. When she wasn't fully occupied with her day job, she sang in a band alongside my daughter, Rachel. That was how we met, I reminded myself.

It would be true to say I had been missing her. The text told me she was going to see Billy Elliott tonight. She and her friend would be spending the weekend doing London: galleries, museums and all that. I decided to tell her what I had planned, mundane though it was. A cosy chat with a sex offender first, then chairing a child protection conference, tonight off to watch Salford. Baby-sitting Georgia tomorrow night, Sunday lunch with the family. Then I added:

Have had a strange phone call, will explain when I see you.

Having texted, I walked on thinking about Marti. I could hardly believe we'd known one another for two years. We had the ideal relationship as far as I was concerned: she took me to the pub; I cooked her tea. We weren't married, didn't even live together. We'd both tried marriage before, twice in her case. I thought back to what my life had been like when I first met her. My wife had left me; I'd been recovering slowly from a stroke; I'd been off work for weeks. The way things had improved since then must be at least partly down to Marti. Taking early retirement from

Salford council had helped too. Now I worked independently, a couple of days a week on average.

A little way further on, I reached Ordsall Tower, a down at heel 1970s skyscraper. As I went into the waiting area, a skinny man with a shaved head followed me in. He was of average height, late thirties at a guess.

"Do you work in Social Services, mate," he asked in a southern accent, unzipping a red anorak that looked brand new.

I turned towards him to be hit by his boozy breath. He took his leather gloves off and stuffed them in his anorak pocket.

"Yeah."

I'd long since given up telling people it was now called Children's Services. Had been for years in fact.

"I thought you looked like a social worker," he smiled, giving off beer fumes.

What do social workers look like, I could have asked.

"If you don't mind," he went on, "could you tell Josie that Simon's here to see her."

"Josie?"

The name didn't ring a bell, but there'd been lots of newcomers recently.

"Yeah, Josie Finch."

"OK, fine," I shrugged.

"Cheers."

He walked carefully to a seat near to an old couple, who looked on warily. I keyed in the security number outside the Children's Services door, wondering whether Josie, whoever she was, would want to see someone who was slightly pissed at ten in the morning.

* * *

I walked through the room where the social work team sat after asking several people about Josie. Finally someone from admin told me she was the auditor and was using the boss's office. I went to a door to the right with a sign saying Angela Bromwich. The latest in a long line of managers since I'd first started at Ordsall Tower, I thought as I knocked and went in.

"Well, that doesn't add up," I heard a voice say from the other side of the room.

The youngish woman in the grey jumper sitting behind the desk had a London accent, I reckoned, well spoken by my standards. Thin, bordering on skinny, she looked like someone who ran marathons. Short, fair hair, neatly cut. Judging by her tan, she had been abroad recently.

"Sorry to interrupt," I said, "Are you Josie?"

She smiled half-heartedly, peering tiredly at me through glasses with red rectangular frames.

"Yes," she said from behind the desk.

I caught a whiff of tobacco, then saw a packet of Benson and Hedges on the desk. Funny how the smell always lingered. Josie was too young for smoking to have affected her looks, I thought, but it would one day.

"I'm Gus Keane," I said. "There's someone in the waiting room asking for you."

She raised her eyebrows.

"For me?"

"Says his name's Simon."

Her eyes opened wide and she looked as if she were holding her breath.

"Simon? How does he know I'm here? And how do you come to be...? What the hell's going on?"

I shrugged, shaking my head.

"I just saw this feller on my way in and he said he wanted to see you. That's all."

Josie stared at me, her face impassive. She wriggled around in her seat.

"Right," I said, unnerved by her silence. "Well, I've passed the message on. I'd better be off, got a meeting. Nice meeting you."

I turned to go.

"No, wait."

I turned back.

"Sit down a minute," she said, "please."

She weighed me up for a while, before speaking again.

"If you have time."

I sat on a hard backed chair. She ran her fingers through her hair.

"Look, Gus, I'm really sorry I was rude. It's just such a shock."

I waited, confident she'd have more to say. I was right.

"Could you try and get rid of Simon?"

"I suppose so..."

She sighed.

"I'd better explain."

She took a moment to compose herself. I knew she was going to start telling me her troubles. People were always doing that, despite my being 6' 4" and having a broken nose (a memento of my Rugby League career). Must be my innate charm. Or something. After a couple of false starts, she began her explanation.

"Well, Simon and I were, like, a couple...we moved in together and stuff..."

She leaned forward, resting her elbows on her desk.

"He was gorgeous in those days. I used to go and watch him play cricket. he looked great in his whites."

Her eyes clouded over with sadness.

"I soon realised he had a drink problem and... Things got nasty, you know..."

Domestic violence, I thought. Worse than nasty. I nodded, wondering how I was going to deal with Simon.

"It was a complete nightmare..."

She looked down at her hands.

"He lost his job because of his drinking," she went on. "We got into debt –

he'd lost a load of money through reckless investments and..."

She sighed in exasperation, obviously reliving the whole thing.

"When I tackled him about the money," she went on, "that just made him worse."

She flexed her fingers so the knuckles cracked.

"The weird thing was in other ways he was really tight-fisted. Bought his clothes from charity shops, then sold them on..."

Josie stopped talking suddenly, as though realising the irrelevance of that last remark.

"Eventually," she said, "I left him, got an injunction, you know, all that. He's not supposed to contact me at all."

"Right."

She stifled a tear then went on.

"I moved up here last year. I thought I'd covered my tracks, but he must have found out somehow."

I'd come across this sort of thing depressingly often since I'd started in social work so knew what questions to ask.

"Is there a power of arrest with the injunction?"

"Yes, but I don't want him arrested unless it's absolutely necessary."

"But surely..."

"If you can get him to, well, bugger off, maybe he'll think he's got it wrong and I'm not working here."

I was thinking he should have been arrested, but Josie wouldn't want some macho looking bloke lecturing her. There was still the question of what to do about this Simon now.

"The thing is, Gus," she went on, "if he gets taken back to court, I have to go through the whole thing again."

She breathed in slowly and then out again.

"Instructing a solicitor, giving evidence, being cross examined, all that stuff. I'm just starting to get my life together again, I don't want it dominated by Simon bloody Natchow."

She paused for another deep breath, twisting her hands together.

"I just want to be normal."

I couldn't argue with that.

"Right. I'll tell him there's nobody called Josie who works here."

"Thanks," she said, almost smiling.

"It's true anyway. You're just visiting."

"I suppose you're right. Anyway, Gus, I can't tell you how grateful I am. I'm sorry if I was a bit off earlier."

I shrugged.

"I get worse than that every day," I said. "I'd better go, someone coming in to see me, then a child protection conference."

I got up.

"I don't envy you your job," she said.

I didn't envy hers, I thought as I went out. What was that Monty Python sketch? Why Accountancy is not Boring, that was it.

* * *

After leaving Josie, I went to see Simon again.

"Simon," I said, "sorry to be so long. I've asked all over and there's nobody called Josie working here..."

He jumped up.

"She's here, I know she is..."

"She's not," I said.

"Josie, I just want to talk to Josie," he half shouted, trying to speak precisely but failing to hide the slur in his voice.

"I'm sorry," I said, beginning to regret getting involved in this.

"Just let me talk to her," he pleaded, "please, mate."

"I can't let you talk to someone who's not here..."

The old couple looked on anxiously. The woman whispered something to her husband.

"I'm not leaving until I see Josie."

He sat down and folded his arms. He looked so much like my granddaughter did when she was in a mood, I struggled not to laugh.

"Simon, this isn't getting you anywhere. Please go," I said.

"And you're gonna make me, are you?"

He took a half bottle of whisky out of his anorak pocket. Twisting the cap off, he drank deep. I sighed.

"Cos I'm not scared of you, you know," he added. "You think you're hard, I can see that."

He took another swig then spoke again.

"But you come near me and we'll soon see who's hard."

"Are you gonna leave?"

With a final swig, he replaced the cap on the bottle. The bottle went back in his pocket.

"No, I'm fucking not."

"Watch your language, young man," said the woman.

Simon turned towards her.

"Keep out of this, Grandma."

Taking my phone out, I started to dial.

"I'll have to ring the police," I told him.

He sprang up clumsily and lunged towards me. I stretched out my left arm and placed my hand on his forehead. He came to a juddering halt, though his feet kept moving like a cartoon character. I pushed gently but firmly so that he moved backwards. With a bump, he sat back down.

"I'll have you," he said, "that's assault, that is."

I went back to my phone.

"You're witnesses," he said, turning to the couple. "You saw him..."

"We saw you try to attack this gentleman. He merely defended himself."

I held up the phone and spoke to Simon.

"Last chance, Simon," I said, "are you gonna leave or do I call the police?"

He watched me for a couple of seconds, then got up.

"All right, all right, I'll go."

He got up and zipped up his waterproof.

"It's like a police state," he muttered as he slunk off, "this used to be a free country..."

As I watched him go, I knew deep down he would never learn.

"I don't envy you your job," said the old man.

Nobody did, it seemed. Sometimes I was amazed anybody actually became a social worker.

"All in a day's work," I shrugged.

I went back into the office, thinking I still had my normal job to do.

CHAPTER TWO

"Has a Mr Tattersall come in yet, Hannah?"

The young woman on reception smiled, showing perfect teeth. Her unruly mass of dark hair was, I supposed, dead trendy. How would I know? In contrast her red jumper and black trousers looked disappointingly conventional.

"Yeah, just arrived. You're in demand today."

"No rest for the wicked."

"Must be why I'm always so busy."

She looked down at the note she'd made.

"He's got his solicitor with him. Yvonne from Pym and Sigson."

So he'd instructed Marti's partner, had he? Mmm, what was he playing at?

"If you could tell him I'll just be a couple of minutes."

"No problem."

I went into admin and had a quick look at the file to make sure I had my facts right before talking to Tattersall. He had been a peripatetic music teacher. For twelve years he had been going round schools in and around Birmingham, teaching piano and various string instruments, using his position as an opportunity to sexually abuse children. Once he had been caught and convicted, he was sentenced to four years. He'd been released on licence a year or so ago, but he was not on parole now. Since moving to the Ordsall estate just before Christmas he had found it easy to get work as a freelance musician, playing in various bands. The only trouble was, he'd started a relationship with a woman who, surprise, surprise, had a couple of kids. There was to be a conference on the children next week. I went back to reception.

"Karen ought see this bloke with me really," I said to Hannah. "Is she in today?"

I was glad Karen Davidson was the social worker who had been allocated to this case. She was good with kids but could also handle tossers like Tattersall.

"No, off until Monday."

"OK," I said.

In the interview room later, I sat opposite Edward Tattersall and his solicitor. Tattersall was medium height with a dark beard. He was 39, I remembered from reports I had read, but looked younger. He'd got dressed up for this meeting, navy blue suit, white shirt, silk tie. As if ready for action, he sat up straight. As I introduced myself, he stretched his arm across the table and shook my hand.

"I appreciate your seeing me today," he said.

His voice and accent – educated Lancashire – confirmed my first impression that he was a bit of a smoothie. Certainly out to make a good impression.

"I need to be away in a few minutes," I said before we got down to business, "so I'm afraid I can't give you a lot of time."

"I haven't got much time either," said Yvonne.

I'd been wondering when she would say something. Marti's business partner and best pal was overweight, mumsy, and disorganised. Yvonne Sigson tried to look smart and efficient but succeeded only in giving the impression she had flung her clothes on and missed. An impartial observer might have thought she was having a bad hair day, but she always looked like that. The enduring friendship between Marti and Yvonne was the best example of opposites attracting I'd ever come across.

"My client wishes to protest about the violation of his human rights," said Yvonne in a voice more suitable for projecting across a crowded room.

She was, I knew, originally from the Peak District but if she'd ever had a Derbyshire accent there was little or no sign of it now. Whatever she sounded like and however loud she spoke, Yvonne managed to convey an almost complete lack of conviction. She was, according to Marti, more at home with litigation involving large amounts of dosh, steering clear of the more sordid types of crime and children and family cases.

"In what way," I asked.

"I would have thought that was obvious, Mr Keane," put in Tattersall. "You are attempting to deny me a right to a family life..."

"Let me explain, Mr Tattersall," I said, "my job is to protect children."

"But..."

"And part of the human rights act concerns protection of children from harm," I added.

Nice one, I thought.

"You have been convicted of serious offences against children," I continued, "It seems there is a possibility that you will have contact with two children: Freddie and Sarah Attwell."

"My partner's kids. Imogen and I are thinking of moving in together."

"I'm aware of that," I said, "but as I am sure your legal representative has explained, the welfare of the children is the paramount consideration."

We went on in this way for a while. Eventually I got fed up of going round in circles and brought proceedings to a close. Tattersall got up to leave then sat down again.

"Let me get this straight," he said, "I am not allowed to live with the woman I love because a bunch of social workers say so but you employ a murderer."

A murderer? I looked at him, then at Yvonne.

"Surprised, I see," he said. "Obviously only a select few are in on the secret. What do they call it? Need to know basis?"

"I have no idea what you mean," I said, thinking I ought to say something.

"Let me spell it out for you," Tattersall went on. "Somebody who has been convicted of murder – or as good as – is working in this building as we speak."

I tried to make my face a blank. I knew he was talking rubbish, but I was interested in what he had to say. After a deliberate pause he continued.

"Oh, don't worry, I'm keeping it to myself for now. I'm sure the killer and whoever was responsible for their appointment wouldn't like it blazoned forth in the media."

I shrugged.

"Possibly not."

I couldn't quite keep the scepticism out of my voice.

"Apart from anything else," he added. "I have to be careful. If they found out I knew about them I could be at risk."

A smug look crept onto his face, as if to say, 'aren't I important?'

"I'll wait and see what decision you come to about Imogen's kids," he said. "And with that thought I shall leave you."

He got up again.

"I'll need to have a word with Mr Keane about another matter while I'm here," said Yvonne to Tattersall. "So if I can be of further assistance do get in touch."

"I'll bid you farewell," said Tattersall, "and do remember what I said, won't you?"

As he went out of the door, Yvonne heaved a sigh of relief. I thought once again about the nerve of sex abusers.

They were constantly on their high horse about some imagined grievance. The point being to avoid being called to account themselves.

"What was all that about," I asked Yvonne. "And what does 'convicted of murder or as good as' mean?"

"Haven't a clue," she said. "My God, how do you cope with all this stuff? I'm only here because Marti's in London. I drew the short straw."

Her shoulders shivered in distaste.

"Anyway, Marti seems to be having a good time."

"Yeah."

"She misses London, you know," she said. "I think she only stays in Manchester because of you. And her mum of course."

Marti had moved from London after 20 odd years to be near her elderly mother in Liverpool. She had a lot of friends down there and the Big Smoke still exerted a pull.

"She's terribly fond of you, you know," said Yvonne.

I was glad to hear it.

"It's mutual."

"At least she'll be back for your birthday," she smiled.

"Yes," I said.

I was looking forward to Marti coming back rather than my birthday, I thought as I left shortly afterwards.

* * *

At last I can prepare for the conference I thought, a few minutes later approaching Hannah again to let her know where I would be.

"Sorry, Gus," she said the second I arrived, "somebody else wants to see you. What it is to be popular."

Good job I'm paid by the hour, I thought.

"Who is it this time?"

She checked her notes again, then looked up at me.

"Imogen Attwell."

Edward Tattersall's girlfriend? What did she want?

"I can just about fit her in," I said, looking at my watch.

I talked to her in the interview room, where I had seen Tattersall. She sat hunched in a parka as though protecting herself from attack. She had short, brown hair and an air of frailty, looking older than she was.

"This meeting," she said as soon as she sat down, looking at me with sad eyes, "what's it all about?"

She put her hands flat on the table and spread the fingers out. I noticed the thin, white cotton gloves she wore and wondered what they were for. Weirdly they put me in mind of a snooker referee. Karen had explained the meeting to her in some detail, but I didn't mind going through it again.

"So my kids could go on this list," she asked after I had finished, "and they'd be 'at risk', like, officially?"

She shook her head in disbelief.

"That's right," I said.

"But I wouldn't let anything happen to my kids."

The number of times I had heard that or something like it. How could it be more straightforward? This man has abused children; I don't want him anywhere near my kids. You didn't need to be a genius to work that out, did you? It had the added advantage of keeping the social workers off your back.

"It's not a question of your letting anything happen," I said.

She sat back and folded her arms tight around her chest. That childish gesture showed me how vulnerable she was. She'd had kids when she was little more than a child herself. Their father had buggered off, leaving her with two children under three. She'd still managed to give them a good life.

"Not that Edward would harm them. You should see him with them. He thinks the world of them."

Words like targeting and grooming sprang to mind, as the alarm bells in my head got louder.

"You and Edward are thinking of moving in together?"

She nodded and pulled her arms tighter.

"Yeah. He needs looking after," she said. "I hate to think of him living in that Deadbeat Mansions. You should have seen the state of his flat before he met me..."

We were getting off the point.

"But, Imogen..."

"I clean the place for him every week. It's the least I can do for him."

I wondered when if ever Imogen had time to herself. Nearly every time I went in the Co-op she was on the till or stacking shelves. The previous day I had seen her doing her other job, delivering the Advertiser around Ordsall. With two young kids to look after as well, she still found time to clean up after her useless boyfriend. Even so, a lot of people would dismiss her as a chav or a scrounger. Not that that was relevant right now, I reminded myself.

"The important thing is," I said, "if Edward moves in with you, he would have constant contact with the children."

She tutted as if I were being deliberately obtuse.

"But I told that woman who came to see me. If you want me to I'll never let them out of my sight."

"That's not practical, is it, Imogen?"

Especially with a clever sod like Tattersall. Paedophiles targeted women as well as kids. Vulnerable kids, a vulnerable woman, just what Edward was looking for. God, sometimes this job did my head in.

"Not practical? For God's sake. I'll tell you what's practical," she said, getting up to leave. "Edward won't touch my kids. If he lays one finger on them, I'll kill him. And I'll castrate him first."

The child protection conference I was about to chair would be a piece of piss in comparison I thought as Imogen left.

CHAPTER THREE

That afternoon in my spare room that doubled as an office I sat down to update my CV. Before I started I decided to ring Steve.

I started in on my news almost straightaway.

"You'll never guess who phoned me today."

"John Lennon?"

"Not far out. It was a bit like someone coming back from the dead."

"Go on, surprise me."

I paused dramatically. Pity he couldn't appreciate it.

"Tony Murphy," I announced.

A silence followed, while Steve took in the news. Eventually he thought of something to say.

"Murphy? Never. What did that twat want after all this time?"

Steve had a deep, authoritative voice. Even as a youngster he had sounded grown up. The man of the world cynicism he had worked on during his long police career only added to his credibility. If he said Tony was a twat, Tony was a twat.

"I don't know yet," I said. "I've arranged to go for a pint with him Tuesday night."

"You're actually going for a drink with that pillock," said Steve, "I don't know how y..."

I tapped my foot on the floor. I'd been expecting a bit more...what? Interest? Enthusiasm? Curiosity?

"Come on, Steve. I wanna know what happened all those years ago, don't you?"

"No I bloody don't. And why's he turning up now? What's the point?"

A good question, I thought.

"I don't know, but I aim to find out."

"He'll be up to something," said Steve.

The voice of authority again.

"How can you possibly know that?"

I could picture Steve scowling morosely.

"He was always a bit dodgy..."

"Not Tony," I insisted, "some of his family maybe..."

"No maybe about it. His Dad died when he fell downstairs back in the 90s. Rumour was his wife pushed him."

"Yeah?"

"No-one would have blamed her."

"Suppose not."

"His brother was killed in pub brawl in Stockport a couple of years ago," added Steve, determined to finish off the family saga.

Secrets of the criminal classes, just the sort of thing Steve would know.

"Tony was never in any trouble though."

Why was I defending someone I hadn't even heard from for decades?

"Never got caught. I've got a bad feeling about this. Just be careful, that's all I'm saying."

"Be careful?"

I'd heard that expression a lot since Georgia's birth. The grown ups in her life were constantly saying it.

"Yeah. Just before he... went away or whatever he did," Steve went on, "didn't you say Vic Kennelly was after him for money."

I had forgotten that.

"He'd hardly still be after him now," I said.

"No, but it illustrates my point about him being dodgy."

If you say so, Steve, I thought.

"Whatever happened to Brenda," he added.

"I've no idea where she is, have you?"

"No."

She could be anywhere, I thought. She'd probably be married now and have a different surname.

"And what about that Debbie you were going with in those days," he asked. "What became of her?"

"Last time I heard anything about her, she was doing something high-powered for the European Commission."

"You always did get involved with ambitious women," he said. "Talking of which, are you out with the lovely Marti tonight?

I wished I was.

"No, she's working away. I'm off to watch Salford at the new stadium."

"Glutton for punishment, you are."

"You never know, we might win."

"Stranger things have happened. Is your Dad going with you?"

"Yeah."

"How is the old bugger?"

Steve had always been fond of my Dad.

"Fine. He'll be 90 this year."

Steve's amazement echoed my own.

"Give him my love," he said.

"Will do."

"It must be hard watching Salford these days, remembering how good they were when you played for them."

Hard, I asked myself? Compared with what? It had been great playing for a successful team all those years ago, being paid for having fun. But life was pretty good now, I reminded myself.

"It's not too bad."

"Suit yourself," he said. "By the way, I've got a golf day in Didsbury the week after next. Thought I'd come over to yours first. Monday the 14th, I think it is."

"That sounds OK."

"I'll ring you nearer the time. In the meantime, don't get too friendly with Mr Murphy."

"I'll see you," I said before ending the call.

My mam had always disapproved of my friendship with Tony, I recalled, because of his family. Now Steve was warning me off. Surely I was old enough to make up my own mind by now, wasn't I?

I thought about Steve's reaction, wondering why he hadn't been more eager to know about Tony. He never had been one to dwell on the past. There was something to be said for that, though what had happened all those years ago still niggled away at me.

* * *

Seven o'clock found me pulling up outside a block of flats in Weaste. I beeped the horn and waited. A couple of minutes later, a white haired man, tall and upright, came out and walked to the car. Not long ago my Dad would have practically marched but there had been an inevitable slowing down in recent years. Immediately he got in my Peugeot, he asked how 'that great granddaughter of mine' was. I would not have believed anybody could be more besotted with Georgia than me but Dad probably was.

"I had a phone call from Tony Murphy this morning," I said once we were underway.

"Tony who?"

I reminded him who Tony was and after a bit of patient explanation, my Dad began to remember.

"Ferret faced lad, only the size of two penn'orth of copper."

"That's him."

He tutted. I wondered if that were to be the standard response.

"Right bloody gomaloo and all, he was."

That was Tony put in his place.

"Come to think of it," he went on, "Wally Brignall thought he saw young Murphy in Jersey one time."

That was news to me.

"Did he? You never said."

He shrugged.

"It was that summer you went to France, I think. You were away about three weeks. By the time you got back, it must have slipped my mind."

I looked in the rear view mirror before signalling to turn left.

"When was this?"

My Dad thought for a while.

"Ooh, years ago. Late eighties, I reckon. Wally said Tony was doing all right for himself."

That didn't surprise me. My dad continued his tale of what happened on Wally's Channel Island holiday.

"At least he thought it was Tony, he never actually spoke to him."

So it might not have been Tony. Then again...

"But we all know what Jersey means, don't we, Gus?"

"Bergerac?"

He chuckled as I had a sudden vision of the nineteen eighties detective series set in Jersey.

"Not Bergerac, you daft bugger. Money. Tax evasion or avoidance or whatever they call it."

It made sense somehow. Do you sincerely want to be rich, somebody had asked during the Thatcher era. I'd always thought Tony would have responded with a resounding yes.

"Our Theresa phoned the other night," Dad said we'd talked enough about Tony.

My sister had for years insisted on being called Terri, but the message had never got through to her father.

"She'll be a bit warmer than us."

"Oh, aye, forty degrees in Sydney this week."

I'd rather be cold, I thought. We talked a bit about Terri. Even that reminded me of the year Tony left. Terri had flown from Australia for my mam's funeral accompanied by a very fanciable friend, Felicity. It was only as she was about to go back she told us she was gay and she and Felicity were in love. My dad, once he had cottoned onto what she meant, just took it in his stride, saying, 'I knew that, love'.

Meanwhile, I saw my fantasies about an older woman go up in smoke.

Half an hour later, I pulled into the car park of the City of Salford Stadium, the new home of Salford City Reds. It was a big improvement on the Willows but much less convenient. The old ground had been a couple of streets from my dad's place. We got out and went to get a ticket from the machine. Searching in my pocket for change, I heard someone call my name. Turning round I saw a young, black man approach.

"Paul," I said, "good to see you."

"You too, mate. I've not seen you for yonks."

"Do you know my dad, Harry?" I asked.

Introductions made, I put the ticket on my windscreen and we walked to the ground. A few people recognised me, saying 'All right, Gus,' or nodding. Very occasionally I'd get asked for my autograph. These strangers knew things about me because I'd been a professional rugby league player. They were aware, for instance, that my dad had named me after his hero, Gus Risman, who played for the Reds in the thirties. I still hadn't made my mind up how I felt about being called Gus Risman Keane.

"Will we get our first victory at the new stadium," asked Paul as we approached the turnstile.

"We can only hope," I replied.

"Definitely," said my Dad.

I huddled up in my anorak. Watching rugby league was getting harder as I got older, with the cold, the rarity of Salford victories and the discomfort of the seats. I was more worried about Dad but he always insisted he was OK.

"Are you still doing your investigations, Gus," said Paul.

"I've not done any for a while," I answered. "There might be some more work in the pipeline."

"If you need any help, you know where to look," he hinted.

"Certainly do."

I thought back to the time I had set up GRK Investigations with Marti's encouragement and become a private eye. My first case had come from Marti and I'd enlisted Paul's help as an assistant. He'd done a good job then and had made himself useful in a couple of cases since. I remembered what he was like when I first met him. He'd been referred to TRYS, a rugby charity I'd been involved with since I'd signed for Salford. He had got into trouble with the law and was well on the way down the slippery slope. Through his interest in rugby league, we had gradually convinced him there was an alternative. Now he was an upstanding citizen and did some voluntary work for TRYS.

"You'll be finishing your apprenticeship soon, won't you?"

He nodded.

"Yeah, a couple of months. Got a permanent job lined up."

Those words gave me a little glow of pleasure, but soon we got caught up in one of the best matches I'd ever seen. The cares of everyday life were a distant memory as the game ebbed and flowed. I forgot about Tony, Steve and pretty well everything else. After Salford took an early lead, Hull bounced back and led 16-10 at half time. Fighting hard, the Reds equalised before Hull took the lead again. Daniel Holdsworth clinched the match for Salford with a last second penalty. So the Reds got their first win at the new ground and we went home happy.

* * *

I was lost in a dream about Debbie Oldham, where all my fantasies were happening at once, when I heard banging on the door. My head full of distracting images of a girl I hadn't seen since the 1970s, I got up and put on my battered Marks and Spencer's slippers. A glance at the alarm clock told me I had only been asleep half an hour or so.

Maybe the phone call with Steve had led to the dream. I must thank him. But not whoever had broken into it, I thought, as I opened the door in my pyjamas. A woman of

Asian background, carrying a kind of handbag cum briefcase, stood ready to knock again.

"DI Ellerton," I said. "Where's the fire?"

She followed me in. She was casually dressed – jeans, anorak, trainers – and her long, dark hair was loose, all of which suggested she'd been called in on her day off.

"Any chance of a cup of tea, Gus," she said in a Scottish accent.

So it was first name terms today, was it? The previous time I'd had dealings with her, sometimes I'd been Mr Keane, sometimes Gus. Depended on her mood, I supposed.

"Certainly," I said, "when I've got some clothes on."

"Thanks."

"Just go into the kitchen and sit down."

In the bathroom I washed my face, wondering what she wanted. Despite her friendly manner I knew this wasn't a social call. All our previous dealings had been official, mostly to do with the death of Bill Copelaw, my boss at the time. I ran my wet hands through my hair, but still looked as if I had just got out of bed.

Going back into my bedroom, I had a terrible feeling that it would take me ages to get back to sleep once the inspector had finished with me. I looked for clean clothes, asking myself why whatever Sarita wanted couldn't have waited. And why she hadn't phoned first. Dressed in jeans and an Isles of Scilly t-shirt, which I had a feeling had originally belonged to my ex-wife, Louise, I went back into the kitchen.

"Right, tea," I said.

"You're a life saver," she said, "I was just looking forward to a nice, quiet night in when I got the call."

What call was that, I asked myself? I put the kettle on and got a white sliced loaf out of the freezer.

"Marti tells me you make a smashing cup of tea. And you're a great cook."

Does she now, I muttered to myself.

"I suppose you want toast?"

"Please. You know, you'll make someone a lovely wife."

I put bread in the toaster while I tried to remember whether that joke had been funny the first time I'd heard it. We chatted about our families for a bit. By the time Sarita had waxed lyrical about her little boy and I'd got into doting grandfather mode for a bit, the tea and toast were ready. Only when tea had been poured and we were tucking into toast did the Inspector get down to business.

"Do you know a man called Edward Tattersall,' she said.

"Not personally. I've come into contact with him professionally."

She took a sheet of paper out of her bag and unfolded it.

"Have you seen these before," she asked as she handed it to me.

It was a flyer, with a picture of Tattersall on one side. On the other it said:

Protect Our Kids From Paedophiles

Edward Tattersall is a convicted sex criminal. He has abused kids in Birmingham.
Now he is free to abuse Salford children.
Tell Tattersall he is not welcome here. If he stays it will be at his own risk.

I looked at Sarita.

"Bloody hell," I said. "To answer your question, I haven't seen them before. Who's responsible for them?"

She shrugged.

"That's what we want to find out."

I sensed she was holding something back.

"There's more, isn't there?"

She crunched a bit of toast.

"Tattersall's dead body was found in his flat at half six this evening."

"I take it as you're here, he was murdered?"

"We're treating his death as suspicious."

Reassuring to know she was falling back on an old cliché, I thought.

"He had a gig with some band or other and another member went to pick him up. She got no answer to her knock, saw the door was open and went in."

Those words took me back to the day I'd found a dead body.

"The woman who found him had two shocks..."

"Yeah?"

Sarita took another bite of toast and a mouthful of tea, then went on.

"First the dead body, then the news that Tattersall was a sex abuser. She had no idea apparently."

Well, she wouldn't, I thought.

"What do you want from me," I asked.

She got a pen and notepad from her bag.

"Well, what dealings have you had with him?"

While she scribbled rapidly in her pad I told her about Tattersall's relationship with Imogen Attwell.

"Because she has kids, we were planning to have a conference on them next...Tuesday, I think it is."

"Right. Have you actually met him?"

I thought back to the meeting in the interview room, realising he'd only had hours to live.

"He came to see me at Ordsall Tower today, mid-morning it would have been."

"Anybody else there?"

I sipped more tea.

"Just Tattersall's solicitor, Yvonne Sigson."

She raised her eyebrows.

"Yvonne? She doesn't usually deal with that sort of thing."

"Marti's away in London."

"That explains it. What did Mr Tattersall have to say for himself?"

"Oh, you know, we were infringing his human rights..."

"You're kidding?"

I sighed.

"I wish I was. Fellers like him are an insult to all the victims of human rights abuse around the world."

And to the kids he abused, I thought.

"He did say one strange thing though,' I added after a moment's thought.

She perked up at this.

"Oh?"

"He alleged that a murderer worked at Children's Services."

She pulled a face that spoke of confusion.

"Who might that be?"

I swallowed more toast.

"He refused to say. Very mysterious he was. He hinted that he would report the facts to the media if we didn't let him live with Imogen and her kids."

She shook her head in bewilderment as I went on.

"He also suggested that if this 'murderer' learnt that he knew about them, he would be at risk."

She wrote for a bit longer.

"If you want to know my whereabouts for today," I added, "I was at Ordsall Tower this morning, in the afternoon I was here in the flat. I left for the City of Salford stadium about seven. I got back about half ten. After that I was on my own."

The last case we had both been involved in had resulted in strong hints that I was a murder suspect.

"Thank you," she grinned. "I suppose you're going to solve this one for me, are you?"

I shrugged.

"I'll help in any way I can, Inspector. If you'd like to employ me as a consultant, that would be fine. Shall we say a hundred guineas an hour?"

"Shall we say on your bike."

Worth a try, I thought, as she got back to business.

"Was that the last time you saw him, when he came into the office?"

"Yes."

More notes.

"What about the girlfriend…"

She looked down at her book.

"Imogen…"

"She came in to see me a little while after Edward. I don't know if they'd planned it, but that's how it happened."

"What time was this?"

"Before eleven."

She asked me what Imogen had to say for herself.

"She came to plead her boyfriend's case."

I went through the interview with Imogen in as much detail as I could remember.

"Anything else?"

"Now let me see," I muttered, pretending to be deep in thought.

She waited, pen poised.

"Oh, yes," I replied, "she threatened to kill him."

She tutted.

"There's no need to take the piss."

"I'm serious."

She stared at me for several seconds.

"She actually threatened him?"

I picked up the teapot, topping up both our mugs.

"You could say that," I said.

"What did she say exactly?"

I pieced together the conversation in my mind before replying.

"Something to the effect that if he laid a finger on her kids she'd kill him, making sure she'd castrated him first."

CHAPTER FOUR

I looked round the kitchen, wondering how I got there. Waving a sheet of paper, I tried to work out what was happening. What was Debbie doing, lying slumped on the floor. No, not Debbie, it was my mam. God. I looked again. No, it was Tony.

"Are you dead, Tony," I asked.

"It's not Tony," said Debbie, coming up behind me, "it's your mam."

"Mam," I shouted again, panic in my voice this time.

She had fallen awkwardly and lay on her left arm, her head touching the concrete floor. Debbie spoke again.

"Feel her pulse, Gus, she might be dead."

"Loves me like a rock," sang Tony.

"Hear that, mam," I said, "Paul Simon. A song about the way a mother loves her son."

I went over to her, but it was Tony lying there. Debbie lay next to him. I searched for a pulse on my arm but I couldn't find it. I was dead. I can't be dead, I said to myself. "Protect our kids from paedophiles," said the man on the floor.

"Tattersall, what the fuck...?"

I looked again. Tony was lying there, brushing the hair out of his eyes.

"What were you expecting to find," he said, grinning manically.

I blinked and opened my mouth.

"I wasn't expecting to find you."

Then my mother spoke.

Footsteps in the next room drowned out her words.

"Help me, son..."

"Can't hear you, mam," I said, "somebody's coming."

It took a few seconds to realise (a) it was Saturday morning (b) there was someone moving about in the kitchen and (c) I had just woken up. Looking at the alarm clock I got out of bed. 9.30. Who was it? I searched for my slippers, put them on and went out of my bedroom along the short passage towards the kitchen. My mind was still on the dream I'd just had for the first time since around the time my mam died. Just after Tony went missing. That was why they were both in it. If I hadn't woken up the dream would have taken me out of the kitchen and in again several times, getting me more and more confused. In my actual kitchen, I saw Rachel standing at the sink, filling the kettle. Her black coat and handbag were on the back of a chair.

"Hello, Rachel," I said. "This is a surprise."

She would sometimes call round and let herself in, but I was seeing her tonight so couldn't help wondering why she was here now.

"'morning, Dad," she replied. "I was in the area and thought I'd drop in. Tea?"

"Please. I'll just go to the loo."

When I got back, having been through the same routine as I had when Sarita had arrived, I was dressed once more in jeans and Scillonian t-shirt. Rachel had put the kettle on the hob and was sitting at the table, where I joined her.

"Everything all right?"

She looked up at me before answering my question. Rachel had inherited my dark hair and blue eyes, but in every other respect she looked like her mother. This had become more pronounced as she'd got older. Her slim build, the way she held herself, her walk were almost identical. Looking like Louise was no bad thing, I thought.

"Yeah, well..."

She shrugged.

"You're not ill, are you?"

She shook her head. I wondered about Georgia.

"Nor is anybody else," she said as if reading my mind. "It's just that I had a bit of a shock yesterday."

"Shock?"

Hearing the kettle whistle she got up to make the tea.

"I became the second member of our family to find a dead body," she said as she filled the teapot.

"What?"

I went over to her and gave her a hug.

"Are you OK?"

"Fine," she said. "I'll tell you about it."

"We had a gig last night," she said once we were at the table with our tea.

"Right."

"It was short notice, some bloke's 60th, he'd been let down by the band he had booked. We said we'd do it, but we needed a stand-in for Marti on keyboards."

I poured the tea as she talked.

"We managed to get this bloke, Edward. We'd used him once before, he was good."

She paused for a moment to drink her tea. This gave me a chance to chip in.

"Before you go on, Rachel, I know what you're going to tell me."

Her eyes opened wide. She put her mug down.

"How come?"

I told her about DI Ellerton's visit and my dealings with Tattersall. She sighed and picked up her tea again.

"It was a Sergeant somebody I spoke to...Snow, I think her name was. Once she'd interviewed me she said I could go. I've got to provide a formal statement at the police station at half ten this morning."

I assumed Sarita had arrived on the scene after Rachel had been sent home. Even had she been there, the name Rachel Bertrand would have meant nothing to her.

"How are you feeling now," I asked.

Another shrug.

"I'll survive. It's all still a bit unreal, you know. He lived in a really grotty block of flats called Dedby Mansions – somebody has spray painted Deadbeat Mansions on the wall."

"I know it."

"I got no answer when I knocked on the door, then I noticed it was ajar."

This was reminding me all too vividly of the time I found Bill Copelaw's body in his office.

"I went in and there he was in the living room with his throat cut, covered in blood. I went towards him and nearly tripped over a loose floorboard..."

She shook her head as if to rid herself of the image in her mind.

"Rachel, it's OK, you don't have to..."

"No, I want to talk about it."

I nodded.

"Anyway, I soon realised I mustn't touch anything. It was pretty obvious he was dead. So I rang the police and waited."

"Bugger."

"Quite. We had to do the gig without keyboards. Normally Olivia and I would handle the vocals in place of Marti, but I didn't get there till half way through."

It seemed Rachel had had enough of talking about dead bodies.

"Olivia played a blinder apparently."

Well, I thought, that's something.

"Oh, by the way, did you know Danny's bringing his new girlfriend to lunch tomorrow?"

Wonders will never cease, I thought, looking forward to seeing my son. What did this departure from the norm mean? I might find out tomorrow.

* * *

"So you actually, like, found him?" asked Danny in his youth-speaky way.

It was lunchtime the next day. I'd woken up that morning in Rachel's spare room. Looking out of the window, I had seen a deep frost. Since then it hadn't got much above freezing. That made the family Sunday lunch that much more cosy. It was partly an early birthday party for me. I'd been handed cards and presents with strict instructions not to open them until the actual day.

"Yes," said Rachel, picking up a glass of red wine.

She had explained how she had come to discover the late Mr Tattersall in Dedby Mansions. Georgia was having a nap so it was safe to talk about dead people. We were in the dining room of Rachel's four bedroom house in Worsley, not far from where she and her brother had been brought up. Did Rachel's recent move to a bigger house mean more grandchildren might be on the way? It would be another milestone in my ever changing life, I thought.

"Dad's involved in it," added Rachel.

"What," said Danny, now in the middle of a mouthful of Merlot, almost spilling a drop on his denim shirt.

Rachel, her husband Kevin and I all knew what she was talking about. Only Danny and his girlfriend Natalie, who was meeting us for the first time, hadn't a clue what Rachel was referring to. I glanced over to Natalie to gauge her reaction. She sat impassive in her check shirt. No sign of alarm but I was willing to bet she was wondering what she had got herself into. Danny asked the expected follow up question.

"Go on then, what's it all about?"

"Well, did you see the local news last night," said Rachel, "about a convicted paedophile being killed?"

"Doesn't ring a bell," said Danny.

"I saw it," said Natalie, her right hand brushing back her short, red hair. "Somewhere in Salford, wasn't it?"

She'd arrived with Danny about half eleven and had impressed me as quietly confident, with a ready smile and a natural manner. She had made a hit with Georgia from the word go, so Rachel was impressed. Danny had got a job in an IT firm in Macclesfield about six months previously after spending a few years in Brighton post university. I gathered that Natalie and Danny had met on a walk organized by Macclesfield Ramblers. She lived in Bollington, a canal-side village and was Customer Services Manager at Chataway

Phones. She'd talked about being fed up with her job and wanting to do something more worthwhile, whatever that meant.

"Have you had dealings with this guy then, Gus," she asked, turning to me.

Natalie was an outdoor type, I would have said. The old-fashioned expression fresh faced came to mind. She was about 5 foot 6. Danny was even taller than me but Natalie didn't seem to mind him towering over her. Fair like his mother, he bore no resemblance to anybody else in the family.

"Yeah, and I had the police round on Friday night," I said, going on to explain about DI Ellerton's visit.

"At the time I had no idea about Rachel finding him."

"I still can't believe it," said Rachel. "I'd only ever met him once, about a month ago, but I'd never have imagined he was, you know, dodgy."

"It's impossible to tell," I said.

"I know it sounds stupid but what makes it worse somehow is that he was such a good musician," Rachel went on.

That made a sort of sense, I supposed.

"Mind you," Rachel went on, "he knew he was good. He kept on about having played in a top jazz group in the Midlands. Said he had to leave Birmingham when his marriage broke up."

She took another mouthful of wine.

"'Of course I'm classically trained' he kept telling us. As if he were slumming it by associating with us. I was half expecting the Halle orchestra to ring up in the middle of a set."

Rachel was on a roll now, maybe trying to cheer herself up.

"Oh, Edward, we can't cope without you any more."

I thought of Tattersall using his talent to abuse his victims. Rachel looked thoughtful for a moment then got back to Tattersall.

"I remember he went on about knowing something that would cause a great scandal."

"What was that," asked Danny.

Rachel shrugged.

"I don't remember the details and he was pretty vague anyway. I assumed he was just trying to sound important."

Which would have been completely in character.

"What did the police ask you," I said.

"All sorts, how long had I known him, did I know about his offences, could I think of anyone who might want to harm him?" she said. "I couldn't help them really."

Very few people could, I thought. Kevin had been quiet so far. Now, smiling as usual he chipped in.

"Just tell me one thing, Gus," he said.

My Perpignan born son in law, whose name was pronounced in the French way, had been concentrating on his roast beef until now. His accent was a bit more Salford by now, but still mingled with French and Irish from his parents. Apart from his excessive cheerfulness, he was very likeable and a good father. What more could I ask?

"Are you going to be investigating this murder?"

I choked back a laugh. Kevin had been inordinately interested in the truth behind the death of Bill Copelaw. He had seemed to think I had only got involved in order to impress him.

"I shouldn't think so, Kev," I answered. "The police usually manage without me. Hard to believe, I know."

It seemed to me the police wouldn't need a lot of assistance with this one.

"Danny's told me about the other murders you've solved, Gus," said Natalie. "I'm impressed."

I shrugged modestly.

"Thanks. In the case of Mr Tattersall, though, it looks like somebody found out about his past crimes and let a lot of people know."

Danny said what everyone was thinking.

"And somebody thought they'd like to bring back the death penalty."

There was a brief silence before Rachel spoke again.

"We don't always talk about murder, you know, Natalie."

"No," added Danny, "sometimes we go for hours without mentioning suspicious death."

He drank some more wine.

"Strange, isn't it, Rachel, to think only a couple of years ago our family was so boringly conventional."

His sister smiled at him.

"Yes, Mam and Dad were still together, then she went off to London with the most boring man in England."

Natalie looked from Rachel to Danny and back again, looking bemused, while I tried not to think about Brad, Louise's new husband.

"That's no way to talk about Mr Smart-Casual," put in Danny.

"Dad got himself a bachelor flat," said Rachel to Natalie, "a girlfriend and set himself up as a private eye."

Many a true word spoken in jest, I thought. I knew how hard they had found it to get used to their parents splitting up.

CHAPTER FIVE

The following day I left the flat about noon. Marti had texted from court, suggesting lunch. The day had started well – I'd always loved not working on Monday – and looked set to get better. I'd gone through my usual routine: a brisk walk around Salford Quays for 45 minutes, shower and breakfast. Since I'd had a stroke I stuck to the exercise regime religiously.

Outside it was an average February day, overcast but dry and not as cold as yesterday. As I walked out into Salford Quays, pedestrians rushed past me. Why was everybody in a hurry, I wondered? A couple of youths gave me a 'Who you looking at?' stare. I arrived at the tramlines just as the tram to town pulled in. The sleek, turquoise doors opened and I got on. I always thought the trams gave the city a continental air. I could imagine myself in Prague or Berlin, a spy in the Cold War era. Using the orange handrails to help me along, I found a seat at the back.

Minutes later I got off in Manchester city centre and walked to New Bridge Street to a futuristic building dominating its surroundings. Its concrete, steel and glass climbed to the heavens. Approaching the front entrance, I saw the lion and unicorn crest and read Manchester Civil Justice Centre. I could hear the sound of conversation and footsteps inside. Then the automatic door slid smoothly open. A beautiful black woman came out first, carrying a handbag and briefcase, followed by a group of maybe half a dozen people. She took a deep breath, as though relieved to be out of there.

"Marti," I called.

Walking towards me, she smiled and waved.

"Hello," she said, hugging me and kissing me on the cheek.

"Hello to you," I replied.

It seemed ages since we'd got together, in more ways than one. One of the penalties of going out with one of Greater Manchester's busiest solicitors, I thought. Why did I know so many dynamic women?

"Do you fancy The Temple for lunch?" she asked.

"Fine, yeah."

I noticed lines of strain on Marti's face. I kept telling her she worked too hard, but would she listen? Rhetorical question. As always, though, she was totally gorgeous. She wore a formal dark blue suit, cut a bit like a man's – though she did not look in the least like a man. A light grey silk blouse completed the look. I had no real interest in fashion but clothes were one of the things that made me look twice at a woman. I'd liked Marti from the first day I'd met her two years ago. There was also, I must admit, an element of lust in my initial response. Enough to cover a country the size of Wales perhaps. As I looked at her now there was no sign of it going away.

"What happened with your case?"

We walked on.

"Adjourned," she said. "Interim care order. Back in 28 days."

"Right."

"The mother wanted the kids back today," she went on. "I'm sorry for her of course, but..."

She shrugged. Marti had never been able to have kids and I knew how badly it hurt her. The idea of someone having their kids taken away would strike a nerve. Sometimes, I knew, she felt the unfairness that someone like the teenage mother in this case could have kids so easily when she couldn't. Not that she talked about it all that much. The only family she had now was her mother. She had no brothers or sisters and her Dad had died ten years ago. Whether that made her childlessness worse I wasn't sure. I sympathised of course, but I had two kids and a lovely granddaughter. There was always an unspoken 'it's all right for you, you don't know what it's like'.

"What have you been doing," she asked.

"Well, on Friday I had a call from someone I thought was dead," I replied, "and on Saturday I was helping police with their inquiries."

"What the hell have you been up to now, Gus Keane," she laughed, "I turn my back for five minutes."

"Well, the police inquiry you will need to know about," I said.

I told her about Edward Tattersall and Rachel's involvement.

"Poor Rachel," said Marti. "Is she all right?"

"More or less, I think."

We walked on a bit further.

"I never knew the guy," she said. "But the idea of someone being in the band who actually abused kids. And he was standing in for me. God, what a nightmare."

Nightmare was as good a word as any, I thought.

"Have you got any good news," asked Marti.

"I don't know about good," I said, "interesting maybe."

I then told her the story of Tony's phone call.

"Well, you do live, don't you? And here's me thinking you'd be bored without me."

I winked at her and took her hand.

"I'm gonna take the afternoon off," said Marti.

"Great. If you play your cards right, you can come back to my place after lunch."

"In that case," she said, squeezing my hand, "I'd better play my cards right."

We went into The Temple, to be hit with a buzz of conversation and warm air. Right on cue my specs steamed up. I remembered the time, years ago, when I'd tried contact lenses but some sort of weird allergy had knackered that. As we joined the queue of students and office workers at the bar I took my glasses off. Taking a napkin from a nearby table, I gave them a wipe and put them back on.

"What do you want to drink," I said.

She opted for a J2O, apple and raspberry. I tried to catch the eye of one of the bar staff. To no avail. You'd think someone as big as me would stand out, but I seemed to be rendered invisible whenever I joined a queue. I looked along the bank of beer pumps, wondering whether to break my usual habit of not drinking at lunchtime. A skinny woman wearing red glasses was ordering food a little way to my right. Her left hand held a walking stick. She looked familiar, but it took a few seconds to realise who it was.

"Hiya Josie," I said.

She turned her head towards me. After a moment of puzzlement, she smiled.

"Oh, hi," she said, her southern vowels sounding alien among the northern voices. "We meet again."

"Do you know Marti?"

"No."

"Josie Finch, Marti Pym," I said.

The two women shook hands. Josie's brown eyes smiled at us.

"How do you know Gus," asked Marti.

"We met at Ordsall Tower, I was doing the books."

"So you're an accountant?"

"That's right."

Marti looked as if she were about to speak, then thought better of it. The ring tone of her phone sounded from her handbag.

"Sorry," said Marti, taking her mobile from the bag. "I'll take this outside."

As she walked away, Marti answered the call. "Hello, Lily," she said, her voice fading as she went out of the pub.

"What's with the stick," I asked Josie.

"Sprained my ankle yesterday morning, slipped on the ice."

"Nasty."

Josie shrugged, then changed the subject.

"Is Marti a social worker?" she asked.

It was, I supposed, a reasonable assumption that Marti did the same job as me.

"No, solicitor. And a singer."

"A singer? Cool. Like in a band?"

I nodded.

"Yeah, A Lop Bam Boom they're called. They started out doing fifties stuff, you know, now they're classed as a function band."

"A what?"

"They play at functions: weddings, birthday bashes..."

And now, I thought, they're mixed up in a murder, at least indirectly.

"Right. They any good?"

That was an easy question to answer.

"Fantastic. I suppose I would say that. My daughter plays the guitar for them and Marti's..."

"Your partner?"

I wondered, not for the first time, if that were the right word.

"I suppose she is," I said, "we don't live together but we're..."

"An item?"

I nodded. I thought of how well Marti and Rachel got on, even though my daughter was twenty years younger. I remembered all the match-making Rachel had got up to without my realising it. I also recalled how long it took me to realise that, amazing though it seemed, I stood a chance with Marti. Josie changed the subject again.

"How long have you worked in Ordsall Tower?"

"Twenty something years on and off," I answered.

"How do you mean?"

"Well, I got early retirement a couple of years ago," I explained. "Then set myself up as an independent to do odd bits of work."

"So you don't work in Salford all the time?"

"No, I go where the work is. Mainly the Greater Manchester area."

I thought about the recent shortage of work that was putting a strain on my finances. I had another conference tomorrow but nothing else on the horizon. The baby P case in London a few years ago had led to an increase in referrals and more kids being in care. This should have led to more work but it had coincided with the cuts. Ah, well, this way of working was preferable to putting up with the daily grind. Not to mention all the office politics that went with it. It was certainly much better for my health.

"Anyway," I said, "I'll be going to Ordsall Tower tomorrow. Will you be there?"

She nodded.

"Yeah, should take me another couple of days to finish, I reckon."

She turned towards the barman and paid him.

"Better go back to my table. I'm off today," she said, "me and my friend have been getting a bit of retail therapy. Now for a nice, leisurely lunch."

"Sounds good to me."

"Thanks again for, you know...what you did on Friday."

I pictured the appalling Simon breathing alcohol fumes in Ordsall Tower.

"That's OK. Enjoy your day."

"Will do. Catch you later."

I watched Josie limp away, thinking about seeing Tony tomorrow. Again I thought about Brenda, trying to picture her. All I got was an identikit teenage girl from the seventies, complete with flared jeans and long, straight hair. Here I was, older and wiser, in theory at least, still thinking about it. I thought of that expression, 'one day all this will be twenty years ago'. Nearer forty in this case. God.

* * *

Marti came back in, anxiety on her face, taking my mind off the distant past. "What's up," I asked.

"That was Mum's next door neighbour," she said.

"Problems?"

I knew Marti had been worried about her mother for a while.

"Mum's had a fall."

Marti's mam had reached the age where people 'had a fall' rather than just falling over.

"She's in hospital," Marti went on. "Possible broken ankle. I'll have to go and see her, probably stay for a while."

I put my arms around her and gave her a hug. Marti would have to drive to Liverpool. Inevitably I thought of my own parents: my Mam, who had died when I was eighteen; my Dad, 'marvellous for his age,' everybody said. How long would that be the case? There was always something.

"Right," I said. "We'll nip to my place for a quick sandwich before you set off."

"I'd rather leave straight away."

"No," I insisted. "How do you think your mother would feel if she knew you'd skipped lunch?"

"Oh, all right, I'll have a sandwich."

She sounded resigned.

"I won't be able to go to Liverpool with you," I said, "I'm working tomorrow."

"That's OK."

"Give your mam my love."

"Sure. Oh, Gus, I'm sorry," she said sadly, "we've hardly seen one another for ages."

"Don't worry about it. It's hardly your fault. Right, where's your car," I asked.

"Underground car park."

I thought for a moment.

"I'm off to the gents," I said, "you go and get your car and come back here. Pick me up in the car park."

A couple of minutes later I went out into the Temple car park and stood to the side of a shelter built for smokers. Going inside would have afforded me more protection from the wind but I'd have had to breath in cigarette smoke. I heard a familiar voice from inside the smokers' enclave.

"But she must have recognised me," said Josie Finch in a stage whisper.

She went quiet for a while. I couldn't explain how I knew but it was obvious Josie was on the phone.

"Yeah, I know," she went on. "Anyway, I recognised her."

She coughed as only smokers can. It really was a pointless and stupid habit. Thank goodness Rachel and Danny didn't smoke. Josie spoke again.

"Course I'm sure. A black solicitor who sings in a band. With a fucking Scouse accent. How many of them do you think there are?"

That must have been why she'd asked all those questions, I thought. There was a brief period while Josie listened to whoever was on the other end of the line.

"It's OK for you to say 'don't worry about it'."

What's going on now, I asked myself as I heard the sound of a car horn and turned to see Marti's black Mercedes a few yards in front of me.

* * *

I walked over to Marti's car, lost in thought, opened the passenger door and got in. As I did up my seat belt and Marti drove off, I saw two women approaching Josie.

"You know that Josie we just met?" I asked as we left the car park.

Marti changed gear and glanced in the mirror.

"Yeah."

"She knew you," I said.

"What do you mean?"

I told her about the overheard conversation in the car park.

"You know, she did look familiar," she said. "I couldn't place her though."

"She obviously doesn't want to be recognised."

"A guilty secret," Marti smiled, "fascinating. Another mystery you've discovered. You seem to attract these things."

She slowed down for traffic lights and pulled up behind a 4x4.

"I'm trying to think why or how I met her," said Marti after a pause for thought.

"Could she have been a client?"

She signalled to turn left, frowning in concentration.

"Don't think so. I remember her in some other context."

We drove on a little way before she spoke again.

"No, no good," she admitted. "My mind's a complete blank. That'll annoy me now."

"You've got too much else to think about," I said.

"Maybe. I kind of think it goes back to when I was in London."

"That covers years."

"Yeah."

We turned into Salford Quays.

"It'll come to you," I said.

She nodded, looking round for somewhere to stop.

"I'll be back for your birthday," she said.

I was still trying to forget about that.

"I'd better tell you now, in case I don't get the chance before the day," she went on, "I'm taking you somewhere posh for the night."

"Can't wait," I said.

"Well, you're gonna have to. Have a shave and bring a suit. You look really distinguished in a suit."

She nipped smartly into a parking space. We got out of the car and made our way to the lift in Palace Apartments. As we got into the kitchen my phone rang.

"Hello," I said.

"Hi, Gus, it's Angela."

There was only one reason why the boss would be ringing me.

"This isn't about Tattersall, is it?"

I sat down at the table. Marti took her coat off and went to put the kettle on.

"Got it in one. I've had the cops round."

"So have I."

"You too? I suppose they'll talk to anyone who had anything to do with him."

"No doubt."

I could hear Angela take a deep breath.

"Anyway. There was to have been a conference tomorrow?"

"Yes."

"It would be helpful if you could come in as arranged," she said. "We'll have a meeting anyway, see if there's any help we can give to Imogen and the kids."

"OK. There is one thing," I said. "My daughter, Rachel, found the body."

"Oh, my God. How did that happen?"

I explained about Rachel going to pick up Tattersall for a gig and everything that followed.

"I don't suppose they do CRB checks for a job like that," said Angela. "Thanks for letting me know, Gus, but I don't see it makes much difference. We'll carry on as planned."

"Fine."

"Partly it will be an arse covering meeting."

"We didn't kill him," I joked.

"Quite, but somebody will be demanding an inquiry into how we handled things. And your experience and independence will be invaluable."

She was right of course.

"Thanks," I said. "I'll be there."

CHAPTER SIX

The next day I arrived at Ordsall Tower and went into the social work room, thinking how familiar the shabby partitions dividing the space into teams looked. The notice board was festooned with posters advertising a coach trip to Thwaites brewery, the next Unison meeting and a quiz night. A few people sat behind desks with mugs of tea and coffee, typing away at their keyboards or talking intensely on the phone. I took my waterproof jacket and jumper off and hung them on a hook on the wall. I walked over to a woman aged thirty something with dark brown hair.

"Hi, Karen," I said.

I pulled up a chair and sat next to her, putting my briefcase on the desk. Karen Davidson was as far removed from the stereotype of a social worker as you could get. In her smart grey trousers and white blouse she looked more like a high powered business woman. It was good to see her. She was one of the few people left in Ordsall Tower from the days I worked there full time.

"Hi," she said. "You here for the meeting about Tattersall?"

"Yeah, bit of a shock him dying like that."

She nodded.

"Yeah, but I can't say I'm too upset about him," she went on. "Not many people will mourn a creep who abused lots of kids."

"I don't suppose they will. Some will say he got what he deserved."

"Possibly," said Karen. "Rough justice though. I can't say I'm comfortable with that."

Just then Josie Finch came in, complete with stick.

"Do you know if Angela's around?" Josie asked me.

"She's in," said Karen, "but she's got a meeting with Gus and me soon and going out straight after that."

"Thanks," said Josie.

"She can be a bit elusive, can Angela," Karen went on. "There's been times I've been tempted to ring missing persons."

Josie turned to go.

"Either that or bring Gus in."

Josie stopped and looked towards me.

"Why Gus?"

"Do you not know," said Karen. "Gus is a private eye on the side."

Josie looked from one to the other of us, obviously wondering if she were having her leg pulled.

"Seriously?"

"Yeah, look him up on Google."

Promising to do just that, Josie left us.

"In the meantime, if you see Angela before I do," Josie added on the way out, "could you mention I need a word with her."

"No problem," said Karen.

We watched her walk away.

"Does she look familiar to you, that accountant woman," Karen asked.

"Who Josie? Don't think so. Why?"

What I'd overheard at the Temple the previous day came back to me. Josie knew Marti and Karen thought she recognized her. Strange.

"I just think I've seen her somewhere before," Karen replied.

"How's Emma?" I asked, deciding to forget about this little mystery for now.

Her eyes lit up at the mention of her daughter's name. Being a single parent had somehow softened Karen, knocking off some of the hard edges.

"Happy as the day's long," she said. "One thing about having kids is there's always somebody who's pleased to see you."

I smiled at the thought.

"Although she's gonna have to cope without me tonight."

"Oh?"

"Yes, I'm being allowed out."

Karen had moved in with her parents when eight months pregnant. She reckoned it had worked out better than expected. Certainly babysitting was rarely a problem. She had been in a bit of a state in those days, even going as far as handing in her notice. Then she had pulled herself round and cancelled her resignation.

"The Park Hotel quiz, no less," she explained.

Bugger, I'd forgotten it was quiz night. I should have looked at the office notice board more closely.

"You know how to live. I'm meeting a mate in there so I might see you. Bloke I haven't seen for years."

"You can join our team."

That was a thought.

"I'll see what Tony thinks."

I remembered Karen coming to work at Ordsall Tower as a keen, newly qualified social worker. It was hard to believe she was now mentoring inexperienced workers and doing it well. It hardly seemed five minutes since she'd started herself. The phone on her desk rang. She answered it, listening for a few seconds. A door opened to our right and a woman with carefully coiffured fair hair came out. A few years older than Karen, she wore a straight, black dress with a V neck.

"Hi, Gus," said Angela. "You OK?"

"Fine," I said.

"We could have our conflab in my room," she said. "Just give me five minutes."

Angela began walking back to her office. As she was about to open her door, she was accosted by Josie, who had entered stage right, carrying a handful of printouts. Karen finished her phone call and started to get her stuff together for our meeting.

"Oh, Angela," said Josie, leaning on her stick, "I wondered if I could see you about some...stuff..."

"Difficult at the moment."

"It's quite urgent," Josie added.

"Sorry, Josie," said Angela, "got to dash, try and catch me when this meeting's finished."

"I really do n..."

"For the last time, sod off and leave me alone."

Shock all over her face, Josie stood still, gripping her stick, as Angela turned on her heels. Then she gave me a 'what can you do' look, watching Angela go into her office.

"Josie," said Karen as though taking pity on her, "some of us are going to the Park Hotel quiz tonight. I don't know if you fancy it."

Josie thought for a moment.

"Yeah, why not? Thanks."

Karen said we'd see her there at 8.30. Josie started to walk away then stopped.

"Oh, by the way, Gus," she said, "I did look you up on the internet. You really are a private eye."

"I know," I smiled.

"Cool."

With that Josie left us.

"What's up with Angela?" asked Karen.

"God knows," I said. "She was a bit hard on Josie."

Karen nodded.

"Stress no doubt. You've heard the rumours about her, haven't you?"

"About Angela? No."

I was always the last to hear any gossip.

"Something that's supposed to have happened at her last authority. Derbyshire, Staffordshire, somewhere round that way."

"What was it?"

Karen lowered her voice.

"Financial irregularities."

To say I was shocked was an understatement.

"What, Angela?"

Karen shrugged.

"Allegedly. They reckon it was all hushed up, but who knows?"

Who indeed?

"It would explain how Angela affords all that designer gear," Karen went on.

"I didn't even know it was designer gear," I confessed.

"Oh, yes," insisted Karen, "She'd be lucky to get change from £200 for that dress."

Even someone as unobservant as me had noticed Angela had a lot of clothes. And didn't she have a house in Bramall and a flash car? I was buggered if I knew what make it was though.

"My entire wardrobe wouldn't fetch that," she added.

But you look a lot better, Karen, I thought. Karen had style; Angela didn't. Anyone could see it.

"And she's always off somewhere exotic," Karen went on. "It was the Caribbean at Christmas."

"All right for some," I said.

Angela was well-paid but she had three kids. Maybe her husband was loaded; maybe she owed thousands on her credit card. I thought of my cousin, Vince, who died without making a will. That had meant a nice windfall for me and my sister. Maybe Angela had inherited a few quid. On the other hand, maybe I didn't give two fleas' knackers.

Two minutes later we sat round Angela's desk, waiting for somebody to say something. I took out a pen and notebook. I wrote the names of the children concerned at the top of a clean page, reminding myself of school. Angela, unaffected by her outburst at Josie, decided to make an introductory statement.

"This is just an informal discussion in the aftermath of the death of Edward Tattersall."

We looked on expectantly.

"I'll take a few notes. We don't need a formal chair," she smiled, "but I'm sure Gus will keep us on the right track."

Since I had done the course that meant I could act as Independent Reviewing Officer, I had got used to the job of chairing meetings. Keeping people 'on the right track' was, it had turned out, something I was good at. Angela continued with her remarks.

"We need to be sure we have handled everything correctly. I am also aware that privileged information concerning Mr Tattersall has entered the public domain."

We all looked suitably sombre at these words.

"This may have had a bearing on his death. We need to be certain there has been no breach of confidentiality at our end. Partner agencies have to be just as sure."

She invited Karen to summarise the main points.

"Edward Tattersall moved to the Ordsall estate six months ago," she said, "took a flat in Dedby Mansions."

It struck me now how appropriate the nickname, Deadbeat Mansions was, given it housed a lot of, well, deadbeats.

"I see," said Angela.

"When he moved to our area," Karen continued, "he only had a week of his licence to go."

Crafty swine, I thought.

"Soon after this he began a relationship with Imogen Attwell."

"Karen, what was your impression of him?" asked Angela.

"A bit of a smoothie," said Karen. "Resented any interference from us, but he was always polite. Basically though, he thought he should be able to do whatever he liked."

I nodded.

"I'd go along with that," I said. "And he reckoned we're employing a murderer."

A collective exclamation of astonishment greeted this. I explained what Tattersall had said.

"Well, it wasn't me, guv," said Angela. "What about you, Karen, killed anyone lately?"

Karen shook her head.

"I've felt like killing a few," said Karen.

She got a laugh for that one.

"Anyway, back to business. Karen, what about Imogen?"

"It's been hard to get through to her," said Karen. "Don't get me wrong. She's brilliant with the kids. But she's...under confident, nervy. She has eczema, has to wear white gloves to protect her hands."

Poor Imogen, I thought, picturing her gloved hands in the interview room on Friday. As if she didn't have enough to worry about, all this aggravation had brought her out in a rash. Karen looked down at the notes she had made for the meeting.

"Imogen didn't make the most of her potential at school but she's recently signed up for a couple of college courses. Making up for lost time she called it."

"That's good," said Angela.

"She's an intelligent woman actually," Karen added.

"Except when it comes to men, presumably," put in Angela.

"Tell me about it," retorted Karen.

More laughter. Karen was on form today.

"Edward was always undermining Imogen," Karen went on. "He didn't like her trying to better herself."

Another way of maintaining control, I thought. Karen then went through the original referral: rather late in the day a probation officer from Burnley, where Edward had moved to on release from prison, had let us know Tattersall had moved into our area. On her initial home visit Karen had told Imogen there was to be no contact between Edward and the kids at least until we'd done an assessment and held a child protection conference.

After some more information sharing and discussion, the meeting came to an end. We decided to offer services to Imogen and the kids but didn't think any offers of help would be appreciated. At that stage we were reasonably sure we had done everything properly.

"Thanks everyone," said Angela as we got up. "I'll get the notes distributed asap."

"Oh, Angela," said Karen as she got up, "are you still on for the Park Hotel quiz tonight? I wasn't sure if you could make it."

"Wouldn't miss it for the world," said Angela, "you can tell I don't get out much."

"I'll give you a lift if you like," Karen added, "I won't be drinking."

Angela grinned. I'd never seen her so happy.

"Great. I can get legless. Show the team the real me."

I can't wait, I said to myself. That would be a sight worth seeing. Karen said she'd pick her up at eight o'clock.

"Fine," said Angela. "And I suppose I'd better book a day's leave tomorrow,"

Karen went out and I followed her. It seemed ages since I'd been on a works night out. A few years ago they had been a regular occurrence. What sort of night would we have in the Park Hotel, I wondered. Did Angela know Josie was coming? That should be fun.

PART TWO: 1974

CHAPTER SEVEN

I left the house to get a bit of fresh air on a sunny Tuesday morning in June. Having just about worked out dramatic irony in Macbeth and memorized some quotations, I deserved a break. As I strolled along 'If it were done when 'tis done' still baffled the hell out of me. What on earth was it supposed to mean? It could hardly be done when it wasn't done, could it? I fancied a long, country walk but a stroll round the back streets of Salford would have to do. I'd only gone a few yards when I heard somebody calling my name.

"Gus, Gus."

It didn't register at first, I was thinking about the trial I had lined up for Salford the following week. If I did well they might sign me. Getting paid for playing rugby league, could anything be more exciting? Stopping and turning round I saw a girl with long, dark hair rushing towards me, struggling to stay upright on her platform soles. I waited for her to catch up, noticing the way her blue flares flapped around as she moved.

Looking along West Park street I took in the building site across the road. Ours was one of the few old back to back houses left. All around new houses and flats, all in the same pale brick, had been springing up. Soon my home would be bulldozed and we'd move to Weaste. Only a couple of miles away but it felt like a major change.

"Hello," I said, as the girl got nearer, "this is a surprise."

Brenda McDonald was the last person I would have expected to be running after me in the street. The platforms added at least a couple of inches to her height but she was still a foot shorter than me.

"Have you seen Tony," she asked.

Tony, I might have known.

"Not since Saturday. Me and Steve went to the test match with him."

"Do you know where he is?"

I fiddled with the buttons on my purple granddad vest.

"At home, I suppose. He'll be revising, same as me."

I looked down at my new, brown boots, almost covered by my jeans. Brenda shook her head.

"Oh, Gus," she said, "he's..."

She clutched a crumpled envelope in one hand, screwing up a handkerchief in the other. She dabbed at her red eyes and sniffed, unable to get the words out. She looked even bustier than usual. Her long-sleeved red t-shirt was baggy on her, but if she'd chosen a bigger size to hide her pregnancy, it hadn't worked.

"I was just going for a walk," I said. "Why not join me?"

Anything but stand still while she fought her tears. She shrugged.

"If you like," she said. "Won't Debbie mind?"

Why should Debbie mind? Just because you were going out with someone didn't mean they ruled your life, did it?

"Shouldn't think so."

We turned left down Oxford street towards Ordsall Park. Why did I feel so awkward with Brenda by my side? Well, she was a girl for one thing and a girl I didn't know all that well. And I couldn't help wondering what my mam would say if she saw me out with a pregnant woman.

After a while, Brenda got a grip on herself. Going through the gates we walked in the direction of the swings where I'd played as a kid. Some lads who should have been in school were playing cricket, using a tree as the wicket. Why couldn't Brenda live further away, I asked myself? Then she would have had to bother somebody else. After a while I stopped by a bench.

"Let's sit down," I said.

We sat side by side on the bench. Brenda cleared her throat, twisting the hankie a bit more.

"Now, tell me what's up," I said.

I was about ready to face whatever Brenda had to tell me. As ready as I'd ever be anyway.

"Oh, Gus, I'm so worried about Tony."

"Worried? Why?"

"He's...well, have a look at this."

She thrust the envelope into my hand.

"What's this?"

She sniffed.

"A letter, it's...read it, Gus, tell me what you think."

I took out a sheet of Basildon Bond and unfolded it, recognizing Tony's outsize handwriting. As usual it was hard to read, but I managed to make it out eventually:

"Dear Brenda," I read, "I'm not sure how to put this into words, but I'm going away and I won't be back. I'm sorry to upset you but it's for the best. I just can't take the pressure any more. Everybody's hassling me to do things I can't do. Where I am going perhaps I'll get some peace. Don't look for me; you'll never find me. You'll soon realise you're better off without me. Love, Tony."

What was all that about? It didn't sound like Tony. I pictured him at the cricket, chatting away to Bert and Mavis, a couple of pensioners sitting next to us. By the tenth over he had formed a lifelong friendship with them. Now Brenda and I sat in silence for a while. At last she said something.

"What do you think?"

A good question.

"I don't know what to think."

'What are you asking me for, I'm only eighteen' would have been a better answer. Brenda was a year younger, how was she expected to cope with all this? She was the one going through it, I reminded myself. I'd be able to go away and forget about it once she'd gone. Doing A-level revision began to look almost attractive. Brenda sighed.

"When I got the letter, I wasn't sure what to do."

Who would be?

"I phoned his mother. She'd had a letter too. She had no idea where he could be."

She sniffed and wiped her nose before continuing.

"She didn't seem bothered. Said he'd come home when he was hungry."

Maybe she was right, I thought.

"Honestly, that woman," Brenda went on. "Calls herself a mother."

Tony's older brother was in prison, probably sharing a cell with his dad, so maybe Tony hadn't had that good an upbringing.

"I don't think she's a full shilling, myself," said Brenda, "her husband knocks her about, you know."

I had heard something to that effect, but it wasn't a subject people generally talked about. In spite of living in that sort of environment, by some miracle Tony had managed to stay out of trouble.

"Then I thought of getting in touch with you, Gus."

"I see."

"I didn't go to work – told the boss I was sick – and came straight to your house."

What did she expect from me? It all sounded like Tony playing silly buggers to me, but no way was I going to tell Brenda that.

"Gus, do you think the police are after him?"

I thought for a moment then shook my head.

"Tony? No."

"It's just that...well, you know that bloke who lives in Captain Fold road?"

"What bloke?"

"Sid Pendleton, he interferes with kids..."

I looked at her, disbelief on my face.

"What's that got to do with Tony?"

"A few of the lads in Little Hulton went round and gave him a good hiding. He's in intensive care."

Would Tony do anything like that, I wondered? For him, Steve and me keeping out of trouble was almost a golden rule. We had too much to lose. I'd always thought Tony had got stuck in at school to escape the influence of his criminal family.

"Do you think Tony was one of them?"

More fool him if he was. She shrugged helplessly.

"When did you last see Tony," I asked.

Getting the facts of the matter was comforting somehow.

"Friday night."

I nodded.

"Tonight we were supposed to be going to see Murder on the Orient Express," Brenda explained, "at the Carlton. That was a definite arrangement."

She went silent again. She seemed to be building pauses into this little scene like an actress.

"Gus, I might never see him again."

More dabbing away of tears with the hankie. I did feel sorry for the poor lass, but what could I do?

"How can I be better off without him? Without the man I love?"

The man I love? It was all sounding too grown up for me.

"How will I cope with a baby if Tony's not there? I'll be an unmarried mother."

She put the hankie in her pocket.

"People call them single parents now but it amounts to the same thing," she said. "God, what's my mam going to say if Tony really has gone away?"

'I told you so' was the obvious thing that sprang to mind. Something else I couldn't say to Brenda.

"She went mad when she knew I was pregnant. Only the thought of us getting married calmed her down. We've got a house lined up in Little Hulton and everything."

She got her hankie out again to dry her eyes. The park fell silent. Neither of us knew what to say. I read the letter again, going over key phrases to see if I could find some deeper meaning. But it was just a letter.

"Listen, Brenda," I said after a while, "maybe Tony just needs a break."

"A break?"

Now what could I say?

"He's probably gone off somewhere to think things over where nobody can...make any demands on him."

'Make any demands on him', nice one, Gus.

"What?"

She was obviously unimpressed by my words of wisdom.

"When he does decide to come back he'll be more able to face up to things."

"What has he got to face up to," said Brenda. "I'm having the bloody baby."

There was no answer to that. None of this was fair on Brenda, that was for sure. She got up.

"I'd better go, let you get on. If you hear from Tony, you will let me know, won't you?"

"Definitely."

I walked with her for a while until we got near my house.

"Well, I hope everything gets sorted out OK, Brenda," I said.

"Thanks," she said, touching my hand.

As she walked away, doubtless still worrying about Tony, I heaved a sigh of relief. Was Tony worth worrying about, I asked myself? I was silently cursing him for causing all this bother. At home, I tried to get back to work but it was hard to concentrate. I thought back to the day at the cricket. During the afternoon Tony's mood had changed. He'd rambled on, complaining that his life was ruined; that he didn't want to marry Brenda but was being forced into it; that he'd be stuck in Little Hulton all his life.

"The world was opening up for me," he had said, "now it's closing in on me."

Bloody drama queen, I thought, as I replayed the words in my head.

"It's all right for you, Gus," he had said at some point, "when I'm living in wedded bliss you'll either be at University, with loads of posh birds throwing themselves at you..."

I'd let out a hoot of laughter at this.

"Or you'll be playing for Salford. Either way you'll have the women flocking round you."

I could see his point. Not about the women, but I did have something he didn't have: choice.

CHAPTER EIGHT

The next day I was trying to get to grips with the ablative absolute when somebody knocked on the door. Assuming it was Brenda, I went to answer it, wondering if I could face any more of her angst. I'd tried to put Tony and his letter out of my mind, but it had been impossible. Phrases from it kept coming back to me; I had remembered more of it than I'd thought. If only I could remember Latin grammar as easily. I opened the door, trying to think of something to say to Brenda. This dilemma was rendered irrelevant when I saw a man in blue overalls on the doorstep. Tony's uncle.

"Hello, Vic."

He was only a few years older than his nephew, early twenties perhaps.

"Can I have a word, Gus?"

I asked him in. We went into the front room, where we sat facing one another. My offer of tea was turned down.

"I can't stay long," said Vic, "I'm on my dinner hour."

Thank goodness for that, I thought.

"I just wondered if you'd seen Tony."

Someone else looking for Tony. The expression pain in the arse sprang to mind.

"No, not since Saturday – at the match, you know."

He nodded.

"Oh, yeah, I saw you there, didn't I?"

There was a superficial family resemblance between Vic and Tony. Both were short arses; their hair colour was similar.

"Yeah, a good day's cricket, that," he said, "Good player, that Gavaskar."

"Yeah. He upset Tony though."

"How come?"

He took out a packet of Park Drive.

"On the way to the ground," I explained, "Steve bet Tony 50 pence that Gavaskar would score a century for India. Tony took the bet."

"Tony would have taken any bet. He was always losing money on the horses. PD, Gus," he said, offering me the packet.

I refused. Vic took a box of Swan Vestas from his overalls and lit up.

"At 143 for 7 Tony said it was a dead certainty he'd win the bet," I went on. "Then Gavaskar and Abid Ali started to build up that partnership."

"Yeah, brilliant that was."

I pictured the Indian opening batsman hitting a boundary to bring up his century.

"When Gavaskar got his ton, Tony said, 'that's all I need.'"

Vic grinned.

"I bet he was sick as a parrot. Maybe that's why he's gone off."

Unlikely, I thought, but it was just after the bet went wrong that Tony's mood had changed. Could something as trivial as losing 50p have been the final straw?

"I don't suppose you know where he is?"

"No idea. Have you tried his mam? Or Brenda?"

He put his fag in his mouth and inhaled deeply.

"Yeah, they reckon he's buggered off somewhere," he said.

275

"That's what Brenda told me," I said. "I thought he'd be back by now, exams start soon."

Vic looked deep in thought and took another drag from his cigarette.

"Brenda thinks he's never coming back," he said. "She mentioned summat about a letter."

"Well, she seemed a bit emotional, you know, might have got things out of proportion."

He smoked in silence for a while. For a man in a hurry he was very relaxed.

"It's a bit awkward, Gus, know what I mean?"

I didn't but nodded anyway. What was awkward, I asked myself? If it concerned Tony why should Vic find that awkward? More importantly why didn't people leave me alone?

"I need to see him urgently," Vic went on. "Very urgently."

"Right."

Was it me or was there an air of menace in the room? Vic Kennelly was not a man to cross or so everybody said. Then I remembered a brief exchange of words between Tony and Vic at Old Trafford on Saturday. Vic had stopped en route to the bar to talk to us. Just as he was going on his way, he had stopped.

"By the way, Tony," he'd said, "when are you gonna let me have that money?"

"Couple of days," Tony had replied, "I'll call round."

Tony had answered too quickly, a touch of anxiety in his voice.

"Champion," Vic had said. "Wouldn't want any unpleasantness, would we?"

Tony had sighed as Vic walked off.

"Something else to worry about," he'd said.

Until now I'd thought nothing of it, having got a bit fed up of Tony's whingeing by that stage. But was it one of the 'other things' he had referred to in the letter? If Vic Kennelly wanted money from you, it was bad news. Now that I thought about it, Tony never seemed to be short of money. He'd had several old bangers in the front garden of his house in Little Hulton over the past year or so. They'd be in bits for ages until he had fixed them. Then he would sell them, presumably at a profit. Now the sound of Vic's voice brought me back to the present.

"So if you do know where he is or if you hear anything, you will let me know, won't you?"

The 'or else' was unspoken.

"Listen, Vic," I said, deciding to assert myself, "I don't know what's happening with Tony and I don't want to know."

Vic took another drag of his Park Drive and listened intently.

"I've got better things to worry about. So if I hear where he is I'll tell you, Brenda, his mam. I'll even tell Pope Paul if you like."

Vic got up.

"Champion," he said.

* * *

I got back to my swotting, feeling smug. That was telling him, Gus, I said to myself. I was confident I'd hear no more about Tony until he came back with his tail between his legs. No such luck. Half an hour later another knock at the door. This time a uniformed policeman had come calling.

"PC Downton," he announced self-importantly. "Am I speaking to Gus Keane?"

"Yes."

"Good afternoon, Mr Keane. I'm making enquiries about an Anthony Peter Murphy," the constable went on.

I might have known

"Tony? Join the club."

"Sorry."

"Nothing. Come in."

In the front room he sat on the settee, placed his helmet on the table and took a notebook and pencil from his breast pocket. I offered tea and again it was refused. I sat in what I was beginning to think of as my usual armchair.

"Just a few questions, Mr Keane," said PC Downton, "nothing to worry about."

"Right."

"I understand Mr Murphy is a close friend of yours."

"Yeah, we've known each other since...well, since birth really."

"He doesn't live round here though."

What did that have to do with it? It wasn't as if he lived at the other end of the earth.

"He lived in Robert Hall Street, just round the corner, until about a year or so ago..."

"I see."

"Then he moved to Little Hulton."

Then the PC finally got to the point.

"I don't suppose you know where Anthony Murphy is at this moment in time, do you?"

"No, no idea."

"You're quite sure about that?"

I took a deep breath.

"Absolutely positive. Any particular reason for asking?"

He wrote in his notebook.

"This is part of a current inquiry. We're anxious to speak to Mr Murphy – he may be able to help us."

I nodded. I decided to say no more unless I had to.

"I wonder, Mr Keane," the officer continued, "whether you know Mr Sidney Pendleton?"

The name rang a bell but I couldn't remember where I had heard it before.

"I don't think so."

"You don't remember reading about him in the paper?"

I shook my head.

"I haven't really got time for that, exams, you know."

I hadn't got time to answer a lot of questions either, but maybe I shouldn't say so. He tapped his pencil on the notebook, then spoke again.

"Getting back to your friend, Mr Murphy, his fiancée, Miss McDonald, seems to think he's missing."

"Missing?"

"In the sense that nobody knows where he is."

He licked the tip of his pencil.

"Miss McDonald said she'd had a letter."

I gave another nod.

"Yes."

"She was kind enough to let me see it."

I nodded again.

"Can I ask you, Mr Keane, whether you entered into financial transactions with Mr Murphy?"

It took a while to consider this. All I said was:

"Financial transactions?"

"Come now, Mr Keane, you know what financial transactions are."

Cheeky twat.

"I know what the words mean but I find it hard to think of 'transactions' in relation to Tony."

He wrote down what I said.

"Well," he explained, "did you buy anything from him at all or sell him any items?"

I shook my head.

"No, I did neither of those things."

I thought being precise was advisable.

"I see. On another matter, Miss McDonald seemed to be concerned about her fiancé's state of mind."

Whatever that meant, I thought, wondering what I'd say if he asked my opinion of Tony's state of mind. It was getting a bit much, I couldn't help thinking. If he failed to turn up for his exams would each of his teachers call round in turn to ask for an explanation? Just then I heard the front door open and close. Oh, God, I said to myself. My mam was back from shopping.

"That'll be my mother," I said.

Then she burst in with a shopping bag in each hand. I didn't know whether to be pleased about the interruption or worried about what the hell she would say. When I saw the look on her face, I opted for the latter. She stared at the officer of the law, her eyes resting on his notebook.

"What's going on?"

She undid the buttons on her beige mac, revealing a blue blouse and dark green skirt. She patted her brown hair into place. People said I looked like her; I couldn't see it myself.

"This is PC Downton, mam," I said.

"And what does PC Downton want?"

"I was just asking your son about Anthony Murphy."

My mother harrumphed loudly. She sat down on the other armchair, putting the bags on the floor beside her.

"Tony Murphy," she said as though the name were a swear word, "haven't I always told you he spells trouble with a capital T?"

The PC and I spoke at once.

"If I could just explain, Mrs Keane..."

"Mam, it's not..."

She ignored us.

"Now he's brought the police to the house."

"It's purely routine, Mrs Keane," PC Downton managed to get out. "Your son's not in any trouble."

"Hmm," she said, getting up. "It's all very well for you to say that, but you don't have the neighbours to worry about."

She left the room without explanation.

"Now then," said Downton, "we were talking about Mr Murphy."

I'd have to get used to hearing my friends referred to as 'Mr', I thought, and being called Mr myself.

"Yeah."

"How would you describe his state of mind?"

I wouldn't, I almost said. It wasn't something I had ever thought about.

"Well, he seemed OK last time I saw him. That was on Saturday at Old Trafford cricket ground."

"I see."

The officer wrote a few notes and looked at me expectantly.

"He got a bit maudlin after a few pints."

"Maudlin?"

I thought back to that day again.

"Yeah, feeling sorry for himself. He 'had to' get married and he wasn't happy about it."

More notes followed this.

"And you think that's why he's gone off?"

My mam came in at that point with a tray in her hands. She'd put on the floral patterned house coat that she wore whenever she was at home. She placed the tray with infinite care on the table in front of us.

"Tea, constable?"

"That's very nice."

She began to pour tea into three china cups that were normally brought out only on Sundays.

"To answer your question," I said, determined not to be put off by my mother's presence, "I don't think he's gone off at all. I reckon he'll soon be back expecting everybody to make a big fuss of him."

The tosser, I might have added.

"He may not come back," said PC Downton. "And of course being an adult that's his prerogative."

In other words 'we're not gonna bust a gut trying to find him if he doesn't want to be found'.

* * *

Once again I hoped I might have heard the last of Tony Murphy. A couple of hours later I was disappointed. Another knock at the door. This time it was a bloke of my age. Skinny and tall, just under 6 feet, but still a few inches shorter than me. Steve. Well, that figured.

"Come about Tony, have you," I asked as we went into the front room.

"How did you know?"

I waited until we were both sitting down. Steve brushed his fingers through his light brown hair. It was a little shorter than mine, only just over his ears.

"In the past couple of day I've had Brenda, Vic Kennelly and the police round here."

"Me too."

He shook his head. I looked at his cheesecloth shirt, white with a thin, brown stripe. I quite fancied one of them.

"What the fuck's going on, Gus?"

He tapped his feet on the carpet. I liked his corduroy shoes too.

"How should I know?' I said. "I've had enough. My mam's going spare."

"So's mine," said Steve.

I could imagine that only too well. Mrs Yarnitzky ran the corner shop and was the epitome of respectability. I could see the disapproving look on her face, her arms across her chest. She came from a long line of arm folders.

"The worst part of it is," Steve went on, "this might knacker my chances of joining the police."

"You what? You've done nothing wrong."

He scowled.

"It's not a question of doing anything wrong. Associating with anyone under suspicion could make a difference."

I looked at him for a few seconds, wondering if he were serious.

"Sounds a bit unfair."

"Doesn't have to be fair. I've finished with Murphy after this."

I could have protested, but couldn't see the point.

"I can't afford to get involved with anything fucking dodgy," he said.

Who could, I asked myself.

* * *

Two weeks later the A-levels were over and there was still no sign of Tony. I had come to the conclusion that he really had buggered off. He must have wanted – or needed – to escape Brenda and whatever trouble he had got into with Vic Kennelly. And he had escaped completely enough to avoid being found. Not that the police were looking all that hard. I remembered what PC Downton had said about him being an adult.

My last exam was on a Friday. I got home about 4.15, running through the timetable for the rest of the day. After tea I'd have a bath and get changed. Maybe play that Paul Simon album Debbie had got me for my birthday. Then out. A couple of pints with Steve in the Park Hotel to start with then meet our girlfriends. Can't be bad.

On the mat I picked up a letter. A white envelope addressed to Mr G.R. Keane. Not often I get a letter, I thought. I took it up to my bedroom, sitting on the bed and ripping open the envelope. I saw the letter head first: Salford Rugby League Club. Holding my breath, I began to read.

"Yes," I shouted a few seconds later.

They wanted to sign me. I had to 'present myself' at the Willows next Wednesday at 11.30. A contract would be ready for me. They were also offering me a job with TRYS, some sort of rugby charity. I could go to college on day release if I wanted. There'd be no call for the ablative absolute where I was going. I could be playing alongside David Watkins, the man who had scored in 92 consecutive matches. Sick with excitement, I ran down the stairs.

"Mam," I shouted. "Come and look at this."

No answer. Maybe she was out. I dashed into the kitchen, waving the sheet of paper. Out of the corner of my eye, I saw a figure slumped on the floor. Catching my breath, I looked properly. It really was my mother lying there. A couple of seconds must have elapsed before the fact of her being there properly registered.

"Mam," I shouted again, panic in my voice this time.

She had fallen awkwardly and lay on her left arm, her head touching the concrete floor. I searched for a pulse on my arm before I went towards her. I found the same spot on her arm. Nothing. She can't be dead, I said to myself. Bloody hell. A song from There Goes Rhyming Simon ran through my mind: Loves Me Like A Rock. There was a line about the way a mother loved her son.

Then for some reason I thought of Tony Murphy. Phrases from his letter came back to me: I won't be back; the pressure's too much for me; where I am going perhaps I'll get some peace; you'll never find me. I'd thought he was just attention seeking, then I thought he had simply run away. He hadn't come back, had he? Nobody had found him. Now Tony's letter could be explained in a quite different way. That night the dreams started.

PART THREE: 2012

CHAPTER NINE

"Right, Tony, where the fuck have you been all these years?" I asked about quarter past eight that night in the Park Hotel.

Up to that point our conversation had been a bit of a walk down memory lane, punctuated by much laughter. Now, though, I had tired of reminiscences about buying Hollies records from Snelson's, taking a trip to Wembley for the 1969 challenge cup final, and getting off with two Geordie girls on holiday in Scarborough. Tony Murphy grinned at my question, picking up his pint of Red Devil from the table and taking a swallow.

"I'll tell you all about it," he said.

I looked at the diminutive man in the beige jacket and open necked striped shirt opposite me. I'd forgotten how small he was.

"On the day I left I put a bet on. A fourfold accumulator."

I wondered if I would have recognised him had I not arranged to meet him. The lines criss crossing his face spoke of a lifetime of smoking. He was a bit thin on top and his once red hair was now mostly grey.

"A four what?"

"I bet two pounds on four horses."

When two pounds was two pounds, I thought. You could get about 6 pints for a pound in those days.

"The winnings from the first horse go on the next horse and so on," Tony explained. "All 4 horses won."

He paused as if collecting his thoughts. In the few minutes leading up to this I had learnt remarkably little about Tony; he knew a bit about my family and my job in social work. He went on with his story.

"About five o'clock I went to the precinct to take my library books back. Then I went to Ladbrokes next door to get my winnings."

"Right."

"Nearly six hundred pounds in cash. I'd never seen so much money in my life."

Over three thousand pints, I thought, sticking to that system of measurement.

"That might have made marriage a bit easier," I suggested.

Brenda would have thought so, I might have added. He took a deep breath.

"Maybe," he said, "but as soon as I had the money in my hand, I thought, why don't I go to London now?"

I recalled he had planned to go to University in London after 'A' levels.

"I could just bugger off. Sod exams, sod getting married."

The adult me felt sorry for Brenda and believed in taking responsibility for one's actions, but I asked myself what I would have done in the circumstances.

"The money would more than tide me over while I got settled somewhere. I'd get a job without too much bother."

He explained how he went home for his tea, got some things together and set off with six hundred quid to drive in an old Volkswagen to London.

"How come you never got in touch with anybody?"

"I wasn't coming back," he said. "Nothing to come back for. I didn't want anyone trying to persuade me to come home."

"What about your family?"

He gave a half laugh of derision.

"You're a social worker, Gus," he said, "you must know about, what do they call them these days, dysfunctional families?"

I nodded, remembering the Murphy clan. Everybody had heard of them when I was growing up. I don't think I ever saw Tony's mother again once the fuss about his 'disappearance' had died down. I just got on with my life. Anyway, I soon had other things to worry about.

"What about Brenda?"

He shook his head.

"She'd be better off without me."

A rationalisation if ever I heard one.

"She came to see me when you'd gone," I said.

"Yeah?"

"She showed me the letter you'd sent her. I thought it was a suicide note."

He laughed out loud at this.

"Suicide? Don't be daft. I've always enjoyed life too much."

I could see that now.

"A policeman came round too."

He looked at me in surprise.

"Police?"

I nodded.

"Yeah, an ongoing inquiry or something."

He drank more beer as I remembered how pissed off I had been at the constant interruptions.

"I don't know anything about that," he said, "it was a long time ago."

It certainly was. I thought for a moment. A question came to mind.

"What made you contact me now?"

He shrugged.

"Well, it was a number of things, I guess," he began, before taking another drink and pausing for thought.

"Such as?"

"A mate of mine died a little while ago. Younger than me he was, just dropped dead. Heart."

I tried not to think too much about my health, but Tony's words inevitably brought back the day I'd had a stroke at work.

"It made me think, I can tell you. I went for a check up and the doc was worried about my blood pressure. Put me on medication."

Join the club, I thought.

"I began to think about, you know, what if I died? What would I leave behind? I'd have no... roots."

He looked into the middle distance, waiting a while before going on.

"I thought about my mother. To cut a long story short, I decided to try and find her."

"Is she still alive?"

"Yeah, I caught up with her on Thursday."

"Never."

"I went to our old house in Carrfield Avenue. They told me she had a flat on Kenyon Way."

"How is she?"

"Still going strong. You'd never think she was 80 odd."

I nodded, trying to picture Tony's mother. All I got was a vague image, like a blurred photograph.

"She goes to a day club a couple of times a week, gets to the pub and stuff."

"Great."

"The only relatives she's still in touch with are her brother, Vic and his family."

"I remember Vic. He was another one who came looking for you the day you left. I think he was after money you owed him."

Tony looked blank.

"Don't remember that."

Why should he? Steve had had to remind me. Then Tony laughed.

"I hope he doesn't want interest."

We sat in thoughtful silence for a moment.

"How did your mam react to seeing you again," I asked.

He smiled ruefully.

"Shock."

"I'll bet."

"She recognised me straight away, that was the funny thing. She was in floods of tears but basically she was over the moon."

The prodigal son, I thought.

"Anyway, she asked after you."

"What?"

"Oh, yeah," he said, "she always thought the world of you."

Did she bollocks.

"So I decided it was time...to look up old friends, lay some ghosts to rest."

I nodded.

"And I was coming up here anyway, so..."

We both drank in silence for a while.

"You know, Gus," Tony continued, "I might even look up Brenda as well while I'm here. You don't know where she is, do you?"

"No," I said. "I haven't seen her for years."

After Tony had buggered off, Brenda had been to my house a few times asking after him. Then my mam had died and we'd moved. So had Brenda as far as I could recall.

"Do you think you could find her for me," he asked.

I looked hard at him.

"Seriously?"

I took another swallow of beer.

"Sure. I googled you the other day," he said.

"They can't touch you for it."

"True. The worldwide web told me what an interesting bloke Gus Keane was."

"Yeah, fascinating."

"Top Rugby League player in his youth, independent social worker with a very impressive CV. All good stuff, but the best bit was something called GRK Investigations."

So that was what he meant.

"You want to hire me to look for Brenda?"

"Yeah," he said, picking up his pint. "You're a private investigator, that's what you do, isn't it?"

Tony offering me work, the last thing I'd expected. He drank some more beer and put his glass down.

"Listen, Gus," he said. "I could make inquiries myself, but apart from the fact that you're a professional..."

Don't flatter me, I almost said.

"...I think it would be better if somebody else kind of paved the way, know what I mean?"

"Yeah."

He gestured with his hands.

"I'm not sure how she'd react if I just landed on her without warning. I mean, she could well not want to have anything to do with me."

True enough, I thought, seeing as he left her holding the baby. Literally. Tony looked straight ahead for a few seconds as if daydreaming. Then he seemed to snap out of it.

"She always liked you, you know," he added.

"Who? Brenda?"

He grinned at me.

"Don't sound so surprised," he said, "all the girls liked you, mate."

I shook my head in disbelief.

"First I've heard of it."

He shrugged.

"Bet they still do. Anyway, if you find her, when you find her, I want you to sound her out about seeing me."

I could do that, I thought. If I found her, if she agreed to talk to me and if she then agreed to meet Tony. A lot of ifs.

"You need to bear in mind," I said, "that I might not find her."

"I know, but..."

"If she's married, she's probably got a new surname."

And there must be thousands of McDonalds anyway and a fair few women of a certain age called Brenda.

"I have every confidence in you, Gus."

If you say so, Tony, I thought, as he took his wallet out of his inside pocket. He handed me five twenty pound notes.

"There's a ton on account," he said, "plenty more where that came from."

"Cheers. I'll get onto it as soon as I can."

We finished our drinks. I got up.

"Another?"

As I waited to be served at the bar I thought about what Tony had told me. I had sympathy for him even now, but couldn't bring myself to let him off the hook completely. To abandon Brenda like that. To cast his family aside. Social workers were constantly warned against being judgemental, but it was hard not to be. Odd snatches of what he had said on that drunken Saturday spent watching Sunil Gavaskar make a century were coming slowly back. I got to the bar.

"Same again, please, Arthur," I said.

The landlord's massive frame dominated the area behind the bar, as he pushed his long hair away from his face and got a couple of glasses ready.

"Great win for Salford on Friday night, wasn't it," he said.

"It wasn't half."

"Were you there?" he asked as he began to pull the first pint.

I thought of the thrilling encounter I'd enjoyed.

"Yeah," I said, "I took my Dad. It was a belting match. A last minute penalty settled it."

"Sounds good. It's hard to get to a match these days. I still haven't been to the new stadium."

Arthur watched the beer froth into the glass, then removed the first pint and began to fill the next one.

"You know anything about this Tattersall feller, Gus?"

I hesitated. It was always difficult to know what to say in these circumstances, but Arthur took my silence as a yes.

"I reckon you must do with your job."

I nodded. Arthur gave one last pull on the handle and let the beer settle.

"I know you can't say too much. The funny thing was he used to get in here regular."

"Did he?"

Arthur nodded, topping up the glasses.

"He seemed all right."

I shrugged.

"They don't have horns, Arthur."

"Be easier if they did," he smiled. "In one way, it's good riddance to bad rubbish, but I don't like the idea of people taking the law into their hands."

"Do you reckon that was what happened?"

Arthur stood up straight, placing his hands in the small of his back, as if easing a pain.

"Vigilantes? Oh, aye. Who else could it have been?"

Who indeed?

"If I were looking into it I'd start with Ian Jamieson," said the landlord thoughtfully, "He lives in the bungalow next door to Deadbeat Mansions."

"Yeah?"

"Aye. He knew Tattersall. He knows what goes on all right."

"Does he?"

He nodded.

"And there'll be a few in the Mansions who have something to hide."

Arthur looked at me and winked.

"Oh, by the way," he said, "are you coming to the quiz?"

He passed the drinks over and took my money.

"Possibly. I'll see what Tony thinks. A few from work will be in later."

I picked up the glasses and walked back to my seat.

***

"What happened when you got to London?" I asked Tony back at the table.

He took a long drink from his pint and put his glass down slowly. He seemed to be building up to something. Surely whatever he was going to tell me couldn't be that dramatic, could it?

"The day I got there I went to this second hand car place in Putney, sold my car for cash," he said.

"And?"

He took a swig from his glass.

"Just on impulse, I asked the gaffer if he needed any staff. I've always loved cars as you know."

I nodded as he continued.

"He said he'd give me a trial. He even told me where there was a cheap flat going. I really fell on my feet."

You would, Tony, I said to myself, as he went on with his tale.

"I did a few repairs, washed cars, all sorts really. Then they let me out on the forecourt. I found I was a natural salesman."

That figured.

"I was soon earning good money – I never touched the six hundred pounds or the fifty I got for the car. And I soon accumulated plenty more."

In the meantime, Brenda was probably having the worst time of her life.

"Anyway," Tony went on, "Years later, after I'd travelled a bit, I set up on my own."

I immediately thought of Arthur Daley in Minder and had to make a deliberate effort not to laugh.

"I've got a place just near the Hammersmith flyover now. APM."

"Great stuff," I said, for want of anything better.

"Top end of the market, you know."

"I wouldn't expect anything less," I said.

He shrugged modestly. By the standards of my early life I was well off, but I had the feeling I wasn't in Tony's league. I couldn't think of any intelligent questions to ask about the car business. Tony's remarks about travelling rang a bell.

"Were you ever in Jersey," I asked.

He looked at me in surprise.

"How did you know that?"

"I told my Dad I'd heard from you," I said, leaving out the uncomplimentary remarks, "and he said a mate of his saw you there back in the eighties."

He nodded.

"Yeah, I was there for a few years. In the motor trade. I made some good contacts in the financial world."

So my Dad's idea had been right.

"Well," I said, not being able to sustain a conversation about money. "Are you married, kids...?"

Again he sought refuge in his beer. He shook his head but a few moments passed before he spoke again.

"No, no. One thing I came to realise as time went on was that I'm not a wife and kids kind of guy."

A wife and kids kind of guy? That was a new one, though it did remind me of Louise's words when she left me: 'I need my own space' or some such bollocks. I had, I recalled, been quite happy to be a 'wife and kids kind of guy' at one time. What was I now?

"I could never settle for the safe option," he said. "I'm a risk taker, know what I mean?"

Not really, Tony, I could have said. I didn't think I could face an explanation, but he went on without any help from me.

"It's been tough getting anyone to invest in my business, Gus, as you can imagine. No point in going to the bank since the recession."

I drank in silence as I knew nothing much about investing in anything.

"So I prefer to rely on people I know. The idea is they invest on a small scale, ten or twenty grand..."

That was small scale? I managed to avoid choking on my beer.

"APM gives good returns. Everyone's a winner. So if you've got a spare few thousand."

"Well, you know...," I said.

"It's a fantastic opportunity."

"No, you're all right, Tony," I said.

Which meant: if I had a spare ten grand, would I give it to someone I was in effect meeting for the first time?

"If you're sure..."

"I'm sure."

There was a short silence.

"By the way, Tony," I said, "the quiz is starting later. Do you fancy it?"

"Yeah, go on."

"Great."

"When we lived round here there were no quiz nights," said Tony.

"We had to make our own entertainment."

Tony sighed loudly.

"The only excitement we got was playing whip and top on the croft."

For a moment I was a kid again, playing on the bomb site a few yards from our house.

CHAPTER TEN

For the next twenty minutes or so the pub, relatively quiet earlier, began to fill up for the quiz. Tony and I commandeered two tables and pulled them together. Moments later, Josie arrived, looking self-conscious with her walking stick. She sat next to me as I introduced her to Tony.

"Are you one of these social work type people?" he asked.

"No, I'm an accountant."

Before the conversation could develop, Angela and Karen rushed in from the back. I was surprised to see Angela wearing jeans. But why shouldn't she? Presumably she didn't go around in office gear all the time.

"Hi, everyone," said Angela a little too loudly as she approached.

She had taken advantage of not having to drive by starting on the booze before she'd left home. Dutch courage to face a night out with her staff? Did she really not get out much? Or did she always get tanked up after a stressful day? With her job every day must be stressful. I introduced Tony to her and Karen.

"I didn't realise you would be here, Josie," said Angela.

"No?"

Did Angela look a bit put out? Stop imagining things, Gus, I told myself. Just because she didn't want to admit knowing Marti doesn't mean everybody thinks Josie's dodgy. Plus Angela was a bit pissed already, she was bound to sound funny.

"So glad you could join us," Angela added.

She took her coat off and hung it on the back of the chair. In so doing she revealed a clinging red top. Her jeans were equally tight. She sat down next to Tony, leaning towards him. Karen went over and sat opposite us, putting her handbag on the table.

"You know, Josie," said Karen, "I'm sure we've met before somewhere."

Josie looked thoughtful for a moment.

"I don't think so."

"You must have a double."

Josie shook her head in disbelief.

"Pity the poor cow who looks like me."

I thought again about Josie. Karen seemed to know her and she knew Marti. Angela had told Josie to sod off earlier today. Her 'so glad you could join us' was to say the least unconvincing. What did it all mean if anything? Maybe nothing. Perhaps Angela just didn't like Josie much. No reason why she should. By now, she was showing a great interest in my old friend. She asked about his job, where he lived, his marital status. She thrust her boobs in his direction, in case he hadn't noticed them and was tactile in the way only drunk people can be.

"I see Angela's chatting your mate up," said Josie, after tapping me on the arm.

"She seems to be doing all right as well," I laughed.

The sound of Arthur blowing into a microphone and chanting '1, 2, 1, 2' filled the room.

"'Ey up, we're under starter's orders," I said.

"Your attention, please, ladies and gentlemen," announced the landlord. "Eyes down for the Park Hotel quiz."

A muted cheer went up. Arthur instructed us to identify somebody to write down the answers and choose a name for our team.

"The Whip and Top Wonders," said Tony.

After a few introductory words, Arthur and Phyllis, the barmaid, strolled from table to table with the picture round. Only moderately overweight, Phyllis looked positively svelte next to her boss. Soon our team had a sheet of photographs and enough paper for the answers to the other rounds.

"I think that's Kevin Sinfield," I said to Tony, recognising the Leeds rugby league star.

He nodded.

"Number 5's whatsisface," he said, "plays for City. Goalie."

"Joe Hart."

* * *

Later, as the papers were being collected from the science and nature round, the scores from the first round – general knowledge – were read out. Half a dozen teams were announced before us.

"Whip and Top Wonders, eighteen," said Arthur through the mic.

That put us in the lead thus far.

"Deadbeat Mansions," he continued, "nineteen."

A team of middle aged blokes cheered. The block of flats round the corner where Rachel had found Tattersall's body, I recalled. It had somehow turned into a sort of hostel for divorced men, loners and drifters over the years. I saw Simon Natchow come in and go over to the Deadbeat Mansions table. Bugger. I tried to watch Josie without appearing to. She had seen him too: the flicker of fear in her eyes gave her away. She got up.

"Just off for a smoke," she said calmly, taking up her stick.

Tony got up.

"I'll join you," he said. "I'll leave you in charge, Gus."

Tony caught up with Josie. I thought again about Josie's 'guilty secret' as Marti had called it. What could it be? It must have something to do with Marti being a solicitor, mustn't it? What else would she want kept quiet? Despite having been put in charge by Tony, I would have to leave soon as the pressure on my bladder was becoming urgent. I got up and went in the same direction as Tony and Josie had just gone.

I came out of the gents and went outside in the garden for a breath of air. I saw Josie and Tony smoking a few yards away, deep in conversation.

"Don't worry, Josie," I heard Tony say more loudly than he needed to, "your secret's safe with me."

I pondered those words. What did Tony know about Josie? Did this just add to the mystery? I went back inside. The place was packed by now and there was a nice buzz. If I could only forget about the musician who had been killed, Simon Natchow and Josie Finch I might even have a good time. Or maybe not, I thought, as Simon approached our table. I hurried past him and took my seat again. The team were still conscientiously working their way through the pictures. They had already identified Theresa May, Jessica Ennis and a judge from X Factor, a programme I had never watched. As the quiz continued, Phyllis went round taking photographs on her phone. Simon reached the table and spoke.

"Well, isn't this cosy?"

He looked round the table, then turned to see Tony coming back.

"Oh, look who's here. If it isn't Mr Murphy."

"Mr Natchow, isn't it," said Tony pleasantly.

"Don't you Mr Natchow me, Murphy."

Tony said nothing and took his seat again.

"I'll deal with you later," said Simon.

Tony shrugged and carried on chatting with Angela. Simon looked straight at me.

"Why did you lie to me?"

I ignored him.

"Hey, you, I'm talking to you."

Reluctantly I looked at him.

"There's no need to shout."

"No need to shout? You said Josie didn't work at Social Services."

"She doesn't."

"Then why is she...?"

I'd had enough.

"I'm gonna explain something to you," I said, "and when I've finished I want you to go back to your table and leave us alone."

He sniffed, twisting his features into a look of hatred.

"I contacted the police after you'd left the office yesterday," I lied. "They told me all about you. Asked me to tell them if you bothered me or anybody else again."

"Look, mate..."

"I'm not your mate. They told Josie what happened and she came to see me to find out more."

"Oh, yeah? What's she doing here then?"

I sighed.

"We needed another member for our team."

"You're shagging her, aren't you?"

"That's enough. Arthur!"

The landlord waddled over.

"This bloke causing trouble?"

"Yeah."

"Right. Out."

Simon stood his ground.

"Watch your back, mate, I'm warning you," he said, still talking to me. "That goes for you too, Murphy. And you can tell Josie to do the same. No-one messes with me and gets away with it."

Arthur grabbed Natchow by the scruff of the neck. Simon struggled, kicking his legs, but the big landlord held firm. He frogmarched him towards the front door, which he opened with his left hand. The right continued to squeeze Simon's neck. Without ceremony, Arthur flung him onto the pavement and slammed the door.

"Thanks, Arthur," I said.

"No worries. I can't help feeling sorry for him though."

"What?"

Arthur grinned.

"He landed in a puddle. Now he's gone and got his nice, new coat dirty."

The rest of the table burst out laughing. A couple of minutes later, Josie limped back in and returned to the table.

"Simon has been thrown out of the pub, Josie," I said.

"I've just seen him going through the car park," she said. "I managed to avoid him."

Josie then rubbed her hands together.

"Come on," she said, "let's win this quiz."

* * *

We settled down for a good night out. On the last round of questions we were in with a chance of first prize. We concentrated hard. The final question was 'Who recorded Judy in Disguise With Glasses'? Tony and I were the only ones who knew that: John Fred and his Playboy Band. At the end we beat Deadbeat Mansions by two points. After a bit of chat, Tony went to the bar to collect the prize, £50 worth of beer tokens, from Arthur. This seemed to signal home time for the quiz team. Tony came back to the table and handed the tokens to me.

"Here you are, Gus. That'll come in handy for the next quiz night."

We stood up ready to go, all a bit the worse for drink apart from Karen. Angela clung onto Tony's arm.

"Karen," said Angela, "Tony and I are having a drink in town. We've phoned for a cab, haven't we, darling?"

Darling? My God. This was turning out to be quite a night.

"Sure," said Tony.

"Oh, and Karen, if you see Frank, tell him I went back to yours for coffee."

Karen smiled and shrugged.

"OK, whatever," she said.

Josie explained that her brother was picking her up.

"I'm just off to the loo, then I'll wait for him in the car park," she added.

Karen looked at Josie for a few seconds, a thoughtful expression on her face.

"You've never been to Norfolk, have you?"

"No," smiled Josie. "I've heard it's very flat though."

With that she said her goodbyes and went on her way.

Karen left. So did I, thinking about the part chance played in everybody's lives. If Tony hadn't made his call to me, he and Angela wouldn't now be going off together. It was the same for all couples, I thought. A chance meeting could change lives. I thought of Simon and Josie as I began my walk home. I'd gone a few yards when the rain started, soon becoming a real downpour. Putting my hood up, I heard a high pitched noise behind me. It could have been a scream, a bird or a cat. Or anything really.

CHAPTER ELEVEN

"So this Tony character, was he a close friend?" asked Marti.

It was February 29th. My 56th birthday. A Wednesday. About 11 o'clock in the morning. I'd spent the first few minutes after her arrival at my flat opening presents and cards. We were in my kitchen having a cup of tea and I'd started to tell her about Tony Murphy.

"Yeah, he used to knock about with me and Steve."

"I can't imagine you and Steve with anybody else. You're like twins."

I would never have thought about Steve and me in that way.

"I can't believe he just turned up as if nothing had happened," she went on.

"It is a bit weird," I said. "The more I think about it the stranger it seems."

"In what way?"

"Not sure really," I began. "I think I've been influenced by Steve, you know, wondering what Tony was up to."

"And what was he up to?"

I shrugged.

"Probably nothing. Anyway, I'm not gonna be too hard on him, he's put a bit of work my way."

"Oh?"

I sipped more tea.

"Yeah, he wants me to find Brenda."

She looked baffled for a second.

"Find who?"

I explained about Brenda, the pregnancy and Tony doing a bunk.

"A bit late to say he's sorry, if that's what he has in mind."

"True, but..."

"And when you say find her, is this a job for GRK Investigations?"

"Yeah."

She went quiet for a bit.

"Since when have you been getting work from anyone but me?"

I smiled at her.

"You don't have exclusive rights to my services, you know."

Grinning, she leaned towards me, taking my hand and kissing me full on the lips.

"Oh, no?"

She grinned again.

"Maybe," she murmured, "there are a few exclusive services you might be interested in when we get to the hotel."

"Can't wait."

I finished my tea and recalled something else from the previous evening.

"Do you know what else happened last night," I said.

"What?"

"Tony got off with Angela Bromwich."

"Never."

"Or should I say she got off with him."

She stared at me.

"Angela? She doesn't seem the type."

I shrugged, thinking perhaps anybody could be 'the type'.

"She turned up in skin tight jeans and t-shirt and made a beeline for him as soon as she arrived."

"Bloody hell. Some people are full of surprises. Is he very good looking then?"

How the hell should I know, I wanted to say.

"Well, I don't fancy him."

"That's a great help."

* * *

"Da lat da Da lat da, Da lat da, Da lat da," Marti and I sang in her Mercedes three quarters of an hour later.

The Best of the Proclaimers – a present from Danny – was blasting out at full volume. We were joining in with 500 miles. I couldn't believe I hadn't already got it in my collection. We'd been driving for about ten minutes and were now going through Worsley.

"Nearly there," she said, breaking off from her singing, as she turned down a side road.

That was quick, I thought. We soon came to a sign saying Keaton Hall Country Hotel and turned right down a winding path. Marti eased the car into a parking bay in front of the hotel just as the track finished. A good omen, surely. I hate it when the car stops just before the end of a favourite song. We got out, gathered our stuff together and crunched across the gravel. Now we huddled in our fleeces against a cold wind. It had rained for a couple of hours overnight, but the sky must have cleared. Now the ground was mostly dry but, as the temperature had dropped, we'd been left with odd icy patches. Treading carefully, I looked up at the imposing facade.

"Too posh for the likes of me," I said.

"Don't worry, Gus," said Marti, deliberately exaggerating her Scouse accent, "I'll tell you what knives and forks to use."

"I thought we might be going further afield," I said.

We can't have travelled more than half a dozen miles.

"We can't go too far. I've got to be up early tomorrow to visit a client in Strangeways," she explained.

"You know, Marti," I said as we continued along the path, "Sometimes I suspect you of being a workaholic."

I reckoned I was privileged to be spending just one night away with her.

"I'm no such thing," she replied. "And I'll certainly be forgetting about work for tonight at least."

She'd only got back from Liverpool a couple of hours ago. Her mother was on the mend and being looked after by her neighbour. I'd been instructed not to ask any more.

"It's your birthday," she said, "and I aim to make sure you enjoy it."

She put her arms around my waist.

"After all, it only happens once every four years."

I smiled as I thought of the cards I'd received with Happy 14th Birthday on the front. We approached the front of the hotel where an automatic door opened to admit us. Marti checked in. We went to the lift where she pressed the button for the second floor. As we began our ascent, Marti kissed me.

"Gus," she said, "switch your phone off. When we get to our room, we won't want to be disturbed."

I took the phone out of my pocket. I hadn't got round to switching it on. Another good sign maybe.

* * *

Later we lay together in a four poster bed in a room big enough for a 7 a side rugby match. Our clothes were scattered randomly on the floor in front of us. We were sipping a post-coital glass of Bollinger. The bottle waited in an ice bucket on a table to the left. Places like this always made me think of my Salford childhood. There was a time when staying in any hotel had intimidated the life out of me. And now look at me, I said to myself. My sister had once said, 'We've come a long way from West Park Street'. How right she was, metaphorically at least.

Soon after we got to the bedroom, Marti had warmed me up with the seeing to to end all seeings to. Best birthday present ever? Probably. I sipped more bubbly, enjoying the dry, yeasty flavour. If I had the money I reckoned I could become a champagne socialist. Marti coughed as though preparing for an announcement.

"I've got something to say," she said.

"What's that?"

She put her glass on the table.

"Can't you guess?"

Her accent sounded stronger somehow. I shook my head.

"Give me your hand," she instructed.

I did so. She cleared her throat.

"Gus Keane," she said, stroking the back of my hand with her thumb. "Will you marry me?"

Oh, no. Buggeration. Too late I tried to rearrange my features. She must already have seen the flicker of horror on my face.

"You want to get married?"

That was pointless, I told myself. You can hardly pretend you didn't hear what she said. The smile gradually slipped from her face as she pulled her hand away. I had to say something.

"Well...I'm not sure...you know..."

My words petered out. I looked at the blue and white geometric pattern on the duvet cover as though fascinated. She stared at me.

"You're turning me down?"

The smile had definitely gone. Tears were not far away.

"You're fucking turning me down?"

Her voice was louder now. This was bad: she hardly ever swore. I glanced surreptitiously around, half expecting the people in the next room to bang on the wall.

"I'm sorry..."

"You're sorry? You're fucking sorry?"

"Marti..."

"What the fuck did you come away with me for if you were going to..."

"I had no idea..."

She swigged back her champagne in one go, slammed the glass down on the bedside table and got out of bed. I couldn't stop myself from thinking how good Marti looked naked. The hours she spent in the gym really paid off.

"Why do you think I brought you here? It's 29th February. Leap Year for fuck's sake."

Yeah, but even so, I thought, feeling decidedly thick. I said nothing. She picked up her knickers from the floor and put them on. They almost matched the purple varnish on her toenails. Not that that had anything to do with it.

"I might have known," she went on. "I always end up with a commitmentphobe."

This irked me.

"Commitmentphobe," I said. "What's one of them? It's not even a proper word."

I remembered the women's magazine I'd picked up in the doctor's waiting room on the day of my last check up. Is Your Man a Commitmentphobe? Our Quiz Has The Answer. Commitmentphobe indeed. She had now put her bra on and was pulling her t-shirt over her head.

"Oh, isn't it?"

The t-shirt muffled her words. With a final angry tug she managed to get it on. Seeing her threatening look, I gave up the attempt to defend myself.

"Strange though it may seem," she went on, "A grammar lesson's the last thing I fucking need."

She sat on the edge of the bed to put her jeans on. I got up and began to get dressed myself.

"It doesn't seem that important just now," she went on. "Not compared to the humiliation I'm facing right now."

It should have been 'compared with', but I let it go.

"Marti, you know I've been married once and..."

By now I had put on a pair of jeans, a t-shirt and a cotton jumper.

"Lots of people get married twice," she countered as she put socks and purple suede boots on.

Yeah, including you, I thought. If she'd had her way, I would have made husband number three. Everybody knew the second marriage was usually even more disastrous than the first. What price a successful third one? Mumbling to herself and gritting her teeth, she picked up her suitcase and put it on the bed. Searching in her handbag she pulled out the room key and tossed it over to me. I tried to catch it but the metal tag attached to it hit me in the chest.

"I'm leaving," she said.

"There's no need..."

Taking her fleece from the back of a chair, she put it on. She picked up her handbag and wheeled her suitcase to the door.

"Shut up! And don't try and stop me. In fact, I don't want to see you again. Ever."

With that she was gone. Thirty seconds later she rushed back in, grabbed her dress from the wardrobe and went out again. That went well, I said to myself, as I searched for my trainers. Finding them at the other end of the room I put them on without socks. The phone rang on the bedside table. I ignored it, dashing out of the room and slamming the door.

On the way downstairs the room key jangled in my hand. I wondered what the hell had got into Marti. At times in the last few weeks she'd been quiet, uncommunicative. I put it down to worry about her mother and overwork. Maybe it was partly dissatisfaction about our relationship. The one I had thought was perfect even though Marti was always busy and worked away a lot. The good thing about that was, when she got back, I was always pleased to see her. The rest of the time I was glad to be on my own. If Marti and I had been together all the time how long would our relationship have lasted?

Reaching the foot of the stairs, I heard a car alarm in the distance. I noticed a couple of about my age walking towards the lift. Marti was taking a sheet of paper from the receptionist.

"Hang on a minute," I half shouted.

She began to walk away, struggling with her bags and the dress draped over her arm. As I passed reception I plonked the key on the desk. Marti had by this time reached the front door. Outside I chased after her across the car park. The ground still felt icy underfoot. The blare of the alarm was louder now. To my right a motor bike approached the hotel. Marti quickened her pace as I caught up with her.

"Marti, don't go," I said.

She scurried towards a line of cars in front of us. The alarm stopped suddenly, the resulting silence a shock. The motor cycle found a parking space in the line of cars. The rider, clad in leathers, removed her helmet, her long, red hair tumbling down her back. She sat upright for a few seconds, looking to the horizon like a model doing a photo shoot. Out of the corner of my eye I saw Marti fall and collide with her car. Her keys flew from her hand. I raced over to her.

Taking my mobile from my pocket, I switched it on. There were several messages waiting for me. They'd have to wait a bit longer. I crouched down to see what had happened to Marti. At least she was still breathing. She had landed on her front. I could make out a bruise on her forehead. Her eyes were closed as if in sleep. There didn't seem to be any blood. Was that a good sign? I knew sod all about it. Face it, Gus, you know sod all about anything, I said to myself. I moved Marti's suitcase, which had come to rest on top of her left leg, to one side. The dress she'd only bought yesterday lay in a puddle, smeared with mud. Then my phone rang.

"For fuck's sake," I shouted as I pressed the red button to abort the call.

I stood up and dialled 999.

"Hello, yes," I said. "Ambulance, please, quick...someone's collapsed...she's unconscious, she...her name's Martina Pym...the car park of the Keaton Hall Hotel in Worsley."

I gave the operator my name and put the phone back in my pocket. Marti lay ominously still. Shit.

"It's OK, Marti," I said. "The ambulance will be here soon."

Seeing her car keys under the Mercedes' back wheel, I picked them up. After a few seconds thought I unlocked the car and opened the boot. I put the dress and suitcase in and took out Marti's Barbour and my anorak, which I put on. It was only then that I realised how cold I was. I draped her coat over Marti – at least I could make sure she kept warm. Some vague memory – a film I'd seen, something I'd read – told me you were supposed to do that. Then I saw her handbag on the ground. Stuff had fallen out and been strewn over the gravel. I put a pocket diary, a makeup bag and a purse back in the handbag, which went into the boot with the other things. Slamming the boot shut, I put the keys in my jeans pocket.

Hearing the sound of footsteps behind me, I turned to see the motor bike woman rushing over to me. Close up she looked (a) about 40 and (b) gorgeous. Why notice that at a time like this, I asked myself? The wind blew her hair around; she kept putting her right hand up in a vain attempt to control it.

"Is everything all right?"

I shook my head.

"Not really," I said. "She's...she just collapsed."

She put her hand over her mouth.

"Oh, my God."

I sighed.

"I've called an ambulance," I added. "Let's hope they arrive soon."

"I'm Sally," the woman explained. "I'm the hotel manager. I'm just about to start my shift..."

She concentrated for a moment.

"I'd better go," she said. "Anything I can get you?"

I shook my head. After she left I bent down again and tried to rub some warmth into Marti's hands. I'd never felt so helpless. Not to mention worried sick. And guilty. Sally returned after a few minutes carrying an orange blanket, which she gave to me. I draped it over Marti. Then she handed me a flask and a mug with the hotel crest on it.

"I brought you some coffee," she said. "Might warm you up a bit. That wind goes right through you."

"Thanks."

It was thoughtful of her even if I would have preferred tea.

"What a thing to happen," she said.

Quite, I thought, but I couldn't think of a reply.

"Well, I'd better get back, get changed..."

She waved vaguely in the direction of the hotel and walked away. Then my mobile rang. I answered it this time and immediately wondered why.

"Is that Gus Keane," said a Scottish voice.

"Yes, but..."

"Thank goodness for that. I've been trying to get you for hours."

"Who's that?"

An impatient sigh.

"DI Ellerton, Greater Manchester Police."

Not again, I thought.

CHAPTER TWELVE

What did Sarita want this time? It wouldn't be anything good, that was for sure. As if I didn't have enough to worry about.

"I need to speak to you urgently," she said.

"Well, you can't..."

I wasn't in the mood to be polite. I just wanted her to go away.

"There's no 'can't' about it," she insisted. "We need to interview anybody who was in the Park Hotel last night."

"Sarita, this is the worst possible time."

"Sorry," she said, "I must see you."

The sound of a siren filled the air. I looked up to see an ambulance pulling up next to me.

"What's that," asked Sarita.

"An ambulance," I explained. "I've got to get someone to hospital. Ring back in ten minutes."

I ended the call before she could say any more. The paramedics did their job with care and efficiency – good old NHS, I said to myself – and were ready to go within minutes. I said I'd drive to Salford Royal Hospital in Marti's car. As I carried the luggage out to it, my phone rang again. Putting the cases down on the ground, I answered.

"Gus," said DI Ellerton. "What's going on?"

"I'm just about to drive to Salford Royal. Be there in about 10, 15 minutes. Then I..."

"I'll meet you there."

I didn't have time to argue, but asked her one question. "What's it about?"

"I can't explain over the phone."

* * *

Driving Marti's nearly new Mercedes was different from the ten-year-old Peugeot I was used to. It was much quieter for a start and smoother, easier. I could never enjoy driving but if I could have afforded a car like this it might not be so bad, I thought. As I drove down Barton Road onto the M60 and merged with the heavy traffic, I tried not to picture the scene that had played itself out in the car park just a short time ago. I struggled just as hard not to wonder how Marti was. And now there was this thing with the police.

I kept thinking how good things had seemed not much more than an hour ago. I often told myself this was the best part of my life. But then how do you judge such things, I asked myself as I reached junction 12 and went onto the M602? A few minutes later I was turning right down Stott Lane into Salford Royal Hospital car park.

In reception DI Ellerton got up to greet me, lifting up her handbag cum briefcase from the seat next to her. She was formally dressed again.

"I'm here to visit Marti," I said, getting in first, "she's had an accident."

"Oh, my God."

I explained as briefly as I could what had happened, but not the events leading up to it.

"The paramedics seemed to think it wasn't too serious, but I must see her before I do anything else."

She stood still, deep in thought.

"OK, I'll wait here."

As I dashed off towards the lifts, I wondered whether to tell Marti the police wanted to speak to me. After a bit of thought, I decided not to. She had plenty to worry about as it was. I had visions of her lying comatose on a bed with one of those breathing tubes jutting out of her mouth like on the telly. The ward sister would first of all forbid me to see her. Then, relenting after a quick look at her watch, she'd say, 'five minutes, no more'.

When I finally found the right ward, the nurse I asked for directions pointed me to a single room to the left. No dire warnings not to tire the patient. I found Marti sitting up in bed struggling with the Guardian crossword. A black and blue bruise almost covered the right side of her forehead. In spite of this, she looked remarkably cheerful. Almost weak with relief, I approached the bed.

"You took your time," said Marti, with a smile on her face.

"How are you feeling," I said, ignoring the jibe, which I took to be a good sign, and kissing her on the cheek.

"Stupid," she said.

Not quite what I'd been expecting.

"Eh?"

"Yeah," she explained, "losing it like that. I could at least have hung on to my dignity. Bloody embarrassing."

"I didn't mean that."

She smiled ruefully.

"I thought perhaps you didn't. I'm feeling...OK, I suppose. This bump on my head was hurting but they've given me the most amazing pain killers. I'm as high as a bloody kite."

"What happened?"

She shrugged then winced.

"Well, those boots I was wearing may look good but they haven't got much grip. Especially in the ice. I slid along the gravel, fell over and banged my head."

So that's why she ended up on the ground. She'd come a cropper like Josie Finch, I thought. Would Marti need a stick too?

"I thought you'd had a heart attack or something."

"Fortunately not. My left leg collided with the car," she explained, "then my suitcase fell on top of it. Result: mild concussion, severe bruising on my left leg — bloody severe actually, I can hardly move it — and I might have pulled a muscle as well."

Could have been a lot worse, I thought.

"Only trouble is," said Marti, "they're going to keep me in for a couple of days to keep an eye on me."

"I should bloody hope so."

"What about mum and my appointments?"

"Can't be helped," I said.

Marti frowned then moved around a bit. She seemed to regret making the effort.

"God, I'm gonna be laid up for ages," she complained. "I'll be hobbling about like mum. We'll be a couple of crocks together."

Another sigh.

"'I'm worried about Martina,' she'll be saying, 'she's had a fall'."

I laughed at the thought.

"It's not funny," she said, starting to laugh herself, "I won't be able to drive or anything."

"If there's no bones broken you'll be mobile again in a couple of weeks."

She scowled at me.

"If that's meant to cheer me up, Gus Keane, it doesn't. Two weeks! I'll be dead of boredom by then."

I shrugged. There was no talking to some people. At least she'd have plenty to moan about.

"Oh, can you get me some clothes, nightie...and my kindle."

I committed those things to memory.

"Don't worry," I said, "I'll look after you."

We looked at one another for a moment.

"If you'll let me," I added.

"I'm gonna have to, aren't I?"

She took my hand and squeezed it, taking a deep breath.

"I'm glad you're here," she said, "In spite of everything."

"Good."

She wriggled about a bit more, as though trying and failing to find the most comfortable position. There was still an air of unreality about all this, I couldn't help thinking. But it was real enough; it had actually happened.

"Anyway," she said. "I need some sleep. You can go now."

I leaned over to kiss her on the lips. Her response was quite promising.

"Thanks for coming, Gus," said Marti as I walked away. "I'll see you tomorrow."

* * *

In the hospital reception the Inspector was pacing the floor, drinking from a cardboard cup. Seeing me she stopped pacing.

"I've managed to get hold of a room," she said.

She offered tea or coffee, but I'd rather go without than insult my taste buds with a drink from a machine.

"OK. Follow me."

Functional plastic chairs had been placed apparently at random around the room we'd been given. As we pulled up a couple of them to a table, I looked round. It seemed to be some kind of staff room. The Inspector took out a notebook and pen from her bag.

"Right," she said, sipping something that, judging by the smell, was meant to be coffee. "Were you in the Park Hotel, Salford, last night?"

"Yes. I was with an old friend, Tony Murphy, hadn't seen him for years."

"Anybody else?"

"Well, it was quiz night. A few people from work had a team and Tony and I joined them."

At Sarita's request, I went through the names of the quiz team, but she interrupted before I could mention Simon Natchow.

"So Josie Finch was a member of the team?"

I nodded.

"When did you last see her?"

This didn't sound too good.

"I'm not sure exactly," I said, thinking hard. "It would have been just before I left the pub."

She wrote a note before speaking again.

"What time was this?"

I shrugged.

"About 11, I suppose, maybe a bit before. I can't tell you to the minute."

"So when you last saw her, where was she?"

I tried to picture the scene.

"On the way out...the back way. She said her brother would be picking her up soon in the car park."

"What happened next?"

What had happened next? Nothing that stood out certainly.

"Well, everyone else left...and I went to the gents. I walked home."

She took more notes.

"Look," I said, "are you going to tell me what this is all about?"

I couldn't wait any longer.

"Josephine Elizabeth Finch's brother, Laurence," Sarita announced formally, "found her body in the Park Hotel car park at ten past eleven last night."

"Bloody hell."

"We're treating her death as suspicious."

Life's a bugger, I said to myself, she wasn't old enough to die. I thought of all the things she hadn't done and the pain her parents must be feeling.

"That must have been a bit after I left," I said, "I remember it started to rain around then."

She pulled a face.

"Which made it even more of a bloody nightmare. Anyway, what can you tell me about Josie?"

I took a deep breath and tried to collect my thoughts.

"A surprising amount," I said, "seeing as how I only met her on Friday."

"Go on."

"I take it you've heard about Simon Natchow?"

"The ex-boyfriend, yes. Do you know him?"

"He arrived at Ordsall Tower on Friday just as I did," I explained. "He asked if Josie was in. I'd never heard of her at that time, but said I'd try and find her."

I pictured Simon in his red anorak, remembering the smell of drink on his breath.

"Anyway, when I found her she told me Simon used to knock her about. I presume you know that."

She wrote more notes.

"Yes, we're aware of that," she said.

"I told him nobody called Josie worked at Ordsall Tower. He got stroppy and I asked him to leave."

"Right."

"I threatened him with the police and he went off muttering."

I edited that bit, omitting the part where I pushed him back in his seat.

"The next time I saw her was Monday lunchtime in the Temple."

Sarita looked up from her notebook.

"Monday, you say?"

"Yes."

I went through the events of that lunchtime, particularly my overhearing Josie speaking on the phone about knowing Marti.

"Mmm," said the Inspector, adding a few words to her book, "are you sure about this?"

"Course I am."

"And did Marti know her?"

I shrugged.

"She thought she looked familiar but couldn't think how she might know her."

If what I had told her meant anything to Inspector Ellerton she wasn't saying.

"We'll need to talk to Marti about this."

"I'd appreciate it if you could wait a while."

I wanted Marti left in peace to recover.

"Quite."

"Let's get back to Natchow. Did you see him last night?"

She must have known this by now, but I would tell her anyway. I went through what happened when he approached our table.

"So he definitely threatened her?"

"Yes."

She sipped more ersatz coffee before continuing.

"Did you see Natchow when you left the pub or on your way home?"

"No."

"Did you see anyone?"

"Well, I suppose I must have seen someone. Nobody I can remember particularly."

More notes followed. She sat back in her chair.

"Do you know where your friend, Mr Murphy is now?"

"Not really, he was staying at the Midland, that's all I can tell you."

"Where did he go after he left the Park Hotel?"

"Back to the hotel, I presume. They were getting a cab."

"They?"

"Yeah, him and Angela Bromwich."

"What?"

"Yeah, they'd got friendly as the evening wore on."

She took yet more notes.

"But..."

She stopped herself in mid-stream. Don't tell me, I wanted to say, Angela said she'd gone to Karen's for a nightcap. DI Ellerton said nothing. I couldn't help wondering if Angela's husband would find out about her and Tony.

"But what," I asked.

"Nothing," she said, "I just thought of something I have to do. To get back to Mr Murphy, I need to speak to him. Perhaps if you see him, you could let me know. And tell him to get in touch."

"Sure."

On my way out, I pondered all the things that had happened that day. Josie Finch was dead. I couldn't help thinking I hadn't heard the last of her. I got to the car park and, opening the car door, I began to consider the exact nature of my relationship with Marti. She had seemed friendly enough, affectionate even. We did, though, soap opera style, need to talk. It could wait, I told myself.

CHAPTER THIRTEEN

The next morning after my usual walk, shower, bowl of porridge and blood pressure medication, I went to the spare room, sometimes known as my office and started work on the task of finding Brenda. Not rating my chances of success at all highly, I took the phone book from the bookshelf. This was on the basis that a direct approach might be best. If, as seemed likely, this didn't work, I would go online. It might even be worth going round the Ordsall estate on the off chance somebody might remember her or her family.

Undaunted by the number of McDonalds in the book, I focused on the ones with the initial letter B. I took out my mobile and began dialling. After I'd said 'can I speak to 'Brenda, please' a dozen times and got the reply 'wrong number' the odds got longer. Quite apart from the problem with the surname, this approach was based on the assumption she was still in the Manchester area.

"Could I speak to Brenda, please," I said again.

"Speaking."

Was this thirteenth time lucky?

"Hello, my name's Gus Keane..."

"Who?"

I repeated my name.

"Do I know you?"

I thought it over. The voice didn't sound right. I asked if she had lived in Salford in the seventies.

"Salford? Certainly not."

She'd put the phone down before I could offer an apology. I decided to abandon the phone calls at least temporarily. I put my mobile away and switched on the laptop. I googled Brenda McDonald and waited. There were thousands of them, mostly in the USA. Too many to cope with. I added UK and tried again. It still listed Brenda McDonalds from California and New York City and told me various women of that name were on Facebook and Linkedin.

I scrolled down pages of McDonalds and then went back to the beginning. After another look I saw Brenda McDonald Secretarial Agency. It was worth a try, I decided, clicking on the link. Getting into the website I saw it was a business in Sheffield, a place I liked. Rachel had been a student there and, apart from time spent trying and failing to find my way round the one-way system, I had fond memories of the city.

What to do, I asked myself? I went to the contact section and wrote down the phone number. Digging out the mobile again, I dialled the familiar 0114 code for Sheffield. After half a dozen rings a south Yorkshire voice answered.

"Brenda McDonald agency, how can I help you?"

Another hurdle to jump, I thought.

"Could I speak to Brenda, please?"

A slight hesitation before the woman spoke again.

"Who should I say is calling?"

"It's Gus Keane."

There was silence for a couple of minutes. I thought I'd been cut off. Then another voice said:

"Gus, is it really you?"

"Yeah. Is that Brenda? From Salford?"

"Certainly is."

Even over the phone I could tell this was a different Brenda from the gauche teenager I had known. Her confidence came bounding across the wire.

"This is a surprise, Gus. How are you?"

"Fine, what about you?"

"Fine, you know...but I don't think you've phoned to have a chat, have you?"

"No. I've got something to tell you."

I was relieved not to have to go through a lot of polite exchanges. I took a deep breath and got on with it.

"I had a call from Tony Murphy on Monday morning."

There was a sharp intake of breath from Brenda.

"Bloody hell," she said.

"Just what I thought."

"Well, where is he? Did he...?"

"I saw him Tuesday night in the Park Hotel..."

"Bloody hell," she said again. "Sorry, I don't usually swear so much. It's just been so long since I thought about that place. You must be still living in Salford then?"

"Yeah. Salford Quays. Tony's living in London – he's up here on business."

"Did he tell you why he went off all those years ago?"

"Yes."

I went on quickly before she asked me to say any more.

321

"He asked me to trace you and..."

I wondered what to say next. Brenda cut in.

"And what?"

"Well, he wants me to...sound you out about you and him seeing one another."

I waited, wondering if I'd explained it properly.

"Why doesn't he contact me himself? Why ask you to do it?"

A good question, I thought.

"Well, one reason is I'm a private investigator..."

"Never..."

"The other is he wants somebody to pave the way. A third party if you like."

Neither of us spoke for a while.

"I see," said Brenda, "in a way, you know, this could be quite good timing. Serendipity, do they call it?"

"Shouldn't wonder."

Must look it up later.

"Well, if you want to come and see me, I'm up for it. I can explain properly then."

I agreed to go to Sheffield that afternoon. So I'd managed the first two parts of my job. Nice one, Gus. She suggested I go to her office and gave me directions from the station. I gave her my phone numbers and e-mail address.

"Great, I must dash, Gus," she said, once we'd got the meeting organised, "see you later."

I ended the call with a lot to think about. Tony's reappearance must trigger off so much in Brenda, I thought. Tony was just a friend to me, maybe former friend would be more accurate. To Brenda he was or had been...what exactly? Boyfriend, lover, the father of her child. I was reminded of my feelings for Louise. She was the mother of my children. If nothing else joined us together that would. Forever. I looked at my watch. Plenty of time to go and see Marti before I left for Sheffield.

* * *

I walked onto the ward feeling a bit more relaxed. Marti was reading today's Guardian. A glass vase on the bedside table contained the flowers I had ordered. Hearing me come in she put the paper down and smiled. She looked rested and the swelling on her face was subsiding.

"Hiya," I said, handing over a carrier bag and kissing her.

"Hi. Thanks for the roses, they're lovely."

She rummaged in the bag.

"Oh, you brought the stuff too. Thanks."

"That's OK. I went round to your house last night."

"What's new in the outside world?"

For once the answer 'not much' wouldn't suffice.

"You know Josie Finch,' I asked.

"Josie Finch," she said, looking puzzled for a moment. "Oh, the mystery woman. What about her?"

"She's been murdered."

"Murdered? God, whatever next?"

I explained about the quiz and being interviewed by Sarita, who Marti knew quite well through her work. In fact, she knew all the police officers in Greater Manchester and all their private affairs.

"Have you thought any more about how you came to know her," I asked.

"No," she replied. "Not the best of times for remembering things. My brain hurts."

"I told the DI what I overheard in the Temple car park. They'll want to see you at some point, but I've managed to stall them."

She took my hand, settling herself in a more comfortable position.

"They won't get much out of me unless I have a flash of inspiration."

We talked a bit about Natchow and the threat he had posed to Josie.

"I managed to trace Brenda as well."

Again, she didn't catch on straight away.

"You know, Tony's ex."

I told her of my plan to go to Sheffield.

"She must have got a shock," said Marti.

"She said it was serendipity. I looked it up in the Concise Oxford Dictionary: the occurrence and development of events by chance in a happy or beneficial way."

Marti looked at me.

"Happy or beneficial?"

We would see.

* * *

I got the tram to Manchester Piccadilly that afternoon. The 14.20 to Sheffield was on time and as it pulled out I was safely ensconced in my seat in carriage B, reading A Little Death by Laura Wilson on my Kindle. Was there some significance in the title, I wondered? Could any death be called little? Regardless of that, I got so involved in it I found it hard to drag myself away to look at the Peak District scenery.

I did break off from reading at New Mills. Brenda had been on my mind since I had arranged to meet her. She still was. What would she look like? Did I even remember clearly what she'd looked like at 16 or 17? She was small, I remembered that much. She had to be to go out with Tony. I'd half decided to tell her as little as possible of what Tony had told me. It was his responsibility to explain what he'd done. It was my job to listen to Brenda. If she wanted to see him, or indeed if she didn't, I would let Tony know and leave it at that. I wasn't going to try and persuade her either way.

* * *

The Brenda McDonald Secretarial Agency was on the third floor of a glass and steel tower block near the Crucible Theatre, where Louise, Rachel, Danny and I sometimes used to watch the snooker during Rachel's student days. At about twenty past three I went up in the lift and walked along the corridor, mildly affected by that queasy anxiety that used to come upon me before job interviews. I knocked on the glass door, opened it and went in. In a cramped room a woman of about twenty odd sat behind a desk, talking into the phone. She sounded like the one who answered my call the previous day.

"Well, if you'd like to send us your CV," she was saying.

She broke off to look across at me, giving a brief smile and indicating a chair behind me.

"I won't be a minute," she said, covering the mouthpiece. "Just take a seat."

I sat down, took off my anorak and looked at the framed certificates on the cream walls. It seemed Brenda had won quite a few awards in the recruitment industry.

"That's right, yes," the secretary went on, "look forward to hearing from you. 'bye."

Putting the phone down, she gave me her full attention.

"Sorry about that, how can I help?"

"Gus Keane to see Brenda."

She looked at me appraisingly.

"So you're the famous Gus."

"Hardly famous."

She picked up the phone and pressed a couple of digits.

"You're famous here, Brenda's talked of nothing else since yesterday... Brenda, Gus is here... Fine, will do."

She put the phone down again.

"She says tea or coffee?"

"Tea please," I smiled

"Just go through that door behind me."

Getting up I squared my shoulders and took a deep breath. That job interview feeling came back as I walked towards the door. I wondered for a moment whether something more formal than jeans and trainers would have been more suitable. Too late now. Giving a peremptory tap, I opened the door and went in. Brenda was sitting behind an impressive oak desk. Smiling, she got up and walked towards me.

"Gus," she said, arms open wide.

She gave me a hug.

"It's good to see you."

Taken aback by this effusive greeting, I waited until she had released me before I spoke.

"Good to see you too, Brenda."

We stood for a moment in the middle of the room, looking at one another. She was stockier, having thickened out a bit, but by no means fat. Looking at her grey skirt, her black and white jumper and short hair, expertly cut, the word well-groomed seemed appropriate. Her whole demeanour was what made the biggest impact. It confirmed the impression I had got over the phone. I am a confident, successful woman with enviable social skills, she seemed to be saying.

"You're looking good," I said.

"You too, Gus."

Just as we had sat down on armchairs at a low table near the window, the receptionist came in with a tray.

"Ah, here's Zoe with our tea."

There was a pause while Zoe fussed around, making sure we had everything we needed. After she had left, Brenda engaged me in conversation as she poured tea from a brown pot. Soon she knew about my marriage, divorce, kids, granddaughter.

"What about you, Brenda," I asked when I finally got the chance, "are you married."

"No, I've lived with a couple of guys," she said with a wry smile, "No kids with either of them."

She explained this in a straightforward way, so it was difficult to tell if she minded or not.

"I suppose that made me easier to find," she went on, "I've always been McDonald."

It certainly had, I thought.

"You being here now, and everything that led to it," she said, "well, it's brought back a lot of stuff..."

She picked up her cup and drank, looking away for a second.

"But I am really glad to see you. I always liked you," she added, echoing Tony's words in the Park Hotel. "I thought you were a good influence on Tony."

Fat chance, I thought.

"For years I thought of getting in touch with you," she went on, "but Tony...he buggered up a lot of things for me for quite a while."

I bet he did, I said to myself. She sighed and drank more tea before continuing.

"The baby I was expecting...Tony's son...I had him adopted."

"I had no idea," I said.

I shook my head at the sadness of it all as she went on.

"I could never have coped...or I convinced myself I couldn't."

She sighed again and looked round the room.

"Maybe it was my mother who convinced me."

That I could believe.

"You know what it was like, Gus, with a staunch Catholic family," she added, "It would have been shameful enough to be pregnant to a Murphy."

She thought for a moment, then spoke again.

"I remember hearing about Tony being mixed up with a gang who beat up a paedophile... something like that anyway."

"That rings a vague bell," I said.

"So he wasn't the sort of lad my mam and dad had imagined me going down the aisle with..."

She smiled ruefully.

"Still, that would have been better than no wedding at all."

I wondered at the attitudes of 40 years ago, the hypocrisy, the sitting in judgement on ordinary human flaws. Brenda went on.

"I never really came to terms with losing my child. I was always wondering how he was."

I thought of the niggling worry about how Danny and Rachel were that was always there at the back of my mind. How much worse must it have been for her?

"Anyway," she said, suddenly smiling, "a few weeks back, my boy contacted me."

"Brilliant."

"We met last week. His name's Adam."

I could see tears starting in her eyes.

"He's an architect in Southport. Married, 2 kids, Jake and Chloe."

"So you're a grandmother."

"Yes," she smiled.

She spent a moment composing herself.

"He asked about his dad, of course. I said he'd abandoned me and I had no idea where he was."

True enough.

"He was so disappointed,' she said, "he was planning to try and find Tony. Maybe there's no need now."

With a name like Tony Murphy he would have had a job, I thought.

"I was gonna tell him his father was a waste of space, you know, but I didn't want to upset him any more."

"So what do you want to do about Tony," I asked. "Do you want to see him?"

She nodded, stifling a tear.

"I do want to see Tony. Not for my sake, but for Adam's."

She took a deep breath and went on.

"I need to tell him about his son, find out if he wants to meet him."

"Right."

She sat up straight.

"And I want to tell the bastard what I think of him."

* * *

On the journey back I could hardly believe what had happened. Just a week or so ago I'd no idea where Tony Murphy was. I never thought I would ever see or hear of

Brenda again. And now look. My next task was to tell Tony the outcome of my visit to his ex-girlfriend. That needed to be done today, but it would have to wait until I got home. I needed privacy.

I recalled my recent anxiety about my lack of work. Now I had been commissioned for one case. Not much but it would have to do for now. It hadn't come from Marti. She had given me all my investigation jobs until now. Did that matter? I contemplated Marti and me a bit more deeply. Did we have a future together? I hoped so, that's all I could say. We were behaving as though we were still a couple but...But what? Marti's accident seemed to have postponed decision making. She might, I supposed, need my help when she came out of hospital. What would happen when she was OK? She obviously wanted to marry me. I didn't want to marry her so it was an impasse, wasn't it? Once she had recovered from her injuries would she want to stay with me?

Putting that to one side, I thought about Tattersall and who might have killed him. I felt involved because of Rachel and because I had met the man. If it were a vigilante killing as Arthur had suggested, who were the vigilantes? And how did they find out about Tattersall's offences? It would have been reported in the Midlands papers, but not in Manchester. This thinking was based on the assumption that his paedophilia had led to his death. He could – in theory at least – have been killed for another reason. What he had said about a murderer being employed in Ordsall Tower came back to me. He had hinted this might put him at risk. Who killed him was sod all to do with me, thank goodness. Still, DI Ellerton might actually call me in as a consultant. Yeah, and Elvis might be running a pub in Lower Broughton.

* * *

That evening I visited Marti in hospital again. She confirmed she would be fit to go home tomorrow. Back at my flat I rang Tony.

"I've found Brenda," I told him. "She's in Sheffield."

"What? Well done, mate. How did you manage it?"

I chuckled knowingly.

"I have my methods."

"Like what?"

I gave another little chuckle. I was enjoying this.

"Trade secrets, Tony. The important thing is I've just got back from seeing her."

"You work quick, I'll give you that."

Another satisfied customer, I thought.

"She's looking good," I said, "done well for herself."

"I'm glad to hear it."

So you should be, I thought.

"I think we'd better meet soon. I'll give you a full report then."

"Right, where and when?"

I thought for a moment.

"If you're still at the Midland, I'll see you there in half an hour."

I'd had to curtail my experience of how the other half live when Marti walked out on me in the Keaton Hall Hotel. Now I could make up for it.

"Fine. Come up to my suite. I'll order a bottle of Scotch."

I grimaced at the thought of whisky.

"Make it red wine and you're on."

CHAPTER FOURTEEN

Thirty-five minutes later I got off the tram at St Peters Square in the centre of Manchester, a matter of yards from Tony's hotel. I stood by the tourist signs to Castlefield and the Opera House. Lost in admiration, I stared at the Midland, an Edwardian listed building several storeys tall. Taking up a whole corner, it was more impressive at night, its lights standing out against the darkness.

I went into the foyer with its checkerboard marble floor, its pillars seemingly holding up the ceiling. I went up two floors in the lift and turned right. Tony answered my knock straight away and ushered me into the second posh room I'd been in that week. We could have sat at a small dining table but opted for two armchairs that engulfed us. We faced one another across a small table, as Tony poured two glasses of Rioja.

"Cheers," we said, clinking glasses.

"What a night last night," he said, "that Angela, what a raver she turned out to be."

Did I want to hear this? Not really. I had a sure way to change the subject.

"Have you heard about Josie?"

He looked blank as I savoured the wine.

"Josie?"

"She was at the quiz at the Park Hotel, about thirty, glasses."

He didn't look any the wiser.

"What about her?"

"She was murdered."

"Murdered? Shit."

I explained the circumstances.

"I remember her now. Walked with a stick. So this happened just after we left the pub?"

He shook his head in disbelief.

"Yeah," I said. "The police want to see you."

He looked aghast.

"Me? What for?"

I wondered at the extremity of his reaction.

"They're talking to anyone who was at the Park Hotel that night."

He gulped at his wine.

"You didn't tell them where I was, did you?"

What was up with him?

"I said you were staying here."

He sat deep in thought.

"The last thing I want is the cops sniffing round," he said.

His left hand stroked his chin.

"They only want to know if you saw anything. You went for a smoke with her didn't you?"

He sipped more wine and thought.

"Yeah, that's right."

"The police will want to know what you talked about."

"How the hell should I know? Just general chit chat as far as I remember. She went on about her boyfriend. Oh, and something about getting into trouble when she was young."

I was about to ask him what kind of trouble he meant when he spoke again.

"I did see her as I was leaving though. We got in the taxi, Angela and I, and I realised I'd forgotten my fags. I went back to get them. As I was getting back in the taxi I saw her going into the car park."

That must have been minutes before she died.

"Anyway, enough of this," said Tony. "What gives with Brenda?"

"She runs the Brenda McDonald Employment Agency."

He grinned at me.

"Never. I thought she had no ambition. Shows how much I know."

I sampled a bit more of the excellent wine.

"She wants to see you," I told him.

"Sounds good to me."

"I'll give you her details."

I passed over the card Brenda had given me.

"It's up to you to get in touch. Oh and you owe me £155."

He went over to the bedside table and picked up a wallet. Taking a handful of notes out he went back to his chair.

"There you go, Gus," he said, counting out £160. "Keep the change."

"Thanks."

I wondered if that was the end of me earning money for now.

"I'll ring her tomorrow," said Tony, "try and get over to see her soon. Did she say anything else?"

I sipped more wine.

"Plenty, but I'll leave her to tell you when you see her."

He nodded.

"Fair enough."

I looked him in the eye.

"Just as long as you don't go missing again."

He smiled conspiratorially.

"I'm always missing, me."

* * *

About 11.30 the next morning I picked Marti up from hospital in her car. She hobbled out to the Mercedes with the aid of just one stick. The bruising on her face had faded a bit more but she still looked fairly battered. I carried the roses out to the car and put them carefully on the back seat. Marti opened the passenger door and struggled into her seat. Getting the seat belt done up with some difficulty, she took a few seconds to get her breath back.

"OK?" I asked.

"Yeah," she said, "if you discount lack of sleep, and the pain in my leg."

She adjusted her position slightly and put her left leg out in front of her.

"Oh, and my head hurts. I'm not allowed any more pain killers for half an hour."

"You'll be better off at home."

She sighed.

"Yeah. Thanks for coming to collect me. I apologise in advance for being grumpy."

I'd be grumpy if I were in her state.

"What I thought I'd do," I said, "was get you some lunch when we get to your place."

"Right," said Marti. "I'll probably have a nap after that."

We lapsed into silence for a while. I drove on. I thought Marti would nod off before we got to Timperley.

"I'll come over and stay tonight, if you like," I said.

"Yes, please."

That was a relief. I didn't like to think of her on her own.

"I doubt if I'll be able to get my leg over, though," she added.

I laughed.

"The stick would make things interesting."

What did jokey exchanges about leg over say about me and Marti? Did it mean we were back to where we started? Something told me discussion of all that would have to wait until Marti was in less pain.

I left Marti at home sleeping like a baby and went home to get my stuff for an overnight stay. I arrived at Salford Quays, still wondering what had become of Josie and what it was about her past she didn't want anybody to know. I told myself it may be irrelevant to her murder. Simon was the prime suspect. But he hadn't been around at the time of her death, had he? She must have been killed in the few minutes between my leaving the pub and her brother arriving.

* * *

As I got home and put the key in the door I heard footsteps clumping upstairs and, soon afterwards, a movement behind me. As I went in, a man rushed into the flat after me. I turned to face him, my fists clenched.

"What the...?"

He was about forty, at a guess, bulky build. His navy blue overcoat, worn over a grey suit, looked like Sunday best, the sort of thing people wore to church. Maybe he was a Jehovah's Witness, I thought with horror.

"No need for alarm, Mr Keane," he said.

He sounded local.

"What the hell do you mean by..."

Calm as you like, he sat at the kitchen table.

"Get out."

"I won't keep you long," said the intruder.

He smiled ingratiatingly.

"Nothing to worry about. I'm looking for your friend, Mr Murphy."

Trouble with a capital T again.

"Well, he's not here," I said.

I sat down. If you can't beat 'em join 'em, I said to myself.

"My name's Eric Consett, by the way," he added.

I knew Consett was a former steel town in County Durham but, that apart, the name meant nothing to me. I looked him up and down, while I waited for an explanation.

"I need to contact him urgently, it's a financial matter," said Eric. "Just tell me where he is and I'll be on my way."

I shook my head, scowling at the trespasser.

"I haven't a clue," I said. "Now if that's all I'm busy. You know the way out, same way you came in."

He sat still, looking at me, then he spoke again.

"I managed to find out Murphy was staying in the Midland Hotel."

How very clever of you, I said to myself, as he went on.

"I went along there this morning. I was surprised to discover he'd checked out at 6.30."

What was Tony playing at? I only hoped he'd had time for breakfast.

"And?"

"You might not know for certain where he is," said Eric, "but could you maybe hazard a guess?"

"No."

I could have hazarded any number of guesses, but I was buggered if I'd do so for Mr Consett.

"Pity," said Consett pensively. "I was hoping for a bit more co-operation."

He sat back as if making himself at home.

"Cos, you know, Gus – you don't mind me calling you Gus, do you? – this mate of yours is not worth protecting."

Protecting from what? Or from whom? I pondered these questions as he went on.

"Not worth getting into trouble for, if you see what I mean."

"I don't know w..."

"He's been ripping people off all his life," he went on, "but now he's picked the wrong bloke to rip off."

I was prevented from asking what he was on about by a knock on the door. I got up.

"Looks like the US Calvary has arrived, Eric."

"Ah, DI Ellerton," I said, opening the door, "perfect timing. Come in."

As she came in, she noticed my visitor.

"Mr Consett, we meet again," she said.

She looked at me as though seeking explanation for Consett's presence in my kitchen.

"You keep strange company, Gus."

I thought I'd better straighten her out about my choice of friends.

"Your friend Eric here," I said, "has just barged into my home and he's refusing to leave."

"Has he now?"

"He's started to make threats and he's getting on my nerves. As a law-abiding taxpayer I wonder if there's any chance you could do something about it? It doesn't seem a lot to ask."

She took out her warrant card and flashed it briefly at the miscreant.

"Eric Consett, I'm arresting you on suspicion of behaviour likely to cause a breach of the peace."

The big man looked pleadingly at her.

"Come on now, love, there's no need for this..."

Bad move, Eric, I thought. I couldn't see that approach working with Sarita, especially if she were addressed as 'love'.

"... You do not have to say anything, but it may harm your defence, if you fail to mention, when questioned, something which you may later rely on in court. Anything you do say, may be given in evidence. Do you understand?"

With a sigh, Eric responded.

"Yeah," he muttered, turning to me. "I never meant no harm, mate."

Sarita sat down at the table, waiting for a response.

"It was never meant to get this far," he whined.

"You should have thought about that before now," said the DI. "You're already on bail for...another matter. Or have you forgotten that?"

"Course I've not forgotten."

Had my dad been there he would have said Eric didn't know whether to shit or be sick. Luckily he did neither. We sat in uncomfortable silence for a few seconds.

"Now then," said the inspector, 'listen to me. I can call for back up right now and have a couple of uniformed constables cart you off to the station."

Alarm spread over his face. At a guess I would say he didn't fancy that. Sarita went on with her explanation.

"And I can't guarantee you won't be seen going into the station or that word won't get back to Baz Prince that you've been helping police with their inquiries."

His breathing quickened and he bit compulsively at his bottom lip.

"You can't do that," he said, a note of pleading in his voice.

"Worried about what Mr Prince might think?"

He sat in wretched silence.

"Or you can save me a hell of a lot of paperwork," Sarita suggested. "I forget about you being under arrest; you help me with one or two things I'm looking into."

I sat back in admiration. This was good stuff.

"First of all what are you doing here?"

He exchanged a furtive glance with me. That got him nowhere.

"I was looking for a friend of Mr Keane's," said Eric.

"Go on."

He hesitated then found voice again.

"Feller called Tony Murphy. Maybe I went about it the wrong way."

No maybe about it, I could have said. I kept quiet, enjoying listening to him trying to dig his way out of a hole.

"It's a private matter," Consett went on after a bit of thought, "there's no need for the police to be involved."

She raised her eyebrows, looked in my direction, then glowered at Consett.

"I'll be the judge of what is and what isn't a private matter. Right now I need to talk to Mr Keane here. As for you, Mr Consett, I shall want to question you tomorrow at, ooh, 10 a.m."

Eric nodded.

"So I'll expect you to be at home when I call."

"At home? You..."

"Don't worry, I'll come the back way."

* * *

Consett left soon after this, on his face a mixture of anxiety, relief and gratitude.

"You should do something about your security, Gus," said Sarita.

"Security?"

"Yeah, get a chain on your front door and a spy hole."

I looked towards the door, making a mental note to follow the Inspector's advice.

"Good idea. Anyway, who was that feller," I asked.

"Hired muscle," Sarita explained. "The type who's always being told in films he's not paid to think."

Having hired muscle in my own home didn't sound too good, but I decided not to pursue it.

"What can I do for you?"

"I'm looking for your friend Mr Murphy too," said the DI Ellerton.

Isn't everyone, I could have asked.

"Oh, aye. What's he done?"

She shook her head.

"Nothing that need concern you, but he was near the scene of the crime on the night Josie Finch was killed."

"Yeah, I know."

"One of my officers went to the Midland Hotel this morning."

The hotel staff must be wondering what's going on, I thought.

"They said he'd checked out."

Why was that a problem? I'm sure Manchester Police got all his contact details from the Midland.

"Probably gone back to London," I suggested.

I didn't think there was any need to tell her about Tony's shocked reaction at the mention of the police. Nor did she need to know that Tony was a client. And I was bloody sure Brenda would want to be kept out of all this.

"He's not at his London address now."

So what, I wondered. He could have got back by now but could equally have stopped off somewhere en route. I would have done.

"He might be on his way there. He didn't confide his plans to me. He didn't even tell me he was leaving the Midland."

"Really?"

"Yes really. I didn't know him well," I explained. "Hardly at all when I think about it."

I wondered what that Consett bloke had to do with anything. I had worked out from what the DI had said that there must be something suspicious about him. Did that mean the same applied to Tony? More than likely, I concluded.

"I've seen him twice recently," I continued. "Last Tuesday at the pub, you know about. Last night he invited me for a drink in his suite. Other than that I haven't seen him for getting on for forty years."

In other words, I wanted to say, how the fuck should I know where he is or what he's doing or what his plans are? And why should I care? She got up to leave.

"Who's Baz Prince," I asked.

"You don't want to know," she said as she went out.

I did want to know. Maybe she meant I didn't need to know or it was best if I didn't know. There was somebody who might tell me about Prince. I would just have time to phone him before I got back to Marti.

"Steve, I need your help," I said moments later.

"Well, make it quick, I'm just off out."

"What do you know about Baz Prince?"

Steve sucked his teeth.

"You've never got mixed up with him, have you?"

"No. I only heard his name for the first time a few minutes ago."

I explained about Consett getting into the flat and DI Ellerton's visit.

"So Tony Murphy has some connection with Prince?"

"It sounds like it."

"I told you Murphy was a wrong 'un."

"Yeah, now tell me about this Prince character."

"Where to start? He would tell you he's a fine, upstanding self-employed businessman."

I waited for Steve to give me the alternative version, fearing the worst.

"Some say he's a criminal mastermind."

Milk it for all it's worth, Steve, why don't you, I thought.

"Others say he's a right bloody villain who has never got caught. A gangster in common parlance."

"What sort of thing is he into?"

"Again, where to start? Money laundering, major fraud...You know I told you about those gangs that steal cars to order?"

"No."

"You do," he insisted, "I explained it last time I saw you."

As if I paid any attention when Steve was wittering on about cars.

"Anyway, what about it?" I asked.

"For years we thought he was behind that."

Bloody great, I thought.

* * *

About 4.30 that afternoon my phone rang again as I was in the middle of a game of crib with Marti.

"Gus, it's Brenda."

"Hiya, Brenda,"

A stage wait.

"I've seen Tony."

That was quick, I thought. He did stop off somewhere: Sheffield. It was not really on the way, but so what?

"Great."

"He left Manchester first thing this morning. Said he couldn't wait to see me."

That didn't ring true, I thought, but maybe I was just an old cynic.

"How did you get on?"

"Fine, fine, we..."

She sounded lost for words.

"Well," she said, starting again, "we met in my office. It was, er, quite emotional, you know."

She had had a lot to cope with since I had contacted her. There was probably more to come.

"There were a few tears, a bit of anger on my part..."

I could hear her sniffing.

"I'll bet," I said.

"And... anyway, I told Tony about Adam and the adoption and everything..."

That must have taken some doing, I thought.

"I said Adam wanted to meet him."

"What did Tony say to that?"

"Basically that he wanted time to think about it."

What's to think about, I would have said had Tony been in front of me now.

"He said it had all been a shock," she went on, "it was like his life being turned upside down. He'd been used to only thinking about himself all these years."

"What now?" I asked.

"Tony was off to a mate's house in Leighton Buzzard. He was staying with him for a night or two."

That wasn't what I meant.

"And then?"

"He's gonna ring me," she said, "let me know what he has decided."

* * *

Within seconds of our ending the call with mutual good wishes and promises to keep in touch, the phone rang again.

"Gus, it's Angela.'

"Hiya."

I was hoping it would be more work. She wouldn't have any other reason for calling.

"Could you call in sometime. Next couple of days, say?"

I couldn't see any reason why not. For a few seconds I thought of asking what it was about but wanted to get back to Marti. I wasn't exactly consumed with curiosity. I went into my office and found my diary on top of the desk.

"What about Thursday morning? Ten o'clock?"

There was a pause and a riffling of pages, presumably in Angela's diary.

"10.15?"

I wrote '10.15 Angela Ordsall Tower' in the slot for Thursday 8th March.

CHAPTER FIFTEEN

I got to Ordsall Tower at about ten past ten the following Thursday and went straight to Angela's office. Knocking on the door, I went in. I did a double take on seeing DI Ellerton sitting next to Angela.

"Come in, Gus, sit down," said the boss. "You know Sarita, don't you?"

"Yeah. Hiya."

Sarita gave me a smile of greeting.

"I thought we needed somebody from the police side of things," Angela went on. "It's about the Tattersall case. I'm a bit worried the shit's gonna hit the fan."

"Again?"

In social work the shit was always about to hit the fan.

"Have a look at this."

She passed up a copy of the Manchester Evening News to me. I looked at the front page headline:

Paedophile murder: was there a leak?

Did a leak of confidential information from Salford Social Services lead to the vigilante style killing of paedophile Edward Tattersall, 39?

Wondering what his age had to do with anything, I gave the rest of the article a cursory glance. Noting the complete lack of evidence for this allegation, I stopped reading.

"Amazing," I said, "and they're usually so nice to us."

"I hadn't noticed that," smiled Sarita.

I was finding it hard to concentrate. My mind was on other things. Life had settled down in the past week or so. I hadn't been in Ordsall Tower since then. Not too good financially, but it meant I'd been able to keep an eye on Marti. For a few days I'd slept in one of her spare rooms but moved back home when she could manage on her own. I still had no clear idea how things stood between us. Maybe I'd find out tomorrow, I thought, as I was going to be spending the weekend at her place.

"The thing is," Angela said, "I'd like you to look into it for me."

This sounded like paid work, so I listened harder.

"I'll help in any way I can," I said. "What exactly does look into mean?"

Again she picked up the pen from the desk and twiddled it in her right hand.

"Well, see if you can find out how the information got out."

"Presumably it would have been in the media at the time of his conviction."

She put the pen back down.

"True, but only in the Midlands and quite a few years ago. The police are concerned as well. It only takes one person to be a bit careless, leaving a report in the photocopier, taking files home, a stray bit of paper gets dropped somewhere, you know the sort of thing."

"Yes. Where do I come in?"

"Ask around the estate. Use your contacts in the area."

Contacts in the area? She had obviously heard I came from Ordsall. Did she realise I hadn't lived around here for decades? Maybe she saw me as a sort of working class hero relating meaningfully to his community or some similar bollocks. Whatever was behind this request for me to intervene, it still sounded a bit vague. The words needle and haystack sprung to mind, but I wasn't going to turn the job down.

"I'll see what I can do."

She smiled brightly.

"Great. Nobody else needs to know you're doing this and you'll report directly to me. OK?"

"Fine. Where do you come in, Sarita?"

"Well, the same applies to us. We have to be as sure as we can be that we've respected confidentiality."

I nodded, still a bit unclear about her role.

"While investigating Tattersall's murder and umpteen other matters and no doubt curing all known diseases on my day off, I'm expected to find out how the information about our friend Edward might have got out."

"Right."

Nobody said anything for a moment.

"You'll be liaising closely with one another," said Angela.

"I can share some information on a strictly informal basis," said Sarita, "but nothing is to be written down and it should go no further."

Angela and I exchanged a glance.

"Of course," agreed Angela.

"We've discovered the pamphlets came from Tattersall's laptop."

My mouth dropped open. I must have had the type of facial expression that would have led to my mam saying, 'you'll stick like that if the wind changes'.

"Was it a complicated way of committing suicide then," I asked.

"Doubt it," explained Sarita. "It would have been easy enough to get into Tattersall's flat and use his computer."

I saw the sense of that.

"Who would have done that?"

She shrugged.

"How long have you got? Anybody who knew him and knew about his record. Residents of Deadbeat Mansions. Victims' families. The list is endless."

"Was there anything dodgy on his laptop," I asked.

"It took some finding, but yes, there was. And a few memory sticks hidden under the floorboards."

I thought back to Rachel describing how she found the body. Hadn't she said something about tripping on a loose floorboard?

"Nobody knows we found this stuff, repeat nobody and nobody else must be told. It could compromise our investigation."

"Understood. Looking at this in the context of the job you and I have to do," I said, "it seems unlikely somebody from Manchester police or Salford council broke into the flat."

"No, but they might have provided the information."

I thought a bit more.

"True, but the stuff on these leaflets was pretty general, wasn't it? It gives no clue as to where the information came from."

"We'll just have to do the best we can," said Sarita sadly.

* * *

I left the meeting, went into the deserted social work room and sat at an empty desk. I should have been feeling cheered. I could start work on this case today and earn some money. But it didn't feel right. For one thing, I should have been used to the idea that social workers were to blame for everything, but it still pissed me off. For another, there had now been two murders in the neighbourhood and here we were covering our backs about one of them. Was there no room for a human response? I couldn't forget my daughter had found the body.

Still, brooding over it would not do her any good. I had better just get on with it. What contacts did I have in the area, I asked myself, and immediately thought of Paul. When my Dad and I had seen him at the rugby he'd seemed keen. Looking back, I realised that was the day it all started. Tony phoned; I met Tattersall and Josie Finch; Simon Natchow reared his ugly head. Apart from anything else it would be nice to help Paul earn a bit of extra cash. He would be the ideal man to do what I wanted and always seemed to know what was going on. I'd phone him now.

"Paul, it's Gus," I said a few moments later.

"Hey, Gus, all right."

"Fine, I might have some work for you."

"Sounds good. What is it?"

I was about to explain then thought better of it.

"Can we meet," I replied, "and I'll tell you all about."

"Yeah, OK."

We decided on tomorrow lunchtime at the Albert Square Chop House. What else did I need to do to help the investigation? The conversation I had had with Arthur in the Park Hotel on the night of the quiz came back to me. First stop would be the place the obese landlord thought any investigation should start. That was two avenues to explore, I thought, feeling pleased with myself.

* * *

A few minutes later I walked through the Ordsall estate where a lot of social work clients lived. Contrary to popular prejudice I wasn't taking my life in my hands. Nobody tried to knife or mug me, one or two people said hello with a smile on their faces. Most of the houses were well looked after. The city of Salford scored highly in the indices of social deprivation with Ordsall being one of the worst areas in that respect, but it was full of ordinary people trying to get by.

Passing through Robert Hall street, I thought about Tony Murphy. He wouldn't recognise his old stamping ground. What would he decide about seeing his son? I thought I would have heard something by now. If one of them didn't make contact soon, I'd give Tony or Brenda a ring. These thoughts took me to Dedby Street. A squat, three storey block had, it seemed, been stuck on the corner of the street deliberately in order to bring down the tone.

DEDBY MANSIONS said the sign on the front wall. Whoever had thought of the word mansions obviously had a sense of humour. As did the bloke who had sprayed DEADBEAT MANSIONS just below the official name. Being here now reminded me of Rachel telling me she'd discovered Edward's body.

The building had an air of neglect, rather like the inhabitants who had made up the quiz team. A council van pulled up at the kerb and two workmen in overalls got out. I remembered hearing they were doing up Tattersall's flat before re-letting it. Eventually all the apartments would be modernized.

Though the mansions was the scene of the crime, my first stop was the bungalow next door. Arthur had advised that and he should know, I thought, as I went along the garden path and knocked at the PVC door. I heard a chain being rattled inside.

"Yes," coughed a man who could have been any age between forty-five and sixty.

A homemade cigarette dangled from his bottom lip. His sweatshirt was stained with some unidentifiable foodstuff; his track suit bottoms looked in danger of falling down. Incongruously, his white trainers looked pristine. I took out my wallet and showed him my ID.

"Gus Keane," I said, "from Ordsall Tower."

"Ian Jamieson," he said after the most cursory of glances at my photo.

The way he crouched made him look small but I reckoned he was medium height, with very little fat on his bones.

"I wonder if I could have a word about Mr Tattersall."

He took the cigarette out of his mouth and blew out smoke. I hoped it wouldn't make me sneeze.

"Edward? You know he's dead?"

"Yes."

He replaced the roll up in his mouth.

"Come in," he said, "there's bugger all on the telly."

Marvelling at the thought that a visit from me was a rival to daytime TV, I followed him as he walked painfully into a cluttered living room. With a gesture he invited me to sit on a sagging armchair. He took the settee and picked up one of three remote controls.

"Right, what's it all about then," he asked as he switched off the flat screen television.

How to explain why I was here?

"I'm trying to find out how the news of Mr Tattersall's offences got out."

A coughing fit delayed any response from Ian Jamieson.

"Sorry about that," he said eventually, "I'm on invalidity, you know."

"That's OK. I was wondering if you knew he was..."

"A kiddie fiddler? Not until I read it in the paper."

"You didn't receive a leaflet outlining his record of abuse?"

Outlining, Gus, what are you on about? I had a sudden fear that I had written so many reports I was starting to talk like one.

"Not that I know of. We get all sorts of things through the letter box. Anything I get goes straight in the bin."

He puffed on his cig. Feeling I was getting nowhere fast I ploughed on.

"Had there been any talk? You know, rumours? Gossip?"

For a few seconds he concentrated on breathing, an activity he found difficult.

"If there had been I wouldn't have heard it. I hardly set foot out of this place from one day to the next."

If you packed in smoking you might get out a bit more, I was tempted to say.

"How well did you know Mr Tattersall?"

He shrugged.

"Not that well. He used to come round with Simon sometimes."

"Right," I said.

"Simon keeps an eye on me, makes sure I'm all right. He does bits of shopping for me."

The fug of smoke finally got to me. I sneezed and pulled a tissue from my trouser pocket, holding it against my nose. I muttered an apology. Ian went on with what he was saying.

"He generally brings a drop of whisky. It's the only thing that eases my chest."

He wheezed as if to illustrate his point.

"He lets me have stuff cheap and all," Ian went on. "Sold me these for a fiver."

He lifted his feet up to show off his trainers. You'd have to pay me much more than that to get me to wear them, I thought.

"He always keeps an eye on the place when I'm away. I do the same for him."

I was trying to adjust my mind to the idea of Simon Natchow being a good neighbour, while thinking of a way to get back to the subject I had come to talk about.

"Right. Did your friend Simon know Tattersall?"

"He used to go for a pint with him now and again. I don't think he knew anything about his record with kids."

"No?"

He shook his head.

"Well, he wouldn't have gone boozing with anybody like that, would he?"

"And where might I find Simon?"

He pointed to his right.

"Next door, Flat 13, upstairs."

"Dedby Mansions?"

He nodded. Should I go and see Simon? He was or could be a link to Tattersall but I couldn't see him being pleased to see me. Each time I'd met him so far had ended with him being asked to leave. On one occasion he'd been literally thrown out. On reflection I couldn't face Simon today. I'd get round to him some other time. What I did know was that Mr Jamieson was not much use to me. I thanked him and left, grateful to get out into the air. While not exactly fresh it was at least tobacco free and wouldn't get me sneezing.

* * *

That afternoon I was at home reading the Guardian, pleased at the thought of earning some money and thinking about Tony and Brenda. When my mobile rang I thought it was her. I answered with record speed.

"Hello."

"I was wanting to speak to Gus Keane," said a man with a southern accent.

Not Brenda then, I said to myself. Well spotted, Gus.

"That's me."

I thought I heard a sigh of relief.

"I have got the right number then. This is Larry Finch, Josie's brother."

What could he want?

"Hello, we were all sorry to hear about Josie."

"Yes, thanks. Josie told me you helped her when Natchow came looking for her."

"I didn't do much."

"I just wanted to say we appreciate your trying to help."

I was touched that he would take the trouble to ring me about that.

"There was something else I wanted to talk to you about," he went on before I could come out with another cliché.

"What's that?"

"I, well, the whole family, would like to hire you to investigate Josie's murder."

I wasn't expecting this.

"OK," I said.

"Josie told me you were a private investigator."

I recalled the conversation with Hannah and Josie googling my name. It seemed ages ago now, so much had happened.

"It's not something we can discuss properly over the phone, Gus."

"No."

"Do you think we could meet soon?"

After some indecision about where and when we hit upon the next morning at 10.30.

"Josie and I shared a flat. So if you could come here?"

I agreed and wrote down the address and directions. I put a trip to Whitefield in my diary.

CHAPTER SIXTEEN

The next day I arrived at Whitefield. I'd thought about the case all the way on the tram, hoping to no avail that the journey would give me time to develop some insights. With my brief case in my hand, I walked to Preston Lodge. It had the look of a minor stately home that had been converted into apartments. I noticed a To Let sign as I walked along the gravel driveway. At the cumbersome front door I looked down the bell pushes at the side and pressed the third one along with Finch written in block capitals in red biro. After a short wait the door opened.

"You must be Gus," said a balding man of thirty-five or so, who held out his right hand. "Larry Finch."

He was solid looking, not very tall. After shaking his hand, I followed him along a short corridor to the door of a ground floor flat. Once we were inside the living room, I took off my waterproof jacket as Larry invited me to sit down. I declined the offer of coffee. He sat in a chair opposite mine. The flat, I could see, was smart, bordering on the luxurious.

"I was a bit surprised by your phone call," I said.

He squeezed his hands together, swallowing hard, then smoothed down his grey trousers. One of his slippers hung loose from his bare foot.

"The thing is, the police are no nearer to making an arrest."

He took a moment to get himself together, pulling at the cuffs of his open-neck shirt. "We know and they know Natchow did it."

What he said didn't surprise me, but did Natchow do it? He looked at me as if expecting me to say something. So I did.

"You're convinced it was Natchow?"

"Completely, but the police say there's no evidence to place him at the scene of the crime at the right time."

Natchow had, I remembered, left the Park Hotel a good while before Josie was killed. Then I thought of all the women killed by a partner each year; how often domestic violence escalated to murder. He was still the obvious suspect.

"He made her life a misery, Gus," Larry went on. "We kept telling her to leave him, but she went back every time."

A familiar pattern, I thought.

"At first she thought he would change," said Larry, "then she started saying she daren't leave: that he'd kill her."

At that moment I really wanted Natchow to be guilty of the murder. It would be so satisfying to see him put away. At the same time a warning voice urged me to be objective.

"Just when we thought she'd got away from him, he followed her up here from London."

Again he struggled to contain his emotion.

"And now she's dead."

I waited, wondering if he'd be able to go on with what he wanted to say.

"We – my parents, sister and I – can't leave it like that. Which is why we've called you in."

I didn't know what to say so kept quiet.

"We'd pay you the going rate, of course."

"I'd be happy to take the case," I said.

I'd feel guilty if I refused. There was a more worldly reason: I needed the money.

"That's great," he said, almost smiling. "I know you've had success in the past and if you could find something to put that animal behind bars..."

His determination to prove Simon did it would make my job more difficult. But if somebody had killed my sister would I keep an open mind?

"I can't guarantee anything," I stressed, "but I'll give it a bloody good try."

I opened up my briefcase and took out a notebook and pen.

"I'll need some information about Josie first of all. And an up to date photograph. Two would be handy."

"Photo? Right," he said, "I'll go and have a look."

He left the room while I looked round at the paintings on the wall, a Matisse I thought I recognised and a watercolour of a canal scene somewhere. I had no idea who had painted it, but it looked bloody good. When Larry came back he handed me two almost identical pictures of Josie with long hair and no glasses.

"They're the most recent I've got. They were taken on New Year's Eve," he explained, "we had a bit of a party."

What struck me most was how happy she looked.

"Thanks," I said, "now if I could have Josie's full name."

I wrote down Josephine Elizabeth Finch, remembering that DI Ellerton had already told me the name. Her date of birth came next: I worked out she was twenty-nine. She hadn't even lived to celebrate her thirtieth birthday, I thought. These facts would probably not be relevant but it helped to start with something concrete. Next Larry gave me a potted biography of his sister.

"She was born in Barnes, south west London, same as me. Mum and Dad are both GPs. So am I. Josie was the youngest of three. Cassandra is the oldest – she's a consultant psychiatrist."

He stopped again as if wondering what to say.

"Josie didn't fancy a career in medicine. She did accounting at Manchester University, where I studied medicine."

I wrote all this down. Maybe allowing Larry to talk would get him onto something important to the case.

"She always liked it up here, but she went back home after uni."

Another pause while he psyched himself up to go on.

"A mistake as it turned out. If she'd stayed in Manchester she'd never have got involved with Natchow."

The regret and longing in his voice was hard to bear.

"When did she meet him?"

"Three, four years ago. They worked together. He was a bit of a high flyer at the time. Josie was besotted with him. Within six months they had bought a house together. They were both earning good money."

"What did you think of him?"

He shrugged.

"I should explain when I finished university I stayed in this area. I married a local girl, but we split up a while ago."

That explained the flat. Larry looked lost for a while, then re-focused.

"The point I'm making is that I didn't really see a lot of him. When I did meet him he seemed pleasant enough at first."

"At first?"

"Yes. Quiet, thoughtful. He was the kind of guy who considered everything carefully before committing himself. A planner, I'd say."

That sounded so unlike Simon I wondered if we were talking about the same person.

"As time went on," continued Larry, "I began to notice he'd been on the booze every time I saw him. I mean whatever time of day it was."

I wrote this down. If Natchow did kill Josie, his drink problem would have played a part.

"He was totally different when he'd had a drink," Larry explained. "impulsive, touchy. Act first, think afterwards."

That was more like the Natchow I knew and loved. I jotted down Larry's comments. Two sides of the same coin, I thought.

"Then I began to notice the bruising," he went on.

He stopped again, making me feel guilty for putting him through this.

"He didn't just use his fists. He'd hit Josie with anything that came to hand."

I made another note. I would go over what I'd written down later.

"Anyway, one day last year, September sometime, she turned up on my doorstep with a couple of suitcases."

He sighed, near to tears again.

"By that time she'd left him. He lost his job and they'd had to sell the house, so she saw that as an opportunity to get away."

I wrote down more details and waited for him to finish.

"She walked out one day and moved into a flat somewhere. Saw a solicitor, got an injunction..."

"Yes."

"She decided to move to Manchester without telling anyone, even me."

She must have thought that was the only way she could be safe.

"And she's been here ever since?"

"Yes. She got a job with Judson Mainwaring. She really liked it there."

There was still lots more I needed to know.

"Have you any idea how Simon Natchow found out where Josie was?"

He shook his head.

"No idea, it could have been a lucky guess. He knew I was here and Josie knew the area from days at uni. He could have come to Manchester on spec, then maybe he asked around when he got here. I really don't know."

That didn't get me very far, but maybe it didn't matter. It was difficult to know at this stage what did matter. Natchow did know she was in Manchester and had found her, that was the thing to hold onto. In any case it might not be a good idea to focus too much on the violent ex-boyfriend.

"Though I'm not restricted like the police," I said, "I do need to check the facts."

This was as good a time as any to raise the question of how Josie knew Marti.

"One thing has been puzzling me for a while," I went on, "perhaps you can help me."

"I'll try."

"A couple of weeks ago, my girlfriend and I met Josie in the Temple pub in Manchester."

I explained about what I had heard Josie say on the phone in the Temple car park.

"Any idea what that was all about," I asked.

He screwed up his eyes in concentration.

"Yes, she was phoning me. It goes back to when Josie was about fifteen."

Could that be the connection with Marti?

"Was this in London?"

"Yeah, but...I'd better explain. Mum and Dad had high expectations of all of us. It was kind of expected we'd do well at school and follow in their footsteps."

I wondered where this was leading but let him get on with it.

"Josie was a bit of a rebel, I suppose you'd say..."

A rebellious accountant? Whatever next?

"She felt under pressure, I guess, you know what it's like at that age..."

He stared into space, no doubt remembering his bolshy sister, who wouldn't be rebelling any more.

"She was arrested for possession of cannabis. Her and a few girls from school, you know, just experimenting. No big deal, looking back."

I wrote down what he told me then asked a question.

"What happened?"

He shrugged.

"Not a lot," he said. "A fine, maybe probation for a while, I was at university by that time. Josie was in the dog house with Mum and Dad for a while, but it all blew over pretty quickly."

"And Marti was her solicitor?"

He nodded.

"I can remember Mum saying 'she's a coloured lady actually, from Liverpool I think'. I'm afraid a black woman from the provinces was a bit of a shock to the system for Mum."

"Presumably," I said, ignoring Mrs Finch's prejudices, "Josie wouldn't want to be reminded of her youthful indiscretion?"

"Hardly."

That explained that.

"Did anyone inherit anything from Josie?"

He ran his hands through what was left of his hair.

"Mum and Dad get a few thousand, Josie's savings."

"Not Natchow?"

"No."

"This will be hard to talk about, but I'm afraid I must ask you about the events of 28th February."

He breathed in and sat up straight as if in preparation for an ordeal.

"What do you want to know?"

"Well," I began, "tell me what happened when you got to the Park Hotel car park, what you saw, who you saw."

He looked at the wall behind me as he spoke.

"Well, I was running a bit late. Traffic was worse than I'd anticipated. By the time I pulled into the car park, it was pretty empty, just a couple of cars there."

He seemed to think for a bit.

"No people about. I got out of my car and went towards the pub. I couldn't remember whether I was supposed to meet Josie inside or outside."

Was he concentrating on the mundane aspects to blot out the full horror of the experience?

"It was academic in the end. I walked past a dark Fiesta on the left. Something made me stop; there was what I thought was a bundle on the ground."

He swallowed hard.

"I realised it was a woman lying flat on her back. I leant down. That was when I knew it was Josie."

He sat without moving as if frozen in the moment he found his sister.

"I knew she was dead."

"I know the police must have asked you this, Larry, but did you notice anything at all about your sister's body?"

"Well, there was bruising on her face as from a blow," he said, the first time I had heard what had happened to Josie. "There wasn't a lot of blood. It turned out the blow was from Josie's walking stick. Natchow must have taken it with him afterwards. The police still haven't found it."

His right hand was clenched as he carried on with his account.

"What killed her was hitting her head on the tarmac. One of those freakish things..."

He choked on the last words, as I imagined the crack of her skull on the ground.

"Take it easy, there's plenty of time," I said.

He looked down at the floor. I had to go on.

"Did you realise Simon Natchow had been in the pub that night?"

"Not at the time. Josie had told me he'd been looking for her in the office at Ordsall...?"

"Tower."

"That's it, but you know about that."

Shortly afterwards I left him with a promise to report back. Now all I had to do was look into a murder.

* * *

The tram got me back into Manchester Town Centre in time to keep my lunch appointment with Paul. Albert Square always reminded me of the Whit Walks. For years Catholics marched with fife and drum bands from Salford every Whit Friday. They would finish by assembling outside Manchester Town Hall in Albert Square. There they would sing Faith of Our Fathers, a hymn that extolled the virtues of martyrdom. I gave up Catholicism shortly after my mam had died. Now looking back on it, I was relieved to have left it all behind.

A few minutes later, Paul and I sat in the Chop House, eating fish, chips and mushy peas. In his shiny suit, shirt and tie he looked ultra smart. I didn't.

"So what's this job then, Gus," he asked after a bit of social chit chat.

I put salt on my chips. Sod the blood pressure for once.

"Well, there's two jobs now."

"Two?"

I added vinegar and tasted. Just right.

"I only heard about the second one this morning."

Deciding to deal with them in order, I made a start.

"Did you hear about a bloke called Tattersall being killed," I asked.

He swallowed a mouthful of fish, then nodded.

"The child abuser?"

"That's the one. Everybody seems to think he was killed because somebody found out about his offences."

"That's the most likely solution."

"The boss at Ordsall Tower has asked me to find out how confidential information may have got out."

"Where do I come in?"

I drank some water before replying.

"Well, you live on the estate. See if you can pick up anything and pass it on."

He shrugged and put down his knife and fork.

"I'll see what I can do, Gus," said Paul, "but there's loads of rumours, know what I mean? It's a question of working out what's true and what isn't."

I smiled at him.

"I have every confidence in you, Paul."

"I'll believe you, thousands wouldn't," he grinned. "What's the other job?"

I put my knife down on the side of my plate.

"You might have heard about this one too. The murder of Josie Finch."

He chewed thoughtfully on a chip.

"Finch? Was that the lass found in the Park Hotel?"

"In the car park, yeah, that's her."

After a bit more chewing he asked me what it was all about.

"Well, Josie's family want me to look into it."

I told him about my visit to Whitefield that morning and explained the involvement of Simon Natchow. He put forward his opinion.

"Nine times out of ten the boyfriend did it, know what I mean?"

By this time we were well on with our meals and Paul was thinking about getting back to work.

"Anyway, what do you want me to do," he asked.

Good question, I thought.

"The key time was late at night on the 28th February, a Tuesday."

"Right."

"After, say, half ten. If you can find out if anybody saw someone or something suspicious in the area round the pub. Anything unusual on the estate. You know the type of thing."

I handed him one of the picture of Josie Larry had given me.

"That might come in handy," I said.

He looked sadly at the image of the smiling girl.

"I'll do my best, Gus."

"Hiya, Gus," said a female voice as Paul put the photo in his jacket pocket.

Looking up I saw Hannah standing by our table smiling at me. I said hello and introduced her to Paul.

"Hannah works at Ordsall Tower," I explained.

"Cool," said Paul as was his wont, "are you a social worker then?"

Hannah shook her head, making eye contact with Paul.

"No, receptionist."

I looked from one to the other of the young people.

"She does a great job," I told Paul. "We'd be lost without her."

Hannah smiled modestly.

"What do you do, then, Paul?"

Paul considered this for a second as if struggling with a complex dilemma.

"Most of the time I work in IT," he said, "but today I'm Gus's assistant."

I waited expectantly to see if this would turn out to be a good chat up line. If I were any judge that had been Paul's intention.

"Assistant?"

"Yeah, with his private eye work. Have you heard about that?"

"Oh, yeah," she said. "I know all about him stalking the mean streets of Ordsall and Little Hulton."

They shared a laugh.

"What you doing to help Gus then?"

Paul took a thoughtful sip of water.

"I need to make some inquiries on Gus's behalf," he said, "mainly round the Ordsall area."

"Wow," said Hannah. "I live in Ordsall. You'd better interview me."

She fished in her shoulder bag and pulled out a biro. Picking up a table napkin she wrote on it.

"That's my number," she said, "give me a call."

Then she was off, saying something about her dinner getting cold.

"Down to work straightaway," I said. "I'm impressed."

Paul drank some more water.

"That's me, always on the job. In a manner of speaking."

CHAPTER SEVENTEEN

What more could I do about Josie? That was what I asked myself when I got back home that afternoon. I couldn't just leave it to Paul. The answer came to me as I was checking my e-mails. Make a list. It was obvious really. Making a list was either a way of avoiding doing any work or an essential preparatory step to getting the job done more efficiently. Today I decided the latter interpretation was correct.

I sat at the desk and got into business like mode. A notebook was waiting for me on top of a pile of paper as if it knew what was on my mind. I picked a pen from the cracked Simpsons mug that held such things. I remembered an interview I had read with a novelist whose name escaped me. She had said an empty page is the worst thing. I could soon put that right. Five minutes later I had come up with a list. On Monday I would start the investigation.

At six o'clock I arrived at Marti's. She smiled as she opened the door to me, giving me a hug and a kiss. She looked different somehow, certainly more cheerful, and was moving more freely. She looked even more desirable than usual in jeans and a tight, blue top.

"You seem better," I said as we went into her sitting room and sat on the settee.

"I am. This is my first day without any painkillers."

She took my hand.

"I've booked a table at La Gavroche," she added. "A birthday treat."

I tried not to think of my last birthday treat.

"Great. Is that the new French place?"

Named after some really posh place in London, I recalled.

"Yes," said Marti. "I thought since I rather spoiled your actual birthday, I'd try again."

Was it Marti who had spoiled my birthday? Was there any point in apportioning blame?

"So I'm to have two birthdays? Sounds good."

She stroked my hand.

"And later, well, I don't think I'd like to sleep on my own."

"I don't think I'd like to sleep on my own either."

We sealed the deal with a kiss. So far, so good, I thought.

"Now tell me what you've been doing," she said. "I feel totally cut off from the outside world."

She sat up as if expecting exciting stories of my activities. I hoped I wouldn't disappoint her.

"I've been asked to investigate Josie Finch's murder."

I explained what Larry had asked me to do.

"And I think I've solved the mystery of how Josie knew you," I told her.

"Aren't you clever," she said, "Come on then, tell me."

I went through what Josie's brother had told me about her youthful dope smoking. Marti pulled the sort of face that expressed doubt.

"There's more to it," she said, shaking her head. "I remember her from somewhere else, something else, I know I do."

* * *

The following Monday around lunchtime, I was listening to Rubber Soul, waiting for British Gas to come and fix the central heating. As Paul McCartney told someone called Baby she could drive his car, my mobile rang. I muted the sound on my iPod. Thinking it was the engineer to say he was on his way, I pulled the phone quickly out of my pocket.

"Is that Gus," said a woman's voice.

"Yeah."

"Hi, I'm Yarla Chester, Tony Murphy's PA."

Yarla? Was that a name?

"Hello."

"Gus, I need your help."

She sounded breathless, which added urgency to her request.

"What kind of help?"

"I can't talk about it over the phone. Can I see you, like, now?"

"Where are you?"

A better question would have been, what the hell was this all about?

"I've just got off the train in Manchester," she said as if it were a foreign country.

"Yeah, OK. You'll have to come over here though..."

"No problem."

"It's not very warm. Central heating's packed up, I'm just..."

"Give me the address and I'll jump in a taxi, be with you as quickly as I can."

***

Twenty minutes later, I opened my door to a heavily made up woman, carrying a handbag and an A4 envelope. She had dark hair with blonde highlights. Maybe thirty odd, she wore a bright red jacket and skin tight legging type things.

"Hi, I'm Yarla," she said before she came rushing into the flat, wheeling a suitcase behind her.

Then someone else knocked at the door before I'd even managed to close it.

"British Gas, mate," said a man with a pot belly.

Why did everything happen at once? The heating engineer lugged his equipment into the kitchen. I showed him where the boiler was and explained the problem. Then I went looking for Yarla. I found her in the living room. She had taken her coat off and flung it on the settee beside her. The handbag and envelope rested on top of the coat. Huddled into her thick, baggy jumper, she sat with arms folded protectively across her chest. I sat on an armchair opposite her.

"Do you want a drink, coffee or..."

She shook her head violently as if I'd offered her crack cocaine.

"No, let's get started. I'll tell you why I'm here."

Her accent spoke of privilege; her manner exuded confidence.

"I want you to find Tony."

The question 'what the bloody hell's going on' sprang to mind again. Life had taken on an air of surrealism since Tony had come back.

"Find him?"

She nodded.

"He's gone missing."

"Again," I said.

I shouldn't have said that, I told myself, but recalled my mam's words about Tony Murphy, Trouble with a capital T.

"Again," she repeated. "What do you mean?"

"I'll explain later," I said.

"I was going mad, sitting around waiting, so I got on the first train and came up here."

She spoke precisely, her full lips jutting out with each word. It was as though she'd had surgery to give herself a permanent pout.

"Right."

"I said to myself, don't call first, just go. That way I felt as if I was doing something."

"Tell me what's happened."

"Tony came up here last week, as you know," she said. "I was expecting him back on Friday."

"Were you?"

"Yes. He was supposed to come to the office, but he didn't turn up."

"What makes you think he's actually missing."

"Well, I've texted, phoned, called him at home, been to his house...no sign of him."

"Is this unusual?"

"Oh, yes. I mean, he's constantly in touch."

I had no idea if this woman was panicking for no reason. He could be anywhere, I thought. He might have stayed over with a friend on the way home or something. Maybe he'd lingered longer than planned. I put this to Yarla.

"Oh, I forgot to tell you – I'm in such a state..."

"Forgot to tell me what?"

She sighed.

"He was planning to stay with his friend, Barry in Leighton Buzzard but he didn't turn up."

"I see."

"If he couldn't make it, he would have let Barry know. I'm worried, Gus."

"Let me get this straight. You want to hire me to find Tony?"

"Tony told me you're a private investigator."

I nodded.

"And you're his friend."

Was his friend, I could have told her. That was irrelevant. At the moment the more work I got the better.

"Will you take the case?" she asked. "You're not gonna say you're too busy?"

I thought for a while.

"I am pretty chocker," I lied, "but I think I could fit you in."

"Oh, thanks."

She delved into her handbag and took out a purse. She handed me a wad of notes.

"There's about two hundred there for immediate expenses, travel and so on," she explained. "I guess you have, like, an hourly rate or something?"

"Forty pounds an hour," I said, adding a tenner an hour to my usual fee.

She looked as if she could afford it. And I'd always believed in the redistribution of wealth.

"Is that all?"

I cursed myself for not charging more.

"Well, you know, for a mate..."

"Tony said you were one of the good guys."

Some discordant metallic music disturbed the peace and she pulled her mobile out of her bag.

"Mel, Hi," she purred, "just in the middle of something...it's, like, urgent? Manchester would you believe...yeah, speak soon."

She put her phone away.

"Mélange, my sister."

So her sister was called Mélange. Obviously a bit of a mixture. There was a question I'd forgotten to ask.

"Have you been to the police?"

She shook her head, giving a little shiver.

"Not a good idea."

Yarla sighed and sat back on the settee.

"Tony wouldn't want them involved with him in any way."

"OK."

"Tony's a risk taker," she said, as if explaining how to tell the time to a child, "so he kind of takes risks."

I could have just about worked that out for myself. What I couldn't work out was what sort of risks he took and why taking risks was a good thing anyway. I had a strong suspicion it was all meaningless bollocks and Yarla and Tony had both read the same book: Platitudes for Beginners. What would she come out with next?

"He's talked about people being after him."

Not to me, he hadn't. Consett had been after him, though, hadn't he?

"I'm frightened for him."

There was a deep sadness behind her eyes as she twisted her hands together.

"You see, Gus," she said, "Ours wasn't just a professional relationship. We had a bit of a thing going, you know? Not a conventional relationship of course."

Heaven forbid.

"But with a man like Tony, that doesn't matter. Please find him for me, Gus."

Could it be she really cared?

"I'll do my best."

She leaned over to pat my knee.

"You'd better give me some details," I said.

"Fine."

"I'll be back in a minute," I said, getting up.

I came back with a notebook and pen.

"I'll need a recent photo."

She gave me the envelope.

"There's one in there."

I took the papers out of the envelope. Details of where Tony lived, office address, car registration, business contacts, e-mail address and close friends (precious few of them) were included.

"Let me check some facts," I said. "When did you last see Tony?"

"The day he left for Manchester."

"Did he say anything about his plans?"

She stroked her chin for a moment.

"Yes, he was going to contact his mother as soon as possible..."

"He managed that..."

"He rang me after he'd seen her and he said he planned to look you up."

She moved around on the settee then sat still again.

"He had a few bits of business to attend to, but he kept his cards close to his chest as far as that was concerned."

He didn't tell his secretary? Pull the other one, Yarla. If I didn't know where he had been, I was working with one hand tied behind my back.

"Come on, Yarla, you must have some idea where he went and who he saw."

She shrugged in a way she thought was cute. I just found it annoying.

"Really, Gus, I knew next to nothing about his work. I think he just liked having me around. Partly for, well, you know..."

She lowered her eyes in mock modesty.

"...and partly because he thought it looked good to have a PA."

That I could believe, though I was still sceptical. But if that was the way she wanted it, who was I to argue?

"Did Tony mention anyone called Brenda?"

"Brenda? No, he surely didn't know anybody called Brenda?"

* * *

When she had gone I phoned Brenda to tell her about Yarla's visit and what she wanted.

"So she thinks he's actually missing," she said.

"So it seems."

"History repeating itself."

Brenda must be wishing she'd never started this. So much of her past she would rather forget was coming back to haunt her.

"Yeah. Just for the record, do you know where Tony is?"

"No."

I thought what to do next. It would at least give the illusion of action if I went to see Brenda again, so I suggested it to her.

"Yes, if you think it would help, fine," she said. "Why don't I come to you this time? I fancy a day out."

It would be easier for me, certainly.

"Yeah, we could meet at Tony and Dino's on Salford Quays, it sounds appropriate."

Brenda couldn't make it until Wednesday so we arranged to meet there around twelve o'clock for lunch. Once again I entered the appointment in my diary. By the time I saw Brenda again it would be 14th March. March nearly half over and, though I was busy, I wasn't really getting anywhere. Ah, well.

CHAPTER EIGHTEEN

An hour after Yarla left there was a knock on the door.

"Now then," said the man at the door, dressed in a suede jacket and beige polo neck.

"Steve," I said, "you're early."

He followed me into the kitchen, wheeling his suitcase behind him and carrying two bottles of red wine.

"Yeah, made good time," he said, "not too much traffic for a change."

He sat at the table, handing the bottles to me.

"Tea," I asked.

"Good idea."

I put the wine on a work surface by the sink, filled the kettle and put it on the hob.

"How's Dolgellau," I asked, going back to the table.

"As lovely as ever, you should move there, Gus."

I sighed. We'd had this conversation before.

"No," I said, "I agree it's lovely as is most of North Wales, but I'm happy here."

Steve shrugged.

"Suit yourself," he said.

"It's great to visit, but the delights of Salford always lure me back."

He chuckled quietly.

"Anyway," I said, "you've just missed Tony Murphy's PA."

He laughed out loud.

"You're taking the piss."

I shook my head.

"No, she was here, left about an hour ago. Rejoices in the name of Yarla."

"Yarla? God help us. What did she want?"

"She wants me to find him."

"Find...? You mean he's gone missing again?"

"I'll explain, shall I?"

"Go on."

I told him what had been happening on planet Murphy, a different place from where the rest of us lived. I'd got to the point where Brenda told me about the son she'd had adopted when a whistling kettle interrupted me. Getting up, I made tea. Splashing milk into two mugs, I brought them and the pot to the table. Sitting down again, I finished the tale.

"Well good luck with it," he said, "though if he isn't found for thirty odd years I for one won't shed any tears."

Maybe I wouldn't either.

"I told you Murphy was trouble, didn't I," said Steve for good measure.

"Not trouble for me. I've got some work out of it. And believe me I could do with it."

"Is this the only case you've got on then?"

"No, it's one of three actually."

"Three? What are the others about?"

I told him about Josie Finch: a detailed account of her murder, how I came to know her and anything else I could think of.

"Looks like you'll have your hands full with that one. What about the third one?"

I then explained about Tattersall and the need to know how the information about him got out.

"So you haven't been asked to find out who killed him?"

"No."

"In that case the Josie Finch case sounds more interesting. How are you going to go about it?"

I thought for a moment before answering, discarding 'dunno really' and 'I'm still thinking about it'.

"Well," I said, "I've made a list."

"Made a list, eh?"

Did I detect a note of cynicism in his words?

"That's half the battle," he added, driving the point home. "I think we'll have it cracked in no time."

"Bound to."

He sighed and sat up in his chair.

"OK, let's have a look at this famous list."

I went to the spare room and brought back an A4 sheet, placing it flat on the table. I sat next to Steve. On the Copelaw case a couple of years ago I had found his detective's analysis helpful. We perused the list together:

Interview Arthur
Interview Angela Bromwich
Interview Simon Natchow
Interview Tony Murphy
Interview Karen Davidson

"I thought that'd be quite enough to be going on with," I said.

Steve looked down the items again.

"Too true, that lot will take a while."

"How much of it have you actually done?"

"Er, let me see...nothing."

He laughed.

"Well," I said in justification, "I only got the case on Friday and I don't work on weekends if I can help it."

Steve picked up the sheet of paper and held it out as if practising some weird ritual.

"Right. Are we eating in or out tonight?"

I assumed he had tired of the investigation already.

"In. There's coq au vin in the slow cooker."

"Love in a lorry, great."

I laughed dutifully at one of Steve's favourite jokes.

"You can't beat the old ones," I said.

Steve got up, picking up his bag.

"Here's the plan," he said, sounding as I imagined he used to when giving a briefing for Manchester police, "early doors we go to the Park Hotel for a pre-prandial pint and deal with point one on the list."

I should have thought of that.

"And now," Steve continued, "I shall retire to my sleeping quarters to unpack. I take it I'm in the blue room again?"

"I trust sir will find everything to his satisfaction."

As I watched my friend walk away, I could only hope that by talking to Arthur tonight I'd get a lead.

* * *

On the way to the pub later Steve went on about his two favourite things. I did my best to switch off during the first of these: his new BMW. Eventually my lack of response led Steve onto a topic I had more interest in: the form of Manchester United, who were battling it out for the title with City. I had fond memories of the 1960s team with Best, Charlton et al who lit up my childhood. Steve and I used to walk to the ground with my dad. I had supported them ever since, like all true Salfordians, even through the bad times, though Rugby League always came first.

"You know, Steve," I said, "the last time we saw Tony was in the year United got relegated."

"Dark days," he said without the least trace of irony.

"Don't know about that. Salford were doing well."

Steve pulled a face; if I hadn't played for them the progress of his home town rugby league team wouldn't have figured in his life. I'd tried telling him it was part of his working class heritage but he wouldn't listen. Anything that sounded left wing was anathema to Steve, as was any suggestion he was working class.

"Talking of Tony," he said, "what do you reckon has happened to him this time?"

I shrugged.

"I'd say he's just buggered off, leaving everyone in the lurch again. The idea of responsibility is too much for him. He's only bothered about himself."

* * *

As we went inside the Park Hotel, Arthur looked up from behind the bar and gave us a wave.

"Now then, Gus," he said as we got nearer, "I see you've brought Superintendent Yarnitzky, retired, with you."

"All right, Arthur," said Steve.

"You'll be ready for a pint after your long journey from the wilds of Wales."

We ordered two pints of Red Devil. Arthur began pulling them as I looked round the room. Apart from Steve and me at the bar, the only other customers were two couples sat at tables at either end of the room.

"Looks like adulterers' happy hour," suggested Steve.

"Cynic," I said, "they're probably happily married."

Arthur spoke from behind the beer pump.

"Oh, aye, to somebody else."

When the laughter had died down, I decided to broach the first subject on the agenda.

"Arthur," I said quietly as he continued pulling the pints, "have you got time for a word?"

He stopped what he was doing for a moment.

"Yeah," he replied. "Now's the best time, while it's quiet."

It was that all right. The drinkers engaged in illicit encounters were whispering.

"It's about Josie Finch," I explained.

"Oh, aye? What about her?"

"Her brother has asked me to look into her murder."

He pulled the rest of the pint before saying any more.

"Has he? So this is work, is it? Where do you come in, Steve?"

I answered before Steve could get a word in.

"He's my assistant," I said, "he's on work experience."

Arthur laughed as Steve looked daggers at me.

"Just for that you can buy the beer."

We took the glasses Arthur handed to us.

"Why doesn't her brother leave it to the police," asked the landlord.

After a first mouthful, I told him about Larry's frustration that the police had insufficient evidence to nail Natchow for the crime.

"So the family are convinced he did it," asked Arthur.

I got my wallet out and extracted a £10 note.

"Yes," I said, handing over the money. "They want me to prove it."

"Good luck to you, Gus, but if the police can't prove it..."

He gave a philosophical shrug, went to the till and came back with my change.

"Well, let's see what you remember about that night."

He breathed in, then out again, puffing out his cheeks.

"You've got to remember I was busy serving and doing the quizmaster bit."

And any recollection he had would be partial and subjective, but I wasn't going to let that put me off. I moved on to my first question.

"What time did Simon Natchow arrive that night?"

"Pass."

I pulled a face.

"Make an effort, Arthur."

He grinned at me.

"Sorry, mate, I couldn't resist that. Anyway, you were there."

This was going to be hard work, I could see that.

"I know, but I want to check whether you remember it in the same way I do."

"Fair point," he acknowledged. "It was after a couple of rounds of the quiz, so...half nine, just after...give or take."

That sounded about right. I took another drink. It tasted as nice as ever. Maybe being named after Salford Rugby League club gave it a special quality.

"Had he been in before?"

"Yeah, come to think of it he used to come in with that Tattersall now and again."

Was that relevant, I wondered? Should I have tackled Simon about his friend, Edward? A different case, I told myself, concentrate on the matter in hand.

"Had you had any bother with him any other time?"

He wiped the bar while thinking about this.

"Not like on the night of the quiz, but every time he came in he'd already had a few."

"Right."

That sounded like pretty typical, I thought, as I recalled the morning he came into Ordsall Tower looking for Josie. I could see him in my mind's eye, swigging at the whisky bottle he had taken from his pocket.

"He'd get a bit loud, you know," Arthur added, "truculent, I suppose you'd say, but he never really overstepped the mark."

How did you decide when somebody had overstepped the mark?

"After you chucked him out," I went on, "did you see him again?"

"No. I haven't laid eyes on him since then. I don't bloody want to."

"What about your staff? Have they said anything about seeing him?"

He shook his head.

"Sorry. One or two have talked about seeing him around since poor Josie got killed, but not on the actual night."

If Natchow really didn't come back to the pub then somebody else killed Josie, that much was obvious. So I'd better ask different questions.

"Right. Around the time we left," I said, "say eleven o'clock or thereabouts. Did you go into the car park?"

Arthur straightened a towel on the bar.

"No, we were clearing up in here. Everybody else decided to go home when you did."

'So if Simon had come back you wouldn't have seen him?"

"Not if he stayed outside. And before you ask, there's no CCTV."

There wouldn't be, not when you needed it.

"Two people did come back, though," said Arthur after a moment's thought.

"Who?"

"Well, your friend and mine, Tony – he'd come back for his fags and lighter. And that nice lass you work with. Karen. She'd left a scarf on the back of a chair. Said it was a present, didn't want to lose it."

That didn't tell me much I thought as Arthur went on.

"Come to think of it, I've got some photos of the quiz night."

"Right," I said. "Let's have a look at them, see if they trigger any memories."

"Sit down and I'll get the iPad."

While Arthur was gone, we sat at a table nearby and sipped our beers. When he got back he put the iPad on the table and switched on. He found the photos and left us to it. We spent a few minutes looking at a seemingly endless stream of images of people bent in concentration over sheets of paper. There were snaps of people who had noticed they were being photographed pulling funny faces at the camera.

"There's Natchow," I said after a while.

He was resplendent in his red anorak, or as near as he ever came to resplendence. Another shot of Natchow caught the moment when he approached our table.

"They haven't inspired any new insights, Steve," I said. "The trouble is they are all taken inside. The important things happened outside."

I turned to Steve.

"Any thoughts?"

He scrolled through the photos again then stopped after about half a dozen. He stared intently at the picture he'd got to.

"What was she doing here?"

I looked over to him, puzzled.

"She was at the quiz, I told you. That's..."

"I know who she is."

The world was full of surprises, I thought.

"You know Josie Finch?"

Steve looked at me as if I were mad, pointing to one of the pictures.

"That's Josie Finch," I said.

His eyes opened wide.

"Josie Finch? Never in the memory of man," he said, "that's Michelle Adams."

We seemed to be at cross purposes.

"Michelle who?"

Steve tutted.

"Michelle Adams. You must remember her."

"Can't say I do," I replied, looking at the photo.

"She was the girlfriend of Edward Keith, who killed a little boy called Jack Hinton in Norfolk."

That stirred an indistinct memory.

"She covered up for him," Steve went on, "got done for perverting the course of justice. Probably out of prison by now."

I tried to take in what Steve was saying.

"And you think that's her?"

He nodded.

"But she can't be," I countered.

He had another look at Josie.

"Let me get this straight. This woman here," he said, pressing his thumb on the screen, "is the one who got killed in the Park Hotel car park?"

"Correct."

He shook his head in disbelief.

"But she's the image of Michelle Adams."

"I can't believe it," I said after a bit of pensive beer drinking.

"Think about it, Gus," said Steve. "When she got out of prison she would have been given a new identity for her own safety."

The idea that what Steve was saying was actually true began to filter through my brain.

"I suppose you're right."

"This is what happens when you get mixed up in a murder."

"Bloody hell," I said. "Why can't anything be straightforward?"

He chuckled over his pint.

"Cos Gus Keane doesn't do straightforward. I mean, with most murders you just have to look for the Sybil Fawlty solution."

"Sybil Fawlty?"

What was he on about now?

"You know, Sybil's chosen specialist subject on Mastermind: the bleeding obvious."

How could I have forgotten?

"But once you get involved, it gets complicated."

I mulled over the Michelle Adams/Josie Finch dilemma.

"On reflection," I said, "wouldn't it have got out by now? And she would surely have changed her appearance. Grown her hair, dyed it black or whatever, worn contact lenses."

I sipped more beer.

"Probably," agreed Steve.

He looked into the beer in his glass.

"Although it does throw a different light on the murder," he added.

Now what, I thought.

"Whether she is Michelle Adams or not, she looks like Michelle Adams."

I still didn't get it; my brain was beginning to hurt. Steve explained further.

"Somebody else might have recognised her," said Steve. "And, thinking she was an accessory to child murder, sought revenge?"

"Shit."

I thought of people being attacked by vigilantes, who hadn't bothered to make sure they'd got the right person. I tried to work out how this might have affected Josie.

"It still leaves a lot of unanswered questions," I said. "If she was instantly recognizable as Michelle Adams why hadn't somebody had a go before now?"

I thought about the photograph of Josie that her brother had given me. An inkling of an idea crept into my mind. I took out my mobile, found Larry's number and dialled.

"Larry, it's Gus, have you got time to talk?"

"Sure."

I took a second to work out what to say.

"Has Josie changed her appearance recently?"

"Depends what you mean. She had her hair cut short before she went to Tenerife, said it would be cooler."

That fitted with what I'd been thinking.

"In the photo you gave me she wasn't wearing glasses."

"No, she usually wore contact lenses, but she had trouble with them while she was away. Went back to glasses."

I had one more question.

"When did she get back from Tenerife?"

"The week before she died, can't remember exactly. What's all this about?"

Was there an explanation for all this? It might be a complete red herring. Then again, it might not.

"I can't explain now, Larry. It's nothing to worry about. I'll be in touch."

I told Steve what Larry had said.

"So she's only looked like Adams for a short time," he asked.

"Looks like it."

Steve took his phone out of his jacket and began to dial.

"I'll give Sarita a ring."

Do you have to, Steve, I wondered? Question expecting the answer yes. I recalled the time at his home in Dolgellau when he had called DI Ellerton after describing her as his protégée.

"Sarita," he said, "Steve Yarnitzky here."

He smirked as he listened.

"Of course you haven't got time to chat," he said, "a busy working mum like you, but I may be able to help you with your inquiries."

Another pause followed while Sarita spoke.

"Interfere with you? I can't think what you mean, Sarita..."

He looked over at me and winked.

"I'm in the Park Hotel with my old friend, Gus Keane. He sends his love by the way..."

I tried to signal to Steve that I wanted to be kept out of this conversation. He covered the phone with his hand.

"She sends her love too, wonders why a nice bloke like you knocks about with someone like me."

Steve went back to his call, which, in my estimation, seemed to be going on forever.

"We've been looking at some photos of Josie Finch, the lass who got killed...have you noticed she's the image of Michelle Adams?"

He tutted.

"Michelle Adams, the Jack Hinton case in Norfolk...that's the one."

He adopted a serious expression, nodding at intervals.

"That's fine then," he said, "just thought I'd mention it...I'll let you get on. Cheers, Sarita."

He ended the call.

"She thanked me for my call and said she would take my information into account."

CHAPTER NINETEEN

The next day I knocked on the door of a council house a few minutes' walk from Ordsall Tower.

"Hello, Imogen," I said, "sorry to bother you. It's Gus Keane from..."

She frowned, looking me up and down as if finding me wanting in every way possible. She put her white-gloved hands on her hips.

"I know who you are. What do you want?"

I clutched my briefcase, wishing I could get out of the strong wind.

"Angela Bromwich, the manager, asked me to call. Just to see how you are and check one or two things."

Her sigh came up from her furry carpet slippers.

"I suppose you'd better come in."

I followed her into the living room. Cosy, I would have called it. Neat and tidy too, but not excessively so. Tattersall had probably thought a man could feel at home here. Somewhat superior to Deadbeat Mansions anyway. Not that he had been motivated by anything other than true love. Imogen invited me to sit down and offered tea or coffee.

"No, I'm fine thanks," I said.

I took out a notebook from my briefcase, as we sat opposite one another on matching armchairs. On the small table to my right was a library book called Setting Up Your Own Business, a closed laptop and Topsy and Tim's Monday Book. Topsy and Tim, I thought, happy days, as my mind took me straight back to Danny and Rachel's childhood. I almost forgot what I was going to say for a moment.

"I was just wondering how things were since Edward died," I said.

She glared at me.

"What do you think? Some stupid sod couldn't mind his own business and now my boyfriend's dead."

"So you think whoever killed Edward saw one of those leaflets about his offences?"

"Suppose so."

"Who do you think produced the leaflets?"

She shrugged.

"Had you confided in anyone?"

"Confided?"

"About Edward?"

Her face registered scorn.

"Huh. Who would I confide in? What am I supposed to say? 'Oh, by the way, you know Edward? He's been to prison for child abuse'."

It seemed obvious a woman in Imogen's position would keep quiet about it, but many didn't. They took on the role of persecuted victim, bullied by uncaring social workers, and tried to gather a support group around them.

"You don't remember hearing anyone say anything, drop any hints?"

Again she shook her head. She clenched her hands tight.

"Do you need any help at all?"

I knew she had refused help after the meeting we'd had in the office, but she may have thought again. She shook her head, rubbing her bottom lip against the top one.

"No, that Karen offered me counselling, but that would mean going over it all again, wouldn't it?"

"Yes. It's your choice of course."

Which was best, I asked myself? Talking about it until it wasn't such a weight or trying to forget it and getting on with your life? I thought of the counselling I had had a couple of years ago. It worked for me but what did that mean to anybody else?

She stopped in mid-stream as though struggling for the right words.

"At least there won't be anybody coming round checking on the kids now. I just want to be left in peace."

Don't we all at times? There seemed little point in pursuing the offer of help.

"Look, Gus," she said with an air of finality, "if I need any help I'll get in touch, OK? I know you're only doing your job, but having social services on your back isn't a lot of fun."

No, not fun, I thought.

* * *

In Angela Bromwich's office in Ordsall Tower a few minutes later, I told her about my interview with Imogen and what Ian at Deadbeat Mansions said.

"So, no sign of any leak," asked Angela.

"No, I'll keep digging though."

It struck me how different she looked in her dark, formal clothes, than she had at the quiz. This led me to consider again Josie's change of appearance. Would that turn out to be important or not?

"I did want to talk to you about a couple of other things, Angela," I said after a slight hesitation.

"Oh, yes?"

I knew asking about Tony may cause embarrassment, so I decided in my cowardly way to deal with Josie first.

384

"The first concerns Josie Finch."

I explained about Larry's request for me to investigate his sister's killing.

"My, you are in demand."

"I suppose I am," I said. "I should say the family are convinced Simon Natchow did it and want me to prove it."

Looking at my notebook, I scanned the main points I wanted to cover.

"If you could go through what you remember of what happened that night."

She placed her hands flat on her desk and concentrated.

"Well, as you probably know, I had a bit to drink that night," she said, "so I'm not sure how reliable my memory will be."

I waited, confident she would get going soon. She did.

"Well, I remember Natchow coming up to our table. I found him a bit scary. He seemed...I don't know, a bit paranoid. As if people were out to get him...and he was out to get them."

That sounded like Natchow all right.

"What about later? You know, when we were all leaving."

She looked questioningly at me.

"What are you trying to find out?"

I tried to get my thoughts in order.

"Josie seems to have been killed in the few minutes from the people in our quiz team leaving and her brother arriving to pick her up."

She thought in silence for a moment.

"Yes, I suppose she must have been. Now then, let me think, I walked into the car park at the back with Tony..."

She stopped as if giving herself time to get her account right.

"Yes, we were waiting for a taxi. It would only have been a minute or so before it arrived."

What happened in that minute or so and the time it took to drive away could be important?

"Did you notice anything while you were waiting?"

"Only one another," she said, the hint of a blush on her cheek and an 'aren't I daring' twinkle in her eye.

"Just as the cab got there, Tony went back in for his cigarettes and lighter, I remember. When he came back we left."

I plodded on, not expecting anything to come from all this.

"Did you see anything as you left the car park?"

She shook her head.

"Sorry, Gus, I'd like to help, I really would. Nothing springs to mind."

I sighed.

"Did you see Natchow or Josie?"

Another head shake.

"No."

I had been writing in my book and now stopped.

"What did you think of Josie," I asked, having got as far as I could with purely factual questions.

"I don't know that I thought anything about her. Why do you ask?"

What could I say to that? I'm clutching at straws? My mate, Steve think she could be somebody else.

"Well, you and she had a bit of an altercation in the office."

Sighing, she frowned before she responded.

"Yeah, she caught me at a bad time."

I decided to follow this up.

"You didn't seem too pleased to see her at the quiz."

She shrugged.

"I was surprised she was there. And now I think about it I did find her irritating."

"Irritating?"

"Yes. Along with so many other things in my life. She seemed to think her bloody accounts were the most important thing in the world."

She sighed in exasperation.

"She wouldn't leave me alone. I had better things to worry about, quite frankly. I'm on the point of burn out; I'm drinking too much; my home life's a mess since Frank got made redundant and..."

She stopped and slumped back in her seat.

"Sorry, Gus, you don't want to hear this."

She placed her hands on her thighs and let her shoulders relax.

"So there was nothing wrong with the accounts," I asked.

She stared at me, fury on her face.

"What are you getting at? You've heard the rumours, haven't you?"

I looked away momentarily.

"Well, there was..."

She breathed out audibly through her mouth.

"My God, this is intolerable. If people around here paid as much attention to their work as they do to tittle tattle, we'd all be better off."

Play it cool, Gus, I said to myself.

"That doesn't really answer the question," I said.

"OK. There is nothing wrong with the accounts. Judson Mainwaring sent somebody to replace Josie and everything's been signed off."

She drummed her fingers on her desk. Time to move on, I thought.

"I've got just one more question about Josie," I said.

She sighed, then grinned at me.

"You're a cheeky sod."

"I know," I replied, grinning back.

"When you first met Josie did you recognise her?"

She looked genuinely baffled.

"No, should I have?"

"You didn't think she looked familiar?"

"No, sorry."

I left it at that.

"The other case I'm involved in concerns Tony Murphy," I said.

"Tony? That's another thing. I'm sorry the poor girl got killed, really I am, but it has meant the Manchester police knowing my intimate business. I didn't tell them the truth at first, but somebody must have grassed me up."

As long as she didn't know it was me, I thought.

"Anyway, Tony's PA came to see me on Monday. She seems to think Tony's missing."

"Missing? He can't be."

Oh, yes, he can, I said to myself, you don't know him like I do. I explained what Yarla had told me.

"Oh, my God, but..."

She stopped abruptly.

"I'll ask the obvious question," I said. "Do you know where he is?"

"I haven't a clue."

Having decided to try and piece together his movements in the time since I'd last seen him, I made a start.

"What happened after you left the Park Hotel that night?"

"I think you can work that out for yourself, can't you," she said, the faint blush threatening to make a comeback.

"I suppose what I'm getting at," I said, "is where did you go, when did you last see him and do you remember anything that might give a clue as to his whereabouts?"

I paused for breath.

"Mmm," she said. "Well, the first bit's easy. We went to the Midland Hotel. The last time I saw Tony was in the early hours of the morning when I sneaked out without waking him."

"How did you get back home?"

That wasn't really relevant, just curiosity.

"Taxi."

An expensive business, these affairs.

"Right. Did Tony say anything about where he was going next?"

She sat back, obviously bored with my questions.

"Gus, we didn't do a lot of talking. That wasn't the idea. Oh, I know it sounds sordid, but a girl's got to have some fun."

"Angela, think," I instructed, irritated by her vagueness and her asides about her dalliance with Tony. "Tony must have said something about his plans."

She made an effort to look as if she were considering what I had said.

"Well, he was the kind of guy who tries to impress all the time, you know," she said.

I looked at her, willing her to go on. I was already beginning to form my own impressions of what Tony Murphy was like. What I wanted was to find him.

"He said something about having business to sort out, but he invested it with a kind of mystery. So I had no idea what it was or where he'd be doing it."

I jotted down notes.

"He mentioned an old flame he might look up. Even that was meant to be a big deal. To hear him talk, this Barbara or whatever she was called had been pining for him since she was a slip of a girl."

That sounded like Tony. I assumed she meant Brenda, but there could have been a Barbara as well.

"Anything else?"

She shrugged.

"He was stopping off on the way back to London to see a mate."

Brenda had told me that.

"So you can't say specifically where he was going?"

And of course she couldn't.

On my way home, I wondered about Tony and his possible connection to my other two cases. Things had started to happen once Tony came back into my life. Was that coincidence? It was difficult to see how it could be anything else, but maybe I should think about it.

CHAPTER TWENTY

That afternoon found me approaching Dedby Mansions again. I went in at the front entrance and into a damp, chilly foyer. My footsteps echoed as I climbed to the first floor. At flat 13 I knocked on the door and waited. The door creaked open.

"Hello, Simon," I said.

He peered at me as though trying to identify a laboratory sample. It took a while for him to recognise me.

"Oh, it's you. What do you want?"

He tensed as he said the words like a bouncer in a club ready to turn away anyone not suitably dressed.

"It's confidential," I replied. "I'm sure you wouldn't want to discuss your private affairs out here."

Scowling, he held the door open. That approach always worked.

"You'd better come in."

It was only a step into Natchow's living room. I breathed in a mixture of stale sweat, booze and tobacco. As the room's windows were rarely opened the fug had lingered. The place was cleaned even more rarely. Simon moved an out of date copy of the Radio Times and a Daily Mail from a battered chair. It had the same level of taste and comfort as Ian Jamieson's place.

"Sit down."

I sat while he lowered himself onto a green settee that sagged in the middle. This too held a pile of papers as well as a crust of burnt toast.

"Right, what is it?"

In answer I took my wallet from my trouser pocket and handed Simon a card for GRK Investigations.

"What the bloody hell's this?"

"I'm a private investigator," I said.

He looked up from his perusal of the card, which seemed to hold endless fascination for him.

"I thought you were a social worker."

I put my wallet back in my pocket.

"I'm versatile. I'd like your help with a couple of things."

"Like what?"

It suddenly struck me that Natchow was sober. There was a first time for everything.

"Firstly, I want to ask you about the tragic death of Josie Finch."

He leaned forward, his hands joined together and resting on his lap.

"Tragic is right. I only wish I could get my hands on whoever killed her."

He sank back into the cushions.

"Josie's brother has asked me on behalf of her family to look into her death," I said.

He breathed in as though building up to something.

"That Larry, he didn't like me. I bet he thinks I killed Josie."

"He's suspicious."

"Well, I didn't kill her, you can get that out of your head for a start."

He pointed his finger angrily at me.

"I'm gutted about Josie dying, gutted. I still had hopes she'd see sense and we could get back together."

She'd seen sense all right.

"You can help me," I said, "because you knew Josie and because you saw her not long before she died."

He said nothing, seeming to have gone into a trance.

"Who might have killed her, Simon, that's what we have to think about?"

He shook his head.

"Some nutter, that's what I think. She was in the wrong place at the wrong time. Nobody who knew Josie would have killed her."

Somebody did kill her, I reminded myself, and most murder victims are killed by somebody known to them. It might, in Simon's words, be 'some nutter', but the odds were against it.

"When you left the Park Hotel on the night Josie died, where did you go?"

"Here we go again, I went through all this with the police. They wanted to pin it on me too."

I looked him in the eye, hoping that would make him go on talking.

"Oh, I don't suppose it will do any harm to tell you," he said. "It might get rid of you quicker."

He leant forward again.

"I went home, went to bed and fell asleep. The cops woke me up about half two in the morning."

"Right."

"They took me down to the station. Questioned me for hours, they did. Checked the clothes I was wearing that night. Fingerprints, DNA, the lot. Eventually they let me go."

Would I simply have to accept that Natchow couldn't have killed his girlfriend? So who did?

"In the time you knew her, was Josie ever mistaken for somebody else?"

"No, what are you getting at?"

"Just a line of inquiry I'm following," I said with a touch of smugness. "Did she ever meet anyone who thought they recognised her but she didn't know them?"

A look of bafflement spread over his face.

"What is this?"

"Just answer the question."

"The answer's no. Is that all? Because I have better things to do than sit here answering stupid questions."

Such as, I wondered?

"This won't take much longer. Before I go, Simon, can I ask you about Tony Murphy?"

He scowled again.

"It'll save me coming back," I added.

That clinched it.

"Go on then. What's that wanker done now?"

A good question, I thought. The way it was phrased suggested a history of things he'd done which led to his unpopularity with Simon.

"Well, his secretary is worried about him, she hasn't seen him for several days and doesn't know where he is. She's asked me to try and find him."

He pursed his lips.

"I'll tell you what, mate, when you do find him ask him where my money is."

This was becoming more interesting by the minute.

"How did you know Tony?" I prompted.

"When I lived in London with Josie," he said, "I was earning good money and looking for promising investments."

I was wondering why those words sounded familiar when I remembered what Josie said the day I first met her in Ordsall Tower. Something about Simon's bad investments, wasn't it?

"Well," he went on, "I met Tony Murphy down the George and Dragon, you know in Lekeren Grove..."

Can't say I do, Simon, I thought.

"...and I thought, 'top man', you know. Only little but larger than life type of thing. He seemed to know what he was on about."

Talked a good game in other words. I'd met a few like that.

"He was doing all right for himself, you could see that. Had this posh car salesroom in Hammersmith. He was looking for small investors to help him expand."

I'm ahead of you, Simon, I thought.

"Well, the long and the short of it is I invested, correction, gave him twenty grand and I haven't see a penny of it since."

The idea that Tony Murphy was a little twat lodged itself in my mind and wouldn't be shifted. If that were the case, the worst of it was that Steve would be proved right. And my mam. Bugger.

* * *

Later that day I got into my car and headed towards the M602. I slipped a homemade CD in the player. Some Songs it was called. How did I think of that one? The motorways around Manchester – sometimes there seemed to be hundreds of them – were nearly always busy but today traffic was no too bad. As Bob Seger belted out Feel Like A Number, I drove at a steady 65, overtaking the odd lorry, but sticking mainly to the inside lane. There was plenty of time. Within 15 minutes I was driving past the terraced houses on Manchester Road in Walkden.

Before setting out I had checked the electoral register in the library in Robert Hall Street to get Mrs Murphy's address. I hadn't been able to find her phone number, so just hoped she'd be in when I got there. According to Tony she had remembered me when he saw her, which might help. But how would I approach my task? Telling her that her son may be missing again wasn't going to be easy.

Turning left off Manchester Road in Little Hulton I went slowly down Kenyon Way, trying to gauge where the flat might be. When I thought I'd got somewhere near it I pulled into the side of the road. I got out and locked up, walking over to a two storey block of flats, checking the numbers. I found the one I was looking for and rang the bell. Before I'd had time to think a woman in her eighties, short and dumpy, was talking to me.

"Yes?"

"Mrs Murphy?"

She looked me up and down as if working out whether she could trust me.

"That's right."

"Hello, Mrs Murphy. I'm Gus Keane, don't know if you..."

Her eyes opened wide.

"Gus! Come in, come in."

She stepped back and I crossed the threshold. Only the smallness of the lounge stopped it looking like part of a show house on a modern estate. Everything was brand new: the three-piece suite, the burgundy carpet, the flat screen telly on its stand that dominated the room. The walls and skirting boards gleamed with fresh paint, the glass topped table had been polished to within an inch of its life.

"Sit down, I'll put the kettle on," she said, disappearing out of another door on the other side of the room.

I heard her moving about in what I assumed was the kitchen. Some minutes elapsed before she returned with a tray. Jumping up, I took it from her, placed it carefully on the table and sat down again. She sat opposite me.

"You saw Tony then," she said.

"Yes. It was quite a surprise hearing from him."

She smiled again.

"How do you think I felt? I got the shock of my life."

I looked at her. She showed the obvious signs of aging: hair completely white; wrinkles around the eyes; liver spots on the back of the hand. There was an alertness about her though, a kind of toughness that could withstand any number of shocks. Or was that wishful thinking on my part? Was I just hoping she'd cope with the shock I was about to give her?

"I was pleased to see him, course I was, especially when he's doing so well."

A faraway look came into her eyes.

"Oh, but I gave him such a telling off. You wouldn't believe it."

I thought I would believe it.

"Anyway, help yourself to tea and cake. You can be mother."

As I poured tea into Manchester United mugs, she went on with what she was saying.

"I said to him, I said, 'It's not just me you should be going to see. What about Brenda? What about your friends?'"

I took a piece of fruit cake and looked at the framed family photographs on top of cupboards around the room. I thought I could make out a couple of Tony at 18, one with me and Steve.

"Lovely cake," I said.

It was nearly as nice as mine.

"Oh, do you like it? I still do a lot of baking. Anyway, I said you get in touch with Brenda and try and make things right with her. Then you do the same with Gus and Steve."

I was strangely touched at her concern, misplaced as it was. Had I never heard from Tony again it wouldn't have bothered me. It was different for Mrs Murphy and Brenda.

"Right. Er, Tony's secretary has been in touch. She's a bit...she's wondering where he is."

"Oh?"

"Yes, she was expecting him back in London by now and she's asked me to see if I can find out where he might be."

She sighed.

"He'll turn up when he's good and ready."

Was she putting on a brave face or had she developed a philosophical outlook on life during those years when she thought she'd never see her youngest son again?

"When did you last see him," I asked.

"A couple of weeks ago."

"So you just saw him the once? He's not been back since?"

She sipped her tea.

"No, he phoned though. Told me he'd seen Brenda in Sheffield. I'd been hoping he'd have news of my grandson..."

She wiped a tear away with the back of her hand.

"Brenda had him adopted apparently. She has no idea where he is."

Oh, yes, she does, I wanted to say but that would have been like twisting the knife. Tony really was a bastard, wasn't he? Was I to be forever asking myself what the hell he was playing at? It seemed such a pointless lie. What should I say to Tony's mam, that was the question? My dilemma was postponed by the turning of a key in the back door. I heard the door close and the sound of footsteps into the kitchen.

"It's only me, Bernadette," said a man's voice.

"Right."

The man started singing American Pie to the accompaniment of the opening and closing of cupboard doors.

"It's Vic, my brother. He's just brought my shopping."

The uncle who came looking for Tony after he went missing.

"I remember Vic, how is he?"

"All right. Him and his wife help me out a lot. He's a grandfather now."

"Me too."

"Oh, lovely."

We spent some time talking about my family and the chance to talk further about Brenda had gone. Much to my relief. Then the kitchen door opened and a man who looked about sixty odd came in.

"Your shopping's all put away..."

He looked towards me as Mrs Murphy said:

"I've got company."

"All right, mate."

I smiled.

"You remember Gus, don't you, Vic?"

I looked again at the man. Not much hair, a jowly look, a prominent paunch straining against the belt of his jeans. It must be Vic Kennelly, but I'd never have guessed. He stared at me like a man faced with an impenetrable puzzle.

"Gus?"

He shook his head.

"Not Gus Keane?"

"Vic, how are you?"

He shrugged, moving from one foot to another as if embarrassed, then sat next to his sister on the settee.

"Not bad."

"Help yourself to tea, Vic," said Mrs Murphy.

"No, ta, Bernadette. I can only stop a minute. Anyway, Gus, what brings you here?"

I explained about my search for Tony.

"Right. Good luck with that. I haven't seen him since 1974 so I can't help you."

"OK, I'll keep on looking."

Vic got up.

"Gotta be going," he said, "things to do."

His sister started to get up.

"Stay where you are, I know the way out. I'll pop round with the kids tomorrow."

"Oh, smashing."

I got up.

"I'd better be moving too."

Outside Vic and I walked to our cars.

"So that wanker's gone missing again," he said.

"Looks like it."

He shook his head, a look of bewilderment on his face.

"Did Tony tell you why he came back?"

I thought back to our conversation in the Park Hotel.

"He seemed to think it was the right time. He didn't want to die without seeing his mam again. Something like that anyway."

"I'll believe him, thousands wouldn't."

Vic looked thoughtful for a moment.

"Tell you what, Gus," he said eventually, "come back to my house, I want a word with you."

"OK."

"I only live in Astley, I'll lead the way, just follow me."

I drove off in the direction I was facing, turning left down Park Way, passing the place where the Lancastrian had stood, where Tony and I had gone under-age drinking. After a ten minute drive, I pulled in behind Vic's Ford Escort outside a row of houses in Greenland Road in Astley. They dated from the sixties or seventies at a guess. The house next door had a blue plaque on the wall. Ellen Gallagher, Musician and Song Writer Lived Here 1966 to 1969. A proud Salford lass, Ellen was the only famous person I actually knew, albeit through her brother Jimmy. Marti had been in the charts in the eighties – famous for fifteen minutes, she called it – but had given up on a musical career.

I followed Vic into his sitting room, which had had a makeover, just like Mrs Murphy's. The local DIY shops had done well out of them. Vic sat down, indicating the chair next to his.

"Right then," he said without preamble as I sat down. "Did you know Bernadette had come up on the lottery?"

After wondering for a moment who Bernadette was I looked at Vic in surprise.

"No, I had no idea."

I sensed he was leading up to making some sort of point.

"When was this?" I asked.

"First week in January. It was in the papers, radio, telly, the lot."

"Right."

I must have missed it. There were occasional stories about local people winning the lottery, but they never interested me much. I certainly wouldn't have registered their names.

"She was in a syndicate at the day centre, Brierley House. Eight of them won four point something million."

"Bloody hell. She would have got, what 500 grand."

"Nearer 600," he said.

Even better, I thought.

"And you think that's why Tony got in touch?"

"Bound to be," he said.

"Did he say anything when he came to see his mam?"

"No."

"Presumably his mother told him?"

He sniffed, pursing his lips.

"I asked her that and she said she didn't."

After a pensive pause, I asked the obvious question.

"Why?"

He glanced at me then looked away again.

"Again I asked her that and she went 'oh, I never really thought about it' and 'people don't like it when you go on about how much money you've got'."

I waited for the but.

"But...Bernadette's got her head screwed on."

That baffled me. I knew what the words meant, but had no idea of their relevance.

"And?"

"Well, I'm not saying she wasn't pleased to see her long lost son, but I reckon she was still wary, you know, wondering if he'd maybe come back because of the money."

I didn't know her well enough to say either way. On the other hand, assuming Tony found about the lottery win from, say, the Manchester Evening News website in early January, would he have waited until the end of February before following it up? I put this to Vic.

"He always was a crafty sod."

Was he I wondered. I didn't remember thinking that when we were friends.

"He was biding his time," Vic explained. "If he'd turned up the day after the news broke that would have been making it obvious."

"True enough, but what's he going to get out of reappearing after all this time? It's not as if his mam's gonna start handing out loads of cash, is it?"

Vic shook his head as if to say, 'you don't understand'.

"Like I say, he's biding his time. Either he's hoping to be remembered in her will, bearing in mind she's 89, or he'll let slip, casual like, he's in need of money."

The terrible thing was I could imagine Tony doing that. Or maybe trying to get her to invest in APM. I could also believe what Vic said about Tony Murphy's reason for coming back. All that stuff about fear of dying without making things right with his loved ones was an example of what he was really good at. Bullshit. I needed to talk to Yarla again. Maybe this time she'd tell me the truth.

"The thing is, Gus," said Vic, "Bernadette hasn't gone mad with her new found wealth."

"No?"

"She's bought a few things for her house, gave me a few grand, you know."

I waited, knowing he was leading up to something.

"She's told me when she goes, I get the lot."

I was looking at a potentially rich man. Funny, he looked just like anybody else.

"So I'm not too pleased about your mate, Tony, re-appearing after all these years."

He wouldn't have been pleased without the financial considerations, I thought, but it must have been worse now.

"Go on."

"I don't want Tony to have a penny of what's rightfully mine, know what I mean?"

I knew.

"I'd feel I'd been robbed," he added with extra emphasis.

The air of menace I remembered from the day he came looking for Tony all those years ago was making a comeback.

"It wouldn't be the first time he'd robbed me."

He made eye contact, allowing his words to sink in.

"Around the time he buggered off I'd lent him a fiver. He'd put it towards car parts, he reckoned. Pay me back with interest when he sold the motor he was working on."

There'd be a bloody lot of interest by now. I looked round, focusing on the family photos dotted round the room. Did his kids and grandkids know the history of Tony?

"The day he went away," Vic went on, "he called round to my house on some pretext or other. I can't even remember what it was now. What I do know is he left with a betting slip in his back pocket."

Fuck!

"It was on the mantelpiece when he got there, nowhere to be seen when he'd gone. Six hundred quid it was worth. Like a fool I told him about it."

I looked at him in shock for a moment.

"What a bastard."

"You said it, Gus. Just think what that would have meant. I'd just got married, determined to go straight. I was back inside within six months."

He thumped his right fist into his left palm.

"It took me another couple of years to get back on the right track. When I think of him cashing it in and driving off into the sunset."

He looked straight at me as if it were my fault. He spoke again with great intensity.

"So do me a favour. When you go looking for that nephew of mine, don't try too hard."

CHAPTER TWENTY-ONE

"The trouble is, Brenda," I said in Tony and Dino's the following lunchtime, "Tony's a bit dodgy."

"I thought he was."

I summarized what illustrated Tony's dodginess: his mother's lottery win; what Vic had said about him; Consett barging into my flat; his involvement with Baz Prince. Even then I felt I had only scratched the surface.

"Maybe it would be better if you didn't find him," was all she said.

There was a lull in the conversation while I looked around me. I'd been in Tony and Dino's before but it wasn't really my sort of place. All steel and chrome, full of coffee machines making too much noise.

On arrival we'd chatted about how Salford had changed since we were kids, but had soon move on to the reason for our meeting. Brenda had confirmed that she had no idea where Tony was. Now we were coming to the end of our meal.

"Listen, Gus," Brenda went on, "a long time ago I wasted a lot of time thinking about Tony bloody Murphy. Was he dead or alive? Would he come back to me."

I drank some water and waited for her to continue.

"Then I got my life sorted out. Well, as much as anyone can. I'm only interested in him now because of Adam."

There was no more to be said. We talked of other things, paid the bill and went home. I wondered if I would ever see her again.

* * *

"Did you recognise Josie on the night of the quiz?" I asked Karen the next day, thinking of her question to Josie about Norfolk.

We were drinking tea in Ordsall Tower's tiny kitchen, the only place I could get to talk to her in private. I had explained the family's asking me to look into the murder. We had talked about the night she was killed, but Karen hadn't had anything useful to add.

"I thought I did," she said, putting her cup down on the table next to the biscuit tin. "She looked like someone called Michelle Adams. I'd been trying to remember who she reminded me of and it suddenly came to me."

I explained that Steve had also noticed the resemblance.

"Was there any particular reason why you remembered Adams?"

She unfolded her arms as if starting to relax.

"Gary and I were on holiday in Wells-next-the-Sea when it all kicked off," said Karen. "We actually saw Michelle Adams one day."

I took a chocolate digestive from the tin and took a bite, reflecting on Karen's reference to Gary. She rarely talked about her ex-husband. What was he up to now?

"I followed the case when I got home," Karen added, "right up to the time she and her boyfriend were sentenced."

"Right."

"Josie couldn't have been Adams, no way, I realise that now. But just for a moment I convinced myself that she was."

She looked away for a moment.

"But it can't have anything to do with her murder, can it?"

"It could have a bearing on the murder if someone mistook her for Adams."

She took a deep breath.

"God, I never thought of that. What a nightmare. You know all this...I mean these deaths, well, it reminds me of Bill."

"Me too."

We both had reasons to think about the time two years ago when Bill Copelaw was murdered in this very building. He'd been my boss and Karen's lover. The father of her child in fact.

"I've been more or less OK about it for a while or so I thought. Quite positive in fact, but these killings have triggered a reaction."

The past always comes back to haunt us, I said to myself, or so it seems.

"This bloody job doesn't help. I feel so angry sometimes, you know," she said.

I knew about anger, but tried to avoid it now. Bad for my health. I'd had one stroke, I didn't want another one.

"This job, it's...we're supposed to be compassionate and stuff, but some of the people we have to deal with...like Tattersall...sometimes I feel like...ooh!"

The inarticulate shout of rage was the only way she could find to get her feelings out.

"I know," I said inadequately.

"I've fixed up to have some counselling," said Karen.

"Good."

"I need help dealing with...well, not just Bill, but work and stuff that happened when I was a kid."

She looked about to say more but then shook her head.

"This isn't the time to talk about it though," she went on, "I'm too busy."

We left the kitchen soon afterwards. Had Karen been hinting about some kind of abuse in her childhood? If so was it relevant? She'd had the information about Tattersall so could have produced those leaflets. And she had thought Josie was Michelle Adams. How badly had she been affected by whatever happened to her when she was a child? Had it made her want to kill the woman she thought might have played a part in the death of a young boy? That's the trouble with investigating murder, Gus, I said to myself, you're starting to suspect everyone. I had, I recalled, had Karen down on my list of suspects for Bill Copelaw's death. I was wrong then; I must be wrong now.

CHAPTER TWENTY-TWO

The Sunday after my meeting with Brenda, I was thinking about my trip to see Josie's parents in Barnes in two days' time. I should really try and find out what I could about Tony while I was in London. Maybe I should go down a day early. There was, I felt sure, a large part of his life down there that I needed to know about if I were to have any chance of finding him. I got out my phone and dialled Yarla's number.

"Yarla, it's Gus," I said. "I need to see you."

"See me? I don't think I can manage another trip to Manchester right now."

"Don't worry, I'll come to you, should be there early afternoon tomorrow."

"Gus, I'm terribly busy and..."

We're all busy, I said to myself.

"Yarla, things are happening with my investigation," I said, perhaps being a little economical with the truth. "My inquiries so far have led me to believe the answer may lie in London."

"But..."

"It's essential I get a look at Tony's house," I went on, still economical with the truth. "In fact I may as well spend the night there. It'll save you a few bob."

"Gus, I really don't think..."

"If you want me to find Tony, I shall expect complete co-operation."

A loud sigh was the only response.

"And you can reimburse my train fare when I get there," I said. "In cash."

* * *

The next day I caught the ten o'clock train from Piccadilly. I was pleased with myself because I was killing two birds with one stone on this trip. I was determined to make sure Yarla paid a bigger part of the bill than the Finches. She had hired me to find Tony when I would have liked nothing better than to forget about him for a while. Now I was beginning to doubt the version of events that I'd heard from Tony and his secretary. I needed to talk to her face to face. I also wanted to speak to anyone who worked with him or for him. I had already come to the conclusion that nobody really knew Tony intimately because he didn't want them to. His business might, though, give me some insight into where he was, if anything could. His drinking companions down the George and Dragon or whatever it was called might also have a few things to tell me.

As the train pulled out of Piccadilly station, I switched off my mobile and settled down to enjoy the trip. There was something about train rides that I'd always liked. Maybe it was the thought of being carried along without any effort. I didn't have to do anything for a couple of hours. It was a chance to read, listen to music, stare vacantly out of the window or all three. In this case it was also an opportunity to make some money.

I thought about my phone conversation with Yarla the previous evening and her reluctance to see me. What was all that about? I'd said I needed to have a look inside Tony's house but had no idea what I would find there. Tony could easily have taken anything significant with him. Yarla could have done the same. It might still be worth a try. In truth I had no idea whether my journey was absolutely necessary. I felt I had a genuine need to see Josie's mam and dad, but that wouldn't necessarily help me. More than anything though, I had to clear up a couple of points with Yarla for my own satisfaction.

A couple of hours later, clutching my briefcase and trailing my suitcase, I made my way through the crowds to Euston Square tube station and looked for the Hammersmith and City line. The underground was, as usual, hot and crowded, but convenient. I counted off the twelve stops, humming the Gerry Rafferty song when we got to Baker Street. Half an hour later I arrived at APM, which dominated one corner of the Hammersmith flyover. Yarla's words 'you can't miss it' were, for once, only too appropriate. I walked onto the forecourt, glancing at the price tags on the Jaguars, Bentleys and other cars I couldn't have put a name to. Who would want to spend that much on a car, I wondered? I gazed for a moment at the glass fronted building before going in the front door.

Two minutes later I was drinking tea in a poky office. Yarla sat behind a desk strewn with bits of paper. She sighed with what I guessed was exhaustion. The cool image she'd displayed the only other time I'd seen her had slipped a bit. Make that a lot, I said to myself, taking a second look at her.

"Listen, Gus," she said, "I'm snowed under with work and to be honest I don't think I can tell you anything I haven't already told you."

I took a mouthful of lukewarm tea.

"How about the truth?"

She looked up in alarm as if truth were an alien concept. To her, maybe it was.

"I don't know what you mean," she said.

"Right," I said, "I'll ask a few supplementary questions, shall I?"

She gave me an adolescent shrug. For a moment I expected her to tell me she wasn't bothered.

"Why did Tony go and see his mother?"

She looked at the Lake District calendar on the wall to the right. Finding no inspiration there, she cleared her throat.

"Well, you know..."

"It was because he knew she had won the lottery."

"Oh, you, er, found out about that, did you?"

"Finding things out is my job."

I was quite pleased with that statement.

"Right, well," she said before hesitating for a moment. "The thing is, Gus, with the recession and everything there's been a bit of a hiccup with the business..."

She stopped again and moved a few documents around the desk with pointless precision.

"Nothing major, you understand, cash flow and stuff."

"And he thought if he could persuade his mother to help out her long lost son..."

She smiled.

"I knew you'd understand," she said, missing the point.

"The trouble was," I went on, "his mother insisted Tony should get in touch with Brenda and me..."

She put her hands together.

"Just remind me who Brenda is again."

As if she didn't know.

"She's the woman who was pregnant to him in 1974. He didn't want to risk alienating his mam's goodwill before he'd raised the subject of the money."

"You've got it all worked out, Gus."

Don't sound so surprised, I said to myself, I'm not as daft as I look.

"Getting me involved in searching for Brenda was ideal. I can hear him now: 'Look, mam, I've put a bit of work Gus's way', and she'd think, 'oh, bless.'"

I now knew Tony had been hoping I wouldn't find his ex-fiancée.

"Something like that," Yarla admitted.

I psyched myself up for the next bit.

"Moving on," I said. "Let's talk about Mr Consett."

She looked blank and opened her eyes wide.

"Who?"

I sighed again, this time with exasperation.

"Eric Consett, the feller who barged into my flat looking for Tony."

While I explained further, she licked her lips, rubbing her hands together as if she were washing them.

"He could have been anyone."

She continued the Lady Macbeth impression, as I explained further.

"In fact he was representing some of the people owed money by Tony. One of the unfortunates who 'invested' in this very business."

The psychology of Tony's approach was quite clever, if a little obvious. The blokey persona must have helped too. One thing that appeals to anyone who wanted to appear grown-up – almost anyone in other words – is having expertise in certain subjects: cars, property values, how to make the most of your money.

"There's more to it than that," she said.

I waited for more, but she kept quiet.

"What's that supposed to mean," I asked.

She rearranged the papers once more, coughed and leaned slightly towards me.

"Just what it says. If you think this is just Tony ripping off a few grand here and there you could not be more wrong."

I looked straight at her but she would not meet my eye.
"Go on."
She rubbed her hands together again, making me think of obsessive, compulsive disorder.
"It's more serious than that."
"More serious?"
She nodded slowly as if to emphasize whatever point she was trying to make.
"That's right."
"It's something to do with Baz Prince, isn't it?"
Her expression changed. Was that fear on her face?
"What do you know about Baz Prince?"
I looked her straight in the eye.
"As much as I need to know."
She closed her eyes, resting her chin on her hands.
"That's probably too much," she said.

She looked as though she were about to elaborate, but then seemed to give herself a metaphorical shake. Sitting back, she smiled at me.

"Anyway, can I help you in any other way?"
She was trying to turn on the charm but her heart wasn't in it.

"Who else can I speak to about Tony while I'm in London?" I asked.

* * *

My mind was still mulling over my meeting with Yarla as I travelled on the tube to Richmond upon Thames later. Dismissing me with a suggestion that I talk to the staff at APM, she had at least handed over the keys to Tony's house and even paid my train fare without a murmur. That gave me a bit of spending cash while I was in the smoke. It occurred to me she was being too nice and I couldn't quite see why. From Richmond railway station, I lugged my case down the steps leading away from the front entrance and turned left into the town centre.

As I passed House of Fraser, I thought about the members of Tony's staff I'd talked to. All had said what a character Tony was and I'd agreed. What they didn't know was I thought being a character was a bad thing. All too often it was a synonym for prat. Apart from that they were of no help at all. Nobody had any idea where Tony was; as far as they knew he wasn't in any trouble and the last time they had seen him he'd been his usual self.

A brisk ten minute walk brought me to Lekeren Grove off Richmond Hill. Yarla had told me Mick Jagger lived nearby, though I doubted whether Tony said, 'morning, Mick,' to the Stones' frontman as he went for a post breakfast saunter by the river. Tony's house was a three storey affair in red brick. Window frames and sills were painted sparkling white. Worth a small fortune I would have said. I went up the steps to the front door and let myself into a spacious hall. I picked up mail from the floor and put it on the telephone table. The echo of my footsteps on the uncarpeted floor followed me as I went through a door on the left into a living room. Was this what they called minimalist, I asked myself, as I looked at the walls, bare but for a mirror over the unused fireplace.

Deciding not to linger, I took my suitcase upstairs to find somewhere to sleep. Having looked quickly in the two larger ones, I went into the smallest of the three bedrooms. Insipid water colours were arranged asymmetrically on the walls. The single bed was made up as for a guest. Sheets looked clean. I opened the window to let in some fresh air and left my luggage by the bed. Now for some lunch, I thought.

* * *

"So you're a mate of Tony's, are you," said Clive, the bespectacled landlord of the George and Dragon a few minutes later.

The pub at the end of Lekeren Grove was quiet when I got there. In fact I was the only customer. Clive had a southern whine that put me in mind of John Major. Come to think of it, he had a look of the former prime minister. I drank from my pint of Middle's Bitter. A nice drop, I had to admit, though a bit flat on account of the different beer pumps they had in the South. What with that and the funny accent I could never live down here.

"Yeah, knew him when I was a kid, but we lost touch until recently."

I took a bite from my cheese and ham toasty.

"Top man, Tony," said Clive, "one of the best."

"Did Yarla tell you I was trying to find him," I said.

"She did mention some such thing."

That sounded like the sort of thing Major would say. I could have imagined him taking up running a pub on retirement like footballers used to. He might even have suited the blue sweatshirt with George and Dragon stitched across the left breast.

"I was wondering if you might be able to help me," I said, trying not to imagine all the prime ministers of my lifetime in the role of mine host.

"In what way?"

Tell me where he is so I can go home, Clive. What about that?

"Have you any idea where he might be?"

He picked up a pint glass as I heard a door open at the back of the room.

"Well, he could be anywhere."

Anybody could be anywhere, I muttered to myself.

"He's a bit of a law unto himself," said the landlord. "A great character, of course, but one learned not to ask too many questions."

The sound of a door opening interrupted these not very illuminating remarks. Turning to the right, I saw a man in his fifties coming in. His paunch, encased in a waistcoat, seemed to lead the way. His pinstripe suit was as crumpled as his face, his grey hair flopped across his forehead.

"Evenin', Clive," he called with a smile as a second man followed in his wake.

"Quentin, Ollie," said Clive, "what can I get you?"

Both made a mime of careful consideration before making their choice.

"Do you know," said Quentin, the pinstriped one, "for a change I think I'll have my usual."

"So will I," said Ollie, who wore a check sports jacket of the type I thought they'd stopped making years ago.

Clive chortled dutifully at the top notch wit and repartee.

"Large G & T and a pint of special it is," said Clive and set about getting the drinks. "Gentleman here's a private detective."

Quentin clapped his hands lightly together before responding in a fruity baritone, reminiscent of Test Match Special.

"Oh, I say. Really?"

The landlord turned back from the optic and placed the gin and a bottle of Schweppes on the counter.

"He's looking for my friend and yours, Mr Murphy."

Both men at the bar looked at me with renewed interest and respect.

"One of the best, old Tony," said Ollie.

His voice was pitched higher than his friend's, with a hint of cockney. Clive poured tonic into the glass, watching the bubbles rise.

"You're not wrong, Ollie, you're not wrong."

Clive began pulling Ollie's pint, looking at me with polite interest, obviously expecting me to say something. I drank again, wondering whether the two newcomers would be of any more use than anybody else.

"I don't suppose you know where he is?"

Both men let out little chuckles and looked at one another with raised eyebrows.

"Does anybody know where the elusive Tony is at any given moment in time?" asked Ollie.

"Mmm," said Quentin, as if such words of wisdom needed no other response.

"I suppose you've been to APM?" asked Ollie.

I drank some more, thinking this job could turn me into an alcoholic.

"Yes, but I didn't find the people there very forthcoming to say the least."

Another meaningful look greeted this innocuous remark. Both men smirked knowingly.

"Well trained," said Quentin, taking a hefty draught of gin and tonic, "Tony's always kept his cards close to his chest. The, er, merchandise for sale at APM...now what can one say about it diplomatically?"

He looked at the barman for an answer, but he just passed Ollie his beer.

"Let's just say one shouldn't look too closely into the provenance."

"Provenance?"

I thought of that TV series with Ian McShane. What was it called?

"I should say," chipped in Clive, "that these two reprobates are in the antique trade."

Lovejoy, that was it.

"I see," I said. "Do you mean Tony's cars fell off the back of a lorry?"

Maybe it should have been the back of a car transporter, I thought, as eyebrows were raised once more.

"Draw your own conclusions," suggested Quentin. "Tony walked a fine line."

Ollie took a mouthful of beer and rolled it around his mouth like a wine taster.

"He had an unconventional way of raising capital for his business," I said.

Quentin agreed with me.

"He did indeed. Asked all his friends to chip in with a modest investment, ten or twenty K perhaps. I turned him down flat, I'm afraid."

"Why was that?" I asked.

"Well," he rumbled, "I knew I'd be better off putting my money in antiques, something I knew about."

I scratched my nose.

"What puzzles me," I said after a pause for thought, "is what he did before APM Motors."

"What didn't he do, more like," said Ollie.

"How do you mean?"

Ollie placed his glass carefully on the bar as if to prepare himself for some athletic feat.

"Well, old Tone was hard to pin down, do you know what I'm saying?"

"Yes."

"He never said anything too specific about his background. We knew he was born up North but not much else."

Presumably thinking his friend would never get to the point. Quentin took over.

"Tony likes to make an impression, that's what Ollie is trying to say. He's a 'been there, done that' kind of chap."

"Yes," said Ollie, taking up the story, "widely travelled, tried his hand at everything, girl in every port type of thing."

Apart from confirming my view of Tony this told me next to nothing. With Tony the impression, as Quentin called it, was all you got. As far as hard information was concerned, you were only entitled to what he wanted you to know.

The two antique dealers left soon afterwards. I could not see myself finding Tony any time soon, if at all. Having got into some sort of trouble, maybe he had decided to cut his losses. He wouldn't have been bothered about anyone he left behind – look at the way he had treated his mother. He had acquaintances, sure, would have a pint and a laugh in the local, but nobody touched him at a deeper level.

Unless something unexpected happened, I would soon have to give up on the search and tell Yarla I'd been unsuccessful.

* * *

Back in the house, I decided to see what I could find, starting with the bedrooms. It took a matter of minutes to find nothing of any significance up there. The living room was equally lacking in interest, unless you counted The Complete Fawlty Towers. I might watch some of that tonight. It was probably still funny and I could do with a laugh.

I went into the room next door, which was done out like an office. All the furniture was in that pale wood that was fashionable a few years ago. I'd always hated it and absence hadn't made the heart grow fonder. Even a pleb like me could tell it was unsuitable for this old house. I sat at a swivel chair at the computer desk. On the top was an iPod with speakers. The next space down held a laptop. On the left were four shelves (all empty); on the right a small cupboard with a drawer above it.

I searched in the drawer, reaching right to the back. There was nothing there. As I pulled my hand out, it touched the side of the drawer, causing a small panel to spring open. Out dropped a white envelope addressed to Mr AP Murphy. It had already been opened. I pulled out a passport in the name of Conor Whelan, born in Chester. The envelope also contained a wad of twenty pound notes: five hundred quid in all. Hmmm. Opening out the passport, I looked at the photograph for several seconds. Reading from left to right, Conor Whelan was Tony Murphy. Interesting to say the least. I closed the panel then replaced the passport and money in the envelope and put it in the drawer.

A search of the rest of the house revealed nothing relevant. I needed some fresh air so put my coat on and went out. The walk along Richmond Hill gave me time to think. Something was bothering me about my search for Tony Murphy, but I wasn't sure what it was. I went through

Tony's known movements since I had last seen him. He had been to Sheffield. And then what? From the moment he left Brenda nobody had seen him. Nobody knew where he was. More to the point, nobody knew if he was dead or alive.

As I tried to work things out, I admired the views of the Thames. Past the Royal Star and Garter I approached the gate of Richmond Park, watching the deer wandering through the bare trees. Through a kissing gate, I walked onto the Petersham road, thinking about Tony. Where was he? I walked past Ham Polo Club on my right. Not a game for the likes of me, I thought, mulling over what Tony had done over the years. It was possible to construct a valid argument that Tony Murphy had in effect robbed Brenda McDonald of her only child.

She had admitted nursing a grievance since he had walked out on her. The fact it was a long time ago was irrelevant. Tony had only got in touch with her to please his mother. He'd told his mam he didn't know where the lad was. Supposing Tony, far from saying he'd be in touch with Brenda, had made it clear he wanted nothing to do with his son. I thought about an alternative scenario: Tony sees the woman who has hated him for decades and is never seen again. Going towards the garden of Ham House, I decided to turn back. It was an impressive building, but Louise had dragged me through enough old houses to last a life time.

Tony's world was a different one from mine, I thought, as I retraced my footsteps. He was a wheeler dealer, on the lookout for a fast buck, always up to something. What had he been up to with Yarla? I went over in my mind what I had discovered in London. I tried to piece together things Yarla had said, bits of conversation in the George and Dragon and what I had found in the Lekeren Grove house.

Don't forget the Baz Prince angle, I told myself. This gangster, as Steve had called him, was after Tony. Therefore, Tony was in danger. What Prince and his henchmen might do to him if they caught him didn't bear thinking about. So that was two people who might want him dead. A third was

Vic Kennelly, a man with a grievance if ever there was one. And he stood to lose as long as Tony stayed alive. Even Simon Natchow had reason to do Tony harm after being diddled out of twenty thousand quid.

Had one of the four made sure Tony was never seen again? What did the fake passport mean? It was no use to him in the house, was it? If he had buggered off again, surely he would have taken it with him. And all that money. Give over, Gus, I admonished myself, you've spent too long thinking about murder and being told lies. But the idea that Tony really was dead this time wouldn't go away.

I went into the town and mooched around for a bit, picking up a couple of bottles of red wine from Richmond Wine. On the way back to the house I bought ham, cheese, salad and French bread from a delicatessen. Later, having eaten, I watched a repeat of New Tricks followed by the first two episodes of Fawlty Towers. I'd been right: it was still funny. I went to bed in a better mood.

CHAPTER TWENTY-THREE

The following morning around ten o'clock I rang the front door bell of a large house overlooking Barnes Common. I now had to switch my mind away from Tony Murphy to something more important. I knew the coming interview would be tough, for all the reasons I had found social work difficult over the years. Dealing with other people's misery could be disabling, but I told myself they were the ones going through it. Whatever I felt would be a pale imitation of their suffering. I also had a job to do so I had to be objective. Otherwise I would end up letting the Finches down. A fair-haired woman answered. Casually dressed in jeans and jumper, she looked younger than I'd expected.

"Good morning," I said, "I'm Gus Keane..."

"Oh, Gus," she said with what sounded like relief. "Linda Finch. Come in."

We shook hands, then I followed her down a hall lined with pictures.

"Good of you to come all this way," she said, turning slightly.

"That's OK," I said.

In the living room a man in a check shirt and cavalry twills was perched tentatively on the edge of a sofa. It was as though he were visiting this house for the first time.

"Darling, Gus is here," said Linda.

He scratched his grey hair before getting up. He held out a hand as his wife introduced him.

"My husband, Robert."

Greetings done with, Robert sat down again. I sat with my briefcase on my lap on an antique looking armchair, wondering if it came from Quentin's place.

"I'm really sorry about Josie," I said.

They looked at one another. Linda tried to smile.

"I expect you'd love a coffee," she said.

"Tea, please, if that's all right."

Not that it matters, I said to myself, but maybe normal exchanges like that help keep things together.

"You know, I think I'll join you. What about you, Darling?"

He looked at her in wonderment.

"What?"

"Tea of coffee?"

He shook his head.

"Nothing, nothing."

Smiling at me apologetically, she went off to get the tea. I had expected to have to sit in uncomfortable silence so the sound of Robert's voice startled me.

"You're the private investigator, are you?"

"That's right."

He muttered quietly to himself, pursing his lips.

"Larry's idea of course," he said.

Was there a hint of disapproval in his voice?

"Was it?"

"Always full of ideas, always was, always will be."
He stared into space.
"It won't bring her back, will it?"
"No."

The monosyllable seemed like the safest answer. There was no point in elaborating. Robert shrugged.

"Still, it won't do any actual harm, I suppose. If it makes Linda feel 0.0001% better..."

He breathed in audibly as if it were all a great effort. No doubt he found everything a struggle now. Linda came back with two mugs, one of which she put on the coffee table in front of me. She sat on the other armchair, hugging her tea, looking expectantly towards me.

"Now," she said.

I took my notebook and pen from the briefcase.

"Well, first of all I wondered if you'd heard any more from the police."

I decided to edge gently into the details of the murder.

"Well," Linda began, looking towards her husband, who had switched off for the moment, "we have a family liaison person, a very nice, young lady. She keeps in touch from time to time."

"What about the details of their investigation? Anything on that?"

Again she looked to her husband for support.

"They know who did it, can't prove it," he said. "Now it's some nonsense about mistaken identity."

He got up from his seat.

"If you'll excuse me," he said as he left the room.

Linda turned to watch him go, a look of longing on her face as if she wanted to go after him and say, 'it's all right, darling'. Only she knew it wasn't all right. She'd lost her daughter; now her husband was drifting away.

"Sorry about that. Robert's reacted very badly to all this."

"No need to apologise," I said.

Anyone would have reacted badly, I thought. He'd probably reacted in the only way he knew how. Just as she was trying to cope by keeping up the conventions. Larry's way was to bring me in to solve his sister's murder.

"What he was referring to was some idea that Josie looked like a woman who was convicted for helping a man who..."

She couldn't bring herself to say the words.

"It's all right," I said, "I know about it."

I explained about Steve thinking Josie looked like Michelle Adams and ringing DI Ellerton.

"But don't you see," she said, a touch of hopelessness in her voice, "that makes it more complicated and therefore more difficult to..."

She sniffed and grabbed a tissue from a box on the table.

"Sorry, I promised myself I wouldn't cry..."

Cry all you want, love, I wanted to say.

"Larry seemed convinced Simon Natchow killed your daughter."

She nodded, still fighting the tears.

"I know he's the obvious suspect," I said, "but there's no evidence to link him directly to the crime."

"I know but that means it could go on for years without a resolution."

Bloody hell, she was right.

"Let's try and think how we might make some progress," I said, more in hope than expectation. "When did you last see Josie?"

I was on safer ground with factual matters.

"In Tenerife a couple of weeks ago. We'd been there four or five days when she arrived."

That was something I didn't know at least.

"How did she seem?"

"Much the same. She looked different."

I remembered what Larry had told me.

"She'd had her hair cut, I understand."

"Yes and gone back to glasses. She told me some of her friends didn't recognise her."

I wrote that down.

"Did she say anything about being mistaken for somebody else?"

She sighed with impatience.

"No, nothing like that."

"If there is anything in this mistaken identity theory the change in appearance might be important."

"Perhaps."

"Well, one could argue that Josie could only have been mistaken for this Michelle Adams just before or just after the Tenerife trip."

I had thought this out before I came to London. Anyone who saw her in Tenerife or afterwards could be the one who thought she was Adams. Given that she was killed at Ordsall, it was most likely the wrong recognition happened after she started working in Ordsall Tower. Either that or somebody who caught the same flight to and from Manchester. Linda Finch was right: it could get too complicated for words.

"I suppose so," said Linda when I had put those points to her. "In that case, I can't help you. Josie never gave the slightest hint about anybody thinking she was somebody else."

And perhaps whoever killed her – assuming it wasn't Natchow – wouldn't want to give 'the slightest hint' about thinking Josie was Michelle Adams.

"We wanted you to prove Natchow's guilt, but now..."

Natchow didn't do it, I said to myself. He can't have done. Who did? I would simply have to go back over everything I knew to see if there was any way I could work out the answer. I could try, but I wasn't optimistic. Optimism was in short supply lately.

* * *

That evening at Lekeren Grove, after a takeaway chicken dopiaza and a Tiger beer I'd found in the fridge, I settled down in the lounge with a bottle of Aussie Cabernet/Shiraz. I had to stay another night as my cheap ticket meant I had to catch a train back the next day. I picked another Fawlty Towers episode at random, Basil The Rat. I was just laughing at the line about Sybil's specialist subject on Mastermind when I heard the front door open and footsteps in the hall, then a short silence. More footsteps followed then the twisting of the door handle. A man carrying a holdall took a step into the room, as I turned to face him. I paused the DVD.

"Hello, Tony..."

"Gus, what the..."

"Or should I say Conor," I added.

He raised his eyebrows, his mouth slightly open.

"Don't worry, Tony, the passport's in the desk."

He sat down opposite me, taking his raincoat off and draping it on the arm of the chair. I noticed he was wearing his usual smart/casual gear: corduroy jacket, striped shirt, chinos and brown lace up shoes.

"Wine," I suggested.

"Er, yeah," he answered, "I'll just..."

The bleeding obvious, I said to myself, remembering Steve saying that was the solution in most cases. Whatever had made me think Tony was dead? Seconds later he came back with a glass and the envelope that contained the passport. He put the envelope in his bag and the glass on the table. Then he sat down again, while I poured his wine.

"What's going on," he asked after the first mouthful.

"I thought you might wonder."

I explained about Yarla hiring me to find him and what I had found out so far, including his mother's lottery win and his theft of his uncle, Vic Kennelly's betting slip.

"You've been a busy lad," he said.

"Yeah. I've got a few questions for you."

"Go on then."

Where to start?

"First of all, when people 'invested' money in your business how did you manage to divert it to yourself?"

That had been bugging me. I'd feel better for knowing the answer. Tony swigged at his wine and put the glass back on the table.

"No harm in telling you. I can always deny it later."

That was exactly what he'd do, I thought.

"Some of them wrote a cheque payable to APM," said Tony. "It was dead easy to change it to AP Murphy."

Easy peasy, I thought.

"They got a contract promising them seven percent interest," Tony explained. "A lot of them paid in cash. They didn't want anything in writing."

"Unbelievable."

He smirked and picked up his glass.

"Some people's sole ambition is to stop the taxman getting his hands on their money."

I thought of the Beatles song, Taxman.

"There's more though, isn't there," I said.

"Is there?"

"Here's what I think has been happening," I said. "APM has been selling stolen cars provided by Baz Prince. Right?"

"Go on."

Non-committal. Fine if that was the way he wanted it.

"You were making a good living," I went on, "but you were never good with money, were you?"

He sipped his wine and stretched out his legs in front of him. I wondered if he had gambled his money away. Or was he just greedy?

"And you always wanted more," I went on. "Unfortunately that led you into trying to swindle Baz Prince."

I remembered what Consett said the day he came into my flat. Something about Tony picking the wrong bloke to rip off.

"Yarla was in on it," I said. "She had to be. I reckon you were siphoning off a good bit of the money you got for every car."

He said nothing.

"I'm willing to bet Yarla hasn't seen a penny of it. That's why she wanted you found. Not because she was worried about you."

Tony sat forward, picking up his glass again.

"But I didn't want to be found," he said. "Still don't."

That would have been too dangerous with Mr Prince on his trail. Tony sipped his wine like a connoisseur.

"Not a bad drop, that."

I poured myself some more. Tony looked thoughtful for a moment.

"You've done well, Gus. I wouldn't have expected anything less."

He reached inside the holdall again and pulled out the envelope. Taking out a handful of cash, he gave it to me. I didn't ask what it was for. Gift horses and all that.

"I'm expecting a taxi soon, got a flight to catch. Listen, Gus, it's been good seeing you. Just do me one more favour."

He returned the envelope to the holdall.

"Keep quiet about seeing me, at least for a while," he said, 'tell Yarla..., tell her what you like. She'll never find me, I've made sure of that."

I savoured another mouthful of wine. He was right, it was good stuff.

"I'll ring her later. This'll cover her bill," I said, holding up the money in my hand. "You can do me a favour in return."

"Favour?"

The look on his face seemed to say, 'I don't do favours.' Tough, I decided.

"You know, Tony," I said, "I've got a lot to be thankful to you for."

"You what?"

I smiled over my wine glass, before putting it down.

"Oh, yeah, you gave me some work for a start."

We won't go into your motives, I almost added.

"Then by going missing you gave me a bit more work."

He nodded, keeping his eyes focused on me as I explained further.

"And I've got two more cases to work on. I somehow think you coming back into my life has caused that to happen."

He smiled.

"I doubt that."

I nodded.

"So do I really. However, I have been trying to work out what links the cases of Tony Murphy, Edward Tattersall and Josie Finch."

"So what's this favour, Gus?"

"I want you to help me work out these cases. Because in a funny sort of way you're the link between them."

He looked at his watch.

"Why not? You'd better explain about those other two people."

I did so, though Tony still had no idea how he could help. Maybe it was just a case of two heads being better than one. Having mulled over the three cases frequently since I had got involved in them, I now needed somebody to bounce ideas off.

"Let's start with you. Sybil Fawlty told me the answer."

"Sybil Fawlty?"

I held up the DVD box and explained about the line in the sitcom.

"It was 'bleeding obvious' you'd decided to disappear again leaving everybody else to pick up the pieces."

"So, I've been a naughty boy," he shrugged.

"As for the others," I went on, "you were around on the night Josie was killed; Tattersall was a paedophile and you were suspected of beating up a paedophile just before you went missing the first time."

"Sid somebody or other, I remember him," said Tony. "Though he wasn't killed, he just got what was coming to him."

He leant forward again.

"And before you go any further, Gus, I had nothing to do with either Tattersall or Josie whatever her name is."

He was missing the point, if indeed there was one.

"But there's a kind of connection," I said.

"A bit tenuous."

Maybe he was right.

"What about the 'bleeding obvious' connection?"

He shook his head in bewilderment.

"What?"

Once more I tried to bring my thoughts together coherently.

"Well, if it was obvious why nobody knew where you were, what could be the obvious solution for Tattersall and Finch?"

He sipped pensively for moment.

"See what you mean. Well, with Tattersall it's easy. Once something like that gets out, you know, child abuse, well, he becomes a marked man."

I thought about what Arthur had said in the Park Hotel on the night of the quiz. Something about people taking the law into their own hands.

"So you think it was vigilantes? But who put the information on those leaflets?"

Tony looked at his watch again.

"Someone with a grudge who knew about Tattersall's background."

A lot to choose from there.

"What about Josie?"

He scratched his left eyebrow before answering.

"Well, this mistaken identity theory makes it difficult, but as you said yourself, Gus, if an abused woman is murdered, most of the time it's the boyfriend who did it."

Why was it all so impossible?

"I may not be a very moral man," Tony added, "but I've no time for someone who abuses kids or fellers who hit women."

We talked on for a while, finishing the wine as our discussion became more and more rambling. It was a relief when his taxi arrived. I phoned Yarla after he'd gone and told her Tony was safe and well and didn't want me to tell her any more than that. A deathly silence was her immediate response. This was followed by:

"Oh, my God, I'm really in the shit now."

I couldn't offer any reassurance and rang off as soon as I could. I went back to Fawlty Towers muttering the bleeding obvious to myself.

CHAPTER TWENTY-FOUR

The day I returned from London I went back to Deadbeat Mansions to question Simon again, without having a definite plan. Passing the bungalow next door, I stopped, thinking of Ian Jamieson. Could he help me? He hadn't said much of any use when I had asked him about a possible leak of information regarding Tattersall. Arthur had said Jamieson knew what was going on around the area. He might, therefore, have seen something significant. And he knew Simon Natchow.

Deciding on a detour I went up to Ian's front door and knocked. As before the sound of feet shuffling was followed by the rattling of a chain. Then the door was flung open. Jamieson took his roll up from his mouth and cleared his throat.

"Oh, hello, mate, come in."

He made his painful way along the hall. I followed him into the living room, little changed since my first visit a couple of weeks ago. Ian collapsed into his settee, while I sat on the armchair, which sagged even more than before. I opened up my briefcase.

"You all right?" he said.

I hoped his friendly greeting meant he was in a talkative mood.

"Yeah, not bad. You?"

He coughed in answer to this query about his health.

"Mustn't grumble," he said.

Something in his voice hinted that grumble was just what he'd do given half a chance.

"I'm looking into Josie Finch's murder."

I took out a notebook and pen from my case.

"I thought you was with the welfare."

'The welfare', it was a long time since I'd been called that.

"I am but I'm a private investigator as well."

His face lit up and he rubbed his hands, reminding me of Josie on quiz night.

"Private eye? That sounds exciting."

It's not, I felt like saying. Instead I explained about Larry Finch's request for me to look into the case.

"Don't know if I'll be able to help you, mate," he said when I'd finished.

"We'll see. First of all, do you remember much about the day Josie died?"

He took a drag from his cigarette.

"When was it?"

"Tuesday 28th February. She was killed about eleven at night."

He puffed on his fag, sending billows of smoke into the air. A sneeze began to tickle the back of my nose.

"February 28th, eh?"

Leaving the cigarette between his lips, he smoked pensively for a few moments.

"I'd better check."

Getting up with a struggle, he went over to a railway calendar on the wall behind him. Turning back to the February page, he peered at it for several seconds.

"Thought so," he announced, before coming back to his seat. "I was away with my sister in Reigate."

Bugger, I said to myself as I wrote down the details.

"Went on the Monday, back Thursday."

I let out a loud sneeze then pulled a tissue out of my pocket and wiped my nose.

"Right," I said, "have the police been to see you about the murder?"

He sent a shower of ash onto his jeans.

"No, but Simon told me all about it," Ian said, "gutted, he was. He used to live with her, you know."

"Yes."

He wheezed quietly for a bit.

"The police gave him the third degree, know what I mean? But he never done it. He's not like that."

Oh, isn't he, Ian, I could have asked.

"You couldn't wish to meet anyone kinder than Simon," he went on.

Could I bear to listen to a hymn of praise about Simon?

"Just after I got back from Surrey, he gave me a fleece, pair of jeans, t-shirt. Good as new. Wouldn't take any money."

I carried on writing down what Ian was saying until I realised it was pointless. A couple of decades in social work had given me a touching faith in note-taking.

"I'm saving them until I go out somewhere special," he said.

I smiled insincerely.

"I'd better be going, Ian."

I got up.

"Well, thanks for your time."

"Pleasure, mate. Pity I couldn't help but that's the way it goes."

I went out of the door, his voice behind me telling me to call again. That evoked a pang of pity and triggered a memory of my sister listening to Only The Lonely a long time ago. Outside the bungalow, I took a deep breath.

Knowing I would stink of tobacco, I went home. When I got there I began thinking about Marti, who was in Liverpool with her mother. Getting my phone out, I dialled her number.

"How's things over there?" I asked.

"Oh... not too good really. Mum's struggling a bit."

She hadn't looked too clever last time I'd seen her, I thought. The fall had affected her badly.

"She suddenly seems old, you know," Marti went on. "Her confidence has gone somehow. And she gets weepy easily."

Marti sounded near to tears herself. I looked at my watch and did a quick calculation.

"I'll come over. If I get away now I should be with you by four o'clock."

She sighed.

"Thanks. It'll be good to have you here."

Let's hope I can cheer her up, I thought. She'd certainly cheer me up.

* * *

Ten minutes later I was heading out to the M62, thinking about several things at once. Not just Marti's mam but Tony Murphy, Josie Finch and Edward Tattersall. Perversely, my mind kept coming back to Tony, as though he really was the common thread that tied them all together. I gave up my attempt to make sense of it all and put a CD on. I drove on towards Merseyside to the accompaniment of Crowded House, who told me to take the weather with me. Good advice, lads, I said out loud.

* * *

"Gus, I wanted to talk to you," said Marti that evening, after her mother had gone to bed.

Something told me she wasn't planning a chat about world affairs or global warming.

"Oh, yes?"

We were sitting in opposite armchairs in her mother's living room, drinking red wine. Family photos were dotted round the room, including those from both Marti's weddings.

"Well, it's about, you know," she said hesitantly, "us, me and you,"

"Go on," I said.

She gulped her wine, averting her eyes. Plucking up courage no doubt. Finally she spoke.

"Well, where do you see our relationship going?"

That put the onus on me, not where I wanted it to be. My first instinct was to say 'a relationship can't actually go anywhere', but both Marti and Louise had said at different times that pedantry was one of my most annoying habits.

"I don't know really," I said.

My reply, I realised, was truthful, but for Marti probably unhelpful.

"Perhaps you could explain a bit further," I added.

She put her glass down on the table beside her, lining it up on a coaster.

"You obviously don't want to get married."

"That's right."

She put her hands on her lap.

"Would you rather we just lived together then?"

I hesitated, knowing I would have to be honest.

"No, I don't want us to live together."

She sighed in exasperation.

"But that would be the natural next step," she said.

"Not necessarily."

Another sigh.

"What do you want then?"

Assuming she wasn't referring to my burning ambitions or the 500 things I wanted to do before I died, I tried to form a response.

"I want us to go on as we are."

That was clear enough, surely.

"Oh."

It occurred to me that 'Oh' could mean a lot of different things. This one had a bit of an edge to it.

"The thing is, Gus, I'm, I don't know... what you're saying, it sounds a bit temporary."

Everything's bloody temporary, I was about to say. Luckily I realised the fake profundity of the words in time.

"I want, maybe I want reassurance...I don't know, commitment."

"You have that."

I had an exclusive relationship with Marti. Even if I'd wanted to chase other women I doubted if I could be arsed and I certainly wouldn't have the stamina.

"I think it's because of Louise," she said.

Now what?

"What's Louise got to do with it?"

"I think you still love her."

I sighed. Of course I bloody love her, I said to myself, she's the mother of my children. But loving or not loving Louise wasn't the point.

"Marti, I don't want to marry anyone. I don't want to co-habit with anyone. I'm happy as I am."

"That could change though, couldn't it?"

I sighed.

"Anything can change."

Why did people complicate things so much? One thing I was sure of: I could do without this.

* * *

The next day I returned to Salford, leaving Marti at her mother's. We were still a couple apparently. A niggling dissatisfaction followed me along the motorway, all the way into the flat. On the sitting room settee ten minutes after I got back, I sipped a mug of tea and read The Code of the Woosters. I often resorted to PG Wodehouse at times of stress. A harmless addiction, I'd always thought. It was certainly cheaper and healthier than maintaining a drug habit, getting paralytic or online gambling.

Maybe my choice of reading was to blame for my reluctance to get married, I thought. An old lefty like me should disapprove of Bertie Wooster, but I had always envied, maybe even aspired to, his lifestyle. Enough money to live a comfortable life, his own flat, a good social life. He spent an inordinate amount of time avoiding marriage. In fact that was the basis of most of the plots. I wasn't stinking rich and still needed to work, was a grandfather and had a steady girlfriend (just about) but my present situation was the nearest I would ever get to the Wooster lifestyle. Not a bad old life on the whole and I didn't want to change it.

Half an hour's reading settled me down a bit. I thought I'd better get some shopping. As I was getting up, I heard the free paper being pushed through the letter box. I went to get it and glanced at the headline:

MEN HELD FOR PAEDOPHILE DEATH

I went back into the living room, where I learned that three teenagers, one who couldn't be named for legal reasons, had been charged with the murder of Edward Tattersall. Reading between the lines I was able to deduce that it was, as Arthur had suggested in the Park Hotel, a vigilante killing. Tony had said the same. The names of the two youths given in the article meant nothing to me, which was a surprise. When a knock came on the door I guessed straight away who it was. DI Ellerton came with me into the sitting room and sat down.

"To what do I owe this pleasure?" I asked, sitting down with her.

"I've got a feeling you already know about it," she replied, indicating the paper on the table.

"The arrest?"

"Yes, I meant to tell you before now, but I've hardly got time to turn round at the moment."

"Only youngsters weren't they?"

"Yeah, one was just sixteen."

Apart from wondering how a sixteen-year-old got involved in something so mindless, I didn't know what to think.

"It looks like these three lads got the pamphlets I showed you," she said, "the ones that outed Tattersall as a sex offender."

"And that's why they did it?"

She shrugged.

"Apparently. They were drugged up as you'd expect."

I could have understood if one of Tattersall's victims or their parents had killed him, but this was beyond me.

"How did you catch them?"

"Information received as they say. The word on the street was that these three were responsible."

From working with the police, I knew that was how a lot of crimes got cleared up.

"Unfortunately for them they were pretty incompetent," the inspector went on. "They weren't known to us, but they left plenty of forensic evidence."

That seemed pretty clear, though there was at least one unanswered question.

"Did they have any idea who produced the leaflets? Or who delivered them?"

Sarita shook her head.

"No. Or maybe they're not saying."

I thought about the other cases I had been involved in and decided to suggest something to the DI.

"You know what Steve told you about Josie looking like Michelle Adams?"

"Yeah."

Her tone of voice hinted at the question, 'what about it'.

"Well, could these lads have killed her? You know on the basis they thought she was a paedophile?"

She shook her head.

"Unlikely to say the least. They haven't got the nous to plan something like that."

"Who did kill Josie then?"

She closed her eyes momentarily.

"We're getting there," she said, "that's all I can tell you. But going back to the question of who, if anyone, leaked the information about Tattersall, we're no nearer an answer."

We agreed to keep trying. A few seconds after Sarita had gone, an idea came into my mind. It seemed significant but disappeared as quickly as it had come. Probably a legacy of having suffered a stroke, I thought. Things like that were always happening. I tried to recall the thought. It was to do with something I had done, maybe something that had happened or been talked about that might give a clue as to how those leaflets got to those kids. It was no good. I had to accept that nothing would come.

I turned my mind towards the death of Josie Finch, something else I was getting nowhere with. Two questions – who could have killed her and why – swarmed round my head without answer. The culprit had to have been near the Park Hotel on 28th February at the relevant time. Almost certainly they would have a connection with Josie. For want of a better idea, I went into my office, sat down at the desk and took a notebook and pen from the top drawer. I would start with names. A few minutes later I read through my handiwork.

> Arthur: was there but didn't know Josie and why would he kill her?
> Angela: was there, was alone while Tony went back for his fags. Would the taxi driver have seen her? No reason to kill Josie. Pity she wasn't on the fiddle, that would have been an ideal motive.
> Simon: Abused women often killed by their (ex)partners. But no evidence.
> Tony: Why does everything come back to Tony bloody Murphy? He was there and went back for his cigarettes. If he had killed her the taxi driver might have seen him. In any case what motive would he have had?
> Karen: She was there but didn't know Josie and had no reason to kill her. She went back to get scarf. Admits

she thought Josie was Michelle Adams. Motive would have been hatred of abusers and their accomplices.

Larry: He was there, but had little time (neither did anybody else). No known motive. If he had wanted to kill his sister, he had plenty of other opportunities.

That was it. If there had been any forensic evidence against any of those people surely the police would have pulled them in. Sod it, I'd find something else to do. Maybe if I stopped thinking about murder for a while, the answer would come to me in a blinding flash. It was time I tidied up this room, I thought, as I looked around. Get rid of some of the stuff you don't need, I instructed myself, and the old clothes. Half an hour later I had two carrier bags of clothes and a cardboard box of books and CDs, which I took to the British Heart Foundation.

When I got back, I rang Brenda. There was something I wanted to tell her.

"I was wondering," I said after the usual greetings and a quick update on Tony's doings, "whether Adam might want to meet his grandmother. If so, I can tell you where she lives."

"Oh, please, Gus."

I gave her Mrs Murphy's address.

"Adam will be so pleased," she said. "I'll write to her today."

That was better than nothing, I thought. Feeling pleased that I'd done two useful things that had nothing to do with murder, I allowed myself a smile.

CHAPTER TWENTY-FIVE

"Hannah, tell Gus what you told me," said Paul that night.

We were in Hannah's parents' house, sitting at the kitchen table. He and Hannah were dressed up for a night out. It was easy to see they were a couple now. The things I do for people, I thought. Not only was I giving him paid work, I had even fixed him up with a girlfriend. Paul had phoned me earlier to tell me he had some information.

"One night a couple of weeks ago I couldn't sleep," said Hannah.

"Right."

I didn't want to put Hannah off by saying too much. I only hoped she wouldn't go into too much detail about her insomnia.

"Had things on my mind, know what I mean," she continued. "Any road, I went into the kitchen for a drink of water and looked out of the window."

So far, so good, I thought.

"Look, I'll show you."

As if at a secret signal we got up and went over to the window and looked out.

"And I sees this feller in the garden opposite. Over there."

Our eyes followed the direction in which she was pointing.

"He was creeping about. Pouring with rain, it was, he must have been soaked."

I nodded, willing her to get to the point.

"And he, like, had no clothes on."

"Are you sure?"

"Hundred percent. There's a street light nearby. Showed him up in all his glory."

"Glory," said Paul.

"Not really, he wasn't too impressive to tell you the truth," she giggled.

When the sniggering died down, we got back to the point.

"Can you remember exactly what night it was, Hannah."

"It was...," said Paul.

I cut him short.

"Let Hannah tell it."

She took his hand and smiled at him.
"It was the 28th February, pretty late."
"What did he look like, this man?"
Hannah seemed to weigh up this question carefully.
"Hard to say really, he was moving too quickly."
"So you didn't recognise him?"
"No."
"What did he do?"
"Do?"
Yes, Hannah, did he stay in the garden all night, did he go anywhere, did he dance the hoky bloody koky?
"Did he go anywhere for instance?"
She nodded.
"Only into the house. By the back door."
Paul, unable to keep quiet, chipped in.
"You know where that is, don't you, Gus?"
I turned towards him.
"Enlighten me."
"Deadbeat Mansions."

* * *

Interesting, I thought as I made my way home later, but where did it get me? The police would always ask if anyone had noticed anything unusual. Some bloke creeping bollock naked through the back garden of Deadbeat Mansions would come into that category. So would lots of things. Had he been getting a bit of illicit leg over in one of the neighbouring houses? Maybe the husband came home unexpectedly and he had to make a quick getaway. Or was he doing it for a bet? A bloke I used to work with told me he'd indulged in a childhood game called back garden creeping. There could be a nude version, I supposed.

* * *

The next morning shortly after I got up, I prepared Lamb Rogan Josh and left it to cook in the slow cooker. Danny and Natalie were coming round for a meal, having both arranged to get off work early. They would be staying the night. I wondered at the possible significance of this, as

I set out for my daily walk. Pulling up my anorak hood against a persistent drizzle, I went through Salford Quays, which was already busy. As I walked, I dodged people on their way to work. Random thoughts jostled one another in my head. The naked man in Deadbeat Mansion's garden, the leaflets that outed Edward Tattersall, the whereabouts of Tony. I said good morning to a postman pushing his trolley of letters and parcels. As usual he was wearing shorts. Only thick snow forced him to don a pair of trousers. I approached the Lowry Centre, an idea trying to break through the clutter in my mind. There was something significant about that postman. What was it? I tried to imagine him with no clothes on, but that didn't help.

I had to face up to the fact I had got nowhere with Josie Finch's murder. To cap it all, it began to piss down on my walk home. Real Salford rain too. I scurried along, hood up, hands in pockets. A lorry splashed muddy water onto my jeans and trainers. Not since the night of the quiz had I been out in rain like this. I briefly thought of finding somewhere to shelter, but decided to plough on. It was only a few minutes, though no doubt it would seem longer. And I'd soon get dry once I was home.

In my bedroom ten minutes later, I stripped off my clothes and put my dressing gown on. I took the muddy jeans and what was in the washing basket into the kitchen. Once I had loaded the washing machine, I had a shower as hot as I could stand it. Fifteen minutes later I was in the kitchen, eating porridge and catching up with The Code of the Woosters. The feeling of well-being I got from being warm and dry and wearing clean clothes almost made it worthwhile getting a soaking. My mind lingered on that thought.

Having eaten, I went into my office/spare room and took out the notes I had made on the case of Josie Finch. Painstakingly I read through every word I had written. If you wanted to do something you had to work at it. This got me thinking about Imogen Attwell. With her work ethic, she was an example to us all. She'd got involved with a paedophile, but at the time she met Edward Tattersall she didn't know about his offences. As I went through my notes for the second time, something important made its way from the back of my mind to the front.

I got up and looked out of the window. It had stopped raining. I just had time to do what I had to do. First I went to see Ian Jamieson to check a few things. I didn't explain – the less he knew the better – so he must have wondered what on earth was going on, especially when I looked behind his washing machine. I left him in a state of bewilderment. When I got back home, I telephoned Sarita Ellerton and told her I had some important information.

"Fire away," said the Inspector.

So I fired away and told her what I had worked out and what I thought she should do. She took a hell of a lot of convincing.

"You want me to...," she said after I had explained it for the second time.

"Or you can tell Mr and Mrs Finch why you turned down the chance to nab their daughter's murderer," I said.

"OK, you bugger," she said, "I'll come and see you later. Just you sit tight."

"I intend to do just that."

By then it was lunch time. I had a sandwich at home and then spent the next couple of hours indoors just pottering. I'd discovered a long time ago I was a born potterer. The rain started again a few minutes before I heard a knock on the door.

"Hello," I said to Natalie.

"Hi, Gus," she said, pulling down the hood of a trendy, green anorak.

Drops of rain had blown into her face and made her fringe damp.

"Come in," I said. "Where's Danny?"

"He was delayed at work," she said. "I got the train."

She followed me into the kitchen.

"Gosh, it's dreadful out there."

"Sit down, take your coat off."

I thought of the expression my mam had always used: 'you won't feel the benefit'. Natalie put the coat on the back of the chair, then sat at the table, where I joined her. I moved aside a cheese board. A knife lay diagonally across it.

"Something smells nice," she said.

"Lamb Rogan Josh."

"Danny said he hoped you'd make a curry," she smiled.

"His wish has come true," I said, "do you want a drink or anything? Tea, coffee?"

"No, I'm fine, thanks. Before Danny gets here, Gus, I wonder if I could have a word with you?"

My eyes must have shown my surprise. Was this to be another complication in my life? I did hope not. Was she pregnant? In which case shouldn't Danny be telling me? Without anybody saying anything, everybody now assumed Natalie and Danny were an item.

"The fact is I'm thinking of applying to do social work and wondered if you could advise me."

That was a relief. Not that I wouldn't have loved another grandchild, but it was too soon for these two.

"I'll do what I can."

She gave me a proper smile this time.

"Oh, thank you. Actually, I think I will have a coffee after all," she said.

I put the kettle on, wondering if I actually had any coffee, then sat down again. Before Natalie could say any more, somebody banged on the door.

"Sorry," I said, getting up.

As I opened the door a wet and bedraggled man in a red anorak barged past me. Booze fumes wafted in the air. Simon Natchow, I said to myself, that's all I need. Wishing I hadn't forgotten to sort out the chain for the door, I turned towards my unwelcome guest.

"What the fuck you playing at, Keane," he snarled. "You'll suffer for this."

"Simon, get out of here."

He looked at Natalie, who returned his stare. He moved across to her with a speed I wouldn't have thought him capable of. In a trice his right hand snatched the knife from the cheeseboard and his left arm was around her throat. She stifled a scream, looking at me with a mixture of terror and pleading.

"Natalie, try and stay calm. I'll sort it. Just tell me what it's all about, mate."

I hoped I sounded more in control than I felt.

"You know very well what it's about. I've just seen Ian Jamieson."

That was always a possibility, I thought.

"You've been asking about some clothes I gave him."

Keep him talking, Gus, keep him talking, I said to myself.

"Yeah, I hear you washed and ironed them for him."

He gritted his teeth.

"What of it?"

He knew the answer to that, but I carried on the pretence.

"I just thought it was nice of you, that's all. I don't see why me knowing about it should worry you."

"You've been sniffing around things that aren't your business."

I thought for a moment but got no inspiration.

"I'll just switch the kettle off," I said.

I wanted to be doing something.

"Oh, no," said Simon, "you don't catch me like that. It'll switch itself off."

I pulled a chair away from the table and sat down.

"You've called the police, haven't you," he said. "Well, you can just uncall them."

He tightened his grip on Natalie. The knife was perilously close to her throat. I had sharpened it that lunch time. Her eyes flickered round the room and back to me.

She didn't look any less scared. Who could blame her? Come on, Gus, I urged myself, think, you dozy bugger.

"How do you mean, Simon?"

I recalled what Larry Finch had said about Natchow. I could picture Josie's brother explaining it in his flat in Whitefield. This was Simon's impulsive stage; let's hope he gets onto the planning stage soon, I said to myself, and realises he's doing himself no good.

"I want you to call the cops, Keane, tell them you've made a mistake. Or your tart gets it."

Too late, Simon, I thought. Couldn't he see it didn't work like that? Why did he have to be so stupid? Natalie hadn't reacted to being described as my tart. It hardly mattered, did it? I detected a slight tremor in her hands. She licked her lips and stared straight ahead.

"OK," I said, taking out my phone.

I took the phone out of my jeans pocket and found the number I wanted in my contacts.

"How do I know who you were talking to?"

I trained my eyes on the knife and Simon's not very steady hand. I'd have to try and save Natalie. But how? I showed Simon the phone with DI Ellerton's name on the screen.

"Inspector," I said "sorry to bother you again."

"Gus, we're at Ian Jamieson's bungalow, I haven't got time to talk."

"I just wanted to say that the call I made earlier. It was a mistake. I'm sorry."

"You're not making any sense. We've found the stick and..."

"The wrong end of the stick, that's right..."

"What the hell are you on about? Is everything OK?"

"No, not at all...."

"Right. Are you at home?"

"Yes. Well, sorry again. Take care. Thanks again. Bye."

As I ended the call Natchow looked at me. The tense silence was broken only by the steam rising in the kettle.

"He's done what you asked," said Natalie in a shaky voice. "You can..."

"Shut up, bitch," snapped Simon, "I'm thinking."

A high pitched sound could be heard in the background. When it became a full blown whistle, Natchow pulled back in alarm. That was enough for Natalie, who drove her elbow into his stomach and sprang up. Turning round, she gave Simon a half-hearted push, but it was enough to knock him over. She stood there shaking, looking to me for guidance. Natchow stretched out his hand towards the knife.

He grabbed the knife and struggled to his feet, moving towards Natalie again. She backed away in alarm. By then I had grabbed the kettle from the hob and removed the whistle. Thank goodness I'd given up on electric kettles when the last one packed up. Two strides took me within inches of Natchow. I poured boiling water on his hand. He screamed in agony and dropped the knife. I kicked it wildly, watching it slide to the other side of the room. Natalie kicked Natchow in the knee, making him to stagger slightly. Not content with this, she kicked out more fiercely, catching him in the knackers. He crumpled with a groan. He lay on the kitchen floor, one hand clutching his balls.

"Don't move," ordered Natalie, her voice trembling.

She began to sob quietly.

"I'll kill you for this, Keane," grunted Simon.

"Like you killed Josie," I said.

"What if I did? She..."

He stopped talking as Danny opened the door. He must have taken in the man on the floor and his father holding a kettle for some unexplained reason, but he only had eyes for Natalie. He rushed over to her and held her in his arms.

"Oh, Danny, Danny, thank God you're here."

Danny glared at me.

"What the hell's been going on," he snarled. "I might have known..."

He left the sentence unfinished and concentrated on comforting his girlfriend. Whatever he might have known, I might have known it would be my fault. There was no opportunity to hammer out the rights and wrongs, however, as DI Ellerton arrived with back up. We then got caught up with Simon Natchow's arrest, making statements and trying to get over the shock.

It was nearly nine o'clock by the time we sat down to lamb curry, rice and spicy peppers and mushrooms. Not the night we'd planned. I tried to explain to my son and his girlfriend what Simon's behaviour was all about. Natalie persuaded Danny I wasn't to blame for her nearly being killed. I had the feeling he wasn't convinced.

CHAPTER TWENTY-SIX

The next morning Sarita called round as I was getting my breakfast. Natalie and Danny were still in bed. After asking how Natalie was – difficult to say, I replied – the DI joined me for tea and porridge. It was a casual clothes day for her and in keeping with her jeans and leather jacket, she appeared relaxed.

"If we could deal with the Josie Finch case first," she said as she sipped her tea, "I have something else to tell you later."

Though intrigued, I didn't say anything.

"We've sent the walking stick and the clothes away for forensic examination," she explained. "What do you reckon happened then, Gus?"

I took a spoonful of porridge, delicately flavoured with black treacle.

"On the night of the quiz, when Arthur chucked Simon out," I began, "he went home. His clothes were covered with mud."

I remembered Arthur telling us Simon had landed in a puddle.

"Right."

"So he changed into something clean and warm and decided to go out again."

I tried to picture what Natchow did next.

"As he walked back to the pub," I said, "I reckon anger was mounting with every step."

Sarita dug into her porridge – she preferred honey on hers. I was glad to see she had a good appetite.

"He blamed Josie for his humiliation," I went on.

"It's always someone else's fault with men like him," said Sarita.

"He got to the Park Hotel," I went on, "and when he saw Josie waiting for her brother in the car park he must have snapped."

I paused for another mouthful of tea. I pictured Natchow's face contorted with rage.

"He grabbed her walking stick and hit her. I don't know whether he knew Josie was dead; maybe he was just hoping she hadn't seen him."

I pictured Natchow making his escape, stick in hand.

"I think he must have sobered up quickly and started worrying about forensic evidence."

"He doesn't strike me as a thinker," said Sarita.

"But according to Josie's brother, that's just what he is. When he's sober, he plans everything very carefully."

"Right. Carry on."

"When he passed Ian's bungalow next door to where he lived, he saw a way out."

Sarita nodded, eating away steadily, while I thought out the next stage of my narrative.

"He had a key to the bungalow while Ian was away and he let himself in."

I remembered the chain smoking neighbour saying Simon always kept an eye on the bungalow while he was away.

"Once inside he took his clothes off and put them in the washing machine."

"What next?"

"He had a shower then stopped to think again."

"And what did he come up with?"

"I reckon he had been planning to come back for the clothes the next day, but he decided to give them to his friend, Ian instead. That way the police may never know they were his. He still had to think what to do with his trainers and the stick."

Sarita finished her porridge.

"Delicious," she said.

"He couldn't be seen with the stick," I went on, "and wouldn't be able to clean up the trainers enough to remove all evidence. So he dumped them in Ian's utility room behind the washing machine. He just had to hope the police would never look in the bungalow."

"Which we didn't until yesterday," Sarita put in.

"He still had to get home, so he crept out the back in the nude."

"Did that really happen," asked Sarita?

I explained what Hannah had told me.

"Clever sod."

"Then he sneaked into Deadbeat Mansions. When the police came to do tests on his clothes, he gave them what he'd worn at the Park Hotel earlier."

Sarita looked at me.

"And of course," she said, "there was no forensic evidence to be found."

She explained the rain had washed away any tiny traces Natchow might have left on the way to Deadbeat Mansions. Still wondering what the 'something else' was she wanted to talk about, I asked her what had happened to Simon Natchow.

"In custody overnight," she explained, "we can hold him for the attack on Natalie, while we get a case together for Josie's murder."

We went silent for a while. I wondered if the solution to Josie's murder passed the 'bleeding obvious' test. Having gone through the complicated explanation, I was tempted to answer, 'hardly'. But the identity of the killer was indeed obvious.

"Now, the other matter," said Inspector Ellerton.

She cleared her throat.

"I thought you might like to know Baz Prince has been arrested," she said,

"Yeah?"

She smiled as if pleased with herself.

"Picked up by the Met in the early hours of this morning. Thanks to the invaluable assistance of the Manchester force."

I sipped my tea, wondering why she was telling me.

"He was running a gang who stole cars to order..."

"Steve told me about that," I put in, "and I know about Tony Murphy's connection."

She looked at me, raising her eyebrows.

"Do you now?"

I nodded.

"I know everything."

She grinned at me.

"Then maybe you won't be surprised to learn Yarla Chester has decided to co-operate with us."

"To save her own skin?"

She finished her tea.

"Precisely. She dropped Prince and Murphy right in it."

That second name did surprise me. I had begun to think Tony was untouchable and was hoping I'd seen and heard the last of him.

"The only snag is," Sarita went on, "we have no idea where Tony Murphy is."

I shrugged, anticipating her next question.

"Join the club."

* * *

A month went by, taking us well into April. The nights got lighter; the cricket season started, it rained. Lancashire, having won the county championship the previous year for the first time for sixty years, lost their first two matches. Salford City Reds continued to lose more games than they won. I moved out of private eye mode after Natchow's arrest. Local authorities in greater Manchester had got busy and, cuts or no cuts, had to employ me. This, added to the nice bonus the Finches had given me for finding Josie's murderer, meant things were looking up financially.

On a rare sunny day in early May I had just parked myself at an empty desk in Ordsall Tower when Karen came up to me.

"Hiya, Gus," she said, "Imogen Attwell is here, asking to see you."

I looked up from the file I was reading.

"Imogen?"

"Yeah. I asked if I could help but she insisted in talking to you."

"OK."

"I hardly recognized her," she added. "She's had a complete makeover."

"Really?"

I looked at my watch.

"Tell you what, Karen, I've just got to make a quick phone call. Could you park her in an interview room and tell her I'll be with her in a couple of minutes? I'll do the same for you one day."

Karen smiled sweetly.

"Sure."

"Thanks."

* * *

When I saw Imogen in the interview room I realized what Karen meant about the change in appearance. Her hair was cut in a sort of bob similar to the way Louise had had hers done. My ex-wife was always up with the latest fashion so that made Imogen trendy. The purple top and skinny jeans looked new.

"Hiya, Gus," she said like I was her best mate, "you all right?"

Telling her I was fine and having ascertained she was never better, I asked what she wanted.

"Well, I've met this feller and... I wondered if you could check him out."

She explained she didn't want to repeat the nightmare she had with Tattersall. I agreed to look into it and get back to her. She still seemed reluctant to leave so I asked what she was doing now.

"I'm on this course in Walkden about setting up your own business."

"Great."

She was as keen to tell me this as she was to get the boyfriend checked out.

"That's where I met Ryan," she explained. "He's really supportive about what I'm doing. Unlike some I could mention."

"Who might that be?" I asked.

"Someone who never thought I could do anything."

A bit cryptic, I thought, but I knew who she meant.

"What sort of business is it?"

"I make, like, greeting cards, wedding invitations and that. Kind of customised you know. Here."

She delved into her bag and gave me a business card for Immy's Invites.

"Very professional," I said.

After urging me to tell all my friends, she left.

* * *

I went back to the social work room as Karen was on her way out.

"What did you make of Imogen, Gus?" she asked.

"She certainly looked different," I said.

"I got the impression she's happier too. I told her the council had re-let Tattersall's flat at last."

"Yeah?"

"She said I only hope they fumigate the fucking place and replace the loose floorboard. I laughed my head off."

With that Karen went out on a visit. Little did she know it, but she'd given me something to think about.

The full significance of what Imogen had said to Karen didn't really hit me until the next day when I was off on my morning walk. I said good morning to the postman, who was still in his shorts. Half an hour later everything had more or less slotted into place. An hour after that, I was sitting in Imogen's front room. Luckily the results of the checks into her new boyfriend had come in so I had a legitimate reason to see her. She was delighted to hear he was clear, but I had more to talk about.

"Do you remember those leaflets that got delivered about Edward."

She folded her arms in that defensive way she had.

"As if I could forget."

I waited a few more seconds then explained.

"People in children's services have been wondering how confidential information got out."

She folded her arms tighter.

"Yeah?"

Feigned indifference.

"We want to be sure we can keep that sort of stuff secure," I explained.

She sighed with impatience.

"Look, Gus, it's nice of you to call round and thanks for the information, but I haven't really got time to chat, know what I mean?"

"This isn't chatting, Imogen."

We looked at one another.

"Anyone with access to a laptop could have produced those leaflets. Me, you...anybody at all."

"And?"

"Somebody who could produce business cards as good as yours would find those leaflets easy."

She shrugged.

"Suppose so."

"Here's what I think happened, Imogen."

She sat back.

"I can't wait."

I went through everything in my mind, then started.

"Let me explain first that the person who found Edward's body nearly tripped over a loose floorboard."

"Did they?"

She looked away, apparently fascinated by the fireplace to her right, then faced me again.

"The day before Edward was killed, you cleaned his flat. I reckon you noticed the loose floorboard."

Once more she averted her eyes.

"What makes you think that?"

"When you came to see me yesterday," I said, "Karen showed you to an interview room."

"Yeah. And?"

"She mentioned that the council had just re-let Edward's flat."

"Maybe."

"You said something like: 'I only hope they've fumigated the effing place and replaced the loose floorboard'."

She shrugged.

"'Fumigate', is a word you'd use about vermin."

She tutted.

"How the heck," said Imogen, "am I expected to know every word I said yesterday?"

"Let me finish."

She groaned.

"Go on then, Hercule bloody Poirot, let's hear the rest of it."

"I reckon when you were replacing the floorboard you found some memory sticks," I went on. "You knew straight away what was on them. He'd hardly need to hide his holiday snaps or his music collection, would he?"

She looked round the room as if bored by what I was saying.

"Get to the point."

"OK. Had Tattersall been there you might have killed him. Luckily you had a bit of time to think. You didn't want to end up in the nick, leaving your kids motherless."

She looked hard at me.

"Why didn't I just report it?"

"I don't know," I admitted. "Why don't you tell me?"

She looked down at the floor.

"I could only do that if I had printed those leaflets."

A silence built up.

"OK. Speaking hypothetically, say a woman in your situation had found those memory sticks. How would she feel?"

She pursed her lips and breathed in. Letting out a breath, she began to speak.

"Well, she'd feel angry and betrayed. And a bit of a fool."

"Because the dreadful social services had been proved right?"

She looked up again at this and met my eye. I had hit the nail on the head.

"Yeah, that would be part of it. I h... she would have hated you lot for... The thing is the relationship with Edward might have come to an end quite naturally. Who knows? But once a social worker stuck her nose in, it's like you have to stay together on principle."

She joined her hands together, grimacing as if struggling to cope with strong emotions.

"This woman we're talking about, this hypothetical woman," she continued, "couldn't let Tattersall get away with it. She would have wanted to find a way of punishing him without going to Social Services."

She held back a tear before going on.

"I haven't even mentioned the worst part. The guilt. If she'd believed in him when he said he'd reformed, learned his lesson and all the time he'd been...To think I let my kids near that piece of shit."

In her anger she had forgotten to put herself in the position of the hypothetical woman.

"He thought he was better than me just because he knew about Beethoven and all that lot. How did I let the bastard take me in?"

A tear ran down her left cheek. She raised a hand to wipe it away.

"I wanted to show him, show everyone, that I wasn't stupid. Cos I'm not."

I nodded.

"I know you're not, Imogen," I said.

"When I'm at college and they give me work to do, projects, you know, I think, yeah, I can do this."

It was as if she was now glad I'd found out: she'd made her point.

"That's great."

'Yeah, it is."

She managed a smile. I smiled back.

"How did you think of the idea? About the leaflets?"

"When I was fourteen," she explained, "I went to stay with my cousin in Doncaster. One day we found a leaflet on the pavement saying some bloke was a pervert, there was a picture and everything."

I nodded.

"I've been struggling to work out how somebody could have delivered them without anybody noticing," I said. "Then I saw the postman this morning."

"Postman?"

"Nobody would notice someone delivering what they were supposed to be delivering, would they?"

She curled her lip.

"What are you on about now?"

"You were off to your job delivering papers that afternoon. So you put the leaflets in your bag."

She had run out of things to say.

"You had no need to worry about fingerprints," I said, "because of those white gloves you have to wear. The next day you came to see me, still defending Edward, as if nothing had happened."

"There's no way you can prove it," she said.

That wasn't the point. Angela would simply want to be sure there would be no criticism of the department. We could hardly be held responsible for Imogen's actions. And we'd had to tell her about Tattersall's record.

"You may be right, Imogen," I said. "I'm not sure what you did is even illegal."

"What you say I did."

"You probably didn't think he'd get killed," I went on, "a good hiding maybe. Anyway, the neighbours would know all about him. That would give you an excuse to leave him. And if nobody found the memory sticks, an anonymous 999 call would sort that out."

She sat still for a while, saying nothing. Then I left, applying the 'bleeding obvious' test once more. Tony had said 'Someone with a grudge who knew about Tattersall's background' had produced the leaflets. True enough as it turned out but it had been far from obvious until now that Imogen had a grudge. So Tony wasn't a lot of use. No change there then. Anyway, it's sorted now, I said to myself.

* * *

"Well, mam, I'm back," I said the next morning.

I was paying one of my periodic visits to my mother's grave. As usual I wore a suit and tie in a pointless attempt to win her posthumous approval. The sun shone from a clear blue sky.

"Sorry I haven't been sooner," I apologised, "I've been a bit busy."

I told her about my recent adventures. In the past few years I'd taken to confiding in her, something I could never do when she was alive. I told her my dad was still doing well and enthused about Georgia.

"I'm sorry you never met her," I said, "you would have loved her. You would have loved Rachel and Danny too."

Sad, I thought, how things worked out.

"Me and Marti are still together," I said. "Though it's still a bit...up in the air, I suppose."

Not that she would have been interested in my love life. Not after I had brought shame on the family by getting divorced. I looked round at the gravestones laid out neatly, the trees, the flowers left in pots as gifts to the deceased.

"Have you noticed that about life, mam? How nothing is ever resolved. Nothing is ever over."

I moved my feet across the gravel, listening to the crunching sound.

"That doesn't apply to you of course. I keep thinking of all the people who'd been hoping to find love, happiness and fulfilment and ended up just finding death."

I remembered what Tony Murphy used to say about the horses he backed: a dead certainty. Well, there was nothing as sure as death. Then in a weird kind of procession I saw my younger self finding my mam's body; Josie Finch having her life cut short in a pub car park; Edward Tattersall's throat being cut and somehow leading to the liberation of Imogen Attwell. Inevitably I thought of Tony Murphy who had come back into my life, seemingly determined to create havoc. Looking at my watch I realised it was time to go. Danny, Natalie and I had arranged to have a walk by Macclesfield Canal. Danny had more or less forgiven me for the incident with Simon Natchow. I said goodbye and left my mother alone until the next time.

I got back to the flat and, opening the door, saw the mail on the mat. I picked up the bundle and dumped it on the kitchen table. A postcard fell onto the floor. Picking it up I admired the picture of the Swiss Alps. Turning it over, I saw a Greek stamp and recognised the almost illegible handwriting.

Hi Gus
Greetings from who knows where?
Not Switzerland or Greece, I bet.

Thanks for everything. You never know, I might see you some time.

"Not if I see you first, Tony," I said out loud.

THE END

BOOK III

FALLING FOUL

CHAPTER ONE

I rushed through Salford Quays on a warm April morning, looking at my watch and wondering how I had managed to sleep through the alarm. Maybe I had forgotten to set it. Was it old age? Or was I just knackered? It had been a busy weekend, but even so.

I might have still been asleep but for a phone call just after half eight. By the time I'd fumbled for my glasses on the bedside table, registered the time on the alarm clock and began to struggle out of bed, the phone had stopped ringing. I didn't bother to check my mobile for messages; getting to work on time on the first working day after Easter was a greater priority. If it were urgent, they would call again.

As I crossed Trafford road and walked down Ordsall Lane, my thoughts turned to the review meeting I was to chair. Two kids in need of a permanent home. I would have to concentrate on them now and ignore any distractions. My tired brain had got this far when I approached Ordsall Tower, the concrete block that housed Salford Children's Services.

A woman in a leather coat with shoulder length black hair stood outside the building. She brushed at her heavy fringe with the fingers of her right hand before looking round impatiently. The frown on her face seemed to be a permanent fixture. Staring across the road into the middle distance, she moved her bag from one shoulder to the other.

Passing her, I was about to go up the steps towards the front door, when I heard a cry. Turning around I saw a youth, his face half hidden by a hoodie, arrive from nowhere. He grabbed the woman's handbag, accomplishing the task slickly without breaking stride. As the little toe-rag tried to get away, he staggered against the steps, then righted himself. He relaxed his hold on the bag and I snatched it from him. His hood slipped off his head, unveiling a skinny, narrow face. His startled eyes glanced towards the woman then back to me.

"That wasn't supposed to happen,' he said.

And you're not supposed to go round stealing handbags, I thought. His face full of indecision, he stared at me. I was six foot four; he was medium height if that, average build. I knew the broken nose I'd got playing rugby league for Salford gave me an intimidating air. This kid had no idea I was on medication for high blood pressure. Or that I would run a mile to avoid getting into a fight. Having weighed up the odds, he hared across the road right into the path of a white van with Pallister Paving written on the side.

"Look out," I cried pointlessly.

The driver, poor sod, had no chance of stopping in time. I saw the boy slump to the ground, hitting his head on the tarmac with a crack.

"Shit," I said.

The van screeched to a halt, veering to the right. It ended up slewed across both carriageways. Lines of traffic on both sides ground to a halt, the 4x4 behind the van only just stopping in time. Horns blared in a discordant chorus. Like that would do any good, I thought.

Shaking his head in disbelief, the van driver sat in shock for a while before staggering out of his vehicle. Two passers-by ran across to help, one of them already on the phone. I turned and passed the handbag to the woman, who seemed reluctant to take it.

"Are you all right," I asked.

"Of course I'm all right," she scowled.

Charming, I thought, as she turned on her heels and went into Ordsall Tower, muttering something like 'it's too bloody complicated'. It certainly is, I silently agreed. I looked back to the scene of the accident in time to see the bag snatcher sit up. He said something, but I couldn't make out the words. He rubbed a bump on the side of his head. A siren sounded in the distance. Pulling his hood over his head, he jumped up and ran off.

Well, I suppose that's that, I said to myself, time to get back to normal. Thinking about the woman who'd almost lost her bag, I turned back, noticing a clean buff envelope on the ground. It wasn't there a moment ago. Stooping to pick it up, I read the name typed on the front: Vicky Monroe. Whoever she was, she lived in Cholmondeley Road in Irlams o' th' Height. The street where Debbie Oldham used to live, I recalled, smiling at the memory. Then my phone rang. I really couldn't be doing with two calls before I had even got to work. As I answered I saw I had a missed call from Steve at 8.33.

"Hello," I said.

"Hi, is that Gus Keane?"

"Yeah."

"My name's Will Trader," said the caller.

Never heard of you, I thought, and I'm too tired to talk to you. I certainly didn't recognise his voice and his accent was hard to place.

"Your friend, Tim, said you might be willing to help me," he went on.

I didn't have a friend called Tim. Did I even know anyone of that name, I wondered? Not that I had time to argue about it.

"Help you? I..."

"I'm writing a novel with a social work theme," he explained, "and I wondered if you could give me the benefit of your expert advice."

Did I want to be bothered with this? Did I want to deal with it now? Or ever?

"Sorry, I'm a bit busy at the moment..."

"I'll text you my number, you can get back to me..."

If you must, I thought.

"I really have to dash," I said. "Bye."

Hoping I would have a bit of peace for a while, I went into Ordsall Tower. At the reception desk I pressed the bell.

"Hiya, Gus," said a young woman with lots of dark hair.

"Good morning, Hannah. I've got a question for you."

"Oh, yeah," she smiled, "if it's a proposal of marriage, I'm already spoken for."

I shook my head.

"A woman in a black leather coat came in a minute ago."

"Black leather coat? Oh, yeah. She was here for an interview. Fostering and Adoption manager."

That might explain why she had made herself scarce so quickly, but it still seemed odd.

"What was her name?"

Hannah looked down at a typed list.

"Vicky something," she said. "Vicky Monroe. Too young for you, Gus. Right miserable looking cow and all."

I handed over the envelope.

"She dropped a letter outside."

"Oh."

I went into the office, thoughts of a girl who lived in Cholmondeley Road a long time ago and the mysterious Ms Monroe distracting me. If her interview went well, we'd meet again. It was going to be one of those days, I could tell.

***

In the admin room a paunchy man of about my age wearing a beige v- neck jumper over a shirt and tie sat at a desk. I went over to him.

"Morning, Jimmy," I said. "I've just come to pick up some reports."

My old school friend, Jimmy Gallagher, had been appointed head of administration last year, but I still hadn't got used to working with him.

"Oh, hiya, Gus," he said. "What about David Moyes then?"

"What about him?"

"Did you not know? He's got the sack."

"Nobody tells me anything."

I wasn't too bothered about the fate of the Manchester United manager, who would doubtless get a pay out of several million quid to ease his pain.

"Has he? Not surprising really."

It was pathetic, I said to myself, that multi-millionaire footballers paid thousands of pounds a week suddenly couldn't play because they had a new boss. I would never get away with that in my job.

"Who's gonna take over? That's the big talking point," Jimmy went on.

Jimmy behaved a lot of the time as if he had been on a course about what blokes are supposed to talk about. He could bluff his way through a conversation about sport without having any real interest in it, his major hobby being collecting beer mats. A lot of his spare time was spent visiting fairs and exhibitions around the country.

"Who knows?"

Who cares, I could have added. I was much more concerned about Salford Red Devils rugby league team, who had already sacked their coach and were in even deeper trouble than United. I went over to the pigeon holes against the wall and pulled out an envelope with my name on.

"There was a strange carry-on outside as I arrived here," I said.

"What was that then?"

I explained about the handbag snatch.

"So this Vicky could be the new fostering manager," said Jimmy.

"I presume she's got as much chance as anybody else." I thought for a moment.

"Tell you what, Jimmy. Let me know how she gets on, will you? I'm curious."

"Will do."

The phone on Jimmy's desk rang.

"Hello, love," he said. "This is a surprise."

A pleasant one, I thought, judging from the smile on his face and the change in his tone of voice. I had a quick look in the envelope to make sure all the reports were there.

"Oh," he said. "...OK...you're staying the night?"

Jimmy's tone of voice changed again. He picked up a pen and tapped out a rhythm on the desk.

"I know, but...what do you mean 'don't be like that'? I'm not being like..."

He sighed loudly and put the pen down, only to pick it up again.

"But it's only...oh, I suppose so, if you must...yeah, see you tomorrow."

He put the phone down and smiled sheepishly.

"The wife," he said, "I've told her not to phone me at work."

Jimmy had lived on his own for ages until, about ten years ago, he had surprised everyone by marrying a charismatic woman twelve years his junior. With her encouragement he had even done something about his appearance, no longer looking quite such a nerd. His beer belly, though still distinctly noticeable, was now a shadow of its former self.

"How is Caitlin?" I asked.

"Fine, you know, same as ever."

"Great."

"Do you see anything of Louise these days," he asked.

I was sure Jimmy still thought of my ex-wife and me as a couple.

"I haven't seen her for a while," I said.

More to the point, neither had Danny and Rachel. I didn't see why she couldn't tear herself away from her second husband in London to see her children and granddaughter. To make matters worse, Danny and his girlfriend, Natalie, had arranged to go to London over Easter; Louise and Brad had gone to Paris. A mix-up, Louise had claimed. There was nothing I could do about it, but that only made it more difficult.

"Give her our love if you're in touch with her," he said.

"Sure."

I didn't have time to chat so smiled and started to leave.

"I'll see you, Jimmy. Running late this morning."

"Oh, by the way, Gus," he added, "Ellen's flying over today. You'll have to come and meet her soon."

"Great. I'll bring Marti."

"Yeah. And I can get you tickets for her world tour if you fancy it."

"If I fancy it? Try and keep me away."

What it's like to be friends with a rock star's brother, I thought.

* * *

I got back to the flat a couple of hours later, thinking I should ring Steve. I couldn't imagine what he had phoned about this morning, but at least he'd got me out of bed.

"Hiya, Gus," he said. "You ringing about Moyesy?"

I smiled at the way Steve referred to Man U's ex-boss as if he were one of his golfing cronies.

"Should I be?"

"Yeah, that's what I called you about this morning."

I might have known. Steve was a United fanatic, whereas I was just a supporter. And I preferred rugby league.

"What's your expert analysis?" I asked.

Steve wittered on about the woes of his favourite team for much too long. Just as I was losing the will to live he changed the subject.

"You still working?"

I couldn't afford not to, unlike Steve.

"Yeah. I'm on call tonight. Five until midnight."

"On call?"

"Yeah, did I not tell you? I've signed up for the Emergency Duty Team. They get in touch when they're short-handed, you know."

"I have a distant recollection that you took early retirement a few years ago," said Steve. "Or did I dream that?"

I laughed.

"No, you didn't dream it. But as I said at the time, I still need to do some work to supplement my meagre pension. And the EDT pays well."

"Can't be bad. How's Marti?"

"She's fine," I said, "busy as usual."

I had more than once accused Marti of being a workaholic. When she wasn't in court representing clients she was singing in a band called A Lop Bam Boom alongside my daughter. What spare time she had was increasingly taken up with looking after her aging mother. Sometimes I was amazed she had time to see me at all.

"Solicitors are never out of work," said Steve with all the cynicism he'd built up in a long police career. "You haven't made an honest woman of her yet then?"

That, I thought, could qualify as a rhetorical question. Steve knew I had no intention of marrying Marti.

"No. You won't need to compose a best man's speech."

Marti and I had been an item for about four years and people we knew expected us to be married by now. I saw no reason to change the nature of the relationship. While Marti had been keen on marriage at one stage, I was unsure how she felt now. She had become more reticent lately and had even stopped dropping obvious hints about our moving in together.

'She's not got you investigating any murders then," asked Steve?

I thought of my other job as a private eye, which had led me to look into a few murders.

"No. I want to steer well clear of that. A couple of pints on a Friday night is enough excitement for me."

CHAPTER TWO

"I love Andrea to bits of course," said Tim Greenhoff at around ten to seven that night.

I waited for the inevitable 'but' as he scratched his beard thoughtfully.

"But she's so jealous."

We sat on the settee in the lounge of a former old people's home a hundred yards or so from Ordsall Tower. My diary, notebook and pen lay ready on the coffee table in front of me – since its closure, Mangall Court had become an office for the emergency duty team. "If I so much as talk to another woman she goes off on one," he explained. "I mean, I've no idea what she gets up to when I'm not around, but I'm not forever accusing her of shagging every bloke she meets."

His wife had rung on the office phone a few minutes earlier. To check up on him, Tim reckoned. That had triggered his confessional. Now he was doing what most people did in my company: giving me the low down on his problems. The fact that we hardly knew one another didn't put him off.

"It's not only that, you know," he went on. "She's really high maintenance."

Wondering what he meant, I tried to look interested. For someone in his late twenties he sounded suspiciously like a grumpy old man.

"But she seems to think we've got more money than we have. She knows how much – or how little – I earn and she's a primary school teacher. Do the maths."

What was I supposed to say to that?

"But she must have the best of everything," he went on. "iPad, smart phone, top of the range TV...you name it. She's even joined the gym at Dacre House."

Dacre House, eh? Membership of the same health club as Marti would be pricy. "And she's booked us on a Caribbean cruise in August," Tim went on.

"Sounds nice," I said.

I meant the Caribbean, not the cruise.

"You wanna see the price. God knows how we're supposed to pay for it. I'm up to my eyes in debt as it is."

Apart from that, it's a match made in heaven, I said to myself. He sighed and I was hoping he had run out of steam. From a retro settee, I looked round at the huge TV that dominated the room, the old-fashioned music centre, and the sort of furniture that went out of fashion in the eighties.

"That's why I'm on the EDT," he said.

I broke off to answer a call on my mobile. Within seconds it was obvious I would have to go out: two kids needed a foster placement as their mother was being admitted to hospital. I explained the situation to Tim after ending the call.

Hearing a knock at the door, he left the room as I looked for the number of the foster carers I wanted. Having got that sorted out, I was ready to leave. I wasn't looking forward to leaving the warmth of Mangall Court. The temperature had dropped markedly as I had started my shift, so it was now more like November than April.

As I took my waterproof from the back of the chair and got up, Tim came back in. With him was a tall, slim bloke in an overcoat with a velvet collar over a grey suit that looked fresh from the cleaners. He had, I thought, taken a lot of trouble getting ready before he came out.

"This is Will," said Tim as he and his companion sat down.

I nodded, putting my anorak on.

"I rang you this morning," smiled Will, taking off a pair of leather gloves.

He spoke with an air of confidence.

"This morning," I said, puzzled.

"Yeah, about a book I'm working on."

So he was the novelist and Tim Greenhoff was the 'friend' who had given him my name. With friends like you, I don't need enemies, I almost said.

"I thought I'd try to catch you in person," Will went on.

The temptation to call him a cheeky twat was strong, but I resisted. He had a muscular build, the result of regular work outs at a guess, and I didn't want to upset him.

"I'm afraid I can't help you," I said, "I need to go out."

"Pity," said Will, trying to inject genuine regret into his voice. "I'm happy with the idea. I could really make something of it, but I need to make it realistic. That's where you come in."

His boyish enthusiasm was disarming, I thought, but I still didn't have time to listen to him.

"I'm sure Tim would help you."

"But you have the experience, Gus," said Tim.

I shrugged.

"Right. I'm off," I said with some emphasis.

"I'll hold the fort here," said Tim. "Probably get called out myself soon. You'll be out for a while, will you?"

I thought for a moment. With two young kids, probably upset about their mother, this job couldn't be rushed.

"Should think so."

"OK, have fun."

"Hey, Tim," I heard Will Trader say as I went out, "Can I have a look round this place while I'm here? There's a scene in the novel set in an old folks' home, you know."

* * *

As I was about to get into my car, I recognised the man walking past the car park entrance.

"Hello, Jimmy," I said, "What are you doing round here?"

"I've only just finished work," he explained. 'I'm off to get some fish and chips. Caitlin's out."

He huddled up in his waterproof jacket and scarf.

"I'm still working. I'm on the EDT tonight. Just got my first call-out."

"Oh, I see. How does that work then? Is it just you on duty or what?"

"Me and Tim Greenhoff tonight," I said.

"He used to work at our place, didn't he?"

"So he told me. I can't say I remember him though."

"He was only there five minutes. The vacancy on the EDT came up just after he started. It was good riddance to bad rubbish as far as I was concerned."

"Oh? How come?"

"I had my reasons," he said.

I didn't have time to decipher cryptic clues.

"Anyway, I'd better go," I said. "Do you fancy a pint some time?"

"Yeah."

"What about the Park Hotel Friday night?"

"Good idea," he agreed.

We arranged to meet in the pub at eight o'clock. I didn't want to hang around in the cold so began to move away

"By the way," he said, "that Vicky Monroe got the job. Starts first of May."

I wondered what the handbag woman and I would find to talk about when we met again. Before I could comment, I heard someone walking towards me. Turning, I saw a man of about forty with cropped hair.

"Is Greenhoff in there?" he asked as he came to a stop in front of me.

"Sorry," I said, not being able to think of anything else.

"I said, is Greenhoff in there?"

He spoke with slightly less aggression, nodding in the direction of Mangall Court. I shook my head.

"I have no idea."

Jimmy looked on warily. It was obvious this bloke spelt trouble and it would be best if we both stayed where we were until we could get rid of him.

"Do you know?" asked the man, turning to Jimmy.

"What was the name again," asked Jimmy.

"Greenhoff. Tim Greenhoff."

Jimmy thought for a moment before answering.

"Doesn't ring a bell."

"Wasn't there a Greenhoff played for United back in the seventies," I put in. "Two of them, I think, brothers."

The angry man looked from one to the other of us with a vacant stare.

"One of them died last year, the younger one," added Jimmy.

"There's another Greenhoff who's gonna die if I get my hands on him," snarled the man. "Should I tell you what that bastard did to me? I'll tell you what he did. He took my kids off me."

An angry client, that was all we needed.

"Terrible," I said.

"Bloody right, mate," he said, making me wish I had been less sympathetic. "He left his job a couple of weeks later and nobody would tell me where he was. But I tracked him down. I reckon he's in there right now."

He pointed at Mangall Court.

"That's an old people's home," I said.

Luckily, the old sign hadn't been taken down.

"Closed down," said the man. "It's the office for the emergency team now."

"Emergency what?"

He looked at me, amazed at my ignorance.

"It's, like, a team of social workers who deal with anything that comes up out of office hours."

Trying to look grateful for being enlightened, I wondered how to get rid of him.

"And you reckon he works there?"

"I do and I'm gonna get him."

Bugger.

"I don't know much about these things," I admitted, "but I'm not sure that's a good idea. What do you think, Jimmy?"

"I agree, you don't want to put yourself in the wrong, do you?"

He looked uncertainly at us, his original anger slowly dissipating.

"Don't I?"

Handle this right, I told myself and this madman could soon be off our hands.

"No. What I would suggest, er, sorry, I don't know your name..."

"Wayne Dickens."

"Well, Wayne, I reckon you need a lawyer, don't you think so, Jimmy?"

Wayne treated this suggestion with contempt.

"I've got one, fucking useless, he is."

"You're entitled to change your solicitor," said Jimmy. "There's a good one on Salford Quays. Pym and Sigson. Top notch they are."

Wayne hesitated. His adrenalin had got back to normal.

"Yeah, maybe you're right," he conceded. "I'll get along there first thing in the morning."

"Ask for Mrs Sigson," I said.

"Yvonne will kill me," I said, as I watched Wayne walk away.

Marti's partner hated family cases. Still it got us off the hook, didn't it? I reminded myself to tell Tim about Wayne Dickens when I got back.

* * *

I drove off, heaving a sigh of relief. As I got nearer my destination, I heard rattling from the engine of my Peugeot.

I started to wonder if it would get me to where I was headed. The bloody thing was on its last legs and I was reluctant to fork out for repairs or a new motor.

The car got me back an hour and a half later without mishap. I had settled the children with their new carers and would have to arrange someone to visit them tomorrow. Poor kids, I thought, remembering their confusion at being parted from their mother again. Good job you're such a hard bastard, I said to myself, or this job could upset you.

I opened the door of Mangall Court. In the hallway I heard something upstairs. I paused to listen then decided I'd better find out what was going on. As I climbed the stairs, the noise got louder. I couldn't be sure but it sounded like somebody in pain. I got to the landing, trying to make out which bedroom it was coming from. The door with a number three on it was slightly ajar. I leant on the door until it was open sufficiently for me to see inside, managing to do this without making a sound.

A collection of garments was scattered randomly around the room. On the vividly patterned carpet a lacy bra trailed across a black skirt; a white blouse was draped on top of a pair of Manchester City boxer shorts; a pair of trousers lay crumpled in a corner. A naked man with a pimple on his left shoulder writhed on the mattress, straining against the white ropes that tied his hands to the brass bedstead. The woman straddling him, like her partner, had her eyes shut tight. She wore only a red and white scarf knotted round her neck. The frown on her face looked familiar as she forced otherworldly noises out of her mouth with every thrust. I pulled the door to and moved away. The two lovers had been concentrating too hard to take a blind bit of notice of me.

I went downstairs, struggling to contain my laughter. Several questions went through my mind. The principal one was how Tim Greenhoff came to be shagging handbag woman, Vicky whatever her name was. A miserable cow, Hannah had called her. Even in mid-orgasm the new fostering manager looked as if she'd just lost twenty quid and found ten pence.

Ah, well, it's one way of passing the time, I said to myself as I went into the kitchen. Over a cup of tea, I wondered about Tim's wife. He had a cheek to complain about her jealousy. If he indulged in extra-marital shenanigans while at work, what did he get up to on his days off? And what about Vicky? Did she have an unsuspecting bloke waiting at home for her? When Louise had been having it away with Brad I was certainly unsuspecting.

It was half an hour before I saw Tim again. During that time, I didn't dare go upstairs. I was just coming out of the downstairs loo when I saw him and his bedmate approaching the front door.

"All right, Tim," I called.

He turned round guiltily, as did Vicky. She was wearing the same clothes as this morning. She didn't look as if she had cheered up any.

"Oh, hi, mate," he said ingratiatingly. "Wasn't sure if you were back."

"Yeah, been back a while."

"Right. This is Vicky, by the way, a friend of mine. She's in the area and... popped in for a bit."

Popped in for a bit, eh? Another expression to add to the lexicon of euphemisms.

"Hello," I said, trying not to laugh.

She gave a half-hearted wave, no more than a flick of the fingers.

"Hi."

"You've still got your handbag I see," I said.

She looked at me as if I were mad.

"My handbag?"

I said nothing. The penny dropped.

"The less said about that the better," she said in a strong Lancashire accent.

Sorry I spoke, I thought. She turned to leave.

"See you then," I said.

"Sorry about that," said Tim as he closed the door behind her.

I shrugged. We walked back towards the lounge together.

"Nice girl, Vicky. A United fan, but nobody's perfect."

I refused to take the bait; I didn't want to get back to the David Moyes sacking.

"Her turning up was quite useful actually," Tim added.

Useful? And they say romance is dead.

"In what way?"

He looked pensive for a moment.

"Financially, I guess you'd say. We discussed a way I might make a bit of extra cash."

"Before I forget," I said, "I thought I'd better tell you I saw Wayne Dickens outside earlier."

"Bloody hell, what did he want?"

"You."

I explained the altercation with Wayne and how Jimmy and I had got rid of him.

"Thanks, mate," he said. "I owe you."

He shook his head and sighed.

"One of the reasons I applied for the EDT was to get away from people like Dickens. I didn't feel safe."

The constant fear and anxiety nagging away in the background was all too familiar to me.

"The thought of having to deal with the same people for months, years," Tim went on, "it's just..."

He sighed again, unable to put his emotions into words.

"At least with this job, you sort out the immediate crisis and pass it on to somebody else."

There was an attraction in that, I had to admit.

"I'm gonna get out of social work before it drives me mad," he said. "Once I've got a few bob together, you won't see me for dust."

I hope it keeps fine for you, I said to myself.

"Sorry about Will by the way," said Tim. "He talked me into giving him your number."

"You still shouldn't have done it."

He held his hands out in mock supplication.

"I realise that now, but I honestly didn't think he'd bother you. He hardly ever follows up on his brilliant ideas."

"No?"

"Will is always having sudden inspirations. I take it all with a pinch of salt myself. I mean, he calls himself a writer but he's poker correspondent for the Manchester Evening News and that's it."

"Poker correspondent? I didn't know there was such a thing."

Tim grinned at me.

"Oh, yes, all that stuff is big business. You could say Will's a professional gambler."

I had heard of such people, but had never believed they really existed.

"He'll be at the Duke of Earl now."

"Is that a pub?" I asked.

If it was, I had never heard of it, though I vaguely recalled a song by that name when I was a little kid.

"No, it's a casino," he explained, "if I know Will, he'll be there till all hours. Makes a decent living out of it and all."

People are full of surprises, I thought.

"As for the novel idea," Will explained, "Will's probably trying to impress some woman."

"Yeah?"

"At Uni we called him URL."

Before I could ask for enlightenment Tim's mobile rang. Another call out. After Tim had left, I googled URL, which I had an idea was something to do with the internet, and discovered it stood for Uniform Resource Locator. Gratified to know this and feeling more complete as a human being, I still had no idea what it could possibly have to do with Will Trader.

CHAPTER THREE

The next morning about twenty-five past eight I was searching my flat for my diary. Having looked everywhere I could think of without success, I concluded I must have left it in Mangall Court. Bugger. As I got into my car, I cursed my stupidity, finding this sort of thing disproportionately annoying. I didn't think I had any appointments today, but wouldn't be sure until I checked the diary.

I drove round the back of the former residential home and, as I turned right towards the car park entrance a black car came roaring out, almost scraping my door. I caught the merest glimpse of a baseball cap and eyes screwed up in concentration as the driver shot past. I slammed my brakes on and shuddered to a halt. That did my blood pressure no good, I thought, as I felt my heart beat increase. There were some mad bastards about.

Once I had calmed down a bit, I eased my car into a space and got out. On my way into the building I passed Tim's red Fiesta, the only other car in the car park, wondering idly why it was still there at this hour. As I got into the Mangall Court lounge, I noticed a man in a suit walking past the front window. He looked familiar, but I didn't have time to think who he might be.

I saw the diary on the coffee table right away. With a sigh of relief, I picked it up. Flicking through the pages, I checked what I was supposed to be doing today. Nothing. Good, I could go home and relax.

* * *

"I had a hell of a shock this morning, Gus," said Polly, my cleaner, a plump, sixtyish woman.

"Why, what happened?"

We usually had a bit of a chat at my kitchen table before she started cleaning. I employed her when I could afford it and she was glad to supplement what she earned from Salford council.

"Well, it was at Mangall Court."

"Mangall Court? I was working there last night."

Polly paused, chewing her bottom lip.

"Oh, I didn't realise you were on the night duty team."

"Just now and again."

Another pause.

"The other lad who was on, er, is he a friend of yours?"

"Tim? No, not really."

"Well, that's something..."

She went silent, a worried frown on her face.

"What's up?" I asked.

"I'm sorry to be the one to tell you, Gus, but I'm afraid he's dead."

"Tim dead?"

Polly touched my hand in sympathy before she continued.

"I found his body," she explained.

"God. Are you OK?"

"Not too bad."

"You should have stayed at home, Polly. The cleaning can wait."

She shook her head.

"No, you're all right, Gus, it's better if I keep busy."

"What happened?" I asked.

She took a deep breath.

"I went into one of the bedrooms upstairs – about ten o'clock it would have been."

Not that long after I had been there retrieving my diary.

"I looked over to the bed. Well, I couldn't believe my eyes. There was this feller lying there in his boxer shorts."

"Bloody hell."

"And that wasn't all. His hands were tied to this, like, brass bedstead," she said, "and he had a red and white scarf round his neck."

"A red and white scarf?"

"Yeah."

So he'd died in Man City boxers and a United scarf. What was that all about? I thought again about the David Moyes sacking.

"It was funny at first," she continued. "I wasn't laughing long."

She hesitated, as though reluctant to get to the nasty bit.

"I could see something wasn't right," she continued. "He wasn't moving for a start. And whoever had tied him up in the first place wasn't there no more."

She pressed her hands together.

"Any road, I went a bit closer and shook him. Gently, you know."

I pictured the cleaner tentatively nudging the body. With a less tragic outcome it would have been farcical.

"No reaction. I shook him a bit harder. Still nothing. I looked a bit closer. The scarf was pulled dead tight, you know. Under the scarf I could make out a load of marks round his neck. It looked like ... it was all red and bruised."

She closed her eyes at the memory.

"And I thought, bugger me, he's dead."

Poor Tim, he was just a lad. The whole thing brought back unwelcome memories of the day a few years ago when I found my boss dead in his office.

"The police asked me loads of questions," Polly went on. "I was there ages."

"I bet you were."

"Oh, Gus, don't tell anyone I told you about this. The cops said I was to keep quiet."

"Your secret's safe with me," I promised.

"I have to talk to someone," she added, "and you're so easy to talk to, Gus."

I sometimes resented people's tendency to confide in me but with Polly I didn't mind. When she had finished telling me about Tim, I got the tram into Manchester. She liked to be left alone to get on with her job. While I browsed Waterstones in Deansgate for a birthday present for my sister, I thought about Tim's death. What was behind it? Sex maybe. Tim put it about a bit and must have been into weird erotic carryings on. So who had tied Tim up? Whoever it was, had they killed him? Was Wayne Dickens, the angry client, responsible? And who was in the car that nearly took the paint off my Peugeot? Had I seen Tim's killer? Like the song said, more questions than answers.

* * *

About half three the doorbell rang. I went over and looked through the peephole. My visitor was a woman, but her head was turned to the side. I opened the door, keeping the chain on. Looking out, I heard a voice.

"Bloody hell, Gus, it's only me."

I'd had a new door fitted after a violent nutter had barged into the flat two years ago and I had taken no chances since then. Taking the chain off, I opened the door wide.

"Louise," I said. "Come in."

She followed me into the kitchen. We had never worked out an appropriate way of greeting each other since she'd left. The hug and/or kiss that everybody indulged in these days didn't seem right somehow. Louise stood in the middle of the room, looking around appraisingly.

"This is nice."

I realised she had never been to my flat before.

"Thanks. Sit down."

She took her coat off, still inspecting the kitchen, and put it on the back of a chair.

"And so tidy."

"Well, you've got to keep on top of things, haven't you? Do you want some tea or anything?"

"No, thanks."

Louise put her handbag on the table next to the Guardian and a packet of chocolate digestives. She sat down with a sigh.

"How are you?" I said, not knowing what else to say.

"OK," she shrugged. "You look well."

You don't, I could have said. Exhausted, defeated even, would be a better description. She was still recognizably the Louise I had known for thirty odd years. Her blonde hair was as trendy as ever. The long-sleeved pink t-shirt and straight jeans had a certain style. But there was something missing.

"How's Brad?" I said.

I couldn't give a toss about Brad but one had to be polite. Louise sat quite still for a few moments, looking blankly ahead.

"I've left him."

"What?"

"Go on, say I told you so."

She drew circles on the table with her fingernails, avoiding my eyes. I ignored her comment, waiting for her to continue.

"I'm back at Mum and Dad's."

For a moment I couldn't think straight, then thought I'd better say something.

"You're back in Darlington?"

I pictured her parents' Edwardian house in the west end of the town. Louise's mam and dad were in their eighties and, like my dad, were pretty fit. Even so what was happening to their daughter wouldn't do them much good.

"I start work in Durham next week."

"What's brought this on?"

She hesitated and before she had time to answer the bell rang again. I went through the rigmarole with the peep hole and the chain before opening the door to another familiar face. She held up an ID badge.

"DI Ellerton," she announced. "Manchester P…"

"I know who you are, Sarita," I said.

And I know why you're here, I could have added.

"This isn't a good time."

"Sorry, Gus," she smiled.

"Come in."

As we went into the kitchen, I noticed she'd had her dark hair cut short. Otherwise she was much the same. Smartly dressed, carrying her usual briefcase cum handbag.

"This is my ex-wife, Louise," I said when we reached the table. "Detective Inspector Sarita Ellerton."

The two women weighed one another up. Sarita was no doubt thinking, 'so this is his wife'; Louise would be wondering what the CID wanted.

"I was wanting a word in private, Gus," she said.

Her Scottish accent had become less strong over the years, I thought, as she sat down, taking a notebook and pen out of her bag.

"Well, I have no objection if Louise stays," I said.

I didn't want to banish Louise when she'd just arrived. Sarita thought for a moment or pretended to.

"OK."

"What's it all about," I asked.

She then asked the question I had expected.

"Do you know a man called Timothy Greenhoff?"

"I've worked with him. Why?"

The inspector looked from me to Louise and back again. Louise sat forward, all ears.

"Mr Greenhoff's body was found in a bedroom in Mangall Court, Salford around ten o'clock this morning."

Remembering Polly's warning, I didn't let on I knew about this.

"His body? God."

I thought of the bed Tim and Vicky had made good use of the previous night. It had been full of life then; within hours it had become his deathbed.

"Who's..." said Louise.

"We're treating his death as suspicious," said Sarita before Louise could get her question out.

Not the first time I'd heard those words.

"Did you know him well," asked Sarita?

I shook my head.

"No. He was a colleague. We were on the EDT together last night in Mangall Court."

"EDT?"

"Emergency duty team."

Louise looked over to me.

"I didn't know you worked nights," she said.

"I'll explain later."

"When did you last see him?" asked the DI.

"Just after midnight, when I finished my shift," I said. "Tim was on duty until eight this morning."

She noted down my answer before moving on.

"Had you met him before?"

"I could have met him when he worked at Ordsall Tower last year, but I didn't remember him."

She wrote in her book for a while.

"What did you make of him?"

I shrugged, stumped for an answer.

"Not a lot, I hardly knew him."

I could have said he was a randy womanizer, but I was reluctant to get too involved. Getting involved was bad for my health.

"You must have formed some sort of impression," the inspector insisted.

"He seemed OK, went on a bit," I said.

"Went on a bit?"

I might have known a detective investigating a murder wouldn't be satisfied with that.

"Come on, Gus, dish the dirt," said Louise, smiling for the first time since she'd got to the flat.

"Well, he was a bit of a moaner," I said.

"What did he moan about?"

I scratched my left ear and then my right one.

"Last night he was complaining about being short of money."

More note-taking followed this.

"Go on."

Do I have to, I almost said.

"He was...I suppose he and his wife were living above their means. Leading an expensive lifestyle, you know."

She looked directly at me.

"At least that was my impression" I added.

"A lot of addicts have financial difficulties."

And so do most of the population, I could have said.

"I know that. I'm a social worker."

Sarita smiled.

"Quite. What I'm wondering is, did Tim have any sort of...habit, you know, drink, drugs, gambling?"

Was it my imagination or did she put an extra emphasis on the last word? Tim had said something about gambling but that was only in relation to Will.

"I don't know," I replied. "In the brief time we were together I saw no sign of it."

"Right. Who else might know him?"

I thought for a second.

"Anyone who worked with him, I suppose. And he had a couple of visitors in Mangall Court.

"Visitors?"

"Yes, a feller called Will...Trader..."

She cut in while I was congratulating myself for remembering the bloke's name.

"What did he want?"

Her voice betrayed a marked lack of interest as though she were going through the motions. She must get sick of asking questions, I thought, as I explained about Will's novel and the call on my mobile the previous morning.

"He called in at Mangall Court hoping he'd get more out of me, but I had to go out on a case."

"Who was the other visitor?" she asked.

"Vicky something."

Sarita raised her eyebrows.

"What did she want?"

I tried to clear my face of any sort of expression, resisting the temptation to say 'a bloody good shag'.

"According to Tim she was a friend. She was in the area apparently and... called in."

"There is evidence to suggest sexual activity took place in the bed Mr. Greenhoff died in. Have you any thoughts about that?"

I could see I'd have to come clean. Or dirty.

"Well, it wasn't me, guv. It was Tim and Vicky."

Louise and Sarita spoke at the same time.

"How do you know?"

"I saw them."

I explained what happened when I went into the bedroom.

"You say she was wearing a red and white scarf during this sexual encounter?" asked the inspector.

"Yes, is that significant?" I asked, feigning ignorance.

"Everything's significant at this stage, Gus."

"Vicky Monroe, that's her name," I said.

"M,o,n,r,o,e?"

"That's right. She lives in Cholmondeley Road, Irlams o' th' Height."

"How do you know that?"

"I saw her yesterday morning."

I explained about the attempted handbag theft and finding the envelope addressed to Vicky.

"I found out later she was at Ordsall Tower for an interview. She's gonna be the new fostering manager."

The two women looked at one another then at me. Inspector Ellerton spoke again.

"Is there anything else you can tell me?"

"Wayne Dickens," I said.

"Who's he?"

I explained about the angry client outside Mangall Court.

"So this Dickens character had a grievance against Tim Greenhoff?" asked Sarita. "And threatened him?"

"Yeah."

"You don't know where he lives, do you?"

I guessed he was local, but couldn't be more specific.

"Children's Services will have it on record if his children are in care."

She jotted something in her book, then asked me if there was anything else.

"Yes. I had to go back to Mangall Court this morning. I'd left my diary there."

"What time was this?"

I thought for a moment.

"About quarter to nine, I reckon."

Sarita asked what I had seen. I told her about the car making a quick getaway.

"A black car, you say? What make?"

I shrugged.

"I don't know. Like I say there wasn't time to notice anything. Plus I know sod all about cars."

"And you didn't recognise the driver?"

"I couldn't even tell you whether it was a man or a woman."

Her sigh expressed pure frustration.

"Did you notice any other vehicles?"

"A red Fiesta," I said. "It belongs, belonged to Tim."

Now I realised why it was still there after Tim had finished his shift. Sarita went on with her questioning.

"When you went inside Mangall Court, did you see anything unusual?"

Does anybody ever notice anything unusual, I wondered.

"No. It was quiet, but you'd expect that. There was nobody about as far as I could tell. I didn't stay long."

She put her notebook and pen away, stifling a yawn.

"Well, I'd better get on. Perhaps you could come into the station to sign a formal statement – which should include a description of Trader and Monroe – and you'll need to have your fingerprints taken."

With that she was out of the door before I could protest. Not that it would have done any good.

***

"Fascinating life you lead since we split up," said Louise when the inspector had gone. "What was that all about?"

"You know as much as I do. Anyway, you were telling me about Brad."

"Yes, but..."

"So tell me."

She said no more for a while, so I waited, tapping on the table impatiently and looking pointedly in her direction.

"Well, it's been building up inside of me for, oh, I don't know how long," she began. "Six months, maybe even a year."

It was coming to something when Louise started telling me her troubles. I wondered again about the exact nature of my feelings for her. I associated her with the worst time of my life. A week after she walked out, I had a stroke and my self confidence, already low, plummeted even further. Now I took a broader view. We had also shared some of the best times, particularly when the kids were growing up. And she was their mother. That was the most important thing.

"He...he thought he owned me," she went on, "I realise that now."

I had never seen her so subdued.

"I won't go into detail, we'll be here all day, but he resented me having any life of my own."

She sniffed, on the verge of tears by now.

"He was especially difficult when I wanted to see my family. Even a trip to see Mum and Dad made him jealous. And as for you, I hardly dared mention your name."

What did I have to do with it, and where was this leading? Louise swallowed hard, fidgeting with her hair.

"He would make another arrangement every time I wanted to see Danny or Rachel and Georgia. After a while I took the line of least resistance..."

I opened my mouth to speak, but she went on.

"Before you say anything, I know I shouldn't have, but you don't know what it's like."

True enough. I let her get on with it.

"In the end I devised a way out. I applied for the Durham job and used Mum and Dad's address."

"So he doesn't know where you are?"

She shook her head.

"He would have tried to stop me. Once I had decided to leave, I made sure I went along with everything he wanted until I was ready to go."

How had it come to this, I asked myself.

"I didn't even complain when he arranged a 'surprise' trip to Paris for Easter. He knew fine well Danny and Natalie were coming to stay."

Bastard, I muttered under my breath.

"I told him I was taking a couple of days leave when we got back on Tuesday night. I hired a van to take my stuff to Darlo and drove there yesterday. He was at work."

Louise had not once referred to her husband by name.

"Why have you come here?" I asked.

She shuffled uncomfortably on her chair.

"I needed to explain what had been happening. And to make it up with Danny and Rachel."

She was going to try to rope me into this, I could see it coming.

"Good idea," I said.

"Listen, Gus, could you get in touch with them and..."

Various expressions came to mind: on your bike; you'll be lucky; fuck off.

"No."

"Oh, Gus. Please."

I took a deep breath in a vain attempt to calm myself.

"You've got a bloody cheek, Louise," I told her. "This is your problem. Keep me out of it."

She looked down at her hands, shaking her head gently from side to side.

"I know I've made a mess of things and... there's no excuse for...look, what I'm trying to say is..."

Whatever Brad had done to her had rendered her inarticulate.

"I'm just afraid if I contact Rachel and Danny, they won't want to talk to me. So, I thought if you could call them?"

"I refer you to my previous answer," I said.

"Gus," she said, choking back a sob, "if I've ever meant anything to you..."

"For fuck's sake, Louise," I snapped, "don't try the emotional blackmail. It won't work. And there's no point in turning on the waterworks."

By now I knew I would have to do something about this. That was my role in life, sorting things out. Anyway, I couldn't have us joining the ranks of dysfunctional families.

"A phone call's no good," I said. "We'll go and see them together, but you do the talking."

She started to thank me, but I cut her short.

"I'm not doing this for you, Louise," I said.

CHAPTER FOUR

The next morning there was a knock on my door. Looking through the peephole, I recognised Sarita. As I let her in, I made it clear I was in a hurry.

"I won't keep you long," she assured me.

"Good."

We sat down at the kitchen table. I prepared myself for answering more questions and having my answers written down for posterity. Here we go again, I said to myself.

"I just wondered," said the inspector, "if you knew somebody called Francine Ingleby."

"Don't think so."

"Are you sure?"

I had to think for a moment, having had a problem with names since suffering a stroke about five years ago.

"Pretty sure."

I picked up my notebook from the table.

"Tell you what," I said, "I'll write it down, that sometimes helps."

Sarita repeated the name, spelling it out as I wrote. I looked at it for several seconds.

"Sorry, it means nothing to me. Who is she?"

She looked down at her notebook before making eye contact again.

"She's just someone we need to talk to as part of our inquiries."

Yeah, right, I thought.

"She's not another one of Tim Greenhoff's women, is she?"

"I think speculation is pointless at this stage, don't you?"

Not for me, it wasn't. I got up, as did DI Ellerton.

"Who knows? In any case, I've got to be getting to work. Do call again if I can help in any way."

As I left Palace Apartments, I decided to indulge in a bit of speculation in spite of the inspector's advice to the contrary. Where had the name Francine Ingleby come from? Somebody the police had interviewed might have mentioned her. Lots of names would have cropped up by now, so why did the DI ask about her in particular? There must be something special about her.

Had she left traces at the scene of the crime? Fingerprints or DNA? They could only know they belonged to her if she was already known to the police. So either Francine was a convicted criminal or she had been suspected of an offence and they had kept her DNA on file. Interesting, I thought, but thankfully nothing to do with me.

With a shrug I forgot about it and turned my mind to my family. Louise had made her peace with our son and daughter. Just about. Having spent the night at Rachel's house, she would be on her way back to the North East later today. So far, so good, I said to myself, but it wasn't resolved by any means.

* * *

The Park Hotel greeted me with a buzz of conversation. There was a decent crowd in, enough to give the place an atmosphere. A North Manchester CAMRA Pub of the Year 2013 banner was draped over the bar among the horse brasses, not the first time it had won that accolade. There was something about going for a pint on a Friday night.

"All right, Arthur," I said as I got to the bar.

"Not so bad, you know," replied the landlord. "I struggle on. What can I get you?"

"A pint of Red Devil, please."

"For a change," he said, getting a glass and pulling the pint.

Arthur had been a constant presence in the Park Hotel for as long as I could remember. He had taken over the pub when his dad retired twenty years ago or more. Now he looked almost like a parody of what a landlord was meant to be. To call him fat would have been like describing David Beckham as quite well off. Tonight, as on every occasion I saw him, he had put on a bit more weight. I heard footsteps behind me and turned to see Jimmy Gallagher.

"Hiya, Gus," he said, standing beside me at the bar.

"Now then, Jimmy," I said, "usual?"

"Please."

"Another pint for Mr Gallagher," said Arthur, getting a second glass ready and sweeping his long hair away from his face.

"How's Caitlin?" I asked.

"Fine," said Jimmy. "She's picking me up later. She's out at some charity meeting in Stretford."

"It'll be nice to see her."

Arthur looked up from the beer pump.

"I see one of your lot got himself killed," he said conversationally.

'One of your lot' was the way he was wont to refer to anyone connected with social work.

"Yeah," said Jimmy, "a bad business, that."

Arthur paused in his task to let the beer settle.

"Did you two know him?"

"I'd come across him," said Jimmy.

We carried our drinks over to a seat by the window.

"He was a bit of a lad by all accounts, was young Tim," I said. "Not the most faithful of husbands."

Jimmy nodded in agreement.

"Little toe rag. The cheeky sod was always chatting up the women in my team. Some of them are married and all, and a couple are only youngsters."

Disapproval covered his face.

"It's not on, that sort of thing, unprofessional."

Lighten up, Jimmy, I wanted to say. The amount of flirting that went on at work, not to mention the affairs that started there, it was a wonder anything got done. Jimmy had always been a bit strait-laced though.

* * *

As Caitlin got to the pub about ten past ten, people turned to look at her. She came over to our table, putting her arms around Jimmy.

"Hi, love," she said, "had a good night?"

"Magic," said Jimmy with a grin brought on by four pints of the best beer in the universe.

Every bloke in the room must have been asking himself, 'what's she doing with him?' She was one of those annoying people who never looked any older and never put on weight. Nobody would have looked twice at Jimmy, despite his wife's efforts to improve him. His weight had always been a problem, while his once fair hair was getting progressively thinner and greyer. The contrast between the two didn't end with their appearance.

"Gus, lovely to see you," Caitlin gushed. "I hope you've not been getting my husband drunk."

She spoke precisely, as though she had rehearsed her words. I'd always thought she had a bit of a Lady Bountiful air about her.

"He manages that quite well without any help from me," I said. "Talking of which, let me get you a drink."

She pulled up a chair.

"I think I might risk a small Chardonnay," she smiled. "I need a drink after two hours discussing the CAFOD Summer Ball."

On my way to the bar, I recalled the times Louise and I had socialized with Jimmy and Caitlin. Louise said Jimmy was a genuine bloke, but had always been a bit ambivalent about his wife. She fancies herself, that one, Louise would say.

A staunch Catholic, Caitlin ran a not-for-profit fostering agency in Darwen. Not content with this, she spent her spare time doing stuff for charity. Louise said she was too good to be true. Nobody could say that about my ex, I thought, certainly not right now. When I got back to the table with the wine, Jimmy was going off in the direction of the gents' toilet.

"Tell me, Gus," said Caitlin after a sip of wine, "has Jimmy been OK tonight?"

As I took a mouthful of beer I searched the question for hidden meaning.

"Yeah, think so. Same as ever, you know."

In other words, he started out being a miserable bugger and cheered up after a couple of pints. Caitlin pursed her lips.

"I've been a bit worried about him lately. Just the last few days...you know we had some problems last year?"

"No? What kind of problems?"

She twisted the stem of her glass, then picked up a beer mat.

"With our marriage. I can't tell you what it was about, not if Jimmy hasn't said anything. I thought we'd sorted everything out, but as I say he's seemed, I don't know, distracted, worried."

I thought hard about the evening with Jimmy but couldn't remember the slightest sign of anything untoward.

He was never that relaxed at the best of times. On reflection I wasn't surprised Caitlin and Jimmy had had problems. Not just because they were an unlikely pairing, but the words marriage and problems seemed to go together.

* * *

The next day, after a short tram ride, I was knocking at the door of an imposing town house in Timperley. A tall, black woman in jeans and a red top greeted me with a smile and a hug.

Since I had last seen her, Marti had been to Liverpool to see her mother, a constant source of anxiety since she'd broken her ankle two years ago. Now she had a nasty chest infection that wouldn't go away. Once we were settled in the lounge, Marti gave me an update. Her Liverpool accent sounded stronger, something I had noticed before at times of stress.

"So no change really," I said when she had finished.

"I'm beginning to wonder how long she's gonna last," she added with a chilling finality.

I was thinking the same thing about my dad, who wouldn't see ninety again. My mother had died when I was eighteen so I had not really got to know her. I hated the thought of my dad going as well, but it couldn't be avoided.

"Anyway, nothing I can do about it," said Marti. "Tell me what's been happening with you. Cheer me up."

"I'll tell you what's been going on. It may take some time..."

"Sounds ominous..."

"And I'm not sure it will cheer you up..."

"Sounds even more ominous."

I did my best to collect my thoughts.

"It all started the day David Moyes got the sack."

"Oh?"

"It's as if United getting rid of their manager has triggered off lots of other things.

"Such as?"

I went through everything from my foiling of the handbag thief to Tim's murder.

"You poor thing," she said, taking my hand.

I put my arm around her and she rested her head on my shoulder.

"Well," said Marti with a sigh, "you have been busy."

"It's other people who have been busy," I replied. "I'm just an innocent bystander, me."

"Have you heard any more about this murder since Sarita called round?" Marti said later.

"No," I said. "She'll be coming back one day soon. She always does."

"Suppose so. What was the name of the guy who got killed?"

"Tim Greenhoff. Tragic really, he was only young. I wonder how his wife's coping."

"Poor girl."

"Tim said she's a member of your gym. Do you know her? Andrea I think her name is."

She thought for a moment.

"Andrea? Yeah, I think I've come across an Andrea. Dyed blonde hair, tarty looking?"

I shook my head.

"No idea, I've never met the woman."

"I'm sorry for her, of course, but I can't say I've been impressed with what I've seen of her."

"Why not?"

"She sits in the coffee bar after her workout and complains," explained Marti. "They can probably hear her in Piccadilly."

"What does she complain about?"

"Well, it used to be all about her husband and how mean he is, begrudging her every little thing," she said sadly. "'I even have to get the bus to work', she said one day. I don't suppose she's complaining now."

CHAPTER FIVE

The following Monday morning I pulled a jumper over my t-shirt and left my apartment block. I hurried along, thinking about the call from Marti I'd had a few minutes previously.

"Hi, Gus," she had said. "Do you think you could pop over to my office?"

"Sure. When?"

"Now?"

"OK, but..."

"I've got a job for you. I'll explain when I see you. Just get here as soon as you can."

What was the urgency, I asked myself. And what job did Marti have for me? I passed some swans swimming on what was left of the old canal and strolled round the side of the Holiday Inn. With Old Trafford football stadium ahead of me I continued until I got to Dacre House, a steel and glass tower block that could have been mistaken for a five star hotel.

Coming out of the lift on the third floor and walking towards Pym and Sigson, I switched my phone off. When I entered Marti's office, she was sitting at her black ash desk. Next to her was an older woman with shoulder length grey/blonde hair, wearing a white linen shirt and jeans. What the hell was Ellen Gallagher doing here, I asked myself, as I greeted them both?

I was still star-struck in Ellen's presence. I would forever think of her on Top of The Pops in 1967, singing with The Leaders, her black hair flowing down to her waist. Despite her fame she managed to get on with everybody she met. There was 'no side to her' as my mam admitted when Ellen first made it big. High praise from a woman who rarely had a good word for anybody. Now though it was all Ellen could do to say hello. There was a sadness around her normally vivid blue eyes. She sat silent, almost motionless, casting occasional glances at Marti. I asked the obvious question.

"What's up?"

I had only met Jimmy's sister at Gallagher family parties before, but this was no social gathering. An even less observant person than me would have worked that out. I pulled up a chair and sat down.

"Jimmy's been arrested," said Ellen.

Her flat, Mancunian vowels collided with the kind of Californian accent which makes every sentence sound like a question.

"What?"

It was more of an exclamation than a question.

"For the murder of Tim Greenhoff," added Marti.

"What?"

Stop saying 'what', I told myself.

"That's mad," I protested, "Jimmy hardly knew Tim Greenhoff."

"But Caitlin did."

Ellen's voice had a bitter edge. Was she really saying what I thought she was? She couldn't be, could she? Then I remembered Louise's frequently expressed view of Caitlin: too good to be true.

"You mean Caitlin and Tim were..."

Ellen and Marti both nodded.

"Fucking little bitch," snarled Ellen. "Butter wouldn't fucking melt..."

Marti interrupted.

"Ellen, please..."

"You can bet your bottom dollar this Greenhoff guy wasn't the first she'd..."

"Ellen," put in Marti. "Later, OK? Things to do, you know?"

Ellen sat back.

"Sure. Sorry."

"As far as I could understand," said Marti, "Caitlin had a fling with Greenhoff last year."

That explained Jimmy's attitude towards Tim.

"Somebody must have told the police about it," Marti went on. "It all kicked off over the weekend. And Jimmy was arrested last night."

I was still confused.

"How do we get from Caitlin having an affair with Tim," I asked, still unable to believe what I was saying, "to Jimmy being on a murder charge?"

"Well, I'm guessing a bit here, but I do know Jimmy found out about it last year. Caitlin said it was all over."

"And?"

"Well, I reckon the police will say Jimmy must have suspected it had started up again, went looking for Greenhoff at Mangall Court and killed him."

"Jimmy Gallagher kill someone? Impossible," I said.

We looked at one another for a moment, at a loss for words.

"Right. Down to business," said Marti.

That's a relief, I said to myself, somebody taking control. Who better than Marti?

"Jimmy was kept in police custody last night, having waived his right to a solicitor..."

"Silly bastard was worried about the expense," said Ellen. "He must have known I'd cover all the costs."

I knew only too well that in practice legal representation was only affordable to the very poor and those with a rock star in the family.

"He appeared before magistrates this morning," Marti went on. "Remanded in custody. Luckily Ellen managed to reach me in time so I could represent Jimmy in court."

"He can't have done it," I insisted. "There's been a mistake."

"I agree," said Marti. "The mistake is the allegation of murder. What makes it more difficult is the affair between Caitlin and the murdered man."

That must have been what Caitlin was talking about on Friday night when she said they'd had problems. I wasn't surprised Tim had tried it on with her. But for her to be seduced by his dubious charms, that was a different matter. Still, what did I know about it?

"So in the police's eyes, that gives him a motive," I suggested.

"Yeah. We don't know what else the police have got, but I aim to find out."

I nodded.

"I only had time for a hurried discussion with Jimmy this morning," Marti added, "but I've arranged for you and me to see him at eight tomorrow morning, Gus."

I made a mental note of the time, groaning inwardly at the early start.

"Where do I come in?" I asked.

"Easy. You find out who really did it."

I sighed. Why wasn't I surprised?

"Nothing too difficult then?"

Marti smiled at me and handed me a typed sheet. It was a list of names and addresses of people I might need to see.

"I see Tim lived in Doveleys Road," I said.

"And?"

"That leads into Cholmondeley road, where Vicky Monroe lived. Could be significant."

Marti shrugged, obviously not interested in where people lived. She got back to the point.

"In the meantime you can go and see Caitlin. She's expecting you at 11.30 this morning."

"Right."

"Oh, before I forget, you'd better go through everything you told me the other day, you know, what the cleaner said about finding the body, Tim's sexual carryings on, the lot."

"I'll write it all down for you later, but here's a summary."

Marti waited with her pen poised while I told her what she wanted to know.

"Oh, my God," said Ellen when I had finished, "anybody could have killed him."

* * *

I went home and telephoned Steve.

"I need to tell you something before you hear about it on the news," I said.

"What's that?"

I told him about Jimmy's arrest and what led up to it.

"I had my doubts about that marriage from the start," he said.

Neither of us could claim to be an expert on the married state – I was divorced; he was on his second marriage – but that didn't stop Steve pontificating.

"That Caitlin's Cheshire Set through and through," he added.

He meant she thought she was a cut above and I had to admit there was something in that. Brought up in Wilmslow, footballers' wives territory these days, she had always led a privileged life.

"I reckon Jimmy was her bit of rough."

A bit of rough? I was less sure of that. Jimmy was, like me, from a working class background but he was hardly macho man.

"I take it you'll help me in my inquiries if necessary," I asked, remembering how invaluable Steve's police experience had been in the past.

"For the usual fee," he said, "or a pint in the Park Hotel next time I'm over."

"Done."

"That reminds me. I'm playing golf in Buxton early May. I'll call in on the way if you're around."

I was glad to have Steve on my side again. I was gonna need all the help I could get.

* * *

Later, as the Peugeot rattled its way towards Worsley en route to see Caitlin, I tried to make sense of what I knew. What could Caitlin tell me that would actually help the investigation? She could talk about the affair with Tim but where would that get me? Maybe I should ask her about Greenhoff himself, see if she had any relevant insights into his life.

That might be more productive in my search for the real killer. Should I be thinking about an unknown 'real killer'? I at least had to consider the possibility that Jimmy murdered the bloke who was shagging his wife. It was a classic scenario. I couldn't imagine my friend being violent, but didn't they say anyone is capable of murder given the right circumstances?

Caitlin tried to smile as she opened the door to me and led me inside. As she sat on an armchair in her lounge she smoothed down her blue jeans. She twiddled a tasteful silver necklace between her fingers as I prepared to question her.

"As I explained on the phone," I said, "Marti has asked me to look into Tim's murder."

She said nothing and joined her hands together.

"I guess you know this whole thing happened because of me and Tim?"

"Yes. It must be tough for you."

"Maybe it is, but I'm pretty self-sufficient."

Caitlin rarely talked about her friends and family. I knew she was childless and had a sister somewhere.

"Have your family been to see you to..."

"What, rally round poor old Caitlin in her hour of need? Hardly. I wouldn't want them to."

Her words were dismissive with more than a hint of 'nothing to do with you' about them. I took the hint.

"Anyway we need to talk about Tim."

This was the trigger for Caitlin to launch into an account of how she met Tim at his leaving do, having gone along with Jimmy as a sort of duty. They had their first assignation two days later. From then on they met regularly at Mangall Court and the hotels Caitlin stayed in when away for work. She spoke with relish about the affair, betraying no evidence of that Catholic guilt people go on about. The way she waxed lyrical about the complete physical and mental union she and Tim had achieved was almost embarrassing.

"It wasn't just a shag, Gus," she said.

Oh, wasn't it, Caitlin? I wondered if Tim would have said the same, bearing in mind all his other women.

"I've always believed in embracing new experiences," she added. "Jimmy didn't understand that."

A neat reversal of the 'my wife doesn't understand me' cliché, I thought.

"Jimmy found out from someone at work, I think. He reacted so badly I had to end it with Tim," she added regretfully.

"Caitlin," I said, determined to move on, "Jimmy didn't kill Tim. We need to find out who did. Did Tim say anything that might give us the slightest clue?"

She shrugged.

"Nothing strikes me."

"What did you and he talk about?"

"He went on about how much he hated social work, didn't know why he'd got into it. He was short of money as well; said one day he'd be rich."

"How was he going to manage that?

"I don't know."

She didn't say 'and I don't care' but she may as well have.

"When he was with you did he mention anyone called Vicky?"

She looked at me as if I were stupid.

"What, talk about other women when he was with me? How well do you think that would have gone down?"

Fair point, I thought. I was getting nowhere, but that was what I had expected. Though Caitlin had an affair with Tim and had achieved complete spiritual union or whatever she called it, she hadn't got to know him very well. Still, there must be something I could ask her that would elicit useful information.

"Did he get any phone calls while you were with him?"

What I expected to get from that I had no idea. I had to say something.

"Oh, God," she said. "Unless I told him to turn his phone off it would never stop ringing."

"Did anyone in particular ring him?"

"Someone called...Bill, I think it was..."

"Will?"

"That's it."

"Can you remember any of the conversation?"

She shook her head.

"No, Tim always said he'd call him back."

"Who else did he speak to?"

"There was a time I caught him talking to his grandmother."

Not quite what I had been expecting.

"Grandmother?"

She smiled.

"I was at a conference in Glasgow and Tim had arranged to meet me at the Ibis. When I got to the bedroom he was on the phone."

So what, I asked myself?

"When he saw me he said, something like 'I'd better go, see you, gran'."

What the hell was I supposed to make of that?

CHAPTER SIX

The next morning during the journey I told Marti about my meeting with Caitlin. Marti asked a couple of questions but admitted that, like me, she didn't really know what to make of what Jimmy's wife had said.

Twenty minutes later we had arrived at Haddon House Remand Centre in Sale, a prime candidate for the gloomiest place in the world inside and out. After several security checks that made us feel like criminals ourselves we finally got to see Jimmy in the visiting room. He sat in a hardback chair, arms folded, avoiding eye contact. In his ironed shirt, neatly pressed trousers and polished, black shoes he looked as if he were going to the office. After greetings and some explanatory words from Marti we got on with it.

"Right, Jimmy," she said, "I want you to tell me in your own words why the police think you might have killed Tim Greenhoff."

His reply was incoherent and inaudible.

"Say that again."

"Cos he was a scumbag, a waste of space," said Jimmy a bit louder. "The world's better off without him."

Nice one, Jimmy, I said to myself. It was a good job they didn't still have hanging; he would have been tightening the noose round his neck.

"OK, let me ask you a simple question," said Marti. "Did you kill Tim Greenhoff?"

He looked at us with a frown.

"Course I didn't. I wish I had though."

"Jimmy..."

"I bet there was a queue of us waiting to do him in."

Marti sighed impatiently.

"That's irrelevant. Let me have some evidence, that's what I deal in. On the morning of Greenhoff's death, where were you? Where did you go and why?"

Sitting back in his chair and facing us, he took a deep breath and talked. I just listened and took notes.

"Caitlin had an affair with him last year..."

"I'm aware of that."

Jimmy looked at her with a scowl.

"So's everybody it seems. But I want you to understand. Until I met Caitlin I was a bit of a joke, nobody took me seriously. Boring Jimmy, good at his job but too nerdy."

I wanted to tell him he was exaggerating, but that hardly mattered now.

"No people skills. Goes home to his beer mat collection."

I remembered being strangely fascinated by Jimmy's hobby when I was a kid. In junior school he used to show me his collection at playtime and explained all the subtleties in great detail. I always got a warm glow from the thought that I would go to my grave knowing the technical term for beer mat collecting – tegestology.

"My Dad died when I was two. I lived with my mother until I was in my thirties," he went on. "Everybody assumed I was gay."

"Jimmy," said Marti gently.

She was obviously worried about time passing.

"I want you to understand," he repeated. "I was working in the Civic Centre in Swinton when I met her. She was a fostering officer."

He almost smiled as he thought of those days.

"She would always make a point of chatting to me. She brought me out of myself I suppose you'd say."

Marti and I looked at one another, wondering whether to break into his reminiscences.

"At first I thought she was married, but her husband had died. We started going for lunch together. I thought she was just being friendly; I never dreamed she could be interested in me."

"But she was?"

"Seemingly. When the deputy manager's job came up Caitlin encouraged me to apply. She advised me about what to wear, what to say at the interview. I got the job and she invited me out to dinner to celebrate. It went on from there."

It was significant, I thought, that Caitlin made the running.

"I felt alive for the first time. So when this thing happened with Greenhoff, it was..."

The energy seemed to drain out of him.

"What happened after the affair, Jimmy?" asked Marti.

"She said it was all over and gradually things improved. We had counselling – Caitlin's idea – and we got back to normal. More or less."

His face crumpled slightly as if he were about to burst into tears. Somehow he managed to hold it together.

"She said I wasn't paying her enough attention, that she wanted to feel loved. Loved? It had nothing to do with love."

He scratched his head as if trying to work out a puzzle.

"Sex, that's what it was about. Oh, I dare say she was flattered to be pursued by a younger man. It was him who should have been bloody flattered."

He clenched his fists and flexed his fingers.

"The point is she did it because she wanted to do it. What's to say she wouldn't do it again? I just...If I'm really honest, I couldn't trust her again."

He was silent for a moment, his eyes blinking rapidly.

"You want to know about the day it happened? Well, the previous day Caitlin rang me at work..."

He looked at me.

"You were there, Gus..."

I nodded.

"She said she was going out after work for a meal with a friend in Blackburn. She was gonna stay the night so she could have a drink."

Maybe, I thought, if his trust in his wife had not been eroded, he would not have reacted as he did.

"That was one of the excuses she had used when she was, you know... I knew she'd been to see him at Mangall Court a few times when he was working for the EDT."

I wrote down the details extra carefully – we were coming to the crunch.

"I met Gus by chance on my way home. He told me Greenhoff was on duty with him. I couldn't sleep that night, I was imagining all sorts. I got the early bus to work. Then I walked over to Mangall Court before I went to the office, got there about seven. I thought I might catch them together."

"How did you get into Mangall Court?" asked Marti.

"I'm a key holder. I get called out when there's a problem with the building. When I got inside, everything was quiet. Nobody was about downstairs so I went in one of the bedrooms. There was nobody there."

I could see why Jimmy was the number one suspect.

"I picked up a United scarf from the floor – God knows why – and put it on the duvet," he continued. "I went over and touched some white rope tied to the bedposts, imagining Caitlin and him having kinky sex."

His face filled with disgust.

"She was always going on about livening up our love life. As if it was my fault she'd shagged another bloke..."

He waited a while as if he were counting to ten.

"I don't know how long I stood there, but after a bit my phone rang. It frightened the life out of me."

"Who was it?"

"Ironically enough, it was Caitlin," he said. "She was just leaving Blackburn. She'd decided to take the day off and suggested we met for lunch."

"What did you do?"

"I suddenly wondered what I'd say if anybody arrived while I was there. I rushed out. Walked to work."

I remembered Jimmy had never learnt to drive. So it wasn't him in the car that drove away from Mangall Court as I was arriving to look for my diary. I still didn't know who it was.

"Right," I said. "Do you remember Wayne Dickens, the bloke we met outside Mangall Court?"

"Not off hand," he said.

"The feller who was looking for Tim. He'd had his kids taken into care."

"Oh, yeah. What about him?"

"We got rid of him eventually. Did you see him again?"

He shook his head.

"You're sure he wasn't around when you went to Mangall Court the next morning?"

"If he was I didn't see him. I don't remember seeing anybody in particular."

* * *

"The prosecution have got a motive and enough forensic evidence to satisfy any jury," said Marti as we got in the car a few minutes later. "Apart from that, no problem."

I had to agree it did look bad. Could Jimmy actually have done it? "We're gonna have our work cut out with this one," she added as we pulled out of the car park.

"Yeah. I need to think about it, make a plan."

"One good thing: the way Tim behaved, someone else could have had a motive for killing him."

That didn't solve the problem of who actually did kill him.

"I don't like the idea of Jimmy being in that place much longer," I said.

"He didn't look too good, did he?"

Marti dropped me off at home and kissed me.

"I'll have to love you and leave you," she said. "Papers to read, stuff to catch up on. I'll pop round later, we could maybe do something."

"Sounds good," I said.

* * *

Seconds after getting out of Marti's car I had an idea. Instead of going home, I got into my own car and drove to Irlams o' th' Height, thinking about who might have killed Tim. It could have been one of his girlfriends seeking revenge after he had rejected her, but apart from Jimmy and Wayne Dickens, the main person with a motive for Tim's murder was Andrea Greenhoff. Jimmy had, according to the prosecution, murdered Greenhoff through jealousy. Tim's wife had at least as much reason to be jealous and such was society's faith in holy matrimony, the wife was always under suspicion.

Arriving outside the house where Tim Greenhoff had lived, I parked next to his Fiesta, beginning to regret being so impetuous. So much for making a plan, I thought. Even if she were in, would Andrea be willing to see me? She had never met me and I doubted whether her husband had ever mentioned my name. And what the hell was I going to say to her? Play it by ear, Gus, I told myself as I got out of the car and waited hesitantly on the pavement. I rang the bell.

"Will Trader," I said to the man who opened the door.

He stared at me, nonplussed.

"Oh, Gus," he said, "er..."

He ran his hands through his hair and fastened a button on his grey shirt.

"I just wondered if Andrea was in," I explained. "I was in the area and wanted to express my condolences."

I called myself a lying, hypocritical rat bag, but if it helped Jimmy's case, it was justified.

"Oh, sure," said Will. "Come in. Er, you'd better take your shoes off."

I followed him down the hall. As I kicked off my trainers, I noticed he was wearing slippers. We went into the living room.

"I've been calling round from time to time to see if Andrea's OK," he said, "I don't live far away. Sit down."

I sat on an armchair.

"I'll just go and see if she's up to seeing anyone."

With that he left me to it. I looked round at the wedding photos on a chest of drawers. Throughout the room I saw no evidence of even a speck of dust. The flat screen smart TV and the iPod in its speakers on the glass coffee table reminded me of what Tim had said about his wife wanting the best of everything.

"She'll be down in a moment," said Will when he got back, "she needs a bit of time to compose herself. It's all been a shock."

I nodded.

"Must have been difficult with the police and everything."

Will rubbed his hand over his chin and was silent for a moment.

"Yeah," he agreed, "They came to see me, you know."

"Really?"

"Yeah, they knew I'd been to see him at Mangall Court that night," he said. "I had to have my fingerprints taken. For elimination purposes, they said."

"I see. Had you known Tim long?"

"We met at Uni," he replied. "We just hit it off. I'm gonna miss him."

"I'm sure."

"I introduced him to Andrea in fact. She and I have been friends for years, we were in sixth form college together in Chester. Tim came to stay with me one holiday and the rest is history as they say."

The door opened and a woman in her twenties came in, tapping obsessively on her iPhone. Apple's best customer, I thought.

"Oh, Andrea," said Will, "this is Gus, a colleague of Tim's. He was working with Tim the night before..."

She cut into the introduction.

"Nice to meet you, Gus."

I got up and we shook hands. I took in her long, blonde hair, the excessive make-up perfectly applied. Her black leggings and white top looked made to measure. She was barefooted – was this part of the no shoes rule, I wondered, or to show off her toenail varnish? Tarty, Marti had said. I wouldn't say anything so judgemental of course. I was a social worker.

"I just wanted to say how sorry I was to hear about Tim."

She smiled bravely as I sat down again.

"Good of you to come round. Everyone's been so kind. Except for the reporters."

She sat on the settee.

"I'm dealing with all that sort of thing for Andrea," said Will.

Andrea looked over at him with great fondness.

"I don't know what I'd do without him, Gus," said Andrea, smiling at Will. "I call him my press officer."

"It's what Tim would have wanted," said Will.

"You've always been there for me, haven't you, love?"

How the hell was I going to break through this mutual admiration society and get onto what I wanted to talk about?

"You must be relieved the police have made an arrest," I suggested.

"Oh, certainly," she agreed, "at least I can sort out the funeral now. Will's been getting in touch with Tim's family for me."

"They must be distraught," I said.

"Especially his mum and dad," said Will.

"And his grandparents, I'm sure."

"They've all been dead for years," said Will.

That didn't sound right, but now wasn't the time to go into it.

"At least they were spared losing their grandson," said Andrea, "especially as the circumstances were so awful. I can't believe that somebody who worked with Tim could..."

She took several deep breaths before continuing.

"Sorry, I... you know, Gus, part of me hates the man who took Tim away from me, part of me – this is going to sound bizarre – feels sorry for him."

"In what way?"

She paused for a moment.

"Well, his wife must have mental problems, mustn't she?"

How did she make that out? I couldn't think how to respond so kept quiet.

"She told him a pack of lies about having an affair with Tim. I mean she's obviously a fantasist."

So that was how she had decided to play it, was it? That didn't tie in with Tim's remarks about Andrea's obsessive jealousy. And I had incontrovertible proof that he had cheated on her. Perhaps she would accuse me of fantasizing if I told her.

"And he believed her," she said. "I suppose he would, but honestly...as if Tim would ever be unfaithful to me, certainly not with somebody old enough to be his mother."

If you say so, Andrea, I thought. Did she really believe this or was she preserving her husband's memory? Maybe she was fooling herself.

"I see what you mean," I said.

"Still, I'm glad the police have finished their investigation."

"They came to see me, you know," I said, "because I was with him when...at the, er, at the relevant time."

"Of course."

"It's strange but I always feel guilty when I'm talking to the police," I added.

"I think they do it on purpose, Gus. I even thought at one time they suspected me."

She shook her head in disbelief.

"I had to say where I was on the morning it happened. Well, I was either on my way to work or teaching twenty-nine eight year olds. Where did they think I was?"

More head shaking followed this statement.

"How could I have killed Tim when he was the love of my life?"

'The love of my life', that sounded suspicious for a start.

"They asked about, you know, our personal life," she went on. "I told them he had no need to look elsewhere. We were always very...loving towards each other if you know what I mean."

I knew what she meant. Definitely top marks for stamina, Tim, I thought.

"They even made an issue of Tim's life insurance, as if they'd never heard of such a thing."

Motives for killing her husband were stacking up: he was a serial shagger; a liar; she no doubt stood to make a tidy packet out of his death. Apart from that, nothing.

As I left a few minutes later I wondered how Caitlin could have heard Tim talking to his dead grandmother. Why lie about a thing like that, I asked myself without coming up with an answer.

I toyed with the idea of calling on Vicky Monroe, but thought better of it. I decided to try to catch her when she started at Ordsall Tower, where it would be harder to avoid me. And I really did need to make a plan before going any further.

* * *

That afternoon I took out my phone to check my messages — something I often forgot to do. I had not switched it back on after I'd left the remand centre and there were three missed calls from Marti. Had something happened with Jimmy? I rang back straight away.

"Gus, at last..."

"Sorry, I forgot to sw..."

"Bad news, I'm afraid," she cut in. "Mum's died."

"Oh, Marti. God, I'm so sorry."

"She had a heart attack as far as anybody can tell..."

Her words dried up as she struggled to speak.

"I'm in Liverpool," she explained. "Yvonne drove me."

If I had switched my phone on, I could have done that, I thought guiltily.

"I've managed to sort out the funeral," she went on, "It's Friday at eleven o'clock."

"OK. I'd come over now, but I've got to pick Georgia up from nursery at half three," I explained. "Rachel has some sort of meeting at her school. Kev's in Birmingham on business."

"That's OK, Gus, Yvonne's staying with me tonight. We'll probably get drunk and talk about the good old days."

"Good idea."

That made me feel better. Yvonne Sigson, though different from Marti in every way, had been her good friend since university days. Together they had made Pym and Sigson one of Manchester's leading law firms.

"Tomorrow night I'm staying with Lynn, you know, my friend from school."

"Right."

I tried to remember what I had planned for tomorrow but my mind was a blank. I'd check later.

"Listen, I'll call you tomorrow, sort out when I'm coming over. In the meantime, take care."

"Will do."

* * *

The next morning, I phoned Marti again. She reeled off a list of things she would still have to do. Yvonne would ferry her around for a while before she went back to Salford. Then she was having lunch with Lynn. All that had me wondering when I should go to Liverpool and if I should cancel my appointments.

"Why not come over tomorrow, Gus?" she suggested, in effect making the decision for me.

I wanted to be with her now, but could see the sense in what she was saying.

"OK."

We left it at that. I would have to accept that I wasn't indispensable.

CHAPTER SEVEN

The following Saturday I was driving Marti back home the day after her mother's funeral. Sensing she didn't want to talk, I left her to her thoughts. It was a surprise when, about half an hour into the journey, she turned to me.

"You know, Gus," she said. "I've been thinking."

"What about?"

I glanced over to her.

"Once Mum's house is sold and everything sorted out with the will, I'll get quite a lot of money."

"I suppose you will."

An only child, Marti would inherit all her mother's worldly goods. And she was already well off, at least by my standards.

"I thought I might take a sabbatical," she said.

"A sabbatical? What, give up your job?"

"Take a year off, see how it goes. You know what they say, nobody wishes they'd spent more time at work when they're on their deathbed."

True enough, I thought, though I wished she hadn't used the word deathbed. It only made me think of Tim's lifeless body in Mangall Court.

"I've not been taking any new cases since the turn of the year because of needing to keep an eye on Mum. So it wouldn't take long to finish off my existing work."

"Suppose not."

"If you're wondering about Jimmy's case, you'll have it all sorted out before I leave."

"Such confidence," I smiled, hoping it was justified.

Louise, I remembered, had gone off round the world soon after she left me. Was Marti planning something similar?

"I wasn't thinking about Jimmy," I said, "just wondering what you would do with your sabbatical."

"I'd like to develop my music a bit more."

If I were any judge, Marti was a talented singer and keyboard player. She'd even been in the charts with a song she wrote herself back in the Eighties.

"Sounds good."

"I've been writing songs lately," she explained. "I could get a band together, hire a studio and, you know, make an album."

Then what? I wondered.

"I'd really like to try and make a go of being a full-time musician again. Before it's too late, you know."

***

Three days later, after the May Day bank holiday weekend, I reached Ordsall Tower just after three. Before chairing a meeting I hoped to be able to catch Vicky Monroe, who should have started her new job by now. Prior to that, I walked across the social work room, knocked on an office door to the right and went in.

"Good afternoon Karen," I said to the dark haired woman behind the desk.

"Oh, hi, Gus," she smiled.

"I thought I'd see how the new boss was doing."

She took a bundle of papers from the sizeable pile in her in-tray.

"The new boss is OK, apart from being rushed off her feet. Pretty shocked about Tim and Jimmy of course."

I sat opposite her. Karen Davidson had come a long way since she had started with children's services five years ago. I'd always expected she'd go far. How right I'd been. Even as a newly qualified social worker she had dressed like a manager, eschewing the jeans most of her colleagues wore.

"Aren't we all?"

She put the papers down after a cursory glance.

"It's unbelievable. To think Jimmy of all people..."

She shook her head in disbelief. Time to bring Karen into my confidence, I decided.

"Keep this quiet, Karen, but I'm looking into the murder."

"Really?"

I told her about my meeting with Marti and Ellen Gallagher.

"Did you know Tim?" I asked.

"Not very well. The police asked me about him – questioning everyone who worked with him, I suppose – but I couldn't tell them much."

Nobody could, it seemed.

"They asked if I'd been shagging him," she added.

I raised my eyebrows. I knew very little of her recent love life, though she had a four-year-old daughter from a relationship that had ended tragically.

"Not in so many words," Karen explained. "'What was the precise nature of your relationship with Mr Greenhoff?' was the way they put it."

"Did you know about Jimmy's wife and Tim Greenhoff?"

"I didn't know for sure but there were rumours. You know what a hotbed of gossip this place is."

"Yeah."

Every office in the world was, I reckoned.

"I know he had trouble with a bloke called Dickens," I said.

I explained about the problem Jimmy and I had with Dickens outside Mangall Court just hours before Tim's death.

"Ah, yes," said Karen. "That sounds like our Mr Dickens."

"What can you tell me about him?"

"It was one of my last cases before I took over this job," she said. "Parents who struggled to bring up a couple of kids. Not to be too cynical, but it was a fairly common situation."

I nodded, knowing exactly what she meant.

"The kids were being neglected, physically, emotionally, you name it. I tried to work with the parents like you do. I brought in a family worker, got a priority nursery place, tried to help them improve their parenting skills...nothing worked."

A familiar story of banging your head against a brick wall.

"Anyway, Tim was going to take over the case when I started this job and I took him out to meet them a couple of times. This coincided with the decision to remove the kids."

"Tim must have been delighted."

Karen shrugged.

"That's the way it goes," she said. "The trouble was they blamed Tim for everything: 'before you came along, everything was all right,' you know."

I knew.

"Wayne made a few threats, caused a disturbance on more than one occasion," she added. "Next thing you know, Tim's left for the EDT job."

"Right."

"If you want to know more about it, have a look at the file," she suggested.

"Are you sure?"

"Positive," she said, "A newly qualified social worker has taken over. It would help to have your view on it."

That sounded OK and it would help my investigation.

"Right. I won't have time today, but I'll be in touch in the next couple of days," I said. "I've got a conference soon and I want to try and catch Vicky Monroe before that."

"Vicky Monroe?"

"The new fostering and adoption manager."

"You haven't heard then," asked Karen?

I got up to leave.

"Heard what?"

Not more complications?

"She was supposed to start her new job on the first of May," explained Karen, "but she didn't turn up."

I'd thought Dave Moyes being sacked had started everything off, but the handbag snatching incident outside Ordsall Tower was surely more relevant. Things hadn't been the same since the moment I had first clapped eyes on Vicky Monroe. What did it all mean? Was there some connection between Vicky Monroe and Tim's murder?

"Does anybody know why?"

"No. There's been no sign of her. She's not answering her phone. She left her previous authority – Devon, I think it was – a few months back to go travelling so they couldn't tell us anything."

"That's a bit of a bugger."

"What did you need to see her about?"

"I want to ask her about Tim's death."

"Oh?"

At the risk of making myself late, I sat down again and explained how Vicky fitted into my murder investigation.

"So this Vicky was another of Tim's women, was she? I think I might have been the only woman in Greater Manchester he hadn't slept with."

I laughed at the thought.

"Anyway, gotta go," I said.

"If you see Jimmy, give him my love," said Karen as I got up again.

"Yeah."

She smiled sadly.

"I knew Jimmy when I was a clerk in the Civic Centre quite a few years ago. I always felt a bit sorry for him," she said. "He was never very good socially but when he married Caitlin he was completely out of his depth."

I thought Jimmy was out of his depth most of the time regardless of the circumstances, but didn't say so.

"The trouble was she would never just let him be himself."

"Yeah, you're right."

Karen sighed sadly.

"Caitlin doesn't bring her men much luck, does she," asked Karen? "Her first husband dead; Jimmy charged with killing her lover."

* * *

That evening at the flat I finally got round to making a plan. I wrote down a list of names and summarized everything I knew so far in my notebook. That inspired precisely nothing. I thought about what Sarita had said to me, but she hadn't told me anything I didn't already know. I was about to give up when I remembered that the inspector had made a second visit to my flat. She'd asked me if I knew some woman or other. Who was it?

I pictured myself at the kitchen table with my notebook just like now. I'd written the name down, hadn't I? Flicking back in my notebook I eventually found it. Francine Ingleby. How could I find out more about her? It would be no good ringing Sarita. She'd want to know why I was inquiring. Who else might help me?

I was still wondering when my phone rang. It was Steve asking if I'd be around on 12th May. While we were making arrangements for him to come and stay the night, it occurred to me I may as well tap into his encyclopaedic knowledge of all things dodgy.

"I've got a question for you, Steve," I said. "Does the name Francine Ingleby mean anything to you?"

I could almost hear his mind ticking over.

"It does, yeah. I've heard the name recently. Bells are ringing but I can't remember why."

That was disappointing. I'd got so used to relying on Steve.

"Francine Ingleby," he said. "No, nothing. I'll look into it for you, let you know what I come up with when I see you."

CHAPTER EIGHT

That evening I drove to Irlams o' th' Height and went to Cholmondeley Road, to look for Vicky Monroe. I wasn't expecting to find her, but had to start somewhere. There was no answer when I knocked at the door. I rang the bell several times with the same result. From there I went to Worsley to pay my first visit to Ellen Gallagher's house. I was expecting a mansion; instead I found myself pulling up outside a 1930s semi. Perhaps it was more evidence of there being 'no side to her'. She had invited Marti over, partly to talk about the case but also to show her the recording studio she had had built in the back garden. I had a feeling they would have spent the afternoon on musical rather than legal matters.

Somebody shouted 'come in' when I rang the bell so I followed the sound of music to a room where Marti and Ellen were lounging on separate settees, strumming guitars. The setting would have been perfect for an album cover: two singers relaxing in a minimalist space done out like a modern art gallery. Marti must have decided it was officially summer as she was wearing white linen trousers.

They were singing a song of lost love I'd never heard before. Their harmonies were worthy of the Everly Brothers. I sat on an armchair and listened, awestruck. Not for the first time I wished I had some musical ability. I could remember the words of all the Hollies songs and was willing to sing them (badly) after a few pints. But that was it. When the song finished I applauded. Marti gave a mock bow.

"That was fantastic," I said, "what was it?"

They put down their guitars.

"Lost and Lonely," said Marti. "A song wot I wrote."

"Great stuff."

The two women looked at one another.

"Should we tell him the good news first?" asked Ellen. Marti nodded.

"Ellen's gonna let me use her studio," explained Marti. "You know, for the album I was telling you about."

"This lady's got real talent," said Ellen.

I smiled at the rock star, who looked as cool and charismatic as ever in a San Francisco 49ers shirt, straight jeans and cowboy boots.

"You don't need to tell me, Ellen," I said.

They went on to explain their plans to get a band together, rehearse and do the recording sometime soon.

"But now," said Marti after a while, "we have to talk of other things."

I told them how far I'd got – not very, although I didn't quite put it that way.

"If I could only get hold of Vicky Monroe," I said, "we might start to get somewhere."

"Which one's she again?" asked Ellen.

"The one who I saw shagging Tim Greenhoff in Mangall Court."

"Yeah, I remember now," said Ellen.

"The only problem is she's gone missing."

I explained about her not turning up to work on her first day in a new job.

"I've just been to the address I have for her in Cholmondeley Road," I added. "Nobody in, but I'll be going back."

"We've just got to keep trying," said Marti, "you've succeeded before Gus. I have every confidence in you."

Nice to hear, I thought, but not much practical use.

"I blame Caitlin for this," said Ellen.

Neither Marti nor I tried to contradict her. I got the feeling she was climbing back on her hobby horse after a short break.

"Jimmy was just one of her projects," she added.

That was one way of looking at it, I supposed. Jimmy had welcomed the idea of marrying Caitlin, but I sometimes wondered if he really appreciated her attempts to get him to change. I knew it would have driven me mad.

"Maybe I'm a little overprotective of Jimmy," she said reflectively, "but there are reasons for that. A guy I had a thing with a few years back said I was a natural big sister."

She smiled at the memory. I could see the truth of what the ex-boyfriend had said. Nobody messed with Ellen Gallagher.

"At the same time Jimmy was born to be a little brother. It's not just him being nine years younger than me. He kind of never grew up, you know. I guess he'd have a label stuck on him these days, some syndrome or other."

"Maybe," I said.

"What I'm getting at is, what would the lovely and talented Caitlin see in a man like Jimmy?"

A question I'd often asked myself.

"It wasn't his looks," said Ellen, "or his sparkling wit. He was someone she could control, manipulate. When she betrays him, how's he going to react?"

There was maybe a grain of truth in that statement, but on the whole it was unfair. Caitlin hadn't forced Jimmy to marry her. Admittedly he was naive, but is anybody that naive? There was one troubling thing about what Ellen was saying. It was almost as if she were suggesting her brother had killed Tim Greenhoff.

* * *

The next morning, having finally taken the car to the garage to get it looked at, I walked from Salford Quays to the bus stop on Trafford Road near Phoebe Street. It was jeans and t-shirt weather as I boarded the number 79, my mind on Vicky Monroe. I had decided to go to Cholmondeley Road again. As the bus turned left onto Regent Road, I thought back to finding the envelope outside Ordsall Tower on the day of the handbag incident.

The address on that envelope was still the only clue I had. I was convinced it was important to talk to Vicky about Tim Greenhoff's murder. Something told me nothing would make sense until I found her, but another voice in the back of my mind, equally insistent, reminded me I could be wrong. If only she had turned up for work when she was supposed to. It would have been difficult for her to escape me there. Then I would have known one way or the other. Now I was stymied.

The bus went onto Eccles New Road, reminding me of journeys to school. I could call on my dad on the way back, I said to myself, as we got near Weaste. What would he make of it all?

I refused to believe her disappearance was a coincidence. I needed to know more about Vicky. How had she and Tim met and what kind of relationship did they have? Was it just the occasional shag or was there more to it? There must be a link with the murder, mustn't there? Had she killed Tim? Was that why she had to get away?

What would her motive have been? Had he promised to leave his wife and then changed his mind? Had she heard about his other women? If she had killed him, she must have gone back to Mangall Court on the morning of his death. The only problem was, nobody had seen her.

* * *

A For Sale sign was stuck at an angle in the front garden of the house in Cholmondeley Road. It hadn't been there the last time I had called and it was, I noticed, identical to the one next door. I went down the path, rang the bell and waited, passing my briefcase from one hand to the other. I glanced in the window, but couldn't see anyone. After a while I rang again. Though pretty certain nobody was at home I banged on the door as hard as I could to make sure. After another wait, I gave up and turned to walk away. I saw a fair haired woman struggling with two plastic bags, her handbag slung over her shoulder, about to turn into the garden path next door.

"Good morning," she said with a bright smile.

"Morning."

"Gorgeous day."

"Lovely."

In denim jacket and pink jeans, she looked full of the joys of Spring. 'Life's pretty good,' she seemed to be saying. Then we looked at one another and stood still for a moment. We did a double take.

"Debbie," I said.

"Gus, oh, my God...what the hell..."

What the hell indeed.

"You can't still live here, can you?" I asked.

She smiled again.

"Well, tell you what, come in and have a coffee and I'll explain."

"Good idea."

I joined her on the garden path, taking the bags from her, like the gent I was, while she took a key from her jacket pocket.

"Mum and Dad moved into sheltered housing a few months ago," she explained as we went into the kitchen. "I'm trying to sell the house for them. I'm staying here for the time being."

I put the bags and my briefcase down on the table by a pile of mail. Debbie plonked her handbag next to them. I looked round, noticing a cafetière, a teapot and a sliced loaf on a work surface. A pair of walking boots were on the floor, tucked away in a corner, reminding me it was Debbie who had got me into walking.

"Have a seat."

I sat down, looking round and trying to adjust to being in this house again.

"We had some good times here," I said.

"Yes," she agreed, averting her eyes.

Colour came into her cheeks.

"God, Gus Keane, you'll have me blushing."

She began to put the shopping away.

"So what are you doing in Cholmondeley Road after all these years?" she asked.

I told her I was looking for Vicky Monroe.

"Vicky from next door? How come?"

This could take some time, I thought, so tried to keep it brief.

"I'm a private investigator and she may be able to help me with a case I'm on."

"I'm impressed. Tell me more."

I couldn't remember impressing Debbie all that much in the old days.

"She was involved with the bloke who was killed," I said, having explained about Tim's murder. "The solicitor of the man who's been charged with the murder has asked me to look into it."

She sat down, looking puzzled.

"Now she's gone missing," I added.

Her eyes opened wide.

"Missing? Vicky? That's ridiculous."

I was temporarily silenced by this but Debbie had more to say.

"She's in the Scilly Isles."

CHAPTER NINE

"Scilly Isles?"

"Yeah, you know, off the coast of Cornwall."

"I know where it is, Debbie. I've been there, a lovely place."

"So they say. Her bloke has just opened a restaurant and B&B on one of the islands and she's gone to help him run it."

Well, she could have let somebody know, I thought, annoyed on behalf of Salford Council.

"When was this?"

She pondered for a bit.

"Ooh, let's think now. March, it would have been."

"March? Are you sure?"

She nodded.

"Did you know Vicky well?"

Another nod.

"Fairly well. We got to know one another when I moved in here," she explained. "She was always friendly."

Vicky friendly? That didn't sound right.

"She came in for coffee a few times," Debbie went on, "and we got talking. She began to confide in me. People are always doing that."

Join the club, I said to myself.

"She'd been going out with this guy, Hugh, for ages and something went wrong." I wanted to ask about half a dozen questions, but hoped Debbie might make things clear by the time she'd finished.

"She was all set to go back to social work. She'd applied for a job in Salford, something to do with adoption."

"Yes, I ..."

"She'd prepared herself really well, made loads of notes and stuff," Debbie went on. "All possible questions were typed out with detailed answers. She'd used all the clichés, you know, being passionate about making a difference and stuff."

I knew interview panels were impressed by all that bollocks.

"She even got me to do a couple of mock interviews. I knew as much about it as she did by the time we'd finished."

No wonder she got the job, I thought.

"It was all a waste of time as it turned out..."

"But surely..."

"Hugh, the boyfriend, came looking for her. There was an emotional reunion. Terribly romantic."

Romantic? Confusing, more like.

"But she's been back here at least once since March," I said.

"No."

"She must have been," I insisted.

I explained about her interview in April, her appointment as fostering and adoption manager and her failure to turn up for work.

"She'd hardly go to the trouble of returning from the Scillies," objected Debbie, "and having an interview for a job she didn't want."

"But she did," I said, shaking my head.

"This makes no sense at all," said Debbie, rather stressing the obvious.

How did we come to be discussing one of my investigations in such detail, instead of chatting about old times?

"Wait a minute," she said, clicking her fingers.

Debbie picked up the pile of post from the table. Quickly sorting through the junk mail and official looking envelopes, she handed me a postcard.

"That was on the mat this morning when I arrived."

I admired the picture of sunset over Bryher before turning it over to read the message:

Hi Debbie
Still having a fab time over here. Run off my feet but loving every minute. You must come and see us soon – Hugh will cook you one of his specials!
Love
Vicky xxx

"This arrived today?"

"It could have arrived any time since I was last here," she explained. "I've been away for more than a week."

I looked again at the card, trying to decipher the postmark.

"Posted on 22nd April."

I took my diary out of my briefcase and opened it.

"That was the Tuesday after Easter when Vicky Monroe was having an interview at Ordsall Tower."

The day United sacked David Moyes, I thought, and all this trouble started. Debbie shook her head, struggling for words.

"So on the day she sent this postcard she was in Salford?"

"She can't have been," I said, "there must be some other explanation."

"Such as?"

I sighed and tried to work it out.

"Is that Vicky's handwriting?"

"It looks like it. She wrote out her contact details for me before she left."

I thought a bit more.

"Maybe somebody else posted it for her."

"But why?"

For no good reason I could discern.

"Hang on," said Debbie. "There's one sure way to find out."

She took a phone from her handbag.

"I'll ring the restaurant."

I wished I could have afforded to turn down this job. Like many of my investigations, it hadn't taken long to become impossibly complicated.

"Is that Vicky," asked Debbie?

There followed a minute or two of social pleasantries.

"Listen, Vicky, this is going to sound weird, but a friend of mine thinks you were in Salford in April."

She listened for a moment then covered the mouthpiece.

"She hasn't been back to Salford since she left," she whispered.

"Can I have a word with her?"

Having got Vicky's permission, Debbie handed the phone to me.

"Hello, Vicky, my name's Gus Keane. I'm a private investigator."

"Oh, yes?"

"I need to talk to you about one of my cases..."

Out of the corner of my eye I saw Debbie filling the kettle at the tap and plugging it in.

"What?"

Vicky sounded outraged.

"I saw you in Salford on 22nd April," I went on, "you were..."

"Listen, Gus, or whatever your name is," she said, "I came to Scilly in March and haven't left since. I haven't had bloody time for one thing..."

"But I saw you, you had your handbag nicked and I got it back for you..."

"You're mad or drunk or something..."

She spoke with a distinctive West Country accent, quite unlike the 'Vicky' I had met. Debbie got mugs and a jar of coffee from a cupboard then spooned some into the cafetière before getting a jug of milk out of the fridge. Why were ordinary things still going on when I appeared to have landed in a parallel universe?

"No, I'm neither. There's something going on here and I'm gonna get to the bottom of it."

"Well, I hope it keeps fine for you. All I can say is whoever you saw in April, it wasn't me."

I sensed she was about to end the call, but I couldn't let her go without making some attempt to find out more.

"Are you coming back this way any time soon?"

"I very much doubt it and..."

"Could I come and see you?"

She let out a cry of exasperation.

"What for?"

Lots of reasons, I said to myself. Partly to convince myself she was telling the truth, partly because I thought she might just be able to help me.

"To find out more," I said. "I could come over this weekend if I can get a flight."

I knew it would be expensive but assumed Ellen Gallagher wouldn't mind footing the bill. There was silence on the end of the line. I thought for a second she had hung up on me.

"Let me talk to Debbie again."

I handed the phone back to Debbie with a word of explanation and went upstairs to the loo.

"I convinced her you weren't a mad axeman," said Debbie when I got back.

"Thanks."

She poured coffee into the mugs.

"I think in spite of herself, she was intrigued by what you said, as am I, and she's willing to meet you."

She gave me Vicky's phone number and directions to Hugh's Place, the restaurant.

"That's something anyway," I said as I put milk into my coffee. "The move to the Scillies must be permanent if Vicky's selling the house."

"Oh, it's not her house, she was just Will's lodger."

"Will?"

"Yeah, Will Trader."

So Will Trader was Vicky's landlord. Why was he always rearing his ugly head? Before I could consider this point further, Debbie's phone rang.

"Hello...Hi, Vicky...right...OK, hang on."

She turned to me.

"Vicky says there's a room vacant in their B&B while you're over there, do you want to book it?"

I thought quickly and made a decision.

"Yeah."

Debbie spoke into the phone.

"He says yes ...I'll ask...one person or two?"

"One," I said, knowing Marti would be working on her album with Ellen.

Debbie raised her eyebrows at this, as she made the final arrangements with Vicky and ended the call.

"Now then, Gus Keane," Debbie said, sipping her coffee, "as you've reappeared in my life so mysteriously, I want to know all about you."

* * *

I left half an hour later, having told Debbie my life story since I'd last seen her over thirty years ago. I'd learned that Debbie was divorced and had a daughter. She had recently left her job as a translator for the EU in Brussels with a generous pay out. Now she was wondering what to do next and thinking of travelling for a while. She had a brother in Brisbane she wanted to visit. Thinking about all this, I knocked on Will Trader's door on the way to the bus stop. He was still out. I needed to see him, but he would have to keep.

CHAPTER TEN

"So how do you know Debbie?" asked Vicky Monroe the following day.

In bright sunshine we were walking along a gentle incline up a winding path on the island of Tresco. In a couple of minutes we would reach Cromwell's Castle, a 17th century tower. Vicky had turned out to be a bundle of enthusiasm, seemingly unable to keep still. No wonder she was so skinny.

"We went out together when we were seventeen, eighteen," I explained.

A gull flew overhead, its squawk the only sound apart from our footsteps.

"A teenage romance," she smiled. "How sweet."

I pictured Debbie and me in the seventies and wondered where the years had gone.

"Hard to imagine now," I said.

Strange, I thought, that Debbie was back in my life. Even stranger was the thought that I might have married her. Lots of blokes I knew had married girls they'd met when they were barely old enough to shave.

"What broke you up," said Vicky.

I shrugged.

"I honestly can't remember," I replied. "Neither of us said anything. Debbie went to Oxford University. I signed to play rugby league for Salford."

"Really?"

"Maybe we just drifted apart."

And now Debbie was involved in one of my cases. That meant I would have to see her again to tell her how I had got on in the Scilly Isles. Why did the thought please me? Best not to think about that.

When we arrived at Cromwell's Castle we sat on the ramparts and watched the waves lapping on the almost white sand for a few moments before we got round to talking about the reason for my trip. Vicky had presumably offered to accompany me on the boat trip to Tresco, because that would give us the time and privacy to talk. I had told her about Tim's murder but we hadn't gone into it in any depth.

Now I asked her about how she came to be here and what had happened before she left. She tried to explain the sequence of events, including the split with Hugh and her decision to move from Devon to Manchester where she had friends.

"How did you end up living in Will Trader's house?"

"He's, like, a friend of a friend," she said. "He needed a lodger to help with the mortgage, I needed a place to stay."

"What did you make of Will? He seems a pretty calm bloke to me."

She pulled down the brim of her white sun hat.

"Yeah, he is most of the time. I always wondered what went on underneath that urbane exterior."

"Oh?"

"I don't know him all that well," she said, "he was hard to make out."

"How do you mean?"

"I was never sure what he did all day, how he made a living and stuff," she said. "I heard he was a professional gambler."

"Maybe he was. I find it hard to believe he made much out of that but what do I know?

"He talked about writing a novel, but lots of people say that."

"You sound sceptical."

"Not really, like I say, I don't know him all that well. I never thought he was all that happy, you know."

"Really?"

She smiled before going any further.

"I'm probably guilty of the social worker's besetting sin, over-analyzing, reading too much into things, wanting to carry out an assessment on everybody I meet."

I smiled in recognition at this behaviour which I had been guilty of myself, but decided I had heard enough about Will.

"Anyway, what about the other Vicky?" I asked. "Have you worked it out yet."

I was bloody sure I hadn't.

"I'm as puzzled as you are," she said.

"That means very puzzled."

I looked across the blue-green sea to Bryher, the island that ran parallel with Tresco, creating a sheltered harbour for boats. It had always been one of my favourite views when I came here with Louise. I watched the waders skittering along the shoreline as an oyster catcher swooped down to join them.

"I can't believe that someone pretended to be me to get a job," she said. "What would she get out of it?"

She sat with her chin in her hands trying to puzzle out this conundrum. She had dark hair with a fringe so bore a superficial resemblance to the woman who'd impersonated her.

"As it turned out, nothing," I said, remembering that the 'Vicky' I met hadn't turned up for work.

"I suppose so."

In a more fundamental way the two women were completely different. The real Vicky had greeted me the previous day with a smile as if meeting a close friend after a long separation. I could tell her welcome was genuine; what you saw was what you got. I would never have mistaken the two women for each other. Somebody who had never met them might have been fooled, I reckoned. And whoever interviewed her would not have been expecting an impostor.

"Listen, Vicky" I said, "I've been wondering how she got away with it. I mean, procedures for job interviews are really strict these days."

"Yes."

"You have to have proof of identity," I went on. "Show your passport."

"Well, when I got to Exeter Airport to fly over here," she said. "I realized I'd forgotten my passport. As it turned out it didn't matter. They accepted my driving licence."

"Where is your passport then?"

She shrugged again.

"When Hugh and I decided to get back together, I... oh, I guess I didn't want to blow it again. I just wanted to be with him as soon as I could."

A look of shyness passed over her face as if she were revealing too much.

"What I'm getting at is I left in a bit of a hurry," she said, "I didn't tell Will where I was going, just sent a text to say I was moving out. Some of my stuff is still at his place.'

"So your passport could be among that lot?"

"Suppose so. I haven't really thought about it until now. I keep meaning to get in touch with Will, but never seem to have the time."

Where did that get us, I asked myself? No further forward was the answer. It didn't tell us how the impostor had succeeded in passing herself off as Vicky or why.

"This woman, whoever she is, would need to have a reason for doing this," I said. "And it's not only a question of convincing people she was you. She'd also have had to convince an interview panel she was up to the job."

We sat in silence, admiring the view. Then I remembered something Debbie had said.

"Debbie said you'd made lots of notes for the interview," I said, "and you got her to do a mock interview."

"Yes."

And she said she knew as much about it as Vicky by the time they'd finished. But surely Debbie couldn't be mixed up in this, could she? It wasn't her who attended the interview. I give up, I said to myself.

"What about Tim Greenhoff," I said, "did you meet him?"

She scowled at the mention of Tim's name.

"Andrea's husband? Yes, I met him. Look, I'm sorry the guy's dead and everything but he was a total creep."

I smiled at her words.

"At a guess I'd say you didn't like him."

She smiled back.

"Whatever gave you that impression?" she said. "I met Andrea first, she's, like, an old friend of Will. That didn't stop Tim 'God's gift to women' Greenhoff from coming onto me."

"Yeah?"

"I think he did it automatically on the assumption I'd be bound to succumb."

"But you weren't tempted?"

"Was I hell. If I ever get that desperate, you can shoot me."

CHAPTER ELEVEN

The afternoon after I got back from the Isles of Scilly I was at Ordsall Tower, taking an unwieldy file from the cabinet opposite what I still thought of as Jimmy's desk. I'd had regular updates from Marti about his mental state – not good – but hadn't been to see him since my trip to Haddon House. After a moment's thought I sat in my old friend's seat. Nobody else was using it and I could always tell him I was keeping it warm for him. Anyway, I was familiarising myself with the Dickens family for his benefit. Just then my phone beeped. I read the text:

Thanks for the postcard. Can't wait to hear about Scillies trip. I'm away for a while. I'll give you a call when I get back. Debbie x

I had meant to go and see her, but that would have to wait. I opened up the Dickens file and tried to find my way round it. It took a little while as somebody had had the bright idea of changing the layout for the umpteenth time. After half an hour or so I had discovered nothing I wasn't expecting. It was all as Karen described it. Tim had been involved for a month at most. Hardly enough time to invoke such hatred. I noted the Dickens' address and thought for a moment.

I went through the points in my mind: Wayne lived near the place where Tim was killed; he knew Tim was there; he had a strong motive. I thought back to the brief conversation Jimmy and I had had about the footballing Greenhoff brothers. One of us had said the younger one was dead. Hadn't Dickens said another Greenhoff would die if he got his hands on him? If that wasn't a threat to kill Tim, what was?

* * *

A few minutes later, I was knocking on the door of a council house in the Ordsall estate.

"Hello, Wayne," I said, "Remember me."

He looked at me without much curiosity.

"You look a bit familiar. Who are you?"

He scratched his stomach through a faded purple t-shirt. I took a GRK Investigations card from my wallet and handed it to him.

"GRK? What's that mean?"

I didn't see any point in explaining that GRK stood for Gus Risman Keane, or that I was named after my dad's favourite Salford rugby league player.

"I'm Gus Keane, a private investigator," I told him as he continued to peer at the card with some puzzlement.

"Oh, aye?"

Having been shown such overwhelming indifference, I could see this might be hard work.

"I wonder if I could come in and ask you about a case I'm interested in."

He looked at the card again, then back at me.

"What's it about?"

Mentioning Tim's murder now could, I reckoned, put him off.

"It's a private matter. Be better if we talked indoors."

"Come in then," he shrugged.

The living room he took me into was less of a mess than the garden, quite tidy in fact.

"I'm looking into the death of Tim Greenhoff," I said as I sat on a red armchair.

"How can you be?" he asked. "They've charged someone for it. Feller from social services."

"He didn't do it. I aim to find out who did."

He sat in an identical chair and frowned thoughtfully, scratching the back of his left arm.

"The cops have already spoken to me," he said. "I don't see how I can help you."

"I saw you outside Mangall Court not long before Mr Greenhoff died," I said, ignoring his comments.

"I remember you now."

That was something, I thought.

"You were threatening him," I said. "You were angry about your kids being taken into care."

He stared at me, his eyes wide with alarm.

"Now, wait a minute," he said, "let's get one thing straight. I didn't kill the little fucker. I wish I had, but I didn't."

Somebody else who would like to have killed Tim. I remembered Jimmy using almost the same words as Wayne.

"Anyway," he went on, "after I talked to you and your mate, I went home. You saw me."

He sat back and folded his arms, looking smug. l could see he wasn't about to break down and confess.

"I don't know where you went," I countered. "Even if you did go home you could easily have gone back any time. It's not far, about ten minutes walk, I reckon."

"I often go that way," he said, "it don't mean anything."

"Were you near Mangall Court the morning after I'd seen you there?"

I thought it was worth pursuing the point just in case.

"Could have been," he said, "hard to say."

"See anything unusual?"

He thought for a moment.

"The only thing I remember," he said, "was a car going like the clappers. I thought 'he's gonna kill someone'."

"What kind of car was it?"

He belched quietly.

"How should I know? It was a dark colour. Anyway, it might have been a different day."

I didn't think so somehow.

"Like I said, the cops came to see me," he went on. "They must have believed me."

Especially as they had a strong suspect in Jimmy, someone they knew had gone to Mangall Court at the relevant time.

* * *

"How's the investigation going?" asked Steve in the Park Hotel the following day.

He had driven over that evening from Dolgellau, where he'd lived since he retired. As he was gasping for a pint when he arrived, I allowed him to drag me straight out to the pub. Now we were ensconced in the watering hole we'd frequented for about forty years, getting stuck into Red Devil bitter. Not for the first time, I wondered if it tasted so good because it was named after Salford's rugby league club.

"Not too bad, I suppose," I said. "I haven't got Jimmy out of jail yet."

He sipped his pint, looking relaxed as ever in his uniform of polo shirt and Chinos, his thinning hair neatly cropped. Despite not seeing eye to eye about his devotion to golf, cars and Maggie Thatcher (particularly the latter), Steve and I were always comfortable together. We had enough in common to overcome our differences. Most importantly, we grew up together in the back streets of Salford.

"He might have done it."

I drank deep before answering.

"Don't think I haven't considered that. Anyway, there have been interesting developments with Vicky Monroe."

"Vicky who?"

"The woman who got her leg over with Tim in Mangall Court," I explained. "She went missing, remember? I tried to find her and bumped into Debbie Oldham."

"Debbie...?

"A girl I went out with forty years ago."

He concentrated hard for about ten seconds.

"I know the one, fair hair, nice body on her, a bit posh. By our standards anyway."

I explained about Debbie living next door to Vicky.

"What's she look like these days? Old and grey?"

Anything but, I thought.

"I'd say she's worn well," I said, "but more importantly she was able to help me with my investigations."

"Was she indeed?"

I told him what Debbie had said and my trip to the Scillies.

"Bloody hell,' he said, "somebody's been up to no good."

"Yes, but what exactly have they been up to and why?"

"I don't know what to suggest," said Steve.

We drank in pensive silence for a while. Then I remembered something else I wanted to ask Steve about.

"Did you find out anything about Francine Ingleby?"

"Aye, I did," he replied. "First some background. Remember a kids' programme about, ooh, fifteen years ago called Danger Gang?"

"Vaguely. I've got a feeling Danny used to watch it."

"It was about a group of teenagers who got into adventures."

"And?"

"Well, Francine Ingleby was in it," Steve explained. "One of the main characters, she was."

He let a silence develop, possibly to build tension or maybe he couldn't think what to say.

"Young Francine was a good actress," Steve continued, "and her future looked bright. Even when Danger Gang came to an end everyone thought she would go from strength to strength."

"Go on." I said after another pause.

"But she got a bit carried away with all her success. She got into drugs, arrested for possession a few times. So her DNA and fingerprints are on file."

I still couldn't see the connection with Tim.

"But what's..."

"Then she seemed to fade away. Nobody heard much about her for a few years."

I waited, knowing there was more.

"More recently, her name's cropped up from time to time in a couple of investigations. It looks like she may have taken up a new career."

"What?"

"Well, I suppose you'd call her a confidence trickster."

"Yeah?"

"Nothing's been proved, just...suspicions, I suppose you'd say. The trouble is, a lot of the victims don't want to press charges."

"How come?"

Steve picked up his glass again.

"Partly because they don't want to look idiots," he explained, before taking a drink. "One or two of the blokes were genuinely in love with her."

"Right."

"She also befriended vulnerable people who had money in the bank. She offered them care and attention."

"Bastard."

"You said it, Gus. Some of them were, I dunno, grateful to her."

I shook my head sadly.

"Anyway, a mate of mine has just retired from Lancashire CID," Steve went on, "and he told me something interesting."

Though happy in his retirement, Steve still liked to keep up with his former colleagues.

"Go on."

"A feller called Eliott McIntyre came forward a bit ago. He'd had a relationship with this woman. Thought it was the real thing."

I hoped this wasn't gonna be a Mills and Boon saga.

"But it wasn't?"

Steve took another mouthful and put his glass down.

"Far from it. She conned him out of a load of money and he hasn't seen hide nor hair of her since."

Poor bugger, I thought.

"My mate and his team investigated, you know, and found evidence that Francine Ingleby had been in McIntyre's house."

This Francine got about a bit, it seemed.

"The woman he was involved with went under another name, I can't remember what it was."

"But they think it was really Francine?"

Steve nodded.

"Correct. What I can do is put you in touch with the man who was conned."

I smiled at my old friend. Was this a sign of progress?

"Great."

As I spoke I noticed out of the corner of my eye a balding man of about my age marching towards us. He stood out as the only bloke in the pub wearing a tie.

"This McIntyre character can tell you all about it," said Steve. "As he's got nowhere through official channels he might be willing to pay you to find the woman who did the dirty on him."

"Nice one."

The man I had seen a few seconds ago arrived at our table and stood looking at Steve and me.

"Would one of you be Gus Keane by any chance?" he asked in a southern accent.

He was about six feet tall, about the same as Steve, wearing a grey suit.

"That's me," I said.

"I'm Bradley Harton. Any chance of a word? In private."

Steve and I looked at one another, both of us wary.

"It's not convenient at the moment," I replied.

"Not convenient," he said, as though trying to make sense of the words.

"That's right."

"Are you wanting to offer Gus some work," asked Steve.

This time the man looked even more puzzled.

"Nothing like that, no."

We went quiet until Mr Harton finally spoke.

"Oh, come on, stop pretending you don't know who I am."

This was getting beyond a joke.

"I don't know who you are."

"Nor do I," Steve added.

He tutted.

"I'm Louise's husband."

Oh, bugger. What did he want?

"Brad, of course. Sorry but it's still inconvenient."

He pulled up a chair and sat down.

"Are you deaf, sunshine?" asked Steve.

"I don't think it's any concern of yours, Mr..."

"Chief Superintendent Yarnitzky, Manchester Police," said Steve.

As always, he invested his words with great authority. When Steve spoke, people listened. It didn't matter that he was really an ex-superintendent.

"I just want to know where she is," said Brad.

Well, I didn't think you'd come to discuss Salford's prospects in the Super League, I said to myself.

"I can't help you with that," I said.

"Can't or won't?"

Steve and I exchanged another glance. I took Steve's expression to say, 'leave it to me'.

"We are unable to assist you," said Steve.

Ignoring Steve, Brad turned to me.

"She's back with you, isn't she?"

"What?"

Alarm ran through me at the thought of Louise moving in with me.

"She was always going on about you," he added. "Gus this, Gus that..."

I didn't know she cared. He thumped the table.

"God! It was...God!"

He gave the table another punch.

"That's enough," said Steve. "Now would you please go? We're having a quiet drink."

Brad sat tensing his muscles.

"I'm not leaving until I know for certain where she is."

Steve sighed.

"In that case the landlord will make you leave. We're regulars here, valued customers. He won't want us upset. You on the other hand, well, he won't mind losing your custom."

Brad didn't respond. Steve looked over to the bar and beckoned. The landlord came over.

"Problem, gentlemen?"

"This feller's being a pain, Arthur."

"Right. Out."

Brad turned to Arthur, saw the size of him and got up.

"You haven't heard the last of this," said Brad before he sloped off.

I was very much afraid he was right. After Brad's departure, Steve got onto his mate about Eliott McIntyre. I rang Rachel and Danny to warn them about Brad. Rachel agreed to call her mother to tell her about it. I had already arranged for Danny to come and spend the night with me the following day and have a walk the day after. Rachel agreed to come over and have a meal with us to discuss 'the Brad situation'. We had to devise a plan to prevent him from bothering us.

Why the bloody hell couldn't Louise arrange her life better? And if she was going to get married again, couldn't she have chosen somebody more suitable? It still rankled, I had to admit, that she had preferred that pillock to me. His baldness made things worse somehow, when the only thing I had going for me at my age was a full head of hair. Steve and I talked about Eliott McIntyre a bit more and I was told to expect a phone call from him soon. Then we had another pint.

CHAPTER TWELVE

"Maybe I should start by telling you my wife died about six months ago," said Eliott McIntyre the next morning.

"I'm sorry."

Elliott had phoned the previous night and we'd arranged to meet at the Blackburn Darwen Services at junction 4 on the M65 not far from where he ran the family printing firm. Stocky and about a foot smaller than me, he looked about thirty-five.

"Thanks. If that hadn't happened, I would never have met Zena."

"Zena?"

He smiled apologetically, sipping his strong, black coffee.

"Sorry, Zena is the woman who caused all the trouble. The police thought it was actually Francine Ingleby."

I nodded and he went on, having straightened his tie and cleared his throat.

"When Becky died, well, it was as if my life went on hold for a while. But you know what they say, 'life goes on'. Friends were saying I should try online dating."

Exactly what my daughter had suggested to me when Louise walked out.

"It seemed...I don't know, trivial somehow. At the same time, I was lonely."

He stopped talking to drink some coffee. He wasn't finding this easy.

"To cut a long story short," he went on, "I signed up to New Life, a site for widows and widowers."

I had no idea there was such a thing.

"I thought it would be good to meet somebody who understood what I had been through."

He paused again, picking up the spoon from his saucer.

"Zena was the third woman I met. It sounds melodramatic to say she swept me off my feet," he said, "but it's true."

If you say so, I thought, like the old cynic I was.

"She was so cheerful and up beat. Easy to talk to as well. And sexy too. God was she sexy."

Was that what blinded him to her faults? It wouldn't have been the first time.

"Our first meeting was in a country house hotel in the Ribble Valley and we ended up spending the night there."

He looked into the middle distance, a dreamy expression on his face.

"The rest of this story is going to make me look a bloody idiot," he went on. "But I was...it was a time when I was... susceptible, vulnerable."

"Sure."

"And I thought I could trust her. Famous last words."

He took a deep breath and puffed out his cheeks.

"After we'd been going out together for a few weeks I suggested we go on holiday to Australia and New Zealand together. I've got family out there."

"I see."

"She was all for it," he went on. "It was her who suggested we went first class all the way."

"So she gave the impression of having money herself."

"Oh, yes, presumably that was all part of the act."

"What happened next?" I asked.

I knew something had gone wrong, but what?

"The next time I saw her she said she'd done her research and could get us a good deal if we confirmed by the end of that week."

"Right."

"She'd pay for it, but she needed a cheque for my share right away."

So that was it, I thought.

"I gave her a cheque for about eleven grand."

"And?" I asked, when he paused again.

He drank more coffee.

"She told me she was working in London for a few days so she wouldn't be seeing me until the following week."

It was all fitting into place with an awful inevitability.

"That was the last I saw of her. I've still never been to New Zealand."

Time to dig a bit deeper.

"I need to ask a few questions," I said.

"There's more to come."

"Go on."

"I bought my wife quite a bit of jewellery over the years," he explained, "It was worth a lot of money."

"A lot?"

"The best part of a hundred grand,' he said.

You could call that a lot.

"I showed it to Zena and told her I was thinking of selling it. I'd never even looked at it since my wife's death, I couldn't bear to, for one thing, and kept it in a safe at home. Yet I was reluctant to let it go."

"What happened?"

"Just last week, I opened up the safe. I'd decided I would definitely sell the jewellery. Maybe even spend some of the money on that New Zealand trip."

He shook his head disconsolately.

"When I opened the safe, the jewellery wasn't there."

Bugger. The poor bloke.

"And you think Zena, or Francine, was responsible?"

He nodded.

"Who else could it have been?"

I knew enough. We needed to be practical.

"Right," I said. "Have you got a photograph of this woman?"

He smiled ruefully.

"She hated having her picture taken."

How convenient. She had it all worked out.

"What did she look like?"

"About thirty. Dark hair, brown eyes. A touch taller than me. Slim."

Like hundreds of women.

"Did she tell you much about herself?"

"Lots, but it was probably all lies."

True enough, I thought, but what else did we have to go on?

"Just go through it."

"OK. She said when her husband died she moved in with her mother in Accrington. She had an older sister. Let's see...she was a set designer for the theatre, worked away a lot."

Dutifully I wrote all this down but couldn't see it getting me anywhere.

* * *

At half seven that evening I sat down at my kitchen table with Danny and Rachel. She said when she arrived that she would be going home early as she needed an early night.

The reason for that became clear when she told us she was pregnant again. That put us in a good mood, but once I had served up Brazilian Pork Stew, we got onto the unpleasant subject we had to discuss: the Brad situation.

"I rang mum," said Rachel as I poured Shiraz for Danny and me.

Her dark hair was shorter now, with a fringe remarkably like Vicky Monroe's.

"She wasn't pleased," she added when I asked what Louise had said. "She said she was sorry that he bothered you."

"I never trusted that Brad," said Danny, "too much of a smoothie. And he thought nothing of going off with somebody else's wife."

We were getting on dangerous ground so I brought the conversation back to the point.

"I just want to make sure he doesn't bother us again."

I was most concerned about my kids. If he could find out where my local was, he was bound to know where they lived even though he had never been to their houses.

"Is there anything she can do about it," asked Danny?

He brushed his hand quickly through his fair hair, a sure sign he was worried.

"We talked about that," said his sister. "She's gonna make an appointment to see a solicitor. Some woman she was at school with, who specialises in this sort of thing."

It was good that Louise was taking action. I only hoped it would do some good.

"She's worried about grandma and granddad though," Rachel added.

"What?"

I was outraged at the thought he would harass two people in their eighties.

"He can't be that bad," said Danny, obviously sharing my opinion.

Despite being the only person I knew who was taller than me, my son was a sensitive, gentle soul.

"Mum says he'll do anything to get back at her," said Rachel.

From my social work experience and my private investigation work I knew to what depths people could sink.

"We need a plan," I said after we had talked round the subject for a while longer.

"Mum needs to be somewhere inaccessible for a while," suggested Danny.

That was why I phoned my sister, Terri, in Sydney.

* * *

Half an hour after that I was explaining the ins and outs of the investigation I was involved in.

"So you're trying to find Francine Ingleby," asked Rachel when I had finished.

"Yes."

"You'd like that job, wouldn't you, Danny?"

My son looked daggers at his sister. There was something going on between them I wasn't aware of.

"Come on, explain," I said.

"Danny used to fancy her when she was on that Danger Gang."

"Might have done," he said, regressing to the age he was when Danger Gang was on.

Why shouldn't he fancy Francine, I asked myself, or anyone else for that matter? When I was thirteen, I fancied Dusty Springfield. Nobody told me she was gay.

"Well, you may as well have a go at finding her, Danny," I said. "I'm getting nowhere."

He smiled at me.

"We need another cunning plan."

I shrugged.

"If you can come up with one, I'll be eternally grateful."

"Right."

He drank his wine, deep in thought.

"If she's got this scam of trying to meet rich men through this widows' website," he said, "what's to say she's not still doing it?"

That sounded like the germ of an idea.

"Go on," urged Rachel.

He took another drink, which seemed to inspire him.

"Let's assume she's continuing with the scam using another name."

"OK," I said.

"All you need to do is get someone – a man, obviously – to register on the site and date her."

"That's all right in principle," I said, "but how can you guarantee this bloke would ever get to meet her?"

"It all depends on your profile," put in Rachel. "we'd have to make sure whoever you got to do it had it right."

We mulled over the idea for a while.

"Two things strike me," said Danny. "One: this Elliott bloke and Francine are much younger than most widows. So she must have been looking at potential partners in the younger age range. Say under forty."

Rachel and I nodded.

"The other thing is this: there must have been something in Eliott's profile that attracted her. He might have said something that suggested he was well off."

"I'll check with him tomorrow," I said. "You know, this might work."

Rachel intervened at this point.

"There's just one more thing to decide. Who's going to sign up for this dating website?"

"I'll do it," said Danny immediately.

I had rarely seen him so enthusiastic. The expression laid back was designed for my son. Maybe it was the booze taking effect.

"Danny, don't be stupid," said his big sister.

Those words only made him more determined.

"There's nothing stupid about it," he insisted. "It's the best chance we've got. And I'd make money out of it."

Rachel looked questioningly at me.

"Oh, definitely," I assured her. "It's part of the investigation."

I was sure Ellen Gallagher or Eliott McIntyre would be happy to pay.

"I've just thought of something else," said Rachel. "What about Natalie?"

"I don't think she'd fancy Francine Ingleby," smiled Danny.

* * *

Two days later I was on my way to meet Eliott in the Blackburn/Darwen Services again. On my way along the M61 while trying to negotiate the heavy traffic, I thought how to play it. I had discussed it with Danny the previous day on a walk in Ribblesdale. We decided I should tell Eliott that Danny was a member of my staff. This was ostensibly to impress Eliott. I omitted to tell Danny that I didn't want McIntyre to know he was my son. This was partly to protect his privacy; partly because I was still uncertain about getting him involved.

I couldn't forbid him from carrying out his plan – I had enough trouble getting him to do as he was told when he was a kid. He really wanted to do it and he did need the money. A few weeks ago he had told me he and Natalie were saving hard to buy a house together. I wasn't well off enough to give them more than a few hundred towards a deposit, so if I could give him some paid work, how could I not do so?

"So what's this idea you've had, Gus," asked Eliott as we sat down in the café later.

I tried and failed to get my teapot to pour out the tea without spilling, while I thought about the question.

"Well, it came from one of my assistants," I half lied, "we often discuss cases as a team. That usually proves fruitful."

I almost laughed at the idea that I had a team, but I stayed focused.

"The basic plan is to try and make contact with Zena/Francine through the website."

I explained the thinking behind Danny's plan.

"Not a bad idea," he said. "What do you want from me?"

"Did you bring your profile?"

He pulled out a folded sheet of paper from his inside jacket pocket and handing it to me.

"We want Danny to use a similar form of words in the hope of attracting the woman we're after."

I read the profile: 'I run one of the North West's leading businesses, but I know now there's more to life than material well-being' was the sentence that stood out.

Those words made him a sitting duck, the poor sod.

"I told you this would make me look stupid," he said.

I shrugged, not knowing what to say.

"I wanted to give the impression I was a successful man, not some sad loser," he added. "Zena must have worked out straight away I had a few bob."

"Anyway, what's done is done," I said, "what we need to do is make her pay."

And I wanted to talk to her about Tim Greenhoff's murder.

"Sounds good to me."

"Once Danny's joined New Life you and I will need to accompany him on all his dates. Keep out of the way so you won't be spotted, but near enough to see what's going on."

"OK."

He was starting to sound keen.

"You'll have to say if his date is Zena or not."

* * *

The following Saturday morning, I eased my Peugeot into the car park of Lancaster Road playing fields, where I had played rugby and cricket at school. I was to do a coaching session for TRYS, a rugby charity I had been involved with since I signed for Salford in the seventies. A young, black man in a suit was waiting outside the changing room with a familiar looking lad. I got out of the car and walked over to them.

"Hey, Gus," said Paul Winston, "this here's Riley Henderson, who I told you about."

I held out my hand and, after an initial hesitation, Riley took it.

"Riley's been referred by his probation officer," explained Paul, "she thinks we might be able to help him."

Nobody looking at the smartly dressed man speaking with such authority would have thought that a few years ago Paul was on his way to a life of crime. TRYS had helped him see the error of his ways. Now he had a well-paid job in IT in Manchester and was one of TRYS' mentors. To top it all I had introduced him to his girlfriend, Hannah, the receptionist at Ordsall Tower. I was expecting a wedding invitation any day now.

"I think I've met Riley before," I said, "nicked any good handbags lately?"

"Don't know what you mean,' said Riley, though his shamefaced look said otherwise.

"Don't give me that," I said. "Outside Ordsall Tower just after Easter, you snatched a lady's handbag."

Paul turned to Riley.

"What's all this," he demanded, "you told me you were going straight."

"I am, honest," he said, "I ain't done nothing like it since."

I explained to Paul what happened.

"So no harm done, eh," said Riley, suddenly optimistic.

"No thanks to you. You probably frightened that woman half to death."

"It wasn't like that," he insisted, "she was expecting me."

Does anybody arrange to be mugged, I wondered?

"What are you on about?"

"It was all planned," he said, "I was supposed to grab the bag and take it somewhere."

I should have known anything to do with the fake Vicky was bound to be confusing.

"Where?"

Riley shook his head.

"I can't tell you that. More than my life's worth. I do know there was summat valuable in the bag, plus hundred quid for me."

"Something valuable? Drugs, you mean?"

"I had no idea what it was. It was best I didn't know."

What the hell was 'Vicky' up to, I asked myself? It might have nothing to do with Tim's death, but the sooner I found her the better.

"What happened that day," said Riley, "it made me realise I was gonna end up in the nick. I mean I nearly got caught for a start. That van that knocked me over could have killed me."

He sounded sincere but so did every criminal in Salford when it suited them.

"My probation officer suggested TRYS before but I said no. This time I'll give it a real go, I promise."

I looked at him, making him wait.

"Right, I'll take you on," I agreed, "on two conditions. One you stay out of trouble; two you help me and Paul with an investigation I'm dealing with."

"Investigation?"

"I'll explain later."

Shortly after the end of the training session, I instructed Paul and Riley to keep an eye on Will Trader's house. I needed to make sure he was still around. After a moment's thought I told them to do the same for Andrea Greenhoff's house on Doveleys Road. Will could be visiting her there. He might know something about the fake Vicky, as might Andrea and there was still a chance they might lead me to a solution of Tim's murder.

"You do this without drawing attention to yourselves."

"No problem," Paul assured me.

I had faith in Paul, who had helped with other jobs I'd had, so had to rely on him to keep Riley in line.

"Make sure you report anything significant to me," I told them.

CHAPTER THIRTEEN

"Not much to report, Gus," said Paul the following Wednesday at the Albert Square Chop House in the centre of Manchester.

We'd arranged this lunch-time meeting to discuss progress.

"I really need to see Will Trader," I said.

Paul took a hungry bite out of his steak sandwich.

"I haven't see him at home. He's called round to that Andrea's house now and again."

He must be still helping her out.

"Maybe I'll try and catch him there."

I had another spoonful of broccoli and stilton soup and thought about what to do next

"How's Riley doing?" I asked.

Paul took a swig of water.

"Good, yeah. Took to it like a duck to water. Mind you, he's a right devious little fucker. Had plenty of practice at the old undercover stuff, know what I mean?"

I laughed.

"I don't doubt it, Paul," I said. "I don't doubt it."

Paul glanced at his watch. He would have to be back at work soon and he had nothing more to add.

"Anyway, I might have some more work for you if you're free tonight."

That was my main reason for meeting Paul.

"I'll make sure I am."

I gave him his instructions and he promised me he would be at his post in good time. I left the restaurant with Paul a few minutes later, glad to have him on my side.

* * *

That night I was hiding with Eliott McIntyre in a private room in Villa Francesca restaurant in Didsbury. Through the glass door we could see Danny waiting self-consciously for his date for the evening, at a table in the middle of the room. Occasionally he looked nervously at his watch, sipped at his water and glanced at the front door of the restaurant.

Since we'd hatched the plan it had achieved nothing useful. Eliott and I had already accompanied Danny on two dates, but neither of the women looked anything like Francine/Zena. Now, hearing the door open, I tried to see the woman rushing into the restaurant without letting her see me. She wore a black dress, a red jacket and a flustered expression. Danny looked towards her. She smiled and sat at his table.

"Oh, my God," I heard her say, "I'm so sorry I'm late."

"That's her," whispered Eliott.

"That's her," I whispered at exactly the same time.

Eliott looked curiously at me.

"What do you mean?" he asked.

What did he mean, I wondered. More pertinently, what the hell did the appearance of this woman mean? Before we went any further, I took out my phone and made a quick call. Then I stood up.

"Come on," I said.

We joined Danny and his date and pulled up two chairs.

"Nice to see you again, Zena," said Eliott as he sat down. "Or is it Francine?"

She looked from one to the other of us in alarm. I decided to join in the speculation.

"Or maybe it's Vicky?"

She still had her fringe, I noticed, and the same handbag. Some things were beginning to slot into place. A lot weren't though.

"Oh, God, it's you again," she said. "What do you want?"

"I want an explanation from you for a start. So does Eliott here."

"You'll have to want," she replied, getting up from her chair. "I'm off."

I looked out of the window.

"As soon as you go outside somebody will follow you," I said. "In the meantime I'll ring the police to have you arrested. So you'd better stay where you are."

I knew Paul was in place only yards away. On previous occasions Natalie had taken on that role but had phoned me last night to cancel. Francine spoke to Danny who had stayed silent so far.

"What's going on?"

"Do as he says," Danny instructed. "He's a private investigator and I'm one of his team. We work closely with the police."

Nice one Danny, I thought, as with a show of reluctance Francine sat down again.

"The first question is," I said, "what's your name?"

She tutted and ground her teeth.

"Francine Ingleby."

"Right, Francine, I want you to tell me what you've been up to," I explained. "If I'm satisfied with your answers to my questions, I won't report you to the authorities."

She sat back in her chair before she spoke again.

"How do I know I can trust you?"

I almost laughed at the thought of a confidence trickster asking about trust.

"You don't."

She took a deep breath and then breathed out again slowly.

"OK. What do you want to know?"

Where to start, I asked myself.

"I think we'd better move to somewhere more private," I said.

As we made our way back to the separate room where Eliott and I had been sitting I ordered a bottle of house red. Once we were settled at the table behind closed doors, I began the questioning.

"I'm sure Eliott has some questions for you but first tell me why you pretended to be Vicky Monroe."

She scratched her top lip then sniffed before continuing.

"When I needed to be in Manchester I stayed at Will's place – he's my second cousin twice removed or something. I slept in the room that used to be Vicky's. It was a handy place for me and Tim to get together if you know what I mean."

The coy smile that accompanied this gratuitous piece of information didn't suit her.

"Anyway, Vicky had left a load of stuff behind so I had a good nosy round. You never know what might come in handy, do you?"

She smirked annoyingly.

"There was nothing obviously valuable, but one day a letter came for her from the Council. I opened it of course. She'd been called for a job interview, something to do with fostering, adoption whatever."

She yawned as if bored already.

"At first I was gonna ring the council and tell them she wasn't coming. If I'd done it straight away that would have been that, but I never got round to it. After a bit I thought it might be a laugh if somebody went along in her place."

It didn't sound all that funny to me.

"Don't know where that idea came from, but I did remember I'd found a load of notes she had left in a drawer. You know, a list of possible questions with the answers all typed out."

I was ahead of her but wanted the full explanation.

"I thought if I got away with it I could sell my story to the tabloids. I mean, if somebody unqualified could get themselves an interview, in theory a paedophile could infiltrate social services."

It was beginning to make a barmy kind of sense. A headline like, 'Are Our Kids Safe?' would attract a lot of attention.

"Did you tell Will about this?"

"No, I thought I'd see how it went. If it had worked out I'd probably have told him to make sure he didn't give the game away."

Francine glanced quickly round the room as if seeking a means of escape.

"I did bring Tim into it though, with him being in the business. He knew somebody who was an expert in fostering and he got some tips off her."

Caitlin, well, what do you know, I said to myself.

"I swotted up the questions and answers," she went on. "Vicky had left her passport behind. I reckoned I could pass for her, no problem."

"I'm still amazed you got away with it," I said.

She shrugged.

"You forget I'm an actress. I still do a bit from time to time, but it doesn't pay as well as crime. It was just like rehearsing for a part. I memorised the script, practised the accent until it was just right. Piece of piss."

It was almost funny that a good actress could get a job she knew nothing about. I had often complained that too many jobs went to people who could talk a good game and little else.

"Once I got the job I thought I'd put in a few weeks then sell the story to the Daily Mail," said Francine, "or the Sun or whatever."

"So why didn't you turn up for work?" I asked.

She tutted again, louder this time.

"Because of Tim getting himself killed. The cops would soon find out I had been to see Tim at that old people's home."

And they would learn a lot of things she wanted to keep quiet, I thought.

"As soon as I heard about the murder," she continued, "I went round to Will's and cleared every trace of Vicky from the house. Dumped it in a skip apart from the passport. Got a few quid for that."

I'd better remember to tell Vicky about the passport. Francine sat back smugly.

"Can I go now?"

I shook my head.

"Not yet. Where were you when Tim was killed?"

"How should I know? I've no idea when that was."

"The morning after your interview," I explained. "Around eight o'clock as far as anyone can tell."

I was guessing a bit there.

"Fast asleep in bed. Now can I go?"

I wasn't letting her off that lightly.

"There are a few more things we need to know about," I said, "like the eleven grand you owe Eliott. And the matter of some rather expensive jewellery."

"I'm sorry about that, Eliott," she said, trying a sweet smile, "nothing personal, but a girl's got to make a living."

"Never mind about being sorry," said Eliott, "I want my money back. And my wife's jewels."

"A bit difficult, I'm afraid. Cash flow problems, you understand."

Eliott cut in.

"Cash f..."

"As for the jewellery, I haven't got it no more."

Eliott looked to me as if for guidance.

"Where is it?" I asked.

"Good question. I gave it to Tim but what he did with it I have no idea."

That really baffled me.

"Where does Tim fit in?"

"You remember that kid trying to nick my handbag?"

"Yeah, and I know it was a put up job."

"How do you know that?"

"It's my job to find things out," I said. "But go on with what you were saying."

"Well, the jewellery was in the bag; the guy in the hoodie was supposed to take it to someone who could find a market for it."

"'Too complicated', you called it," I said, remembering her words as she went into Ordsall Tower. "You were right, weren't you?"

She sighed.

"Yeah. The fence didn't want me going to his place cos I'd been there too often. Paranoid pillock. Anyway, when I saw Tim that night I told him to take the stuff to the fence in return for a cut of the proceeds. I assured him there was plenty more where that came from. Blokes on dating websites always have something worth nicking if you know who to target."

"Someone like me," said Eliott ruefully.

"Sorry," said Francine sounding anything but, "like I say, it's business."

"Coming back to the jewellery," I said, thinking out loud, "either the police have got it or whoever killed Tim took it away with him."

At that point the door to our private room was flung open. DI Ellerton came in with two uniformed constables.

"Sarita," I said, "there's the woman you want. Francine Ingleby."

The inspector began to caution Francine. It would be true to say she wasn't pleased.

"You lying bastard," she hissed at me. "You'll be sorry."

As the PCs marched Francine away, a waiter brought a tray. "Bottle of house red," he announced as Sarita said she'd see me later.

* * *

I got back to my flat to find DI Ellerton knocking at the door.

"We've got your friend, Francine in a cell overnight," she said as she followed me in.

We sat at the kitchen table again. We'd have to stop meeting like this.

"She's been charged with fraud and burglary."

"What about claiming to be a social worker when she isn't?" I asked.

"We could get her on that too. Social services aren't sure they want to press charges, bad publicity, you know. Pity, I've never come across it before. Might have been interesting."

I yawned, suddenly tired from having to concentrate for so long.

"Francine wasn't saying much to us," the DI continued. "Can you tell me what she told you? It's not acceptable as evidence, but it might suggest another line of questioning."

"Sure."

I explained as far as I could what Francine had been up to.

"Did she say anything about Tim's murder?" asked the inspector.

"Yes, but not much. Says she was in bed at the time he died. When she talked about it she made it clear she wasn't overcome with grief. Seemed to find it a bit of an inconvenience."

"Quite a girl, young Francine," said the DI. "We've had our eyes on her for a while."

CHAPTER FOURTEEN

"I've got a guy called Ed Richards with me," said Marti the next day.

She had rung me when I was on my regular morning walk through Salford Quays. I had just reached the BBC building when the call came through.

"Who's he?"

"His father, Frank Richards, was married to Caitlin Gallagher," she said. "He read about Jimmy being charged with the Greenhoff murder."

"Yeah?"

"My name was mentioned in the article. He made a special journey from Bristol to come and see me because he reckons he can help in Jimmy's defence."

"How exactly," I asked doubtfully?

"It's too complicated to go into right now. I told him I had a private detective looking into the case."

In other words, Marti had fobbed him off.

"And you want me to see him," I asked.

The 'why buy a dog and bark yourself?' principle, I thought. Still, I was paid by the hour, what did I care?

"Got it in one. He's staying at the Holiday Inn. Could you meet him there at eight tonight?"

"Yeah, why not?"

There was nothing to stop me from seeing this feller. I wouldn't be seeing my girlfriend, that was for sure. It had been days since we'd even been in the same room. I may as well go out and earn some money, though I couldn't imagine how it would do any good. At the same time, I didn't have any better ideas.

"And you're not to say anything to Caitlin about this," Marti added. "She has no idea he's contacted me."

"Right."

That made it sound intriguing. I was almost looking forward to meeting Mr Richards.

"By the way," Marti added just before ending the call, "Francine Ingleby is out on bail. Staying at the Ordsall probation hostel."

* * *

"Do you know what happened to my dad?" asked Ed Richards a few hours later, brushing his hand through his brown hair.

The bar of the Holiday Inn with its grey walls and modern furniture wasn't exactly the cosy pub I would have chosen, though it had the advantage of being only two minutes' walk from my apartment.

"I know he died."

Ed sipped at a glass of scotch. I guessed he was in his mid-twenties though the anxiety on his face made him look older. We had spent the minimum time necessary on introductions, getting drinks and finding a table well away from the handful of other customers.

"He killed himself," he said, going back to his whisky to hide his discomfiture.

"God, I'm sorry."

No wonder Caitlin never talked about her first husband.

"Or at least that was the official verdict," he added.

I drank some Australian Shiraz and waited. It seemed best not to push him. He tugged at the collar of his striped shirt, then fiddled with the buttons.

"I think Caitlin murdered him."

A stunned silence followed. No doubt because I was stunned.

"Tell me about it," I suggested gently. "If you want to."

He cleared his throat.

"I should say I'm serious about this. It's not just a mad theory."

It did sound mad but anything was possible.

"When Dad left me and mum for Caitlin I was only seven. Then when I was thirteen he died."

I wondered momentarily about Caitlin's Catholicism. Her faith hadn't stopped her from having at least two affairs with married men. Or marrying a divorcé.

"In the intervening years I didn't see much of Dad so I never really got to know him. I guess I feel cheated."

He recited the facts with no obvious emotion but there was a tightness in his voice as though he had to overcome a physical obstacle to get the words out.

"Understandable."

"When I did see Dad, his new wife was hardly ever there. I can only remember meeting her a handful of times."

After a gulp of scotch, he went on.

"Dad worked in banking, one of the high ups, you know. In financial terms he was generous. He seemed to think that was all I needed from him."

He rubbed his hand over his chin, looking round the room for a moment.

"In effect Mum was a single parent. She didn't remarry until I was twenty, twenty-one."

He fell silent, clutching at his glass. I thought about the people I had met during this investigation. There's no such thing as normal, I was told on my social work course. Ed Richards was the latest person to prove that to be true. There was something unconvincing about him. Here was a man who accused his stepmother of killing his Dad, but so far he had, in my estimation, just wanted somebody to talk to.

Could anybody in the case be trusted? At least one, Francine Ingleby, turned out not to be the person she claimed to be. That made me question the wisdom of taking anybody at face value, including Ed Richards. For a mad moment, I toyed with the idea of asking to see his ID, but an aversion to looking an idiot made me think better of it. Still Ed had said no more. Maybe he needed encouragement.

"Carry on with what you were saying," I said, "when you're ready."

"When my father died my mother refused to answer my questions about exactly what happened. I gave up asking in the end."

"Right."

"At first I thought maybe she was trying to protect me," he said. "All she did was make me more determined to find the truth."

Was what he was telling me the truth or just his version of it, part of his obsession? Not that he had told me much.

"You've given me remarkably few facts so far, Ed," I said. "And nothing you have said has convinced me this is any concern of mine."

He took a deep breath.

"Facts? OK I'll give you facts."

He leaned towards me, putting his elbows on the table, then pointing with his right index finger.

"On the day Dad died," he said, sounding now like an up-and-coming manager giving a presentation, "a colleague from the bank came to his house to pick him up. They were going to a conference in Leeds."

He sat back slightly.

"There was no answer at the front door. He looked round the back, but there was nobody around. He went down to the shed at the bottom of the garden. Dad had it done out like an office apparently."

He bit at his bottom lip before drinking more whisky.

"When he opened the shed door, the poor guy got a hell of a shock: Dad was hanging from the ceiling."

"Terrible," I said.

What else could I say? I kept quiet for a while, not sure whether Ed would say any more. Would he be too distressed to go on?

"I assume you've told the police about your suspicions," I said.

"Yes, for all the good it did," he said, a look of cynicism on his face. "They wouldn't take me seriously."

"Ed, could you tell me why you think he was murdered?"

He looked around the bar before continuing.

"Well, Caitlin gave evidence at the inquest that Dad had been depressed for a while, you know, listless, tearful, had mood swings. He had trouble sleeping."

I drank more wine and waited for him to say more.

"She claimed she'd begged him to go and see his GP," he added scornfully, "but he always refused."

He looked at me as if expecting inspiration.

"Suicide among men is becoming increasingly common," I said, "and one of the factors is a reluctance to seek help until it's too late."

He smiled sceptically.

"That's where she was clever," he insisted. "She'd know all that stuff because of her job."

I sighed.

"Maybe your Dad really was depressed."

He shook his head vehemently.

"He'd shown no sign of having mental health issues until he got involved with Caitlin."

This was beginning to sound like a classic case of paranoia.

"Depression can strike at any time," I countered.

The poor feller was in denial. He needed help, but like his father he would not accept it. His Dad, in his eyes, had abandoned him twice. Once for a woman; once by dying. If he killed himself it meant he hadn't cared enough about Ed to stay alive. The son might find murder, terrible though it was, more acceptable. At least that meant Frank Richards hadn't chosen death.

"Listen, Ed," I said, "I know what it's like to lose a parent when you're young."

I shivered at the memory of walking into the kitchen forty years ago and finding my mother lying dead on the floor.

"If you're gonna suggest I need therapy or something, save your breath. Anyway, there's more," he said. "Dad was planning to leave Caitlin."

"Go on."

"I talked to a lot of Dad's colleagues from HSBC. They all said he showed no signs of depression."

Would they have known what to look for, I wondered?

"I managed to trace the guy who found Dad's body. He said he thought Dad might have had an affair with a colleague. He wouldn't give her name, said she had moved abroad after Dad died."

I raised my eyebrows at this.

"He said he knew Dad had got fed up with Caitlin's controlling ways, not to mention all her affairs."

That didn't tell me much: a possible affair with an unknown woman.

"She couldn't stand the thought of Dad leaving," he went on, "not because she loved him, but it would have hurt her pride."

A huge leap, I thought. I didn't know Caitlin well enough to say how she would react to rejection, but to suggest she was a murderer still seemed far-fetched. In any case, having an affair didn't necessarily mean he was leaving.

"And Caitlin inherited a big house in Northwich," he added.

He was into his stride now; I was beginning to wonder if I would ever get away.

"Just think, Gus," said Ed, "would he kill himself if he were about to start a new life?"

He might or he might not. There was no logic to mental illness. That's why it was an illness.

"OK, even if I accept what you're saying," I said, "as far as I can see everything you've said is beside the point as far as the death of Tim Greenhoff is concerned."

Again he leaned forward.

"No, no, not at all," he insisted. "Supposing she killed Greenhoff too."

"What?"

"If he was going to dump her, she wouldn't stand for that."

It was my turn to shake my head.

"And she somehow plotted to throw suspicion on Jimmy? She could hardly have known Jimmy was going to Mangall Court that morning."

"Jimmy being arrested was just chance, a bonus if you like," he replied,

I could just imagine Jimmy's reaction to the suggestion that his being banged up and facing a life sentence was a bonus. Eventually I got away from Ed and promised to look into his claims and get back to him. I had no intention of spending too much time on it though.

It struck me as I walked back to my flat that Caitlin was getting the blame for a lot of things. Ellen Gallagher held her responsible for Jimmy's arrest and imprisonment; Ed Richards had her down as a double murderer. Not only that, but if he were to be believed, she was only too happy to let her husband take the rap for Tim Greenhoff's death even though she killed him herself. What was it Francine Ingleby in her guise as Vicky Monroe had said? It's too bloody complicated, that was it. Too true, Francine, I said to myself.

* * *

The next morning Will Trader opened his front door to me. It was almost a shock to ring the bell in Cholmondeley Road and have it answered by the householder.

"Good morning, Will," I said, taking in the straight-legged jeans, the v-neck t-shirt that showed off his muscles. Again I got the impression he'd got up early to make sure he looked right.

"Gus," he smiled, "I was expecting you. Come in."

His words wrong-footed me. I tried not to show it, deciding not to respond. But what was he on about? He opened the door wider. I followed him down the hall and into the dining room. He sat at a light oak table, picked up a piece of toast from a plate and took a bite.

"I wondered when you'd be back."

"Oh."

I pulled up a chair and sat opposite.

"You didn't think your little performance fooled me, did you?"

"Performance?"

He chewed thoughtfully on his toast.

"When you claimed to be popping round to express your sympathy to the grieving widow."

Oh, that performance, I said to myself. I'd thought it had been quite good at the time. Will didn't agree, I could see that.

"After you'd gone, I did some research and found out you're a private detective."

What if he had seen through me? It hardly mattered.

"I reckon Mr Gallagher's brief has hired you."

"I can neither deny nor confirm that, Will. Client confidentiality, you understand."

He drank from a mug of coffee.

"Whatever. So what do you want today?"

I wondered when we'd get round to my reason for interrupting Will's breakfast.

"I talked to Francine Ingleby the other day," I said.

"Fran?"

"Did you know she's on bail?"

He stared at me open-mouthed, almost spilling his coffee as he put the mug back down.

"Bail," he said, "you're kidding! What's she been charged with?"

He took another mouthful of toast, making a loud crunching sound as he bit into it.

"Fraud, burglary..."

"Heavy stuff," he said.

He looked quizzically at me, picking up his mug again as I told him about the probation hostel.

"I must go and see her."

"She's your cousin, isn't she?"

"Third cousin, I think, something like that. What's this all about anyway?"

"I was asked to look for Vicky Monroe," I began. "I found her in the Scilly Isles, where she has been since March."

"So that's where she is."

"I'd already worked out that the "Vicky Monroe' who attended a job interview in April at Ordsall Tower was an impostor."

Will did not respond to this.

"The obvious candidate was Francine Ingleby," I went on.

"What are you on about?"

I told him about the letter that had come for Vicky while Francine was staying with him.

"Francine decided to go to the interview, claiming to be Vicky. She got the job."

He chuckled quietly to himself.

"Only Fran would have thought of that. Only Fran would have got away with it."

"So you didn't know about it?"

He shrugged.

"Nobody tells me anything. How do you know about Francine?"

Again I pondered what kind of an answer to give him.

"Contacts," I said. "It's amazing what you can find out if you know the right people."

"I dare say."

Will went quiet for a while, looking as if he were trying to solve some complex puzzle.

"I'm just trying to work out what actually happened here," he continued. "Someone has masqueraded as a social worker, gone to an interview and actually got the job. Surely Social Services would want to keep that quiet."

That was exactly what they did want. Maybe I shouldn't have told Will about it, but I needed to know whether he was involved in Francine's little plot and couldn't take her word for it. I still had a feeling there was a connection between Tim's murder and Francine going to that interview. I could be wrong; I probably was wrong.

"An interesting lady, Francine," he continued. "Quite fanciable too."

So Will had the hots for Francine Ingleby, did he? Dismissing this thought, I moved onto another topic.

"She was also involved in a scam that involved online dating."

Was Will complicit in this, I asked myself? Surely he couldn't be as innocent as he looked?

"Really?"

I explained what I meant, before telling him about surprising Francine in the restaurant where she was meeting Danny. Will gave another shrug, not interested, it seemed.

Now was a good time to introduce Tim's death into the conversation. That was what I was most interested in.

"Do you think any of this has a link to Tim Greenhoff's murder?"

"You must think so, Gus. Otherwise you wouldn't be here."

"Interesting, isn't it," I said, "Francine has a connection with Tim; you were a friend of his; you know Francine."

"I once met David Cameron," said Will, "which is about as relevant as what you're going on about. It has nothing to do with the murder. Jimmy Gallagher will soon be doing life for it."

I paused for thought.

"Maybe. But supposing he didn't do it?"

"Unlikely, I would have thought. You're biased of course. I happen to know James Gallagher is a friend of yours. Maybe you should choose your friends more carefully."

If Jimmy wasn't my friend, would I still believe in his innocence? I didn't have time to answer hypothetical questions.

"Let's stick to the point," I said, "Francine went to Mangall Court not long before Tim was murdered – as did you – and gave him some very valuable jewellery."

He poured himself more coffee.

"Jewellery? Why on earth should she..."

I cut in.

"Did Tim say anything to you about it?"

He shook his head.

"Time to go, I think," I said, getting up.

Will opened the front door to let me out.

"I see you've sold the house," I said, indicating the SOLD sign in the garden.

"At last," he said, "be nice to have a few spare quid. Now I can sort my life out."

"Good."

"I hope you're not going to bother Andrea again," he said.

"Difficult to say," I replied.

"I would suggest you leave her alone," he said, an edge in his voice I had never heard before. "She's had enough to put up with."

"I may not need to see her," I said. "Depends."

I did not say what it depended on because I didn't know.

"I thought she might be, I don't know…"

He stopped in mid-sentence as if reluctant to put into words what he was about to say. He sighed before saying any more.

"I know they say never speak ill of the dead and all that and Tim was my friend, but you must have worked out by now he was a lousy husband."

I looked him in the eye.

"He was always boasting about his conquests, you know. And Andrea would complain long and hard about Tim. I did what I could to console her. I just wasn't comfortable with the whole thing."

Poor old Will, I thought, stuck in the middle of a flawed marriage.

"I thought she might even be…"

Again he couldn't say the word.

"Relieved that he's not around anymore," I suggested.

He nodded.

"You seem to be saying she wasn't relieved," I said. "In spite of Tim being a less than perfect partner."

"She's taken it badly, been off work for a while. I just want to protect her."

CHAPTER FIFTEEN

I drove home from Will's house, wondering about all the different strands of the investigation and whether they made sense. Acknowledging gloomily that they didn't, I tried to work out what to do next. It was difficult to think straight as I was distracted by the rattling from the car's engine, which had returned with a vengeance. As I approached the traffic lights on Trafford Road, the noise stopped. So did the car. Like its owner, it was knackered.

At least, I told myself, I was not far from Salford Quays. Even so I only got home an hour later, having called out Green Flag, who towed it to a garage. More expense, I thought, as I sat with a cup of tea in my living room. There was nothing for it but to get another car now. Could I afford it? Did I have any choice? I couldn't do either of my jobs without a car. Nor could I get to see my family easily.

Forgetting about the car, I played over in my mind what Will had said about expecting Andrea to be relieved at Tim's death. Digging a little deeper, I wondered if he meant he suspected she had had something to do with the murder? I couldn't get away from the idea that Tim's wife had several motives for killing her husband. Reminding myself she was on her way to work while her husband was being killed led me to another question. If it wasn't Andrea, who did kill him? I was no nearer finding that out than I was when I started. Names ran through my mind: Andrea, Wayne Dickens, Caitlin, Francine, Jimmy, Will Trader, even the real Vicky Monroe. They were all characters in a drama; all linked by this young man who had been killed.

What were the connections, I asked myself? Sex and money were the main ones. They were Tim's twin obsessions, but they didn't apply to Dickens. He was concerned only with revenge for having his kids taken into care. Sex, though, was the obvious motive, given that Tim was strangled with the scarf he used in his erotic games. I couldn't say why but I wasn't convinced by that argument. It was too obvious. So many people involved in this, especially Tim himself, were out to make a fast buck. Was money behind it? Speculation, Gus, I said to myself, mind games you don't have time for.

I continued to turn everything over in my head. Ed Richards' accusations had succeeded only in confusing me even more than I had been before. Time for another list, I thought, going into the spare room. I tapped a pen against the desk top, then I began to write. Three or four minutes later I crossed out what I had written. Now I couldn't even manage a bloody list. Bugger.

* * *

That afternoon while I waited at the Salford Quays tram stop, a dark car pulled up.

"Hi, Gus," said Caitlin Gallagher, "can I give you a lift anywhere?"

"I'm going to Bolton," I said more in hope than expectation. "Getting the train from Victoria."

"Jump in," she said. "I'm off to Darwen but I can take the scenic route through Bolton."

"Thanks."

I jumped in, grateful that Caitlin was willing to go out of her way.

"I've just been to a meeting at Ordsall Tower," she said as I did up my seat belt. "Somewhat tedious but it's got to be done."

She shot off at great speed, forcing me back in my seat and making me wonder if I really was grateful. At least I wouldn't be late, I said to myself, though the old saying 'better late than never' sprang to mind.

"How's the investigation going?" she asked.

She accelerated again, reminding me of another car ride about four years ago. On that occasion the driver had been a teenage girl in great distress, but she had been careful compared with this supposedly mature woman.

'OK," I said, "I think I'm beginning to get somewhere."

Caitlin's mad driving also brought to mind the car that had shot out of the Mangall Court car park on the morning Tim had died, but it couldn't have been her in that car, could it?

"Are you sure?"

"Positive."

Not a completely honest reply, but whoever said honesty was the best policy was wrong. I looked over to her.

"You sound surprised," I said.

She smiled.

"I am. You know, Gus, I've thought about this a lot. I have this terrible feeling Jimmy did it."

Now it was my turn to be surprised.

"What?"

"Oh, I know he's protesting his innocence," she said, "and it's hard to imagine Jimmy losing control."

It certainly was, I thought.

"I've lived with Jimmy for a long time," she explained as if speaking to a child, "and he's so...uptight, keeps everything bottled up."

I vaguely recalled hearing that about somebody else, but who it was I couldn't have said. Surely we all do that, I said to myself. If we didn't keep things bottled up we'd be prey to anger, lust, greed, all sorts of things. Some people were, I told myself, including the killer of Tim Greenhoff.

"I'm afraid my relationship with Tim became Jimmy's obsession and might have tipped him over the edge."

All perfectly possible but to hear his wife saying these things shocked me profoundly. Shouldn't she find it a bit harder to believe this of her husband? Or was that a bit Stand By Your Man?

"Poor old Jimmy can scarcely cope with a predictable routine let alone anything in the least unexpected," she added. "That's why those wretched beer mats mean so much to him. They offer an escape from reality."

She roared onto the M602, immediately heading for the fast lane and staying there. She alarmed me even more by removing her left hand from the wheel and brushing it through her hair. This revealed a wire going into her left ear.

"I didn't realise you wore hearing aids," I said.

"You weren't supposed to see that," she said, smiling to hide her embarrassment. "I only got them last week. It's a hereditary problem from my mother. It makes me feel old."

It was something I associated with people over the age of seventy but I didn't tell her that.

"So anyway, Gus," said Caitlin, "you intend to continue trying to clear Jimmy's name."

"Yes."

I only hoped she wasn't about to ask me how the hell I was going to manage it.

"It's good for him to have a friend like you," she said, "even in a lost cause."

As if being scared shitless by her dicing with death on the motorway wasn't enough, I had to listen to her casting doubts on my chance of success. What was Caitlin's motivation in telling me her views about the investigation? If Jimmy was sent to prison for life how would she react?

At last the helter-skelter ride was over and Caitlin dropped me off at Bolton Children's Services. I'd have to get the train back, but that suited me fine. It would take longer but I had more chance of getting home in one piece.

CHAPTER SIXTEEN

On the following Monday I picked up my post and yawned as I sat down at the kitchen table and went through the junk mail. Stuck in the middle of the pile was a postcard with a picture of Sydney Harbour. Turning it over I read:

Hi Gus

I've decided to go travelling again. Fetched up here yesterday. 23 degrees and it's supposed to be winter! I'll be off to Tasmania next week, then New Zealand for a while. After that who knows? Maybe I'll get my head straight one of these days! I hope you're OK, looking forward to seeing you when I get back.
Love Louise xxx.

Brad might be reading his card at this moment, I said to myself. That should keep him quiet for a while. I looked at the clock on the wall opposite. Nearly half nine. Time to go.

* * *

"What happened with Ed Richards?" Marti asked from behind her desk at Pym and Sigson. "I read your report of course, but we've not had a chance to talk about it."

That statement showed how little we had seen of one another lately. I couldn't remember when we last got together socially. It had taken a while to organize this meeting, even though it was essential to my investigation. I explained Ed's allegations against Caitlin without much enthusiasm. I still couldn't work out what good seeing him had done.

"A bit far-fetched, isn't it?" asked Marti. "Caitlin killing her husband and Tim Greenhoff."

"Yeah. Apart from anything else, Caitlin was in Blackburn around the time Tim was killed."

"Ah, well," she said resignedly, "it was worth a try."

I started thinking about what else I had to tell Marti about the investigation when my phone rang. Pulling it from my pocket, I apologised. Seeing the caller was Louise, I pressed the red button, reluctant to speak to my ex-wife while Marti was there. I was about to put the phone away then stopped and looked at it for several seconds. It was significant in some way. Gradually the idea surfaced from the back of my mind. I looked at Marti.

"Mobile phones," I said.

"What about them?"

I sat up, suddenly alert.

"I've been making the assumption that Caitlin was in Blackburn around the time of Tim's death," I went on.

"Yes, but..."

"Jimmy told us she rang him from there."

"Did he?"

"Yes, when we went to see him in prison that time," I reminded her. "So we only have his word for it, don't we?"

She sat up too.

"I suppose so but why would he lie?"

I could see I'd have to make myself clearer.

"No, it's not a question of Jimmy lying. She told him she was at her friend's house, but if she used her mobile she could have been anywhere."

She looked thoughtful for a moment.

"Yeah, suppose so."

Thinking furiously, I tried to create an alternative scenario. Caitlin could have got up early and made her way to Salford to see Tim, surprise him. Maybe he wasn't pleased to see her. He could have been expecting Francine to pay a return visit. I put this to Marti.

"Come on, Gus, you're not starting to take Ed Richards seriously, are you? Caitlin could have used her friend's phone, which would show she really was in Blackburn."

That was certainly feasible, I had to admit.

"Do people ask to use their friend's phone these days when everyone has a mobile?"

"Maybe there was no mobile signal."

"That's possible, but there's no point in speculating any more," I said. "Would you have a list of calls Jimmy received on the morning of the murder in your file?"

"I can check," she said, before picking up the phone on her desk.

She had a short conversation with her secretary, who promised to ring back in a couple of minutes. I was in the middle of telling Marti about the rest of the investigation when her desk phone rang.

"Caitlin definitely used her mobile to call Jimmy," said Marti as she put the phone down.

"Right."

We looked at one another as if uncertain what to say.

"So, is this good news or bad?" asked Marti.

"I'm not sure," I replied. "Probably neither."

How could we draw any conclusions until we found out where Caitlin was at the time? She could still, for all I knew, have been in Blackburn. Marti broke into my thoughts.

"You'll have to ask Caitlin."

"Suppose so," I agreed.

But if she said she was nowhere near Salford when Tim was strangled, there was no way of proving whether she was telling the truth. I knew I would have to see Caitlin again, but was reluctant to have any contact with her. Why was that, I asked myself? It wasn't for any reason that could be explained. I'd just have to get on with it.

"Actually, Gus, there was something else I wanted to talk about," said Marti.

"What's that?"

"Well, you know the album we're doing? It's going really well. Ellen say she likes it a lot."

"Great."

"Anyway, Ellen wants me to join her band on the world tour," she said, sounding a little breathless, "you know, play keyboards, do backing vocals, even sing a couple of numbers."

"Wow."

She re-arranged the papers on her desk before she said any more.

"I just wondered how you felt about it."

That wasn't the question I was expecting.

"How I feel about it? Well, it's brilliant, isn't it?"

She took a deep breath.

"So you don't mind?"

"No, I..."

"I'll be away for months."

We looked at one another.

"I'll miss you," I said, "course I will, but it's what you want to do."

"Yes, but it's a bit daunting."

I smiled at her. Most things people want to do are daunting, I thought.

"For someone with your talent it'll be a piece of piss."

"Thanks."

Marti grinned, suddenly looking years younger. Then she moved her papers around again. She was about to speak then fell silent.

"I was just wondering what's gonna happen to us," she said eventually.

We made eye contact for a moment then looked away again.

"Us as a couple rather than individuals?" I asked.

"Yes," she said. "I was thinking maybe this was a good time to, you know, think about whether we have a future together..."

"Or not?"

I put into words what I thought was on her mind. She sighed, whether with relief that she'd brought what had been bothering her out in the open or with sadness I couldn't say. I looked out of the window behind Marti, which afforded a view of Salford Quays. I had no idea if Marti and Yvonne had chosen their office with this in mind, but it was certainly impressive. And it distracted me briefly from thinking about what Marti was saying.

"We don't have to decide now but..." she said.

But what, I wondered? I would need time to mull over what Marti was saying. It would take a while to get used to the idea, because, whatever she said, I knew the decision had been made.

* * *

"Well, mam, here I am again," I said.

A wind blew over Weaste cemetery, ruffling my hair. I straightened my tie, checking the crease in the trousers of my suit. I always obeyed what I thought would be my mam's dress code for these visits. She had never got used to casual clothes.

"A lot's been happening," I went on. "That always seems to be the case. I've been thinking about you. More than usual, I mean. Ever since I met Debbie again."

Debbie was one of the chosen few: people my mam actually liked.

"I was going out with her when you died," I said. "It was quite a year. Two general elections. Harold Wilson won them both. Now people would say 'Harold who?'"

Forty years ago, I said to myself. All that time without my mother.

"Then when Ed Richards told me about his father dying when he was thirteen," I continued, "that also reminded me of you."

There was a parallel with my own experience that had made me empathise with Ed.

"I think when Marti goes off on this world tour that'll be it for us," I explained. "How do I feel about it? Sad, I'd say. Yes, definitely sad."

It was easy to tell I wasn't happy by the fact that Cocktail Time was my current choice of bedtime reading. I'd gone back to re-reading PG Wodehouse yet again to bring a smile to my face.

"I'll cope though, Mam, no need to worry."

I looked round at the gravestones, hundreds of them, all with their story to tell – if only they could talk. The peace of the place was comforting somehow, as was the thought that I could confide in my mother. I'd never been able to when she was alive. Maybe, had she not had a fatal stroke when I was eighteen, we might have developed a more equal, trusting relationship. Like the one I now had with my dad.

"Then there's the question of Jimmy Gallagher. What do you think of that, mam? You used to feel sorry for Jimmy; you said he always seemed so hopeless."

It's a long way from hopeless to killing someone, I thought.

"I'm struggling with this one, mam, I have to admit. There's so much information, so many possible theories. That's all they are, theories."

I sighed loud enough to be heard by any passer-by. Luckily I was the only person here.

"Oh, and Louise is having trouble with her second husband."

Why was I telling her this? I knew what she'd say: 'Serves her bloody right, Gus. She wouldn't recognise a good man if he jumped up and bit her on the nose. I tell you something, if my son's not good enough for her, she can sod off.'

"And so say all of us," I said, wondering whether Brad would sod off.

CHAPTER SEVENTEEN

Just after I got home from the cemetery my phone rang.

"Hi, Gus, it's Debbie."

The last person I had been expecting.

"I'm sorry not to have been in touch sooner, too much going on. I'm staying with a friend in the Peak District at the moment, but I'll be back home some time tomorrow."

"Right."

"Maybe we could meet up some time."

"Good idea."

We spent a frustrating few minutes trying to find a time and date when we could meet. It wasn't as if my life were one long round of wall to wall excitement, but there was always something to do.

"Actually, Gus," said Debbie eventually, "I'm planning a final walk tomorrow while my friend's at work. I don't suppose you'll be free to join me, will you?"

Just what I needed to cheer me up.

"Don't worry if it's too short notice," she added.

"No, no, I can manage that."

"Bring a picnic," she said.

* * *

The next morning about half eleven found me walking in the Peak District with Debbie by my side. I'd got off the train in Hope, Derbyshire where she had greeted me with a hug, telling me how glad she was I had been able to make it. Can't be bad, I said to myself. As we began to climb Mam Tor she asked about my Scillies trip.

"Vicky told me a bit about it of course," she said. "Weird about that woman pretending to be her, wasn't it?"

"Yeah. There have been developments since then," I said, breathing heavily. "God, I'll be knackered by the time we get to the top."

She grinned at me.

"You're getting soft in your old age. It'll be worth it for the views."

I puffed louder, feeling an ache at the back of my knees.

"I'll take your word for it."

I explained about the arrest of Francine Ingleby and the involvement of Eliott McIntyre.

"Does this help you with sorting out who killed Tim Greenhoff?" she asked.

"Not really," I gasped. "Nothing does if I'm honest."

For all that I didn't want to talk about the murder investigation, I had to acknowledge that people were fascinated by crime. Debbie, I could tell, thought being involved in that kind of thing made me more interesting.

"You seem to have reached an impasse," she said.

"Yes," I sighed, resisting the urge to say, 'tell me something I don't know'.

"What do you reckon you're going to do next?"

"Go over what I've already done," I said with a question mark in my voice.

"And then do it again?" she asked.

I looked at her, not quite getting it.

"Eh?"

"Why not go and see everybody you've spoken to already?"

"It's as good an idea as any," I replied.

And I might just turn up something that would break the case, I thought. Plus, I had nothing else to suggest. We stopped talking for a while as we devoted what energy we had left to reaching the summit of the hill.

"Is your girlfriend a walker?" asked Debbie as we admired the view from Mam Tor.

A hang glider soared over us as we looked towards Kinder Scout.

"No, she says she's allergic to the countryside," I said. "I keep telling her how much she's missing."

"She certainly is. This is stunning."

"Anyway," I said. "She's not my girlfriend anymore."

This was the first time I'd put it into words, except at my mother's graveside.

"Oh?"

"It's a long story," I said, knowing that was the sort of thing people said when they didn't want to explain something.

"Right."

The idea of Marti and I splitting up just added to my sense of dissatisfaction with life. I was getting nowhere with the investigation. My social work career earned me a crust and occasionally gave me a sense of achievement. On the other hand, it messed with my emotions and left me believing that most human problems were just intractable.

One reason for coming out today – apart from feeling flattered to be asked and enjoying walking – was to get away from things for a while. And I was enjoying Debbie's company more than I did in the old days, when I was overawed by a girl whose dad had a car and who sounded all her aitches. Now I no longer was that desperate adolescent longing to make an impression.

* * *

"Who'd have thought we'd be here after all these years?" said Debbie when we stopped for a picnic about halfway round the walk.

"Yeah, it does seem strange."

"To think we've both been married, had kids and all that," she added, unpacking her rucksack and taking out a sandwich box. "Do you still see your ex?" she asked.

"Just lately I've seen too much of her."

"How come?"

I began to tell her about the trouble with Brad.

"God," said Debbie, "he sounds a nasty piece of work."

You said it, Debbie.

"Anyway, me and my son and daughter came up with an idea that might scupper the lovely Brad."

Debbie drank some water as I took a plastic bottle from my rucksack and poured wine into a cup.

"Go on," she said, "tell me about this idea."

"Right. We wanted to give Brad the impression that Louise was somewhere he couldn't get hold of her."

"And?"

"My sister, Terri lives in Australia and sent Louise some postcards of Sydney," I explained, "Louise wrote on them, sent them back to Terri and she put them in the post. I got one, so did Rachel and Danny. The fourth went to Brad."

"What a clever idea."

"In Brad's card she was to say something like she had to get away for a while and she was sorry it didn't work out between them."

"I see," she said, "you know, Gus, your life seems very complicated. I always thought of you as a pretty straightforward kind of guy."

"I used to be," I said with a hint of regret in my voice. "Still am if only people would let me."

She looked at me with a smile.

"Well, I promise not to complicate things any further," she said, lightly touching my hand. "Unless you want me to of course."

Our eyes met for a moment.

"I'll let you know," I said.

* * *

"Oh, it's you," said Andrea Greenhoff, as she opened her door to me two days later, dressed to kill even at nine in the morning.

I had begun to act on Debbie's suggestion to see a few people for the second time. As I arrived at Andrea's house, I noticed a For Sale sign. It was boom time for estate agents in Salford, it seemed. A bright red sports car was parked outside. The '14' on the number plate told me it was brand new. I took a closer look and saw it was a Peugeot, but it was as unlike mine as you could imagine. I recalled Tim complaining loudly about having to make do with a five-year-old car. He would never get the benefit of driving something really flash, I thought sadly.

"Yes," I said.

"And what does the private detective want this time?"

She folded her arms as she spoke, screwing her mouth up as though issuing a challenge.

"I wondered if I could have a word with you," I answered.

"You've got a cheek."

She adjusted her stance, staring straight at me. Still the challenge was there.

"People say that."

There was no point in being too apologetic, I decided. If she sent me packing, I'd cope. Up to now she had shown no sign of doing so. I waited.

"Come in," she said eventually. "I'll be glad of the company if I'm honest."

That last remark took me aback. I didn't respond, thinking I'd let her explain in her own time. She led me into the living room, where once again I was struck by the unnatural tidiness. Had nobody been in here since my last visit?

"Will said you'd been off work," I said.

We sat in matching armchairs. Andrea sighed and looked blankly around the room.

"That's right. Finding it all a bit much."

"I'm not surprised."

"I went back for a couple of weeks, trying to get back to normal, you know. But there is no normal anymore."

There never was, I said to myself. What was I expecting from Andrea? Surely not a pearl of wisdom that would help me crack the case – that would have been wishful thinking – but something remotely useful would be nice. It was time I took control, I thought, and steered the conversation in the direction I needed it to go.

"Do you still think Jimmy Gallagher killed your husband?"

"Yeah, I suppose so. You know, Gus, at the end of the day it doesn't matter who killed Tim. He's still dead. I just wanna...I just want it to be over and done with."

So did I, in the sense that I wanted to have solved the mystery of who killed Tim and to have got my friend out of prison. Would it ever be all over for Andrea? She would always be the woman whose husband got murdered.

"You weren't exactly honest about Tim were you?" I asked. "When I first came to see you, I mean."

She twisted her hands together and swallowed nervously.

"In what way?"

"You made out he was a saint," I explained. "I know he was a serial adulterer and you were obsessively jealous. Not that I blame you."

She stiffened, as though holding in some great burden.

"Have you any idea how humiliating this is?" she said. "Having everyone know the details of your private life. Fuck! Yes, OK, Tim would shag anything that moved but I loved the bastard."

This release of emotion seemed to flood the room. Her shoulders slowly slumped as the anger left her.

"Me and Tim understood one another," she said. "We both went into jobs that didn't suit us. I thought teaching would be safe and secure. It was what I felt I needed at the time."

Did Andrea want to make some kind of point? Or was she just glad of a chance to talk about Tim?

"I'm not sure why Tim went into social work. He did social anthropology at university. He was fascinated by different cultures, how people define stuff like madness, how we treat anyone who's different."

"All that's important."

"Yeah, but you know better than me the average social worker doesn't have time to worry about philosophical nuances."

I remembered what Tim had said about his hatred for social work.

"We both came to realise we basically wanted a nice lifestyle," she went on. "He was always looking for ways to make a fast buck. He did that for me as much as himself."

She was near to tears now.

"He never quite managed it. The poor sod was worth more to me dead than alive."

She closed her eyes, tensing her muscles as though trying to contain some powerful emotion.

"I've got to get away, Gus, I've just got to. As soon as the life insurance pays out, I'm gonna take the money and run."

It was only after I got back home that I wondered about Andrea's new car. There was something not right about it but, true to form, I couldn't work out what.

CHAPTER EIGHTEEN

"I did some digging into Frank Richards," said Steve, the next day on my living room settee.

He had just arrived from Dolgellau en route to another golf course. The next day he would be playing a round in the Abbeydale club near Sheffield. Rather him than me, I thought, much as I liked Sheffield.

"Did you come up with any surprises?"

He sipped his tea and bit into a digestive biscuit.

"No. There doesn't seem much doubt that it was suicide," Steve went on. "The rope he hung himself with was what killed him. No evidence the body had been moved. He'd had a skinful, but wouldn't you if you were gonna end it all?"

I didn't want to think about that.

"In theory somebody could have put him up there and kicked the chair away," Steve continued, "but it's unlikely."

Was this another blind alley, I wondered? It was always unlikely to bring any concrete results, but I still was disappointed. Would I ever get anywhere?

"The investigating officer came away with a positive impression of Caitlin," said Steve.

"Yeah?"

"She was shocked but not surprised, that was how he put it. You know, she was aware he had mental health issues but maybe didn't realise how serious they were. She felt guilty, thought she should have tried harder to get him to accept help."

"Sad really," I said.

"She was worried about the effect on Frank's son apparently," Steve said. "He was only a lad at the time."

That didn't square with what Ed Richards had said. Maybe Caitlin had said what was expected of her. That hardly made her a murderer.

"That line of inquiry's a dead end then," said Steve. "Where do we go from here, Gus?"

I began to wonder if it were worth pursuing the question of where exactly Caitlin was at the time of Tim Greenhoff's death.

"I still want to find out if Caitlin was in Blackburn at the relevant time. It doesn't look like there's anything in Ed Richards's allegations, but if Caitlin was lying about her whereabouts..."

"Go on."

I explained again about Jimmy's wife staying the night with a friend and ringing Jimmy on her mobile on the morning of the murder.

"The question is," I added, "where was she when she made that call?"

"Have you asked her?"

I shrugged.

"I don't trust her," I said, realising for the first time what my problem was with Caitlin. "I need something more objective."

Steve thought for a moment, then snapped his fingers.

"Sarita will know, won't she?"

I looked askance at him.

"I can hardly ask her."

He raised his eyebrows.

"I don't see why not. She'll have worked out by now you're investigating the Greenhoff case."

"Yeah?"

"Course she will. She's bound to have checked Caitlin's whereabouts. And you helped her with Francine Ingleby, didn't you?"

While I considered this, Steve took out his phone.

"I'll give her a call."

I let him get on with it. I knew he was right: the police wouldn't take Caitlin's word without making inquiries. It was their job to be suspicious. Anyway, Steve always said Inspector Ellerton was one of his protégées and would do anything for him.

"DI Ellerton? It's your old friend and colleague, Steve Yarnitzky here...don't be like that, Sarita, you know you're always pleased to hear from me...I've got your boyfriend with me...Gus, who else?"

He looked over and winked at me.

"You remember how helpful he was in the matter of Francine Ingleby...he's after a quid pro quo...that's your actual Latin...unfortunately you youngsters haven't had the benefit of a classical education like what Gus and me have had...he wants to know where Caitlin Gallagher was at the time of Tim Greenhoff's murder...come on, it's not much to ask..."

He picked up his cup, listening carefully, and drank before responding.

"Thanks, Sarita...I shall let you get on..."

I signalled to him to hang on.

"No, just a minute, Sarita..." said Steve.

I told him to ask her if she had found out anything about the car I saw speeding out of the Mangall Court car park on the morning of Tim's death. Steve passed on the question.

"Right," he said when he'd ended the call.

"What did she say?"

"Caitlin was definitely in Blackburn when Tim was killed. They checked with her friend, Lavinia something. They had breakfast together that morning. She remembered Caitlin making the call to Jimmy."

Well, that got me precisely bloody nowhere, I said to myself.

"And the car belonged to someone who had parked while she went shopping. A bad driver obviously. There's plenty of them about."

"So I can cross Caitlin off the list," I sighed. "I reckon I've now got to the point where I feel as if I have missed something."

"Something being?"

"If I knew that I wouldn't have missed it, would I? Whatever it is will provide the answer."

He smiled and looked at me quizzically.

"And with one bound Jimmy will be free?"

"Something like that."

* * *

Two days later as I strolled along Salford Quays the sun was out, a scattering of people milled about with smiles on their faces and at least momentarily life felt good. I hadn't gone far when, swerving to avoid a pushchair, I heard a voice.

"Gus! Over here, mate."

I turned to my left. A man in a dark blue jacket was waving at me. It took a few seconds to recognise him.

"Will," I said as I approached him.

He held out his hand, I shook it and sat next to him on a metal bench.

"What are you doing round here?" I asked.

"This and that, you know."

I detected a slight slurring in his speech. Looking at him more closely I noticed his jacket was crumpled and he had not ironed his pink shirt with his usual care. He rubbed at the few days' worth of stubble on his chin.

"Drowning my sorrows," he added, making his meaning only marginally clearer.

"Sorrows?"

"Let me buy you a drink," he said, "tell you all about it. I usually pop in to the Holiday Inn around lunchtime."

For the second time in a few days, in fact for the second time in my life, I went to the bar of the Holiday Inn.

"Women, eh," said Will Trader as we sat at a table. "Why do we bother with 'em?"

He poured red wine into two glasses

"It beats me," I said, humouring him.

I drank and wondered what he would say next. Would I finally hear something useful?

"They're so..." he began before stumbling to a halt and raising his glass. "Your very good health."

"Cheers."

He sat back and surveyed the room.

"Where was I? Women..."

I had no idea what on earth he was on about, so let him witter on in the hope he would give me a clue or two. A resigned frown crept across his face.

"It's all gone tits up again, mate," he added.

He lowered his head, swigging more wine.

"I thought I had it all worked out," he went on. "I came into a bit of money a few weeks back. Can't tell you how, not that it matters. So I thought with that and what I had from selling my house, I could settle down with the girl of my dreams. Live happily after."

He shook his head, closing his eyes for a moment. I wondered about the woman who had turned him down. He'd given nothing away about his private life and it didn't look as if he was about to start now.

"Or possibly not," he added.

"What went wrong?" I asked.

His response was a cynical laugh.

"I spent a load of money on her, Gus. And I mean a load of money. I thought that was what she wanted."

He made an expansive hand gesture that nearly knocked his glass over.

"And was she grateful? Rhetor...rrr...rhetorical question. Oh, the words 'thank' and 'you' may have passed her lips, can't remember. But she wasn't grateful in a deeper, more meaningful sense, you know."

The wine was sliding down quite nicely and though the surroundings weren't to my taste, I told myself I could happily sit here getting gradually pissed. I rarely drank during the day, but when I did I enjoyed it. Not that I was doing it for pleasure, far from it: the consumption of cabernet sauvignon was essential for my work.

"This is what gets me about women," said Will, returning to his theme for the day. The spotty youth from behind the bar brought two cheese and ham toasties, spending far too long placing the plates on the table and arranging the cutlery. After the last 'no problem' he left us to it. Will picked up from where he'd left off.

"She reckoned if she couldn't...she didn't...you know. At any rate, 'So long, Will, it's been good to know you' is what it amounted to."

He took off his jacket and flung it onto the chair next to him.

"I dunno," he said, "you try to help people and where does it get you?"

"It's no good expecting anything from people, Will," I said, playing the part of the wise, older man.

He waved his glass in my direction.

"You said a mouthful there, mate. Well, I'll tell you something, I'll get my own back one day, you see if I don't."

He poured more wine for us both before continuing to harangue me.

"Why do I never have any luck, Gus? In any bloody thing that's really important, that's what I mean. What's that saying? Lucky in cards, unlucky in love. Well that's true of me. I've made enough to scrape a living with what I've won in that casino."

Blinking his eyes slowly, he pursed his lips, allowing his shoulders to slump.

"Anyway, that's enough about me, as the saying goes," he said. "What about you, Gus, what you up to these days? You still investigating Tim's murder, are you?"

He was approaching the 'you're my best mate' stage of drunkenness.

"Yeah, I..."

"You getting anywhere?"

Tempted to tell him I was on the verge of a breakthrough, I thought again.

"I'm on the verge of a breakthrough," I said anyway.

The strange thing was I did think I was nearly there. That was why I had told Steve I was missing something that would lead me to the solution.

"Well, the answer's obvious to me, Gus," he said, topping up our glasses. "James Gallagher, guilty as charged."

"He didn't do it," I insisted.

Maybe if I said it often enough it would turn out to be right. Will smiled patronisingly.

"Yeah, whatever. The important thing is, Tim's dead. He was my best friend."

With the awful feeling he was getting maudlin, I drank my wine. I'd make this my last glass. He could drink the rest of the bottle himself.

* * *

"I thought I'd look for a new car," I said to Marti in her office the following day.

We'd spent several fruitless minutes discussing the investigation and she had asked me what I was doing for the rest of the day. Small talk, I said to myself, it's come to that.

"There's no need to do that," she said, "you can use mine when I go on tour."

She found it difficult to repress a smile when she said 'on tour'.

"Are you sure?"

"I won't need it. I was going to ask you to keep an eye on the house while I'm away, so you may as well look after the car as well."

"OK."

I should have protested, at least half-heartedly, but I couldn't afford to. Marti smiled and took my hand, while I tried to imagine myself driving a Mercedes and failing. Still, didn't they say you could get used to anything?

"And I want to make sure I see you again when I get back in spite of...you know."

I smiled back.

"Oh, we'll see one another, I'll make sure about that."

"Great. Listen, Gus I want to explain."

"Explain?"

She rolled a pen between her fingers, before saying any more.

"Remember when I proposed to you?"

I thought back to that day and Marti's anger when I said no. At the time I had thought that was it, but for a while she'd behaved as if nothing had happened.

"Well, when I had got over the shock of rejection, I took stock. I thought I'd handled it all wrong, so decided to bide my time."

"Hence the hints about us moving in together."

She nodded.

"Yes, you see, I was sure you would change your mind in the end."

Was that arrogance or logical thinking? Most people in a relationship ended up living together, didn't they?

"When mum died it made me realise nothing stays the same. And now I've got other opportunities, I guess I have taken stock. The idea of having a relationship isn't so...?"

"Important?"

"Maybe."

A silence developed. I had no idea what to say. As things threatened to get awkward, Marti spoke.

"In the meantime you've got to get Jimmy out of prison."

It was a relief that the discussion about me and Marti had come to an end. We couldn't change anything whatever we said, and there was no point in talking round the subject.

* * *

I opened the door of my flat the following afternoon just before one.

"Hi, Gus," smiled Louise.

I looked her over as she strolled in as if she owned the place. She was looking good, it had to be said, in a red top and check trousers. Certainly more lively than the day she'd come to tell me about Brad. What did she want? Not more problems, I hoped, I wasn't in the mood. We sat at the kitchen table, me wary, her apparently at ease and happy.

"I just thought I'd come and see you," she said, pushing her sunglasses up onto her head. "I'm staying with Rachel, but she's at work so..."

She picked up a CD from the table and examined it. "What's this?"

I was tempted to say, 'what does it look like?' or something equally churlish, but decided to rise above such things.

"It's an Elvis compilation my sister sent me."

"Oh, she made me an identical one when I was staying with her that time."

I'd forgotten that Louise had spent some time with Terri when she was on her round the world trip. How long ago was that? Must be four or five years. God.

"Can we put it on?" she asked.

"Sure."

I went over to the CD player.

"I must send Terri something to thank her for helping me out over the Brad crisis," she added. "What do you think she might like?"

I shrugged.

"I'll have a think."

"Right. How is Terri?"

"Fine, I haven't seen her for too long. I'm trying to save up to fly out and see her one day."

"I hope you manage it."

She looked round the room for a while as if inspecting it. Luckily she had once again come calling on the day Polly had been to clean.

"I don't suppose there's any chance of a drink, is there. Red wine if you've got it," she said as The Girl of My Best Friend started.

"Sure," I said, getting up.

"Oh, I love this one, so haunting."

I came back with a bottle and two glasses and poured Chilean Merlot for us both.

"Cheers," we said.

More daytime drinking, I thought. I was developing bad habits.

"You know," said Louise, "Terri was telling me there's a line in this song, 'the way they kiss, their happiness' and she thought it said 'they hardly miss'."

While we talked about other misheard lyrics, Louise reached into her bag, pulled out a white envelope and handed it to me.

"That's to show my appreciation, you know, for all your help. I feel safe for the first time in ages."

I pulled out a thank you card and a twenty pound HMV voucher.

"Thanks, that's great," I said.

"I wasn't sure what to get, so..."

This was the ideal gift for me, allowing me to choose what I wanted. It was so unexpected that I was lost for words for a moment.

"This is fine." I said eventually. "We could have lunch if you like. I've got some lasagne in the fridge. Home made. It only needs heating up.

Her face lit up.

"Lovely."

I had long suspected she only stayed with me as long as she did because I could cook.

"Gus," she asked as I prepared the food, "we are friends now, aren't we?"

I looked over to her and smiled. The first sensible thing she'd said for a while, I thought.

"Sure."

Over lunch and more wine we gradually relaxed, serenaded by the king of rock'n'roll. She referred briefly to Marti and me – she'd heard from Rachel we'd split up – but I had no wish to talk about it. Then we chatted inconsequentially about her job before we got onto my investigation.

"Sounds dangerous. You will be careful, won't you," she said as I told her all about it.

For the first time since we ceased to be married we weren't restrained by hidden agendas and stuff from the past that could never be resolved.

"Course I will."

She took another mouthful of wine, as did I. I reckoned we had both reached the optimum level of intoxication. Louise smiled at me.

"Because I'm still very fond of you, you know that, don't you?"

I didn't know any such thing, I was tempted to say, but this wasn't the time for bitterness.

"It's mutual," I said.

Two things struck me: I still fancied Louise something rotten – I couldn't see that changing any time soon – and it was nice having somebody telling me they were 'very fond' of me, warning me to be careful. The album moved on to a song called Treat Me Nice.

"I like this one as well," said Louise. "It's very...what can I say?"

She began to sing along, something I remembered her doing whenever she'd had a drink. Then she reached out and took my hand.

"Do you ever want someone to treat you nice, Gus?" she whispered, leaning forward slightly.

"All the time."

She smiled at me.

"I haven't been very nice to you, have I?"

"No, you haven't, you bugger."

After the slightest of hesitations, she kissed me. Or I kissed her. We kissed one another.

Quite some time later, Louise got out of bed, took my dressing gown from the back of the bedroom door and put it on. Turning to look at me, she gave me a wink.

"We've still got it, haven't we?"

I smiled back, nodding in agreement. A sensible, mature man would have agonized over the significance of what had happened. However, one thing I had discovered in life was that sensible, mature men didn't have much fun.

"Certainly have," I said.

She waltzed out of the room, singing Treat Me Nice. When she returned with a bottle of wine and two glasses, she had moved onto another song. Would she go through every Elvis song? It was only after she had left that I got the strong feeling she had said or done something that would help in the investigation. Once I had worked out what it was, I'd be laughing.

CHAPTER NINETEEN

The next morning I got up early, determined to sort out the murder once and for all. I sat at my desk and typed out a list of suspects. This time I got to the end.

Andrea Greenhoff
Motives: money and jealousy. She couldn't have killed Tim because she was on her way to work at the time Tim probably died. Jimmy went to Mangall Court at seven o'clock and stayed for, what, fifteen minutes. I was there at quarter to nine for five minutes. Polly found the body at ten. So Tim was probably murdered between eight o'clock and nine thirty.

Francine Ingleby
She had been to Mangall Court a few hours before Tim died there. She could easily have gone back. The question is, why would she kill Tim? Maybe her affair with Tim was serious in her eyes. Was he going to finish with her? With Francine, money was more likely to be the motive. Tim had no money though. Where was the jewellery she had stolen and given to Tim? Wherever it was, what did it have to do with anything? Nothing probably. She was helping Tim to make

money; he was helping her to make money too. No motive there.

Wayne Dickens
On the face of it he might be the best suspect. He had an obvious motive and had threatened Tim several times. There doesn't have to be a financial motive or a sexual one. I had thought the scarf was evidence of a sexual motive because of what I had seen Tim getting up to in Mangall Court with the woman I thought was Vicky. The murderer could just have used the scarf because it happened to be there. Wayne lives near Mangall Court. It wouldn't have taken long to get there to kill Tim, but there was the question of how he got in the building.

Will Trader
He was in Mangall Court earlier, but he must have left while I was out. He was friendly with Tim and Andrea. He could have gone back to Mangall Court, but why should he?

I would have included Caitlin Gallagher at one time, but as I now knew for certain she was in Blackburn at the time of the murder there was no point. Unless she hired somebody to kill Tim. Unlikely to say the least. I read through the list again. It didn't take me very far. Still, I thought I was missing something.

What was it Louise had said that had my mind racing for a clue? I replayed the conversation we had over lunch, trying not to think about what happened afterwards. We had talked about misheard lyrics, hadn't we? The sort of daft thing we used to talk about when we were young.

Had somebody misheard something or what? Wait a minute, I said to myself, Caitlin has trouble with her hearing. And there was the mystery of Caitlin hearing Tim Greenhoff talking to his dead grandmother. The most likely explanation was that she thought he said 'Gran' when he actually said something else.

Feeling stiff from sitting down too long, I stretched my arms out and tried to loosen up my shoulders. Then I came up with the answer. He must have been talking to Francine Ingleby. 'Fran'. Pity it got me no further in finding out who killed Tim Greenhoff.

Maybe Louise hadn't said anything very important. Yet I still had a feeling she had. I looked again at my list and after a while I saw what was missing. I grabbed my coat and went out, hoping I was right. Did Elvis have the answer?

* * *

"Good morning, Ms Ingleby," I said.

The frown on Francine's face matched the overcast sky.

"Oh, shit, what do you want now?"

I had caught up with her just after she had come out of the probation hostel, a squat brick building on Regent Road about a quarter of a mile from Ordsall Tower. Over shabby blue jeans she wore the same leather coat I remembered from the first time I saw her.

"Just a few questions," I said pleasantly. "I won't take up much of your time. I'm sure you're busy."

She looked to her left as though she had seen something of note.

"Too busy for you," she said.

"What about Will Trader," I asked, "are you too busy for him?"

"What you on about. I haven't seen him for weeks."

"So you were never in a relationship with him?"

She looked at me with scorn.

"Will Trader? I can just see myself. Anyway, don't you get chucked in prison for shagging your cousin?"

A black car pulled up a few yards ahead of us. The front passenger door opened. Francine ran along the pavement and got in the car, which roared away.

So much for that, I thought as I watched the car disappear into the distance. Another theory knackered. Unless Francine were lying; but in this case she'd have no reason to do so. Will had said he fancied Francine, I was sure of it. Was that what he said, or was my memory playing tricks with me? It wouldn't be the first time. Maybe he'd just said she was fanciable or something, which wouldn't mean a thing. I had convinced myself Will was bitter about Tim having sex with her, bitter enough to kill him. What a load of rubbish.

I'd had a half-baked idea based on The Girl of My Best Friend, confronted Francine Ingleby for no good reason and ended up more confused than ever. All before nine o'clock in the morning.

* * *

About four o'clock that afternoon DI Ellerton was sitting in my kitchen.

"Do you know where Francine Ingleby is?" she asked without preamble.

"No. Why do you ask?"

"You were seen talking to her this morning."

Trying and failing not to interpret 'seen talking to her' as in any way sinister I told her the truth.

"That's not surprising. I did talk to her."

She took a note then looked up.

"She's gone missing."

I'd worked that out for myself but refrained from commenting. Sarita sat slumped on her chair and let her jaw drop. Her eyelids drooped so much I thought she'd fall asleep there and then. I couldn't recall seeing anyone so exhausted or fed up.

"What did she say to you?" she asked.

"Hardly anything, just wondered what I wanted, said she didn't want to talk to me."

She had a look on her face I would have described as sceptical.

"Nothing more?"

"Whoever saw me must have noticed Francine was only in my company for a matter of seconds before she got into a car."

She tapped her pen on the table top, screwing her face up in concentration. Predictably she asked if I had recognized the driver, remembered the number plate and what direction they were heading. I got the distinct impression my answers were of little use.

"What did you need to see her about?" asked the Inspector.

"I wanted to appeal to her better nature," I lied.

The sceptical look came back with a vengeance.

"I was going to ask her to return the money she had stolen from Eliott McIntyre, mainly for his sake, but on the basis it might mean she got off with a lighter sentence. It was Eliott's idea."

I don't know if the DI believed me, but if she didn't, we would both, I felt sure, get over it.

* * *

"Are you never gonna leave me alone?" asked Andrea Greenhoff about nine o'clock the following morning.

She was on the pavement washing her car as I walked past her house.

"I'm just passing," I said. "On my way to see a friend."

She put her sponge into the bucket on the ground and raised her eyebrows. There would have been no point in telling her I was on my way to Debbie's parents' house in the next street to help her load up her car before the removal men arrived. As a reward, she had invited me to her new flat for a meal on Friday night.

"So you've not come to cross examine me?" asked Andrea.

"No," I said, glancing at the suds dripping down from the roof of her car. "Your Peugeot's a lot smarter than mine."

She shrugged.

"It's not really right for me. I need something more practical. I've put this thing up for sale, that's why I'm washing it."

Strange behaviour, I said to myself.

"Why did you buy it then?"

"Somebody bought it for me," she said, "since you ask."

I stared at her, unable to hide my amazement. That was what was wrong with her having a Peugeot RCZ: she got it before the insurance money had come through. At least I now knew how she'd been able to afford it.

"Somebody must love you. Who was the generous benefactor?"

She looked me in the eye, hesitating as if wondering whether to answer my question. Whatever it was about me that encouraged people to open up had worked again.

* * *

Later, I sat in my living room, listening to a song on the Elvis CD that had taken on added significance once more. When I left Andrea I had a lot on my mind. I knew what she had told me was important but I needed to think about it. It was a good thing I'd had to spend a couple of hours at Debbie's house before getting back to the flat. That had given me time to go through everything carefully, and stopped me from doing anything precipitate. I still hadn't decided what to do when my phone rang.

"Hi, Gus, it's Louise, just wondered if you fancied lunch or anything..."

"Good idea," I said, unable to stop myself speculating about what 'or anything' might mean. I was about to invite her to the flat, when I made a decision.

"I'm just on my way to the Holiday Inn," I said, "can you meet me there?"

"OK," she replied, "about twenty minutes?"

I was out of the apartment five minutes later, my mind working overtime, piecing things together as I walked. By the time I arrived at the Holiday Inn I had a good idea what to do and say. I looked round the bar, taking in the scattering of people drinking and chatting. Bugger, he's not here, I said to myself. I got myself a glass of house red and took it to a table at the back of the room.

Frustration at not being able to carry out my plan made me restless. I picked up a coaster, turned it around in my hand and put it down again. I looked at my watch, took a sip of wine, put the glass down. Ten minutes crawled by before I saw the man I wanted come in. To add to my frustration he looked in every direction, but the right one. I waved towards him.

"Will," I said just loud enough.

He waved back, smiling, before getting a drink from the bar and joining me.

"I thought I might find you here," I said.

"I'm obviously becoming too predictable."

But I've discovered you're anything but predictable, Will, I was tempted to say, not if I'm right about one or two things. I went through what I wanted to say in my mind, but before I could speak, Louise came in. She wore a leather jacket over a blue t-shirt, a silk scarf draped carelessly round her neck.

When she got to my table, she kissed me. As I introduced her and Will to one another, I saw out of the corner of my eye a smartly dressed man with not much hair enter the bar. Having established we were OK for drinks, Louise started to make her way to the bar.

"You're supposed to be in fucking Australia," shouted the man I had just seen coming in.

He stood in front of her, blocking her way.

"Brad please..."

"And you said you weren't going back to Gus Keane."

Gripping her by the shoulders, he shoved her backwards with all his might, pinning her against the wall. Her scarf floated to the floor.

"Lying bitch, you'll be sorry," he snarled.

I saw the fear in Louise's eyes and leapt to my feet, but Will was quicker than me. Getting there ahead of me, he picked up the scarf and quickly looped it round Brad's throat. Louise watched for a moment as a choking, gurgling sound came from her husband. She dodged round the two men, flinging herself into my arms.

"I'll teach you to hit a woman," said Will, managing to sound as if he was holding it together, although his actions suggested he had completely lost it.

I watched in guilty fascination for a while. Among all the thoughts that swirled around in my head two dominated: one, what I was witnessing confirmed all my suspicions; two, wouldn't it be nice if Brad were to die right now?

"Are you OK?" I asked Louise.

"Yes, I think so," she sobbed. "I'm sorry, Gus, I bring you nothing but trouble."

"No need for you to be sorry, it's that toe rag who's to blame."

I looked again at the two men. Will still hadn't let go of the scarf and I began to think that Brad really was going to die.

"Will, that's enough," I said to no avail.

I repeated the request, raising the volume. By now seriously worried, I got up and tried to pull Will away from Brad. At first I made no impact and began to wonder how we'd explain the presence of a dead body in the Holiday Inn. I strained against Will until at last he moved away.

"That'll do now," I said, "he can't do any more harm."

Brad slumped to the floor, writhing round the carpet. Rasping coughs struggled out of his mouth as he gulped for air. Will stood over him, breathing hard, a look of grim satisfaction on his face. I took out my phone and called the police.

"Come and sit down, Will," I said when I had finished, "I want to talk to you."

He obeyed, moving like a zombie, taking deep breaths as though in pain.

"Sure you're OK, Louise," I said, taking her hand.

"Fine."

Her tears had subsided but she didn't look fine.

"I have to ask Will some questions," I added.

house in Worsley for the time being, having decided married life wasn't for him. There was more to it than that, but would Jimmy ever tell me?

Now I thought of how straightforward my life used to be. Would I go back to how it was? Silly question, I said to myself, you can never go back. Anyway, everything was OK or as near as made no difference. I was about to see a musical legend from the best seat in the house. We had even been invited to the after show party. I wondered momentarily what it would be like seeing Marti again. Once more I looked round the packed auditorium. I had finally made it to Australia and had just the right amount of complication in my life. With this thought, I turned to the woman on my left.

"All right, Debbie?" I asked.

THE END

If you enjoyed this book, please let others know by leaving a quick review on Amazon. Also, if you spot anything untoward in the paperback, get in touch. We strive for the best quality and appreciate reader feedback.

editor@thebookfolks.com

www.thebookfolks.com